MONTANA MAVERICKS

Wed in Whitehorn

Welcome to Whitehorn, Montana—
a place of passion and adventure.
Seems this charming little town has some
Big Sky secrets. And everybody's talking about...

David Hannon: He'd come home to Whitehorn for family's sake, then found himself drawn to the murder mystery in town. So he flashed his FBI badge and got himself a new partner—pretty Gretchen Neal!

Gretchen Neal: Special Agent Hannon sure *looked* good, Gretchen conceded as she agreed to a pretend engagement to capture the bad guy. And then Gretchen discovered he wasn't all about country clubs and consorts—this Kincaid relation was anxious to settle the past...but would it leave room for a future?

Storm Hunter: He'd returned to Whitehorn to set the record straight about big brother Raven. So he met Summer, Raven's secret daughter. But then Storm met Jasmine— and suddenly he was fighting a growing attachment to a woman with *Kincaid* blood running in her veins....

Jasmine Kincaid Monroe: How could she make the magnificent Storm Hunter see her as more than a baby? Perhaps by turning virgin seductress she could tame the Storm—for a time. But would she be able to hold him once his brother's murderer was revealed?

Raven Hunter: When the bones of this Kincaid rival turned up, everyone started talki~~ng~~ between Native American ~~~~ who once defied her fami~~ly~~ disappearance all those ye~~ars~~

D0819373

MYRNA MACKENZIE,

winner of the Holt Medallion honoring outstanding literary talent, believes that there are many unsung heroes and heroines living among us, and she loves to write about such people. She tries to inject her characters with humor, loyalty and honor, and after many years of writing she is still thrilled to be able to say that she makes her living by daydreaming.

Myrna lives with her husband and two sons in the suburbs of Chicago. During the summer she likes to take long walks and during cold Chicago winters, she likes to think about taking long walks (or dream of summers in Maine). Readers may write to Myrna at P.O. Box 225, LaGrange, IL 60525, or they may visit her online at www.myrnamackenzie.com.

CHRISTINE SCOTT

grew up in Illinois but currently lives in Ballwin, Missouri. When this former teacher isn't writing romances, she spends her time caring for her husband and three children. In between car pools, baseball games and dance lessons, Christine always finds time to pick up a good book and read about love.

She loves to hear from readers. Write to her care of Silhouette Books.

MONTANA MAVERICKS

MONTANA
Bred

Myrna Mackenzie

Christine Scott

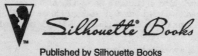

Published by Silhouette Books

America's Publisher of Contemporary Romance

If you purchased this book without a cover you should be aware that this book is stolen property. It was reported as "unsold and destroyed" to the publisher, and neither the author nor the publisher has received any payment for this "stripped book."

Special thanks and acknowledgment are given to Myrna Mackenzie and Christine Scott for their contributions to MONTANA BRED.

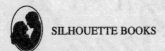 SILHOUETTE BOOKS

MONTANA BRED

Copyright © 2002 by Harlequin Books S.A.

ISBN 0-373-48492-5

The publisher acknowledges the copyright holder of the individual works as follows:

JUST PRETENDING
Copyright © 2000 by Harlequin Books S.A.

STORMING WHITEHORN
Copyright © 2000 by Harlequin Books S.A.

All rights reserved. Except for use in any review, the reproduction or utilization of this work in whole or in part in any form by any electronic, mechanical or other means, now known or hereafter invented, including xerography, photocopying and recording, or in any information storage or retrieval system, is forbidden without the written permission of the editorial office, Silhouette Books, 300 East 42nd Street, New York, NY 10017 U.S.A.

All characters in this book have no existence outside the imagination of the author and have no relation whatsoever to anyone bearing the same name or names. They are not even distantly inspired by any individual known or unknown to the author, and all incidents are pure invention.

This edition published by arrangement with Harlequin Books S.A.

® and TM are trademarks of Harlequin Books S.A., used under license. Trademarks indicated with ® are registered in the United States Patent and Trademark Office, the Canadian Trade Marks Office and in other countries.

Visit Silhouette at www.eHarlequin.com

Printed in U.S.A.

CONTENTS

Just Pretending   13
Myrna Mackenzie

Storming Whitehorn   247
Christine Scott

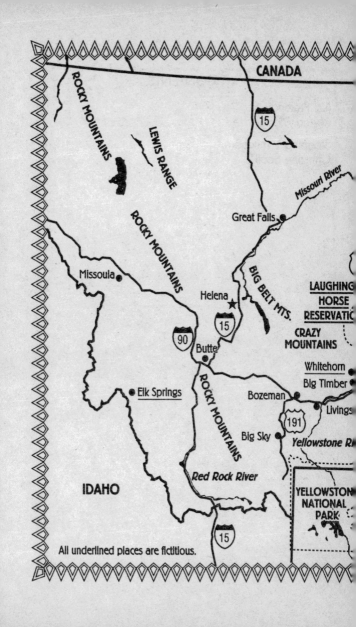

CANADA

ROCKY MOUNTAINS

LEWIS RANGE

ROCKY MOUNTAINS

Missouri River

Great Falls

Missoula

Helena

BIG BELT MTS.

LAUGHING
HORSE
RESERVATION

CRAZY
MOUNTAINS

Whitehorn

Butte

Elk Springs

ROCKY MOUNTAINS

Bozeman

Big Timber

Livings

Big Sky

Yellowstone R

Red Rock River

IDAHO

YELLOWSTONE
NATIONAL
PARK

All underlined places are fictitious.

MONTANA MAVERICKS: WED IN WHITEHORN
THE KINCAIDS

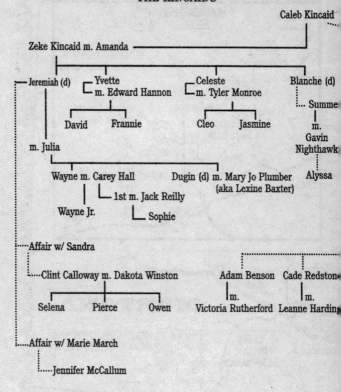

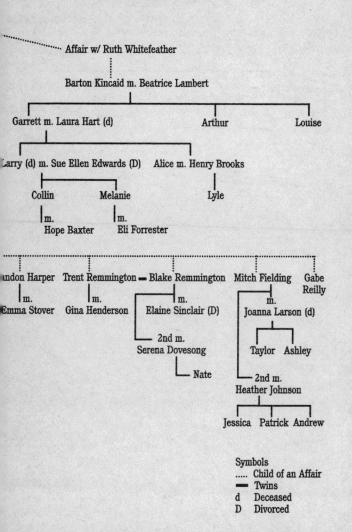

Affair w/ Ruth Whitefeather

Barton Kincaid m. Beatrice Lambert

Garrett m. Laura Hart (d)   Arthur   Louise

Larry (d) m. Sue Ellen Edwards (D)   Alice m. Henry Brooks

Collin   Melanie   Lyle

m.   m.
Hope Baxter   Eli Forrester

Brandon Harper   Trent Remmington — Blake Remmington   Mitch Fielding   Gabe Reilly

m.   m.   m.   m.
Emma Stover   Gina Henderson   Elaine Sinclair (D)   Joanna Larson (d)

2nd m.   Taylor   Ashley
Serena Dovesong

Nate   2nd m.
Heather Johnson

Jessica   Patrick   Andrew

Symbols
..... Child of an Affair
— Twins
d   Deceased
D   Divorced

Just Pretending

Myrna Mackenzie

One

The town of Whitehorn, Montana, didn't look as though it had just been kicked in the teeth, David Hannon thought as he pushed through the outer doors of the police station. The July sky was blue, the sun was out, the mountains in the background were spectacular, and the town appeared to be every man's vision of the perfect place to settle down. But, of course, if everything in his hometown had been perfect lately, he wouldn't be here. At least not on a search for the truth.

David moved beyond the sunlight and into the station. He removed his dark sunglasses, smiled down at the middle-aged woman sitting behind the desk and told her who he was and who he wanted to see. She scribbled his message down on a scrap of paper and excused herself.

"Hey, Hannon, it's been forever. Good to see you," a booming voice called, snagging his attention as David walked further into the room and grinned at the deputy sheriff heading his way. "But if you wanted to catch any of those weddings your family's been staging lately, you're too late. Of course, the way your clan has been falling, there might be something Cupid's slipped into the water supply. Better watch out. You could be next. Just another smooth bachelor fallen facedown in the wedding cake."

David shook his head, still grinning as he reached out to shake his old friend's hand. There *had* been a couple of unexpected weddings in his family in the past few months. But that wasn't why he had returned.

"Reed, it's great to see you, too. And you're right. I only wish I could have made it here in time for both Frannie's and Cleo's weddings, but I couldn't get away at the time." It was the truth. It had nearly killed him that he hadn't been able to get here in time to see the sister and cousin he was crazy about each take their turn walking down the aisle.

"So, you missed the weddings and now you're here for..."

"To see my home and family, kiss the brides, congratulate the grooms on their good fortune, say hi to all my old buddies," he said. "Do a little nosing around while I'm here."

"Thought so," the man said. "Can't blame you. I'd be doing the same, if it were me, considering all the things that have been going on."

Another deputy showed up and slapped David on the back. "David, it's good to see that pretty face of yours. You don't come around nearly enough. Means less women fainting at your feet, more dates for me, but still we've all missed you, bud. I couldn't help but hear what you said. That nosing around you're talking about have anything to do with those bodies that were found at the future resort/casino site out on Kincaid land?"

David tilted his head, reluctant to say too much until he knew which way the clouds were rolling in. "I thought I'd see if I could help out."

"In an official capacity? FBI send you to assist?"

More like they hadn't stopped him. His superior had known where David was going when he requested a leave of absence and he also knew what was going on here in Whitehorn, but David was overdue for some time off.

Still, it was a mark of Phil's confidence in his professionalism that the man had okayed the leave without question. "Don't get in too deep, Hannon, or I'll have to call you back," was his only comment. David didn't plan to give Phil any reason to do that, but he fully intended to get at the truth of what had happened here in his hometown.

"Yeah, are you here as Special Agent Hannon or simply as David Hannon, one of Whitehorn's favorite wandering sons?" another man asked with a chuckle.

"We'll see," David answered with a shrug and a grin. "Who's the chief investigating officer on this one?" A lot would depend on how open-minded and cooperative the officer was.

The men exchanged a few sidelong glances. "That would be Detective Neal. Over there," one man said.

David turned and looked toward the back of the room where his old friend had pointed and met with a sea-green-eyed stare and a pair of raised delicate blond brows. She was tall, slender, very crisp, her white blouse a sharp contrast to her black pantsuit. Her outfit and her demeanor said she was no-nonsense, just as her position required her to be. Nothing unusual about that. David had worked with plenty of female special agents, trusted his back to more than a few. Some of them had been colleagues, some friends, some more. None of them had ever made him think of hot nights and tangled sheets and drinking champagne from a woman's lips. Until this second, that is. This lady detective was definitely a very special case, and she was frowning at him right now. She made one last comment to the person she'd been conversing with and started walking his way.

"Detective Neal?" David asked the man standing next to him.

"Very definitely, Hannon. Have a care. Gretchen's relatively new to the area, but she's one of the best. Worked the streets of Miami for a while. She's knowledgeable, she's fair and caring, but she's tough. You may be able to charm most women with a single crook of your finger, but Gretchen takes her work very seriously and if you don't do the same, she bites."

The man's words were teasing, but David could hear the respect in his friend's voice.

"I wouldn't imagine the sheriff would give his biggest case to someone who didn't know how to do the job. Rafe's too smart for that," he agreed.

"She know who and what you are?" the man asked.

"Could be. Or maybe not. Catch you later," David said quietly as he strode toward Detective Neal.

He didn't know what the lady knew about him other than that he'd sent a note asking to see her, and those killer green eyes told him nothing. She moved across the room with purpose and efficiency, studying him as she advanced.

"Mr. Hannon?" she asked, looking down at the note the officer at the desk had taken to her. She stepped up beside David and he noted that in spite of his six-foot-one-inch frame, she didn't have to look up very far to stare into his eyes. "You must be related to Frannie, then?"

"My sister," he agreed.

"Frannie was one of the first people I met when I arrived here," the lady said with a carefully polite smile. "She made a stranger feel welcome. But you didn't come here to talk about your family. You're here on police business, I'm told. You know something of one of my cases? You have information you'd like to provide to the authorities, perhaps, Mr. Hannon?"

Her voice was the cool smoky kind that could make a man think about bed when he should be thinking about business. Her thick, honeyed hair moved as she spoke, brushing her jawline. David had an undeniable itch to reach out and sample the silky texture of the tempting shimmery stuff. Like a curious child, he mused. Or a man in the mood to get his face slapped. He tilted his lips up in a bemused grin.

"I'm here on a matter of public concern, Detective Neal," he said, schooling his thoughts to the matter at hand. "You're handling the Raven Hunter murder and the death of Peter Cook. I understand that both bodies were found on the site of the future resort/casino being built in the area and that Peter Cook was one of the employees on the site. I'm here to look into those cases."

She raised one brow. "What reason would you have for doing that, Mr. Hannon?" she asked, that boudoir voice quiet but firm.

"David," he said simply. "Special agent. FBI," he added, removing his credentials from the pocket of his sports jacket and flashing them. "I have reason to believe I could be of service here."

"I see."

He doubted that very much, but he could see something. Those beautiful green eyes had narrowed. He'd at least gotten her complete attention.

"I haven't heard anything from the Bureau indicating that you were on your way, Mr. Hannon," she said, ignoring his suggestion that she call him by his first name. "You're telling me you've been assigned to my case for some reason?"

"I don't recall putting it that way."

"Just what way would you put it, then? If you're not here officially, why would you offer your services?"

"This is my home. I have an interest."

"And Jeremiah Kincaid, the chief suspect in the Raven Hunter murder, was your uncle."

David nodded his agreement. "We weren't close."

The lady took a deep breath. "There was animosity between you?"

The slight look of hope in her eyes had David smiling. "Nice try, Detective, but no, I wouldn't say that. I didn't really know Jeremiah well. He didn't take much interest in his sisters' offspring. The man had…other interests." The wary look that crossed the lady's face told David that she knew exactly what he meant and that she was wondering if the family traits were passed down through the male bloodlines. His uncle had been an infamous womanizer.

As for David, he'd been blessed with more than his share of female companionship, and he hadn't failed to notice that while Gretchen Neal did her best to shelve her femininity during working hours, she couldn't hide that rose-and-cream complexion of hers. But just because he'd noticed the lady's skin, that didn't mean he was anything like his disreputable uncle.

David held out his hands in a gesture of surrender, but he arched one brow in obvious challenge.

"Look, Detective, I'll be honest. I'm interested in this case because this is my hometown. It's no secret that the people on the Laughing Horse Reservation have wanted to build this casino and resort for a while and that it will bring them much needed revenue. It's also no secret that this deal has been made possible only because the people from the rez and a few private investors have joined forces to cross reservation lines and build some badly needed bridges between the town and the reservation. Like everyone else here, I want that to succeed. Finding bodies on the affected land has put a halt to that construction and those bridges for now, so, yes, I have an interest in that sense. But I'm also interested because all these 'discoveries,' these bodies, seem to have upset my aunt Celeste tremendously. Jeremiah was her brother, Raven was the father of her niece, Summer, and this brings back memories of her sister Blanche's death, as well. She's naturally upset, so much so that she isn't sleeping. She isn't eating right, I'm told. If I can help in any way, assist with the case and help move things more quickly, I'd want to do that.''

"There's no reason for you to get involved. This is a homicide. Not an FBI matter. Raven Hunter's remains weren't found on the reservation, and the Whitehorn force is an excellent one. We're capable of handling this alone." Gretchen Neal's tone and her demeanor projected absolute calm. She was good, but not good enough to hide that trace element of annoyance in her eyes. She was in charge here and she didn't like the implication that she needed outside help to do her job.

"I'm not implying that you're not capable, Detective," David said, keeping his voice cool and soothing. "That doesn't mean that this department, just like any other law enforcement agency, couldn't use a little assistance when it's offered gratis. You can't tell me that this special arrangement doesn't follow standard procedure, because Whitehorn has never really been known for doing that. You've got Rafe, a county sheriff, in charge of officers in the town and deputy sheriffs out into the rest of the county. Those jobs have always overlapped, and territories have been crossed when it was necessary to keep the citizens of the area safe. It's a maverick setup that makes Whitehorn special—and effective. Why not take it a step farther and get a little help from another agency, as well?''

The smallest of smiles lifted her lips and David had the feeling that he'd been given an unexpected gift. Her smile transformed her face, making her eyes light up. He had an urge to take a step closer. He squelched it, sure that this lady who was fighting so hard to keep him out of her investigation definitely wouldn't want him in her personal space.

''You like to argue, don't you, Mr. Hannon?'' she asked with a touch of laughter in her voice. ''Well, you're right, I can't debate the procedural issue, but that doesn't mean it's a good idea to take on volunteer officers. We've had plenty of work trying to keep the site uncontaminated. People seem to want to flock to a murder scene for some reason. I'm sorry, but in my book, you'd be another warm body wandering over the site.''

She stood her ground, her green gaze apologetic but immovable. David had to give Gretchen Neal credit. She wasn't going to let just anyone waltz in here and start calling the shots. He could see why Rafe Rawlings had put her in charge.

He raised one brow. ''You make a good point there, Detective Neal, but I can assure you that won't be a problem. In my line of work, dead bodies show up more often than I care to remember.'' As always, David did his best not to think back on those scenes. Moving on was the only way to get past the memories and deal with the job effectively. He didn't like sloppy work any more than Gretchen Neal did.

''Ms. Neal,'' he continued. ''I assure you I'll keep my warm body out of the way as much as possible. I'm here to help, not to hinder.'' His voice swooped low on those last words, almost the way a man would speak to a lover, and the lady blinked. She raised her chin higher, the slightest touch of rose in her cheeks just about the only hint that she was anything other than calm. He understood her consternation. He'd been a loner for most of his life and he knew all about that need to hold everything close, that unwillingness to give up even one thread of control to anyone.

For one second, one very brief second when she looked up at him, David could have sworn that the look in Gretchen Neal's eyes spoke of vulnerability. Immediately the shades came down on her soul.

"I'm sure you mean well, but I—that is, I really don't know you, Mr. Hannon, so I can't very well take your word on that, can I? Would you take me on without question if the circumstances were reversed?"

A low chuckle sounded behind her and David was glad for the interruption. She made a good point, an excellent point, but he wasn't sure just how he would have answered. Gretchen Neal was an eyeful and an armful—and a good cop, according to her co-workers and his own gut instinct. David had the feeling she'd be a hard lady to turn away from.

"Easy, Gretch," Rafe Rawlings, sheriff and owner of the low chuckle said. "I know this guy. He's clean. How've you been, David?"

"Busy," David said with a smile as he shook hands with the sheriff. "But probably not as busy as you appear to have been lately."

Rafe shrugged. "I hear you're going to give us a hand. In an unofficial capacity, that is. Just heard from Phil Baker."

"In an unofficial way," David agreed.

"Rafe, have you considered the problems? This case is personal for Mr. Hannon," Gretchen said.

Rafe held up one hand. "You know almost everyone in town, Gretchen, and so do I. All our cases are personal."

"They're not family."

"David's a pro. One of the best and brightest. He'll handle it."

She opened her mouth, then shut it again, but her eyes were worried when she hazarded a glance at David. Clearly she wouldn't take her argument to the next step, blatantly questioning his professionalism, but she still didn't like the situation.

"It's a good move, Gretchen," Rafe said quietly. "David's lived here all his life. I know him. He cares what happens here. He'll make a good partner. You lead. He'll assist. Tomorrow will be soon enough to start. You're a pro, too, Gretch. Get over your objections by the morning. That's an order."

She sighed and nodded slightly. "You're the sheriff, Sheriff."

Rafe smiled, his eyes crinkling at the corners as he said goodbye and strolled away.

"Partners?" she whispered, her consternation evident.

David wanted to smile at the break in her voice, but he restrained himself. This lady didn't want him around at all, and he'd already won the battle. No point in aggravating the good detective.

"Get to know me, Neal, before you decide I'm the enemy. I'm interested in the truth," he said quietly. "And I intend to follow this through to the end no matter what that truth may turn out to be."

He also intended to discover another truth if he could, David thought as he bid her good-day. What was it about Gretchen Neal's soft green eyes that made him want to step in close and risk her bite? Just once before this case was closed, he hoped he'd get the chance to find out.

She'd argued too hard, Gretchen thought when David Hannon walked away, and she knew the reason. It wasn't because of his personal connection to the case, although she'd been right to question it and Rafe had been right to set her straight. It wasn't even because of the implication that she could use help from an outside agency, although her pride made her like to think that she could close this case alone. It did have something to do with the fact that this man was clearly going to be difficult to work with. He was going to want to lead. She could tell that already. Even more than that, though, her resistance was because of her reaction the first moment she'd turned and seen David Hannon. There was something about that dark sweep of hair, those intense emerald eyes, that made a person feel as if he knew what sensual dreams flitted through her thoughts when she lay sleeping and open and vulnerable. He had a strong jaw and a mouth that was a slash of sinful temptation. He looked like a man who drank a lot of champagne out of a lot of women's slippers—and liked it.

Her breath had caught in her throat in a completely unprofessional way. It wasn't that she was unused to men giving her those speculative looks. She spent a lot of time with men. Most of her time, in fact, and she liked men. She liked dating, but she kept work and play very separate. She never got involved with other law enforcement officers. She never got involved with *anyone* too deeply and what's more, she didn't like feeling and doing things that just weren't smart. Having a physical reaction to David Hannon was plain stupid and unacceptable. Especially if she was going to work with him in close quarters.

And she was, it seemed, because when she arrived at the station the next morning David was there before her. When she walked up to her desk and found him lounging in her chair, studying a file, his tall, dark good looks hit her like an express train at full throttle. The man was smooth, James Bond smooth, with that wicked half smile and those deep knowing eyes that had, no doubt, convinced a good number of women that virginity was a very bad thing to hang on to. She'd just bet he knew how to use that face, that body and that convincing, seductive way of talking to get whatever he wanted, just as he had yesterday. Good thing she was a pro, Gretchen thought. She'd gotten past the wallop her first glance of David Hannon had given her and now she was back in charge. Of herself and this case. And she would remain that way.

"Ready to take me on?" he asked sweetly.

She smiled back at him just as sweetly. "I'm always ready and able to handle anything."

He raised one brow and grinned knowingly. Gretchen felt her heart trip over a speed bump too quickly, but she ignored the feeling.

"Let's get started, Mr. Hannon."

"David."

"David," she reluctantly agreed.

He waited, a patient smile on his lips.

"All right, okay, yes, I'm Gretchen," she finally said, reaching for the folder. "Shall we go...David?"

"Thought you'd never ask." He stood, looking down at her, and for one swift second she wished he were a little less tall, a little less broad-shouldered and polished. Maybe then she could think of him as just another cop of sorts. Must be the way he wore those sports jackets so elegantly or the fact that his white shirt looked good against his tanned skin.

"I'll fill you in as we drive," she managed to say, leading him out the door of the station to her plain white unmarked car. For one second, he headed for the driver's side, then paused, a sheepish smile on his face as she stopped dead in her tracks.

"Sorry, Gretchen."

"You're used to being in charge." Her words were resigned.

He shrugged, an admission of the truth. "I'm sure I'll get used to being second in command in time."

The last thing David Hannon was, was anyone's assistant. He was a man who knew how to lead and who liked to lead, and he was being gracious now by not pointing that out.

Gretchen sighed. "We'll both get used to it, David. Orders are orders."

As they cruised down the short streets of Whitehorn and out into the rolling, rugged country beyond, David studied Gretchen's profile. She was soft, fresh, a green-eyed beauty clad in another pristine pantsuit of stark navy. The dark suit and white blouse offset the golden glow of her hair, which feathered over her collar. Gretchen Neal might be a hard-edged detective, but she was packaged in the softness of a very womanly body. A delicious contrast.

She intrigued, and he was used to women intriguing. He'd grown up in Whitehorn, surrounded by his father and a number of females. His aunt, his mother, his sister and all those female cousins. Asthma had made him sickly, a victim of his condition, as a boy, and he'd grown used to a life surrounded by attentive, caring women. A life without close friends his age, it was true. He hadn't been able to do most of the things other kids had done. Still, he'd learned a lot about women in those years and he'd learned still more as he'd grown up and grown healthy. Women fascinated him and he'd enjoyed sampling more than his share. Gretchen was different, though. He could see that right from the start. Her shell was hard, as it had to be, but the core of her…well, that part of her fascinated him immensely. He very definitely wondered what exactly lay under that keep-your-distance armor of hers.

"You grew up in Miami?" he asked, his voice low and coaxing.

Her hands tightened on the wheel. "I grew up everywhere for a while. An army brat, but yes, we landed in Miami when I was ten."

"How'd you end up here?"

She turned for just a second to look at him and she shrugged, a small smile on her face.

"Trying to soften me up, David?"

He smiled as she turned back to the road. "Maybe. Mostly I'm just interested in knowing who you are. It's important for partners to know something of each other, don't you think? I'm responsible for your life from here on out. You're responsible for mine."

She glanced his way again, a dawning respect in the look she gave him. "You're right. It's very important to know whose hands you're placing your life in. I know I came on a bit strong yesterday, but I felt it was necessary, David."

"I never doubted your methods, your motives or your abilities, lady," he said seriously, truthfully. "Rafe chose you."

"And you. I'm sure you *are* good at what you do."

He tilted his head at her somewhat hesitant compliment. "How'd you end up in Whitehorn, Gretchen? This is a long way from the mean streets of Miami."

She smiled broadly for the first time, tilting her head up with pleasure, her smile sliding into her eyes to light them up like pale green flames, and David felt a zip of heated sensation shoot straight through his body. "My grandmother lived in Elk Springs. I used to come visit her, and it was an instant love affair between Montana and me. I moved to Elk Springs for a while four years ago, but Whitehorn was a natural when Dakota Winston retired from the force. I love the size of the town, the location, the people, the mountain scenery surrounded by ranches... It's home for me now, the best I've ever known."

"No family here?"

Her low laugh filled the vehicle, an entrancing sound. David figured the lady might con a few criminals into surrendering just by seducing them with that laugh. "I have family everywhere," she confided. "Three brothers and four sisters. I don't remember a time in my life until now when I actually had a room to myself. Right now they're all scattered, but we keep in touch. We're as close as a phone or a modem or an airport can make us."

He eased back more fully into his seat, relaxing as he stretched his long legs out, pleased that she'd let down her barriers just for a moment.

"So now you know me," she said.

He had a feeling she'd just shown him the sheerest part of her surface, and that she didn't intend to show him much more. Gretchen Neal was cautious.

"And what about you?" she asked. "You're one of the Kincaids. Your family runs the Big Sky Bed & Breakfast. Your father is an architect. Your sister is a banker. One cousin runs a day care center. Your entire family is practically royalty in this town."

"We're just people, Gretchen."

The lady actually rolled her eyes. "You believe that, don't you?"

"It's true."

"David, after you left the station yesterday, every woman in the place was looking in the mirror, trying to see if she'd looked her best when you were there. This is not normal behavior around the station, in case you didn't know that. You're— Well, I'm sure you know what you look like and when you add that to the allure of being a Kincaid, that makes you a temptation to most of the women around here. Especially to those looking for husbands."

She sounded and looked somewhat flustered. David raised one brow. "Just most of the women? Gretchen, you wound me. Deeply."

Her chuckle tempted him to lean closer. "Sorry, I'm just…immune. Some of us are wedded and bedded to our jobs. Marriage isn't an option for me."

That got his attention. "So you're dead set against marriage. Interesting. Is it because of your job?"

She took one hand from the wheel and held it out, palm up. "Not really. And don't get me wrong. I like men just fine and I'm not anti-marriage. It's a perfect choice for some people, but it's not for me. I've already had my family, and while I adore every member of the Neal clan and I'd go out on the skinniest limb for any one of my brothers or sisters, I'm just not prepared to go that route again. I raised babies when I was still very young, I changed diapers, took temperatures, dried eyes and monitored curfew to help my mother out. Now I'm done with that. I like living alone and being free to make my own choices. And I intend to go on doing just that. I'm a lifer now, a loner. So don't get panicky, Hannon. The women in the station may bat their eyes at you and run to get you coffee if you purr at them, but you're safe from me."

He chuckled. "You may find this hard to believe, but in spite of being a Kincaid, I don't expect anyone, under any circumstances, to fetch coffee for me. And as for being safe from you, well..." He held out both hands. "Somehow I just wasn't all that worried that you were going to crawl across the gearshift and onto my lap."

David was surprised and entranced by the slight blush on her cheeks. She was tough, but not that tough. She didn't want to get married, and it sounded as if she had good reasons. He had some good reasons of his own, the chief one being that he'd been a loner way too much of his life to be real good at maintaining a relationship for very long, not to mention all the bad relationships he'd watched his friends get embroiled in. But marriage, a wife, kids, had a certain dreamlike fantasy appeal to him. He wished he had the ability to make a go of it. Unfortunately, he didn't. Besides, right now, there were more important things to consider.

"You think we've dropped enough barriers to enable you to trust me with a few of the details of the case now?" he asked.

Gretchen felt the low hum of David's voice go through her like a touch that could seduce every secret out of her. But of course, they were working together on this case. It was time to give her assistant some assistance.

"You know that a resort casino is in the plans, and that part of it is going to be built on Kincaid land?"

He nodded. "The land belongs to distant relatives. It's destined to be inherited by Gabriel Reilly Baxter, Garrett Kincaid's youngest grandson."

"Yes, the Kincaid portion, about fifteen acres, will house a hotel and spa, and the other half of the devel-

opment being built on thirty acres of the Laughing Horse
Reservation will consist of the casino as well as some
honeymoon cottages up in the mountains. It's a joint venture, one that makes sense, I suppose. The Cheyenne provide land that can be used for a casino and the private
investors chip in the funding. Lyle Brooks has rounded
up some silent investors to finance the project, and Lyle's
in charge of much of the operation. You're friends with
him?''

David frowned. ''Why do you say that?''

She shook her head, strands of her hair catching on
her lips. She carelessly freed it and gave him a look.
''Lyle's another distant relative, isn't he? Another Kincaid, a grandson of Garrett Kincaid's, and a member of
the country club set I'm sure you belong to.'' She wanted
to apologize for what had to sound like an accusation,
but she had to place all her cards on the table.

''You could have mentioned those things to Rafe yesterday.''

''Rafe knows what I know. It's obviously not a problem for him.''

''And for you?''

She studied him, a small frown between her eyes. ''It's
just something that needed mentioning.''

''No need to apologize,'' he said, even though she
hadn't done that. ''You're right. It needed mentioning. I
suppose that's why Rafe put you in charge. You don't
avoid the tough questions even though it would be easier
to do so.''

''No, I don't, but I do try to be fair.'' It was the best
she could do. He needed to know that she would still be
cautious, but that she would trust him as far as she could,
given the circumstances.

''I'm beginning to see that, and I agree that you need

to know more of my background. The fact is that Lyle and I don't share martinis at the country club. We come from two different sides of the family and until very recently, long after I moved away, Lyle's side lived completely in western Montana. I don't really know the man."

Gretchen gave him a nod. He supposed that meant that she trusted him a little bit anyway. Or maybe it merely meant that she didn't see any point in arguing about what she couldn't change.

He stared at her, trying to decipher that almost unreadable expression she worked so hard at maintaining.

"All right," he said. "So Lyle is heavily involved in the resort/casino deal and then a skeleton shows up when they begin to dig the hotel site. I've heard that much and also that there was a bullet lodged in the rib bone. The bones belong to Raven Hunter, a Native American who went missing from the reservation thirty years ago."

"A man who had made Jeremiah Kincaid angry by falling in love with Jeremiah's sister, Blanche," she added.

"You didn't add the obvious—that Blanche was my aunt and she died in childbirth. The baby she gave birth to is my cousin, Summer. It's an old story, one the Kincaids don't talk about too much. And now there's a body and an old murder to solve. Anything I should know that wasn't in the file?" David asked.

She shook her head. "We've already interviewed those people in the area who might have had a link to Raven in any way. Old friends, your mother, your aunt, people on the rez who came in contact with him. It's all there in black and white, what little there is. Right now the case is more or less on hold while we wait for Jackson Hawk, the tribal attorney, to locate Storm Hunter,

Raven's brother. We need to find out if Storm knows any more than we do about what happened all those years ago. But Storm's been gone from the area almost as long as Raven has.''

David blew out a deep breath. "With the passage of time and the two principals both deceased, this case will be a challenge. And Peter Cook?''

"A construction worker,'' she explained. "It appears that he slipped and fell into the hole he'd dug. Until we know more, excavation has ceased completely.''

"Any new leads coming in?''

She had to smile at that one. "Every day. Ghosts. Aliens. People who claim they were out walking their dog in the middle of nowhere and they heard a rustle in the bushes.''

His smile indicated a knowledge of what she was talking about. He'd been doing this for a long time, too. "Any likely leads, I guess I should have said.''

"Not yet.''

But at that moment, the radio crackled and the dispatcher came on. An armed robbery in progress. Just outside of town on a road they'd passed minutes ago.

Gretchen spun the car around and headed for the scene.

A hundred yards from their destination, she slowed and David got out of the car. As she came around the side, he pinioned her with a look. "I'll go in through the back door,'' he said, his voice barely stirring the air. "Stay outside the front in case someone tries to make a run out that door.'' He moved silently back into the trees and toward the house.

Gretchen blinked. Obviously there was a problem here with chain of command. But David was already moving and she would not risk his life by stopping to stamp her foot and assert her authority.

At least not this moment.

She pulled out her weapon and approached the house.

Two

It was broad daylight but the shades on the little cottage had been pulled, blocking out most of the sunshine. David slid up to the kitchen window and peered in, but the curtains covering the windows were too thick to see inside.

"Don't touch those. Go away from here. Leave me and my things alone," he heard an elderly woman plead.

The sound of shoes shuffling on a bare floor drifted out, followed by a loud cracking sound and a grunt.

The woman squealed and David shoved against the thin wood of the door, which fell open beneath his weight. His gun was drawn as he bulleted through the entrance. He hoped that Gretchen was armed and ready as he got his first glimpse of the big, beefy man whirling toward the front door where she would be waiting.

"Freeze. Police," David ordered.

The man spun around, hands high, his eyes rolling back in his head.

"Don't shoot," the man called as Gretchen came through the front door, holding him in the sights of her 9 mm.

"Thank goodness you're here," the elderly woman said. "I didn't know what to do when I heard someone in the house."

"Mr. Adkins?" Gretchen asked, slowly lowering her gun to her side.

The man hung his head. David looked at Gretchen. She motioned for him to put his gun away.

"He was stealing cookies I made for the church bake sale," the woman declared. "I had to slap his hands to make him drop them."

David looked down at the red prints on the man's wrists.

"I wasn't stealing anything," the old man said.

"You're in my house, aren't you?" the woman demanded. "And you're armed. You've got a big rock in your pocket. I saw you studying it like you were going to throw it at me."

Her words jarred something in David's memory. "Mr. Adkins? Earnest Adkins?"

When the man didn't answer, David looked to Gretchen, who nodded.

David let out a sigh. He gazed at the man he'd once known rather well. Time had made changes.

"That rock in your pocket," David said, moving in closer. "I don't suppose you had a particularly good reason for carrying it around, did you?"

The man looked up, his eyes not quite recovered from the fear of having two guns trained on him. He nodded slightly. "Of course I did. A man carries rocks for a reason. Good reason, too. Just look at this. Isn't it a beaut?" he asked, pulling the rock from his pocket.

David gazed down at what really was a fine specimen of milky dolomite. "Mr. Adkins used to teach science at the high school. He studies geology," David explained.

"He was still stealing my cookies," the lady mumbled.

"He came into your house?" Gretchen asked gently.

"Yes," both man and woman said at once.

"The door was open and a cat came in," Mr. Adkins said. "This lady had left the cookies on the ledge and that big cat was all set to help himself. I was simply moving them," he said indignantly.

"I don't see any cat," the woman whined. David didn't, either, but the slight itch behind his eyes told him that there was one nearby.

Gretchen must have sensed the cat's presence, too, because a small smile lifted her lips and she looked around as if she expected to find whatever she was searching for.

"Oscar," Gretchen suddenly called. A grumbly purr rolled out from behind the kitchen door. Gretchen pulled it back and the biggest, blackest cat David had ever seen strolled out, nose in the air.

"Your buddy?" David asked Gretchen, who was smiling at the cat.

"He gets around the neighborhood. Sometimes he gets into places he shouldn't be."

"The man still had a rock in his hand," the elderly woman stated.

"Always do," Earnest Adkins said. "Ask him," he said, motioning to David. "You're David Hannon, aren't you? I recognize you now that you've put the gun away."

"I was a member of the science club. I've still got a few rocks Mr. Adkins passed on to me when I was there. He's an expert in local rocks and minerals," David told the two ladies. "Not that it's any excuse for trespassing," he said firmly, frowning at Earnest. "Since you don't know Earnest, would it be safe to guess that you're new to the area?" he asked the woman.

The lady let out a sigh and nodded. "Just a couple of months. My husband died last year and I came here to start out fresh, to get away from the city. You—you were just saving my cookies from that cat?" she asked Mr. Adkins.

"Maybe I should have knocked first," he admitted, "but Oscar was moving pretty fast."

A slight blush rose on the woman's still-pretty face. "I suppose I should thank you, then," she said. "And apologize to the two of you," she told Gretchen and David. "I'm used to living in the city and that's made me too cautious, I guess."

David shook his head. "You were right to call when you felt threatened. It's always smart to be cautious, especially when there's an uninvited stranger in your house," he said, looking pointedly at Mr. Adkins, who mumbled another apology and gripped his rock more tightly.

"But this is embarrassing, now that I know the truth," the lady said. "What can I do to repay you two for taking the trouble to come over here?"

David knew the woman wouldn't be happy if he told her that he needed nothing, so he took the easy way out. "I'm sure I should just issue the standard 'No thanks necessary, ma'am,' but…what kind of cookies did you say those were?"

The ploy worked. The lady laughed. "Double chocolate chip, and yes, please have some. You, too," she said to Gretchen and Mr. Adkins. "It's the least I can do. It won't hurt me to bake another batch."

David hazarded a glance at Gretchen then. One brow was raised in a rather superior, knowing smile as if he'd just done something brilliant. And later, when they said their goodbyes and left the cottage headed for the car, she placed her hand on his arm.

"Thank you for being so gracious to her."

David pulled up short, staring down at the woman—the detective, he corrected himself—standing before him. He could feel the warmth of Gretchen's slender fingers through the layers of cotton shirt and sports jacket. It was a tantalizing feeling, knowing that only a few bits of cloth lay between his skin and hers. An inappropriate feeling, he reminded himself. They were partners. They needed to work together like a machine, not twine together like man and woman.

"She was uncomfortable. There was no need for that. If something real and dangerous should ever occur, I wouldn't want her to hesitate about calling the authorities," he said simply. "And let's face it, while I'm rather partial to Earnest, he can't be entering people's houses even to save their cookies from stray cats."

Gretchen nodded and they walked on, but once David had climbed back into the car, she didn't start the engine. Instead she turned to him.

"I appreciate the way you wrapped up this call," she said, "but I think we have a definite problem here, Hannon."

He turned and stared into a pair of stubborn green eyes. Her chin was up, her lovely lips were firm, her arms were crossed.

For five whole seconds they simply studied each other. Then he held up both hands. "You're upset that I invaded your territory. You want to lead."

"It's my job," she said simply. "I intend to do it and do it well."

He stared at her for a few seconds more.

"I'm sure you're used to calling your own shots," she said pointedly, "but—"

"I am," he agreed. "And I can't promise not to step on your toes from time to time, but I'll make an attempt not to overstep my boundaries too often. I'll do my best to try and curb my basic instincts from now on."

Gretchen took a long and audible breath, but she merely nodded.

"I'm sure we'll get the hang of this in time. It takes practice for partners to learn to work as one body."

He stared at her hard, the vision her words called forth lodging in his mind immediately. A woman, a man above her, thrusting into the softness of her body, making himself a part of her very being. The thought nearly made him groan, and he fought it. He labored to keep his breathing even as he watched the woman seated not two feet away from him.

As he studied her, her eyes suddenly widened slightly as if she'd read his thoughts. Her breathing picked up a tad, but she didn't drop her gaze from his. She sat as if frozen.

David struggled, pushing the temptation of the image of himself braced above Gretchen to the farthest corner of his mind. "I can't quite believe you said that," he finally managed to say, his voice quiet and reasonably controlled, an amused but still somewhat ragged smile on his lips.

"What?" The word was released on a breath. Gretchen sat up straighter, higher.

He smiled in earnest now. She knew darn well what he meant. "Gretchen, has it occurred to you that this is not going to be easy?"

She sighed slightly, rubbing at the frown that formed between her delicate brows. "I think that pretty much says it, yes," she agreed.

"Why do you think that is?"

"I suppose it's because I've been a rather reluctant participant in this partnership and also because you don't like taking orders from a woman."

He shook his head slowly. "I've worked with many

women in many contexts. Taking my directives from a woman isn't a problem. Having a relationship with a woman isn't a problem. Generally speaking, I keep my private and public life separate."

"We're not going to have a relationship."

"Exactly."

She took a deep breath, waiting for him to finish.

"However," he continued carefully, "I think it's only fair to warn you that wrong and stupid and completely out of place as it may be, the fact that you are a fine detective hasn't quite made me forget that you're a desirable woman, as well."

She didn't move. She almost didn't appear to be breathing. But he saw her swallow, then blow out a long, slow puff of air.

"Why are you telling me this?" Her voice was low. Sexy. Suspicious.

He shook his head slowly. "I'm telling you because we *are* going to be working as partners. I'll trust you to protect my back. I want you to be secure in the knowledge that I intend to protect your life at all costs, but don't expect me not to react as a man to a woman if you're going to make provocative comments."

She stared at him for long seconds. Then she nodded slowly. "Fair enough. I'll try to think before I speak."

"And I'll try not to initiate any…unwarranted bodi ly contact."

"Yes," she said on a cracked whisper. "Touching wouldn't be smart. It would make working together very difficult. Impossible."

"I know that, and that's my point. Finding the thin line we need to walk in the middle of the road is going to be difficult, Gretchen. My fault. My apology."

"Maybe we shouldn't be working together at all."

"Maybe. Except this is your case, and I fully intend to be on it."

"Rafe might feel differently if he knew we were going to have problems."

"What are you going to tell him? That I'm having trouble keeping my lips away from those of his top detective?"

He wasn't even leaning close, but he could feel her presence as if she had wrapped herself around him. Her soap-clean scent enticed him. He forced himself to keep his hands at his sides.

"No. I wouldn't tell him that. What's between you and me is…between you and me, Hannon," she said, releasing another long breath. "We'll deal with it together. We'll work through it."

He raised his lips in the slightest of smiles. "I know women who would have been hyperventilating in a similar situation. You're an admirable lady, Gretchen."

"I'm a good detective, too, David."

"Never let anyone say any different. I liked the way you manhandled Earnest into repairing a few things around Mrs. Barton's house. A good solution for both of them."

She smiled. "You're not trying to flatter me, are you, David?"

He lifted one brow. "Detective Neal, you wound me. I was completely sincere."

"Thank you very much, then," she said, starting the car. "So, Agent Hannon, do you think it's possible that you're ready to take an order from me now that we've established a few truths between us?"

He held out his hands in defeat. She was being a good sport. He had laid his cards on the table in such a way that she might well have been flustered or angry. He had told her the truth, he'd gotten in her face and she was dealing with it, but she still hadn't given up one millimeter of her authority. He could see why Rafe had put her in charge.

"Just say the word, Gretchen."

"That's a lovely sound, David. Since you're being so cooperative, let's go get lunch at the Hip Hop Café. And no cookies for you, partner. You've had enough for one day."

David smiled at Gretchen's attempts to move the conversation onto a lighter plane.

"You're a hard woman, Gretchen Neal. A real tough lady."

"I am," she said more soberly. "And don't you forget it."

He wouldn't. For her sake and the sake of this case, he would do his best to forget that Gretchen was a woman and simply think of her as the partner who was going to help him crack the Raven Hunter case. He hoped something enlightening would happen very soon.

"Gretchen, are you sure the dress is going to fit by the time the wedding takes place? Maybe you should just come in for one more fitting just to be certain. The wedding's still a few weeks away."

Gretchen heard the rising panic in her friend Pamela's voice and did her best to try and put herself in her friend's shoes. No dice. Gretchen had been a bridesmaid more times than she had fingers and toes, but she never had been a bride and never would be, just as she'd told David yesterday. Still, she did want Pamela to be happy…

"Pam, I promise you this dress is absolutely going to fit. It fits right now and I'm the same size that I've been for the past ten years. Everything's going to be okay, hon. Really.''

"Oh, Gretch, I'm sorry. It's just…I want everything to be so perfect. You know?''

"I know, Pam.'' And she did know that much. Enough of her friends and cousins and sisters had gotten married in the past few years for her to be very familiar with this need for the most beautiful, perfect day of all eternity. "And, Pamela?''

"Yes?''

"Everything is going to be just wonderful. You love Raymond, don't you?''

"Gretchen, you know he makes my sun rise every morning.''

"And he loves you more than he loves anything else. More than baseball and basketball, which is saying quite a lot for a sports nut like Raymond.''

Her friend giggled on the other end of the line. "All right, all that's true.''

"Then what more can you ask for, Pamela? The day is going to be perfect even if it rains elephants from the sky. You're marrying the man of your dreams.''

A long silence hung on the line. A nice silence.

"Pam?''

"You're right, Gretchen. It's going to be a wonderful day. Only one thing could make it more perfect.''

Uh-oh. Gretchen had heard this line before. She knew just where her friend was headed.

"It's not going to happen, Pam. I've told all of you, I just don't want to get married.''

"Not even if you met a special guy?''

"If I meet a special man, we'll date, we'll share our thoughts, we'll probably make love, but in time it's going to end. I'm just not cut out for husbands and babies. I like my job. I like my life. That's just not going to change. Nothing's going to change.''

She was right about that. But it still meant that every time someone asked her to stand up in a wedding or to attend a wedding or even mentioned the words wedding or marriage or husband or children, all her friends and loved ones were going to wish she were different. They were going to try their best to get her to settle down and make them feel that at last she'd fit herself into the world the way they wanted her to fit.

But Pam wasn't talking. Perhaps she was getting the message. Finally.

''You're thirty-two, Gretchen. You want to be alone all your life?''

Gretchen couldn't help chuckling at that. ''Pam, hon, I have seven brothers and sisters, more cousins than is probably legal, and friends all over the country. Almost all of them are generous and loving. Like you, Pamela. They share their lives, their homes, and their children, and I absolutely love that. How could I be lonely? And why do I need to raise my own family when I can just share in everyone else's whenever I feel the need?''

''Gretchen—''

''Pam, stop. Right now. I'm so happy for you and Raymond. I'm glad you're getting married and living the life you want. Be happy for me, too. I have everything I could ever need or want.''

More silence.

''Okay, Gretchen, I *am* happy for you. I'm truly happy if you really do have everything you want.''

Gretchen felt herself relax a bit. She and her friend talked a few minutes longer, but when they finally hung up, a frown formed on Gretchen's face.

''I do have everything I want,'' she whispered. ''But

just once, just one time, I wish I could show up at a
wedding with a man on my arm.'' She wouldn't, of
course. Asking a man to travel any distance with her to
a wedding implied a closeness that she just didn't want
to encourage. She had enough trouble with men who
thought dating a female detective meant a lot of things it
would never mean. But wouldn't it be great to show up
with a date? Maybe then all her friends and family would
believe that she was truly happy living a life with no ties
outside of work. All she needed was a little help from
the right kind of man.

Unfortunately the right kind of man didn't exist in
Whitehorn. The only way she was going to find a date
for this wedding would be if one fell from the sky and
disappeared just as quickly the day after the wedding.

Three

It was definitely good to be home, David thought, sitting on the long porch of the Big Sky Bed & Breakfast that night and gazing out at the tall pines that stretched away for miles. He, along with his mother and father had stopped by for an overdue reunion with the remaining members of the family, taking the short walk across the sloping lawns that separated their home from the Big Sky. Now evening had dipped the stars in silver and cast them out over the sky to shine down on the elegant old manor house where Celeste and Jasmine still lived and where so many guests had found peace and beauty.

"You missed this. At least a little, didn't you? Admit it, David," his sister Frannie said, leaning back in her husband Austin's arms and gesturing to the crowded porch where all the people he loved best were now gathered.

David drank in the scene and noted how relaxed his sister seemed. At last. She clearly loved her husband. Marriage suited her. "I missed *you*, squirt," he told her. "Missed all the torment of having you chase after me."

"Humph," she said with a twinkle in her eye. "You and Cleo and Summer used to torment and tease Jasmine and me. Wasn't it true, Cleo?"

"Mmm, absolutely," her cousin said, linking her hand in her husband Ethan's as she nodded her agreement at Frannie. "And wasn't it tons of fun?"

Her chuckle floated out on the night and his cousin Jasmine joined in. "It *was* great fun."

"The best," Summer agreed. "Remember when David wrote a play for us and we insisted he play all the male parts?" she asked. She smiled up at her husband, Gavin. "David spent his life practically surrounded by women," she told him. "Must have been a bit harrowing at times."

"Or…maybe not," Gavin said, staring around at the quartet of beauties gracing the porch.

"It did have its moments," David admitted. "I got to meet any number of young ladies I might otherwise not have had access to. And you were all very understanding about being forced to share your space with a mere male."

"Was it a pain having to deal with all our feminine foibles?" Jasmine asked, prodding her cousin. "Be honest, David, now that we're all grown up."

He turned and smiled at her and marveled at what a lucky man he had been. "The truth, Jasmine? It was pretty great. We were all very close, and no, I didn't mind at all being the only guy other than Dad most of the time. You all spoiled me shamefully, you know."

"Like you didn't spoil us," Cleo drawled. "You did. You and Uncle Edward." She sat silent for a full five seconds. Then she raised her brows speculatively. "So which of our friends did you want to meet that you didn't tell us about?"

David ran one hand over his jaw, not bothering to hide his grin. "Well, let's see. I would have killed to have Edith Darrowby run her fingers through my hair when I was twelve."

Cleo crowed. "I seem to recall her doing that very thing on this front porch one summer when you were home on spring break."

David raised one brow and smiled. "My, what a good memory you have, Cleo, love."

"Yes," she said softly. "Considering how many women you've kissed, it's amazing I remember one specific lady. We've missed you, David. You kept us from getting too serious."

"And you were always ready to defend any of us even when we didn't deserve it," Frannie added. "We've all missed you, big brother. Don't stay away this long again," she said, rising to give David a hug.

He gently kissed her cheek, then took a quick step to open the door that his aunt was struggling through with cups and saucers. "Aunt Celeste, why didn't you tell me you were carrying that? I would have done it for you. Now come on, turn those things over to me."

Celeste gave him a long, patient look. "That's why I didn't tell you. I wanted you to have time to visit with the children. Besides, you know I'm as strong as they come, and your parents are helping me out in the kitchen. Edward is carting out the coffee and Yvette has the cookies. Now you just settle back this one night and let us all look at you and talk to you. Don't fuss over us, David," she said, gently slapping his hands away as she set down her burden.

"Yes, dear, don't fuss. Indulge tonight. You and Edward can go back to being the big, predatory protective males in the morning. You know we eat that stuff up," his mother said, offering her cheek for his kiss as she followed Celeste through the door.

"What's a guy to do?" David asked his father as Edward moved out into the night.

"Simple enough, son. Just enjoy being surrounded by the women who love him," Edward advised, setting down the urn he was carrying and wrapping his arms around his wife. "Just enjoy."

And he did, David thought later that night as he lay in bed. Now, as an adult, he could take pleasure in his family so much more than he'd been able to as a boy. Growing up, he'd been loved, he'd appreciated, but his illness had set him apart from the world in many ways. He'd wanted to be accepted the way other boys his age were, but he hadn't been able to do the things other boys had done. And so he'd retreated into solitude in public. He'd made himself a world within walls and only come out within the heart of his family. He'd even come to enjoy being a loner; he'd thrived on the solitude and the barriers he'd erected. But now?

"That's gone, that's done," he whispered. He didn't ever want to build those kinds of immovable walls again. He loved the world and being a part of it. He wanted all the joys of companionship and joining and belonging. Still, he knew there were flaws to parts of the plan. Years of holding himself aloof had taken their toll. He never dated a woman for long; he always had the urge to move on soon after the start of a relationship.

Secretly he might want to try for the kind of closeness and marriage his parents had, but he knew it was just the kid inside him still wanting something he couldn't have. The truth was that he would never allow himself to offer love or marriage to a woman. Not when he couldn't sustain the feelings a relationship needed to survive. Promising a woman his heart and then asking for it back just wouldn't be fair or right.

So, no, he didn't want to be a loner anymore, and yet in some ways he still was one and probably always would be. Maybe—just maybe—he and Gretchen Neal had something in common, after all.

* * *

"Whoa, hang on there. Gretchen, you're not going to tell me that this little scrap of fluff is actually *your* dog?" David asked the next day. He lifted his lips in a half smile as he followed Gretchen into the door of the small white cottage and was immediately assailed by a bit of white fur, big brown eyes and frantically wagging tail dancing around his feet. "I'm surprised. A tough lady like you. This little guy is not exactly standard-issue watchdog," he said, raising one brow.

Gretchen rolled her eyes. "I told you that you didn't have to come with me. I explained that I was perfectly capable of carrying in a bag of groceries on my own."

"In other words, uninvited guests have no right to insult your pet?" David asked with a grin, depositing the bag on the kitchen table and bending to scratch beneath the little dog's upturned chin.

"Exactly," Gretchen agreed, watching his easy way with her pet. "Goliath is a very intelligent creature. He knows when he's been insulted."

David looked down at the obviously eager wriggling of the pink-tongued little animal.

"Of course. I can see that. Looks really put out to me," he said with a wink at his new canine pal. David rose to his feet and looked at Gretchen, whose mouth was twitching in an obvious bid to hold back a smile.

"Well, he usually gets offended very easily," she insisted. "He doesn't ordinarily get this exuberant over some mere man walking through my door," she said, as if men were swinging through her door every darn hour of the day. The thought sent a small arrow of irritation spiraling through David. He thrust it aside. Gretchen was, after all, a splendidly lovely lady, and she was a woman working in a world filled with testosterone-laced males. It only stood to reason that she'd slayed her share of his own sex, and anyway, he had no business butting into that part of her life. He'd told her that he wouldn't.

"I'm sure you're right about your little friend here," David said with a nod. "I can see he's probably chewed up his share of male ankles. Probably only spared me because of the groceries I was carrying," he said. "But, Gretchen?"

"Hmm?"

"'Goliath'? You really call this little pretend puppy Goliath?" He looked pointedly downward and down farther still to the floor far below where the tiny white tail swished against his shoestrings.

She shrugged. "I thought he needed a little help. Everyone can't have the advantage of being tall and strong," she reasoned, looking pointedly at David.

"You thought he needed a little assist," he said, wondering if the lady knew just how much her words revealed about her. "Where'd you find him?"

Gretchen blew out a breath as she reached into the first bag of groceries and pulled out a head of radicchio. "The humane society. I was looking for a Lab," she explained. "Or a Shepherd. Maybe a St. Bernard."

"Tough-guy dogs," he surmised.

"Well, yes. Why not?"

"Absolutely. Smart dogs to keep around."

"I know, but then—"

"Goliath looked at you with those big caramel-brown puppy-dog eyes that said 'I need help.'"

Gretchen glanced back over her shoulder and leveled a long cool green-eyed stare at him. "Believe me, I'm not such a pushover as that, Hannon. You don't work the streets of Miami and survive if you fall for every pair of big beautiful eyes that look at you beseechingly."

"I'm sure you don't," he said, moving up behind her.

He wondered just what all she'd seen in those years in the city. He was pretty sure much of it had been ugly. There was a telling tiny scar on her wrist and one just beneath that firm little chin of hers. Maybe from falling off a bike as a kid—or maybe from having a knife held a bit too close for comfort. Any way he looked at it, he was positive that she'd learned the survival skills every cop in that sort of situation had to learn. Emotional retreat. Develop a tough patina. Never get too involved. She had those eyes that looked right through a man to read secrets he didn't want read. She had that closed-off look she could turn on whenever she needed to. And yet... He looked back down to the tiny dog worrying a rubber bone as if the chew toy were a criminal Goliath was trying to cuff.

"They were going to put him down. He was too frantic, too untrainable for most people," she explained apologetically. "It was probably foolish for me to take him, but—" She lifted a shoulder in a helpless gesture.

"You did what you felt you had to do," David said, holding out a box of rice to Gretchen, trying to ease her out of her discomfort by returning to the mundane task at hand. She took the box from him, her fingers brushing against his. Cool satin licking against his skin. At the stroke of her bare flesh against his, he felt a slight tremble go through her—and felt his own answering tremors deep inside. Unusual for him, he thought for about the fiftieth time since he'd met the woman. He always kept things light, easy. It was the way he liked things, the way things suited him, but he was relatively sure that nothing was going to be easy with Gretchen—on any level. She had too much to prove where he was concerned, too many barriers. One of those sprang up now. He knew when she made the effort to control that trembling his unexpected touch had brought on. She was right. It wouldn't do for the two of them to mix up the personal and the professional. They'd already discussed that issue.

And so he withdrew his hand, ended the contact that sent sensation in a warm arc through his body. He resisted the impulse to move closer, to step right into her space and drag her body up against his in a long, slow slide. He turned away and helped her finish shelving the groceries.

For long, languid seconds there was only the sound of cans clicking against cans, the whoosh of boxes being slid into place on the wooden shelves.

"David?" she finally asked.

He looked up and met the question in her eyes.

"Do you really think you can remain objective when this case is so tied into your own family?"

His brows drew together. He knew she had the right to ask although she'd already asked the question once before. It was a question that bore repeating given the gravity and the sensitive nature of the situation. Indeed, she had the obligation to demand the truth from him considering her responsibilities. But he knew her question was intended to raise a personal barrier as well as a professional one. She was letting him know that while he affected her breathing, she wasn't going to let it matter.

"I'm a firm believer that the truth frees people," he said. "I may not like the answers we discover, but I'll do my best to make sure that we do, indeed, discover the whole truth. You'll have my full cooperation no matter what. You can trust me, Gretchen."

But he could see that there was still uncertainty in her eyes. There would probably always be uncertainty there until he could prove—if he could—that he meant what he said. She was wishing she had been sent any other man than him. Still, she took a deep breath and looked away.

"Down, Goliath. Sit," she said softly but firmly when the little dog hopped around David, hoping for another chin scratching.

The dog immediately whimpered, but he did as he was told.

"I thought you said he was untrainable," David said.

She shook her head. "I said that he was considered untrainable. I happen to believe that anything is possible if a person is determined enough."

He smiled. "And yet you're working with me when that really wasn't what you wanted. You think you're going to be rid of me?"

She smiled sweetly. "You don't live in Whitehorn anymore, David, do you? Don't you think that if I really want to be rid of you, all I have to do is wait?"

David felt the impact of her smile—of her words—like a ball peen hammer to the chest. He forced a mock-sweet smile to his lips. "Ah, Gretchen, my dearest detective, what a wonderful, ripping way you have with words. Tears at a man's heart just to hear you speak."

She smiled back ever so innocently. "Oh, partner, I'm so glad we understand each other so well. Your candor is refreshing. Still, it's late and we have lots of miles to cover in the morning, so go home now. I wouldn't want to have to sic my attack dog on you."

David looked down at Goliath, who was still obediently sitting.

"She's pretty bossy, isn't she, buddy? Guess I'd better get out of here before she starts ordering me to sit, too." The little dog whimpered and wiggled slightly, obviously wanting a goodbye pat but not willing to leave his post.

Gretchen looked at the two doleful males in front of her and let out the grin she'd been holding back.

"All right, Goliath. Go ahead," she said with a small shake of her head.

The little dog bounded over for a touch from David and received what he was looking for.

"You need some male companionship, buddy, you let me know," David said. "Or maybe some tips on how to worm your way past some bigger dog into a lady's heart."

"David," Gretchen drawled as the maddening man raised his brows and gave her that warm seductive smile she was beginning to know too well. Really, this man was just way too smooth for her to ever feel restful in his presence. He'd obviously been born to reel women in with just a look.

"Gretchen," he drawled, imitating her tone. "Tomorrow I want to see the construction sites where the bodies were found. We'll go right after morning coffee at the Hip Hop Café."

She nodded before she realized he was calling the shots again. Automatically she opened her mouth to protest.

He tilted his head slightly and gave her a serious, questioning look with those deep emerald eyes of his that sent a spark zipping through her entire body.

"Yes?" he asked, his voice low and sexy.

He was playing a game with her. She knew that. She could either fall into the trap by arguing with him or she could refuse to play. Gretchen was absolutely positive that David was a master at the game of winning a woman's attention. She was good at what she did, but so was he. And she was in way over her head right now in this cozy space with David Hannon's broad shoulders filling up her kitchen and her vision.

Shaking her head, she dismissed the subject. "Thank you," she said instead. "For carrying in my groceries."

"Thank *you*," he whispered back.

Confusion had her opening her eyes wider.

"For taking in a sickly little runt even though I know darn well he wasn't what you really wanted. Even though you were probably kicking yourself all the way home, and he's probably caused and will continue to cause you no end of trouble."

Gretchen was pretty sure they weren't really talking about Goliath anymore.

"I can handle trouble, David. I welcome trouble."

He grinned again, then moved out the door and pulled it almost shut behind him. "That's good, Gretchen," she could swear she heard him say just before the door clicked shut.

She couldn't help smiling. She couldn't help wondering why her skin felt alive and tingling even though the only touch she and David had shared had been slight and over too quickly. But there was something about the lazy way the man looked at her, that made her feel that he had touched her time and time again. There was something about the quiet, deep tone in his voice when he said her name, that made her feel he'd been thinking about what it would be like to slide his naked skin over hers.

"The man is definitely right," she whispered to no one in particular. "It's a good thing you know how to handle trouble, because top-notch agent though he may be, David Hannon is going to be a major source of very deep trouble."

And as she climbed into bed that night, another thought traipsed through her consciousness. It was a good thing she'd never taken a man like David to one of her friend's or relative's weddings. He was just the kind of man that would make people start urging her to think seriously about getting married lest she fall prey to some dangerous man with hot eyes and hot lips and deliciously seeking hands.

Maybe someday, she thought, she'd find the right man to haul off to one of those weddings. For now, though, she had to think about taking David off to examine those construction sites.

They had two bodies on their hands—and no answers to their questions.

They had barely gotten their coffee at the Hip Hop the next morning when Lily Mae Wheeler called across to their table.

"David, how are your parents? And your aunt? Your sister and your cousins? And those nice young men Cleo and Frannie married? I haven't been out to the Big Sky in a billion years."

David did his best not to laugh as the elderly lady leaned forward more and more with each question. The long bright dangling beads that dripped from her ears shook with each movement, but even more amusing was the fact that his mother had just been complaining that Lily Mae had been out to the Big Sky way too much lately. Her excuse was that she was checking up on the family and the newlyweds, but Yvette was sure that Lily Mae just wanted the latest dirt on what had happened between Jeremiah Kincaid and Raven Hunter thirty years ago.

"Everyone is doing great, Lily Mae," he said gently, all too aware that half of the lady's nosiness stemmed from the fact that she was alone after being widowed and then divorced twice after that. She could be a wicked gossip and cruel, but at the heart of all of that was a kind of pathetic need to be the center of attention. He knew that, but it didn't mean he was sharing any information the lady didn't need to know. Such as the fact that his aunt was so worried about this case that lately she could be heard quietly pacing the floor on certain dark and lonely nights. "The Big Sky has its usual complement of summer customers out to view the beautiful Montana scenery."

"You obviously love the view, too," Lily Mae said, shaking her head. Her glow-in-the-dark temporarily red hair, unlike her earrings, was wrapped around her head and therefore immobile. "How can you stand to live in the city after growing up out here?"

"I miss it every single day, Lily Mae," David said quietly, and he was surprised to realize how much he meant that. Not that it mattered. His work was important to him, and his work was elsewhere, but there was something about home…

"The city's not so bad, Lily Mae." Gretchen's soft voice brought him out of his reverie. He turned to look into her determined green eyes over her coffee cup. He wondered if she meant what she said, or if she was trying to defend him from Lily Mae. A touching thought. Probably not true, however. More likely Gretchen Neal was simply trying to convince him that he'd be better off scurrying back to Atlanta as soon as possible.

"Well, you grew up in the city and yet here you are," Lily Mae argued. "Although I hear you're taking a trip to Helena soon."

Gretchen froze. A small, almost imperceptible groan slipped through her lips, and she had an undeniable urge to reach across to Lily Mae's table and shove the words back into her mouth. How had the woman found out? And why did she care that Lily Mae knew?

"A bridesmaid again?" the woman was saying, shaking her head sadly. "How many times does that make now?"

Gretchen looked into the eyes of her friend Emma who was waiting on the next table. "I'm sorry," Emma mouthed, and was instantly forgiven. Gretchen knew all too well how good Lily Mae was at worming secrets out of people.

She somehow managed to smile at Emma and shrug her shoulders. But it was difficult. She knew Lily Mae's condescending tone too well. She'd heard it from any number of people lately. As if everyone thought she couldn't get a man of her own. As if they didn't understand that she just didn't want to get married. Ever.

"I've rather lost count of how many weddings I've stood up at, Lily Mae," she said, telling the truth. "I guess I'm just lucky, though, to have so many friends who love me enough to want me to be a part of their weddings."

She managed to keep the defiance out of her voice. She managed to keep from even looking toward David. It didn't matter that it was her own choice not to wed. People looked at the fact that she had stood up at so many weddings as somehow humiliating. *She* didn't feel that way. She loved celebrating with her friends and family, but she hated that pitying tone people like Lily Mae sent her way. She hated knowing that even those closest to her worried about the fact that she was a perpetual bridesmaid well on her way to living her life alone forever.

"I'm sure you're right, dear," Lily Mae said, patting Gretchen's hand. "But it's a shame you haven't gotten married yourself, Gretchen."

"Lily Mae," David drawled. "Bite your tongue, sweetheart." David's voice was low and sexy as he leaned forward, close enough so that Gretchen could feel the warmth of his skin next to hers. "If Gretchen had gotten married, she would have ruined the nighttime dreams of half the men in this town."

Gretchen sucked in a deep breath of air. She saw Lily Mae's eyes go wide. The woman leaned closer. "What do you mean, David Hannon?"

He gave the lady a slow, sexy smile. "I mean, Lily Mae, that there are a substantial number of male animals in this town who moan in their sleep over restless dreams of Gretchen Neal. There's just something about a woman who's good at her job, who knows what she wants and doesn't want, and who happens to be beautiful, as well, that makes a man feel kind of crazy on a dark and lonely night. Something irresistible. It gives a man a goal, something to warm himself with in the winter and hold close to him in the summer. The way I look at it, Gretchen is performing an important civic duty by keeping the hopes and dreams of all of us single males alive. It makes a man sit up a little straighter and behave a bit better if he knows that a woman like Gretchen may pass by at any moment. If she were already married, well, she'd be some other man's woman and we wouldn't care so much. I'm sure the crime rate in town might take a small leap or two."

Gretchen realized that the whole café had gone quiet and that Lily Mae still hadn't answered. It was the first time in a long time that anyone had stunned the woman into silence.

"Now if you'll excuse us, Lily Mae, Gretchen and I have some important business to attend to. The woman is leading a criminal investigation, you know. She doesn't have time today to think about getting married."

"No, of course not," Lily Mae finally said, placing her long, ring-covered fingers against her chest. "Gretchen's going to find the murderer who still might be on the loose. I only mentioned marriage because I thought Gretchen would make some man very happy."

"Thank you, Lily Mae," Gretchen said, going along because she knew deep in her heart that the woman didn't really mean to be cruel. "I'm sure you'll make some man happy again, too, someday. You're a much better cook than I am. That's for sure."

The woman beamed. She didn't even seem to notice that David and Gretchen, her audience, had gotten up and were walking toward the door.

Gretchen was all the way back to the car and seated before she turned to David. "Thank you for saying all that, even if it was a little embarrassing and absolutely untrue."

He turned to her and smiled that melting smile. She was almost getting used to the way her breath came too hard and fast by now.

"It was the least I could do for my partner," he said quietly, brushing aside her gratitude.

"I did feel like I had a partner back there," she admitted.

"You do."

"Yes, I guess I do," she said, starting the car and pulling out into traffic.

"And, Gretchen?"

"Yes, David?" She kept her eyes on the road and the contented smile on her lips.

"For the record, I meant what I said back there about you not letting other people influence what you do.

You're a strong, independent woman and you know your own mind and what you feel is best for you.''

"Thank you, David. I'd say you're rather strong and independent, too.''

She could almost feel his grin. "That's been said about me. Yes, it has,'' he agreed. "And Gretchen?''

She took her eyes off the road and turned to him just for a second. His eyes were narrowed, intent on her own eyes…and lips. Especially on her lips. She took a deep breath and grasped the wheel harder as she looked away.

"I meant every other word I said, too,'' he repeated. "Any man who spends any time with you and doesn't imagine you naked in his arms at night is lying.''

His words made her voice freeze in her throat. She should remind him that they were working together on a case, that he was assisting her. She should tell him that what he was saying was inappropriate for the situation.

"And any woman who looks into those bedroom eyes of yours and doesn't see a bed at her back would be less than truthful, too,'' she heard herself saying instead. But when she turned and saw the lazy intent in those very same eyes, she shook her head. "But now that we've both admitted that we're attracted, David, I think we'd better also both agree that it would be all wrong for us to act on our desires. We do have to work together, after all, and I'm sure you've got plenty of women waiting for you back in Atlanta. You want to get this case solved, after all, don't you?''

His smile was slow when it came, laced with sex appeal and the danger that was an inherent part of his life. "You're a very wise and perceptive lady, Gretchen Neal. I do want to solve this case.''

"Then let's do it,'' she agreed, wishing her words hadn't been so shaky. Because for all that she knew she was right and staying away from David Hannon's body was the only way they could operate together, there was a part of her that had been unleashed today. She wondered how long it would take her to banish the vision that had formed in her mind, of David braced above her as he lowered himself and joined his body to hers.

"This is where Raven Hunter's remains were found," Gretchen said, carefully skirting the yellow police tape that protected the area from further contamination. "They had spent two weeks clearing the land when his bones were discovered. Until then no one had known exactly what had happened to him. Even now, with a bullet in his ribs, we can't be sure whether he was killed on this site or whether his body was brought here after his death. With Storm away, we don't know much about what happened in the last few hours he was alive."

"But we do know that he and Jeremiah had not been on good terms. Jeremiah had tried to pay him to leave town and desert my aunt Blanche. Everyone had assumed that he'd left town right after that."

"That part of the story is pretty well documented, yes."

"And no other evidence was found other than the bullet wedged into the rib. No weapon. No other clues that we could use."

"There were rocks found over the skeleton. More than there were on the rest of the site. Possibly intentionally placed there. But then, you know that already. You've read the file. The area's been thoroughly searched."

"I know. I'm just wondering what might have been damaged or missed in those first few days when the digging was going on, if there were any clues that might have been lost that could still be recovered."

She shrugged her agreement. "We'll keep trying. In the meantime, all we can do is wait for Storm to show up so we can interview him."

"How about the other site? What do you know about the Peter Cook case?"

"At this point we don't suspect foul play. The evidence indicates that the man died in a fall at a site where he had every reason to be. And there were no witnesses that we've been able to locate."

She stopped, but apparently she hadn't stopped soon enough. David's brows rose.

"You don't suspect foul play, but you're not completely sure this is a case you can close without nosing around a bit?"

She shook her head as David waited for her answer. "It's nothing, really. Absolutely nothing that would ever matter in a legal sense. Just a strange feeling. Peter Cook was an experienced outdoorsman."

Nodding, David acknowledged her doubts. "Not the kind to slip under normal circumstances?"

She shrugged. "Everyone has accidents now and then. Still, I do have a disturbing feeling about all of this."

"Who wouldn't? There *have* been a number of strange events taking place in Whitehorn in the past few years," David conceded. "Murders. Kidnappings. Far too many for a town this size. I thought all that was done, that all the pieces had been tied up tight, but now here we have it. A thirty-year-old murder and another death, both on Kincaid land. More trouble on the home front."

"I'm sorry your family has gone through so much," Gretchen said gently, and David was sure she meant what she said.

He shook his head. "Don't feel sorry for us, Gretchen. We're a happy bunch, for the most part. But this has got to affect Summer to some extent. She lost her mother a few weeks after she was born and thought that her father deserted her. Now there are questions about Raven to be answered and all the upheaval of reliving the antagonism between her father and her uncle, but Summer's very happy now that she's married Gavin. He'll help her deal with this. It's Aunt Celeste I'm worried about. She's just not well. This is taking too much of a toll on her."

"We'll solve it, David. Together. How can we miss? The FBI's finest and Whitehorn's first lady of crime fighting?"

He looked up at her from where he was down on one knee, studying the dirt that had beheld so many secrets over the years. Behind her, the beautiful snow-covered peaks of the Crazy Mountains rose up. The picture was breathtaking. A beautiful, intelligent, determined woman standing against a backdrop that radiated strength and vitality and endurance.

"How can we lose, partner?" he agreed. "A team like us is bound to get at the truth in time."

He rose to his feet and stood beside her. She held out her keys. "You drive today," she said. "I'm tired."

He looked down into eyes that were alive and alert.

"What you are, lady, is a liar. A lovely, generous liar. And fair. Very fair."

"Remember that when I get bossy next time."

He chuckled as he turned the key in the ignition and roared off down the road, headed toward town.

In the trees not far away from where Gretchen and David had been standing only moments ago, a thin man with dark hair and dark eyes watched them drive away. The cut of his suit was expensive, his tie was neatly knotted, and the look in his eyes was deadly, like a diamondback rattler's on the verge of striking.

"You two think you make such a perfect pair," he said, "but you don't know a thing. Not a thing. Only I know what really happened on this site. Only I know about the sapphires and Peter's disappearance, and only I will ever have the right to know. And the right to claim."

Oh, yes, he had been the forgotten one. His grandfather had turned all that good land over to all those illegitimate grandkids his uncle had begotten. Garrett Kincaid had all but forgotten Lyle Brooks was his grandson, giving him only one puny piece of land that skirted the reservation—and only after he and his mother raised a ruckus. But this piece, little Gabriel's piece, held such secrets. Rich secrets. Sapphire blue secrets. And he, Lyle Brooks, was going to own them, lock, stock, and barrel. He was, and no frigid ice queen of a lady detective was going to stop him. He would do what he had to do to maintain his secrets. After all, after a man had committed murder, he had nothing left to lose and everything to gain. And Lyle Brooks most certainly intended to gain whatever he could in any way he could.

Four

"So you were out walking your dog at six in the morning and you saw something suspicious, Mrs. Adams? How exactly would you describe what you saw?" David watched Gretchen as she stood the next day, her notepad in hand, her sunglasses pushed back on her blond hair, waiting patiently for the agitated woman to answer.

"Well, of course, I know how to describe it, Gretchen. It was that Mr. Babbins down the road. He was picking up his newspaper and he was looking at me real creepy."

"Did he say anything to you? Do anything?" Gretchen's green eyes told nothing of her thoughts. She simply continued to wait for the woman's response.

"No, he just…looked. But he's pretty old, Gretchen, old enough to have been around here thirty years ago. A person worries when bodies start turning up, you know."

"I know, Enid, but you don't have to worry. We're on the job policing the town. We're looking out for your safety. As for Mr. Babbins, I can't arrest him for a look. You know that. I believe he filed a complaint about your dog trampling his lawn a couple of weeks ago. Have you spoken with him about that?"

"Of course I have. I told him that my Buster has no interest whatsoever in his lawn. That man needs a life. He moans over that little bit of grass as if it were a child."

"Maybe it is like a child to him, Enid. His family's

all grown up and moved away. His wife passed away years ago.''

"I know. I know. But he *was* looking at me funny. If Jeremiah doesn't turn out to be the killer, no offense to you, Mr. Hannon, I'd start looking there at Mr. Babbins. Right down the block from my house. He might have other bodies under that lawn of his. Maybe that's why the grass is so green.''

"I'll keep a record of your report, Enid," Gretchen promised as she and David bid the lady goodbye and went on their way.

"That's the fourth false lead we've had this week," David said, shoving his hand back through the heavy dark satin of his hair.

"Poor baby," she said, scribbling on her clipboard. "You must be missing the danger and excitement of the Bureau. Terribly.''

He chuckled. "Still trying to get rid of me, Gretch?"

She shook her head. "No, actually, I really was feeling sorry for you. This must be a bit boring compared to your usual lifestyle.''

"You think watching you twist the citizens of White-horn around your finger could ever be boring? You impress me, lady. Lots of people wouldn't have been nearly as patient with someone who just wants to complain about a troublesome neighbor.''

"No, it's more than that. Everyone's worried since all these strange things have been happening. There's an edginess to the town. Enid was just nervous, and now that she feels she's done something positive, now that someone from the department has come out, listened to her and offered her some assurance, she'll feel a little bit better. It's part of the job, letting people know that you're out there trying to keep the lid on. Doesn't matter whether it's Miami or Montana. That's what people really want to know, that the people in charge of their safety are aware of their existence.''

David watched her as she spoke. Her face was aglow with true satisfaction. She clearly loved her work. He wondered how she'd look if she felt that same kind of enthusiasm for a man, then shook his head at his own nonsense. He'd promised himself he wouldn't go down that road. But he was just about to ask her about her work in Miami when the radio came to life.

"Fifty-two. Domestic in progress at the Sadine place. Neighbors report suspect was yelling and shooting his gun into the trees. When the ammo gave out, he dropped it. No other known weapons. Both parties are in the living room. Entry should be no problem.''

"Copy that. Fifty-two en route,'' Gretchen said, spinning out onto the road. Her voice was tight and hard and she spared David a glance after she'd asked the dispatcher for details. "You ever get involved in a domestic?''

"Not in my line.''

"Ugly stuff,'' she said. "I did a lot of that in Miami. Not much around here, but it happens. Wayne Sadine doesn't get drunk often, but when he does, he likes to hit. He doesn't care who, but if his wife doesn't get out of his way, sometimes she's the one his fists make contact with.''

The words came out sharp and clipped. David felt the muscles tighten in his jaw. He remembered Wayne and he also remembered the tiny woman he'd married.

But when they reached the small, crooked house, Gretchen exited the car like an Amazon intent on eating Wayne Sadine's liver for lunch.

The house was silent. She knocked, then turned the knob as a yell and a slap sounded inside.

Wayne turned and roared as David pushed in front of Gretchen, ready to take the brunt of any blows, but Gretchen was having none of his interference.

"Wayne, you're drunk," she said.

"It's my own house."

"Peggy's house, too. What happened, Peg?"

It was obvious he had hit her, but the woman stood silent.

"Peggy?" Gretchen said gently.

"You know what will happen if you take him in."

"I know we can keep him until morning. He's drunk, he's disorderly, and not only did he hit you, but he was out in the road earlier firing a weapon. The neighbors called in the complaint and they're not going to back down. At least he'll be sober by morning. At least he'll know he can't just keep doing this and getting away with it."

But of course, David knew, the man could get away with it if Peggy didn't walk away from him, and it was just as clear looking at her that she was much too scared to do that.

"Come on, Peg," he said gently. "Let me take you over to the Big Sky for the night. You remember my mother—don't you?—when your mother used to work there. She always liked you. Said you had pretty strawberry hair."

"Don't touch my wife," Wayne roared, and David felt a prickle at the back of his neck. He whirled just in time to see Wayne hurtling his way and Gretchen crouching and kicking her leg up right into Wayne's path. The man fell like a tree that had been neatly sawed in two.

David stared down at the slender woman who had

saved his back. He automatically reached to scoop her up, then changed course and gave her his hand for an assist when he realized what he was doing. No way would Gretchen appreciate being treated as if she were a delicate flower, nor should she be treated that way. The woman had just acted with a speed, an agility and a courage and decisiveness that many big brawny men could never have matched.

Grasping her narrow hand, David gave a tug, bringing her back to her feet. He managed to stop himself from pulling her to him, but he knew that the look he gave her was fierce and tight and appreciative.

She stared at him, sucked in a long deep breath, then turned her attention to Peggy.

"I'll read Wayne his rights and give him a bed for the night when he wakes up," she promised the woman, brushing her disheveled hair back from her brow. "Could I talk you into pressing charges?"

Peggy shook her head. "I know it's cowardly, but I— I just don't think I can do that."

Gretchen opened her mouth, then shut it again. Clearly she and Peggy had walked this path before.

"About the Big Sky," David began, holding out his hand to Peggy.

"No, I couldn't. Your mother wouldn't even know I was coming."

He tilted his lips up slightly. "We'll call her," he whispered conspiratorially. "She'll rush around getting ready for you and be pleased as can be that she's going to get a chance to visit with you. Since your mother passed away, she hasn't had a chance to talk to you."

"Oh, I don't think—"

But some of the hesitation had drained away from her eyes.

"Don't think. Let me call."

And so they stayed. David heated water and Gretchen made tea while they brought Wayne around, then read him his rights.

Edward and Yvette drove up just at that moment.

"David, love," Yvette said. "I'm glad you called. And, Gretchen, I hear you decked him. Good for you. I hope he has a knot on his head to match the ones he must have been born with. Imagine beating on my poor little Peggy. Come here, sweetheart. We're getting you back to the Big Sky and into a nice crisp nightgown and a big feather bed."

David's mother bustled around like a mother hen. David gave Gretchen a knowing look and took charge of Wayne.

"Hit him again, dear, if you need to. I don't want him getting anywhere near Gretchen with those fists" were his mother's last words as she and her husband pulled away with Peggy in tow.

He and Gretchen watched them drive away, then led a limping Wayne to their own car. David turned to Gretchen as they clicked the door shut behind the man.

"That was an impressive kick back there, lady. You get to put those moves to use a lot back in Miami?"

He could see by the flash in Gretchen's eyes and the sag in her shoulders that the overly long day was taking its toll on her. She was both charged up and tremendously tired.

"He was going for your back, Hannon. He had a bottle poised over your head," she said with a sigh. "I didn't have time to think."

"I know," he said quietly. "I could have twisted away, but not with Peggy standing right behind me. Thank goodness for those long, delicious, and very talented legs of yours, Officer Neal. Now, should we get this mess in the back seat into town and a jail cell?''

"Good idea," she agreed. "Almost as good as handing Peggy into your mother's care. That was generous and sweet of both of you."

"My mother is a very generous woman, Gretchen, and with her children grown, she misses taking care of people—except for my father, of course. The B and B helps, but most of her visitors are just passing through. She hasn't gotten to put those deep-seated nurturing skills to use nearly enough to suit herself lately. I'm hoping it will be good for both her and Peggy."

And with that, he gently disentangled the keys from Gretchen's fingers. "You watch Wayne," he said, not wanting her to know that he needed to coddle her a little now that the adrenaline was draining out of her.

She chuckled. "Very smooth, David. I can see that you're used to taking care of the women in your life, but I'm an officer. I can handle stress and fatigue."

"Mmm, I know that. But why should you have to now that you have a partner to share that stress and fatigue with you? Go on, now. I'll let you be the strong one again tomorrow. For now, just watch Wayne."

Hours later when all the paperwork had been done and Gretchen had gone home, David kicked his feet up on the desk and leaned back in his chair. He was glad his mother had come for Peggy. She'd done so much worrying about his aunt Celeste lately that having Peggy around would be a comfort and a distraction for her and hopefully would be a brief respite for Peggy, as well.

He'd wished to relieve some of the stress and tension his family was going through by helping to bring a hasty end to this case, but it was clear nothing hasty was going to happen here. Raven and Jeremiah were both dead and

Storm seemed to have vanished into the past, as well. The mystery was still a mystery and David chafed at his inability to break through the mist that surrounded it. As for this current situation with Peggy, well, it was a help of sorts. His mother was quite simply never happier than when she could bustle around helping a young person find a way in the world. It would be a distraction for her.

But what about him?

David groaned and ran his hands over his eyes, trying to dislodge the picture of Gretchen throwing herself in front of Wayne today, that long elegant leg shooting up to catch him just beneath the chin.

How could a man resist that?

"Resist," he ordered himself. The lady has her life set just the way she likes it and so do you. All those hot thoughts coursing through you are nothing more than that. Ticklish desires. Fantasies. Just like the ones he'd had as a kid. Of playing football back in the days when his body wouldn't allow him to do much of anything he'd wanted it to do. He'd learned early on that he was a kid who wasn't going to be able to run with the pack. He was going to have to go his own route, forge his own trails. And it didn't matter that things had changed once he'd grown healthier and he'd become much taller and stronger than anyone would ever have believed. Some things just shouldn't be approached. Things that added complications to an already complicated situation. Such as touching Gretchen.

The ringing of the phone sent his fretful thoughts flying. "Hannon," he said as he snagged the receiver and brought it to his ear.

"David, how's it going?"

"Sascha? What are you up to, buddy?"

"A guy can't check up on his best friend? His friend who hasn't even called to say hello?"

David smiled to himself.

"Depends on the reason why he's checking up. The last time I saw you, you told me you were living in Bridget Nelson's bed. I thought I might be interrupting something important if I called."

"Good point," his friend said with a deep chuckle. "But right now the lady's asleep and I've been hearing rumors about what's going on in Whitehorn."

"Rumors?"

"Hey, news travels fast. If you can't find info in the Bureau, where can you find it? I hear you've paired up with a career detective. A lady. A very by-the-book lady."

"Gretchen's very talented," David said with a lazy smile. "Anything more you want to know about her?"

"She succumb to your charms yet like almost all the other women I've met?"

"Sasch?"

"Uh-oh. I hear 'back off' in your voice."

"Very good. I knew we were friends for a reason. You know when to butt out."

"You never used to get so upset when I asked about your current lady."

Sascha was right and David was pretty sure he knew the reason. The reason was that Gretchen was not his current lady and wasn't going to be his lady at all.

"She that special, David? You know what I've told you about getting in too deep. Take it from a man who knows way too much about what can go wrong when that happens. And you should know. You were the one who kept me alive when I was going through my divorce."

David felt a frown forming between his eyes. He *did* remember just how broken his friend had been. He and Sascha Fitzgibbons were a lot alike. Men with warm families, but essentially men who trod their own road. Alone. It was the truth. It was why he'd never even told Sascha that sometimes late at night when he was tired, he wished he were different, wished he had the ability to try for a lasting and permanent connection. He didn't. Women were his for the taking much of the time, but once taken, he seemed to tire quickly. Knowing that about himself, he tried not to get too close to any one woman. Not close enough to burn her, anyway.

"David, you're not falling for this Gretchen, are you? You've only known her a week."

A long, tired sigh slipped through David's lips.

"It's not like that, Sasch. Gretchen is simply a very good detective and a very nice lady."

Silence, then a low whistle.

"And there's nothing more to say than that, Sasch. You got that? I don't want any rumors flying around the office about Gretchen, okay? She doesn't deserve that kind of treatment."

"I hear anything, David, the guy who says it will be eating the carpeting on the floor."

David laughed. Sascha was the biggest pussycat he knew. A giant of a man and as gentle as they came. He hated hurting people. That didn't mean that he couldn't fight with the best of them, but he very rarely needed to.

"Thanks, Sascha, and thank you for worrying about me, but I'm all right. I'm technically on leave, but I've still got a case or two going, some stuff I can look into while I'm out here. I owe it to Phil to get something done since he was generous enough to turn his head for me on this thing."

"Oh. Well then. You're working. You're fine."

"I'm fine," David agreed with a laugh. Sascha thought that the Bureau was life itself and, for the most part, so did he. It was just another reason the two of them got along so well.

"I'm fine," he repeated for his friend's sake. "You can go back to the beautiful Bridget."

"Bridget. Isn't that a luminous name, David?"

"It's a beautiful name, Sasch," he agreed as they ended their conversation and hung up.

But it wasn't the name "Bridget" that was on his mind as he glanced out the window later and watched the moon climb through the sky. There was another lady on his mind, and try as hard as he could, he couldn't get her out of his thoughts.

Gretchen was trudging down the street with Goliath, the heavy leaves of the trees dripping shadows onto the sidewalk glowing in the moonlight. It had been a long day and the extra paperwork involved in arresting Wayne had made the day even longer. Not that she regretted the arrest. Peggy might not be able to pull away from the man she'd married and who abused her, but at least she would know that there were people who cared, that if she ever did feel she could make the break, there would be those who would help her.

The thought conjured up a sudden vision of intense green eyes. David had taken Peggy under his wing as if she were a wounded child. He had treated his mother with warmth and solicitousness when she had arrived. And he had insisted on driving when he'd known she was still reacting to the inevitable fatigue that followed the keyed-up moments detectives faced as a part of their daily regimen. He was the kind of man who looked for signs of need in a woman and he responded to those needs. He took care of people, was most likely used to having women falling all over him and relying on him. It was probably what had helped make him as an agent, that urge to make a difference. And yet, his very warmth was what made him dangerous to her, especially when she was tired. It would be so easy to press close into that warmth and snuggle close.

"Not the right thing to do, Neal," she whispered, catching Goliath's attention and smiling at him to urge him onward. When she dated, she always dated men out of her field, men who had barriers as high as her own. A little fun was all she wanted from a man. Not warmth, not someone who responded to her needs. That meant ties, sticky connections, the danger of getting in and not being able to get out, and she always made sure she knew where the door was when she went into a room or into a relationship. No way did she ever want to become the kind of woman who would trail a man around the country and give up most of the things she held dear. That had been her mother, and her mother had been an old and used-up woman long before physical age had taken its toll. That life wasn't for her. The single life held way too many charms and benefits to ever give it up.

That thought was sailing through her head as she neared a small blue cottage and Goliath began pulling on his leash. He barked softly, then whimpered when Gretchen ordered him to be quiet.

"I know," she said sympathetically. "That little Pomeranian with the twitchy tail lives here, doesn't she? But we've got to be careful, Goliath, you and I. Your lady love has an owner who's very particular about whom her pet associates with. It isn't easy, this relationship stuff, is it? Even if you just want to keep things easy and light, things have a nasty way of mixing themselves up. Let's go home, shall we?''

And so they turned toward the home that Gretchen still loved knowing was hers alone. A sense of warmth, of letting go and giving in to the sleepiness that had been waiting at the backs of her eyes for hours kicked in, and Gretchen knew why. She was heading back to her sanctuary. She'd picked out every stick of furniture in her tiny neat house, she hadn't had to make concessions for anyone. There she could do whatever she wanted, say whatever she wanted, live just as she and she alone wanted. It was her idea of heaven, her house, and they were almost back to heaven when she and Goliath ran into David.

Looking up into his dark smiling eyes, she should have been irritated at having her plans interrupted.

Gretchen smiled back. "Lost, rich boy?"

His chuckle slid in and caressed her senses in the most dangerous of ways.

He slowly shook his head.

"Not nearly lost," he confessed. "I saw Goliath's white coat bobbing down the street and I thought I'd stop and say hi," he said, bending to greet the dog.

"Hi," she said. "But what are you doing so far from home this late, David? Were you at the office working?"

"For a while. Mostly, though, I thought I'd come fill you in on Peggy's progress. I know how you feel about this town and being the caretaker of the inhabitants here. My mother's made Peggy an offer. Help finding a job to get her on her feet and independent and in the meanwhile, room and board and all the time she needs to think her life through. A chance to be away from Wayne for a bit and get her world together in a safe environment if she wants it. Peg's considering it.''

He fell into step beside her as they rounded the corner and headed up the walkway to her place. "I'm glad," she said, and her voice floated softly on the whisper of a breeze that lifted the pale tendrils of her hair, a breeze that smelled of summertime grass recently clipped and flowers. "Would you like to come in?" she asked, wondering where those oh so dangerous words had come from.

He gazed down at her. His eyes darkened, narrowed. "Yes." The word came out harsh and fierce. As if he realized that, he folded his hands into fists, took a deep breath and backed off half an inch. "But I probably shouldn't."

He was right. He shouldn't. But he had brought her this news that she was happy to hear. He'd brought it because he knew she'd want to hear it, Gretchen told herself, and for no other reason. So…how could she be less of a good neighbor?

"I'll make a pot of decaf," she said.

"You'll put your feet up and enjoy a few minutes with Goliath. I'm the intruder. I'll make the coffee."

Gretchen smiled. "I thought I was the bossy one."

"You are. Don't let anyone tell you differently."

"Of course I won't. Bossy people generally don't let anyone tell them anything they don't want them to." And as they walked in the door, she unleashed Goliath, washed her hands and went straight to the coffeepot.

David chuckled. "Making a point?"

She was. Men had tried to take the reins from her before. And they'd failed. It was part of the reason why she didn't want to marry. She was too used to going her own way, too used to being the one in charge. She liked being the strong one.

But as David came up behind her and rested his hands

on her shoulders, as the warmth of his hands and his body
and the soap and aftershave and male scent of him drifted
around her, Gretchen couldn't keep her hands from jos-
tling slightly, the water sloshing just a bit.

"David," she drawled in warning.

"Shh," he whispered, bending his head, his breath
warm at her ear. "You've had a long day and you've
had your way, haven't you? You're making the coffee,
aren't you?"

His long, lean fingers kneaded her skin, gently stroking, soothing, sliding over her. The tension of fatigue
fled, the tension of being touched by a man who knew
just how to turn her nerves to fire grew.

"What…what are you doing?" She barely got the
words past her suddenly dry lips.

"Relaxing you. I realize now that I shouldn't have
come over here. You're tired and now you're making me
coffee."

"You brought me news I wanted to hear."

His fingers slid beneath the thin cotton of her blouse.
His skin met hers. Gretchen closed her eyes. She carefully lowered the coffeepot to the counter.

"David?"

He nudged aside thick strands of her hair, placing his
lips against the side of her neck, and she sagged against
him.

Somehow she turned in his arms. She looked up into
those hot green eyes.

"I—" She parted her lips, snagging his attention.

"Tomorrow. We'll worry about the reasons why not
tomorrow," he promised as he caught his hands around
her narrow waist and pulled her high and tight against
him. "For now…this."

His lips covered her own as he claimed her. Hard,

hungry lips that molded to the softness of her mouth, then gentled as he nibbled at her.

David pulled back slightly and she followed him. Gretchen raised her hands, gripped his shirt and found his lips again.

His hands skimmed her waist, climbed her back. He slid his fingers over her sensitive skin, bringing them forward to cup her breasts.

A low moan curled deep in her throat, barely escaping. She leaned closer still.

"Gretchen." The word came out on a groan, just as Goliath barked.

The sudden, unexpected sound sent Gretchen pushing back from David. Her breathing was labored, and David's eyes looked dazed, still cloudy with desire.

Her own probably did, too. She looked away, down at her little dog.

"It's all right, Goliath," she managed to say, knowing that it was not all right at all. She had been kissing David, practically tearing his shirt from him. His hands had been everywhere, delighting her, seducing her. She shouldn't have been enjoying this time with this man in this way. Besides, it was late and both of them had work tomorrow. They had to work together—as partners solving a crime, not as lovers.

She kept her eyes on her dog, collecting her thoughts, enforcing a calm on herself she didn't truly feel. But Goliath wasn't looking at her or even at David. He was dancing in front of the window.

David gave her one last intense look and moved to the window. He was probably making sure she was all right, Gretchen guessed, making sure Goliath hadn't scared away an intruder. The darn man just had way too much protective male in him.

"He probably just saw an owl," Gretchen said. "Goliath's a little high strung."

"You should keep this down at night," David said, pulling down the shade.

"Yes. I should. I usually do, but—"

"But tonight your partner interfered and caught you by surprise."

It was the truth. She hadn't been acting very smart from the moment David had shown up.

She bit her lip.

"Don't do that," he said. "Don't start getting that I-shouldn't-have-been-kissing-a-fellow-officer look."

Somehow she dredged up a smile. "Well?"

"*I* shouldn't have started it," he said, taking the blame. "It was definitely my doing. But you know what, Gretchen?" David moved to the door, a slow smile on his lips.

"What?"

"I don't regret kissing you. Not one bit."

He paused, his hand cupping the doorknob as he looked back over his shoulder. "And I think I should give you fair warning. Someday I'm going to kiss you again when I get the chance. But not tonight."

She raised one brow. "Not in the mood anymore, David?"

He chuckled at that. "Very much in the mood, Gretchen. Which is exactly why I'm leaving. You're tired tonight, and I have the feeling we're both going to need every ounce of energy we can muster when we finally make love."

And with that, he pulled the door open and stepped outside.

Gretchen blinked twice as the door snapped shut behind him. She told herself to breathe.

The man was totally outrageous. But then, she'd known that. What other kind of agent would come in and ask to take part in an investigation he had absolutely no right to be on? What kind of man was David Hannon, after all?

"A very sexy one, Goliath. A man who makes my fingers itch, my toes curl, and every part of my body ache. And that makes him dangerous. No way am I letting my guard down around David Hannon again. I probably shouldn't invite him into my house again, either. And don't go giving me that look. The man is trouble. Big trouble, and we're not looking for trouble, are we?"

Goliath gave a short bark.

But, Gretchen wondered, did that bark mean yes or no?

Celeste Monroe stared blankly out her window of the Big Sky Bed & Breakfast. The night was warm but slightly breezy. That should have made it pleasant, good sleeping weather, but there was no way she could sleep, Celeste knew, turning to pace up and down the deep carpeting of her room. The dreams were chasing her again.

Something was wrong with this case regarding Raven Hunter. Something really bad. Something she should remember. Why couldn't she remember any of it?

Every time she thought of Raven or Jeremiah, she felt fear. Cold droplets of sweat trickled down her back, dampening her nightgown. Nausea rose up within her.

There were so many questions rattling through her head. How could she sleep?

She knew that Jeremiah was being blamed for Raven's death. Something wasn't right with that. If she could only remember what it was, if she could fill in the blank spots, dredge up the parts of that long-ago nightmarish night that eluded her.

She didn't know what had happened, but she knew one thing. She loved her nephew desperately and she didn't want him digging into this case. Nothing good could come of that.

If only she could remember why. If only she knew why her sister Blanche had come to her in those restless dreams she'd had. *A day of spiritual awakening,* Blanche had said. Soon she would have an awakening.

The only question was, Did she really want to have an awakening? Which was worse, the truth or the nightmares? And what if David discovered the truth and it was as bad as she feared?

What if what he discovered was unchangeable, unforgivable, as awful as the constant tremors running through her led her to believe?

Dark pain and anguish filled her soul. Regret. Fear. So much to lose. So much to flee from. She'd been fleeing for a long time.

Only now there was news. Evidence of sorts. Something that might jar the memory and let everything come flowing back to her somehow. And now David had come home to find out the truth.

She loved him. He was her nephew and she loved him almost as much as she loved her own children. Fondly. Ferociously. She would sacrifice her own safety for his, she loved him that much. But none of that mattered, because she didn't want him here. Not like this.

Somehow she had to find the answers he was seeking before he did. If she did that, maybe she could be ready. She'd go to the station. Maybe that would help her remember. And maybe she could finally find some peace and some rest.

Five

"You didn't have to climb the tree to get the cat, David. This isn't the sixteenth century. We have machinery that lifts us right up into the branches. Amazing stuff."

David heard the curt tone in Gretchen's voice and couldn't help smiling.

"Worried about me, Gretch?"

She let out her breath in a whoosh as they finally made it back to her office. She'd been silent all the way back to town. Now her eyes were flashing green sparks when she turned to him.

"Yes, David. Of course I'm angry. Weren't you the one who just a week ago said that you were now responsible for my life and I was responsible for yours? How do you think I would feel if you fell out of that tree and killed yourself?"

"I don't have to ask. I know, Gretchen, that you would feel you were somehow to blame."

She stood there looking up at him silently with those light green eyes of hers and he wanted to take her in his arms and tell her not to worry. He wanted to crush her softness beneath his hardness, to wrap her up in white sheets and roll with her in a big bed. He wanted to chase those shadows from her eyes.

"You could have fallen," she reiterated.

"It wasn't that far, Gretchen," he said gently. "I've climbed much higher, been in a thousand times more danger.'' It hadn't been that high, although she was probably right. It would have been much simpler and easier to wait for the right equipment, but the child on the ground had been worried, and even Gretchen had looked a bit concerned about the tiny gray kitten up in the tree. And besides, darn it, he'd just needed some activity, anything to chase away the restlessness that had been edging into him lately. His hands were tied on this case. His hands were also tied where touching Gretchen was concerned, it seemed. Because the lady just wasn't at all certain that she wanted his hands on her soft body. And he'd been thinking of nothing all day but that kiss they'd shared last night. He wanted his hands and his lips on her very badly.

She blinked suddenly, as if reading his thoughts, and then finally shook her head. "All right, it wasn't that high," she agreed. "And I'm sorry for complaining. I'm just…a bit tense this morning. I wanted to talk to you. Last night—what happened last night—it shouldn't have. It can't. Not again. You have to know that as well as I do."

He reached out. She backed away a step. "I mean it, Hannon. You're my assistant."

"A temporary one," he told her. "And I don't, in reality, work for you at all. I'm FBI. You're one of Whitehorn's finest. And very fine at that. Exquisite, in fact."

"David."

Her lips mouthed the words just as another voice said the same word behind them.

Both Gretchen and David turned to see his aunt standing in the doorway. Celeste was clutching a large hemp bag, her fingers wrapped around the tortoiseshell handle. Her long rust skirt with the tan leaves besprinkled in the folds flowed out around her as she rocked back and forth on her heels.

"Well, David, here you are," she said briskly in that no-nonsense tone she'd always used to hide the very soft person dwelling inside. "I just…well, since I was in town, I thought I'd pop in for a minute to see you and make sure you were taking care of yourself. Your schedule's so erratic these days, I thought it would be nice to just say hello. Besides, your mother wanted to check and see if you would be home for dinner tonight."

"Aunt Celeste," he said, stepping forward and folding her into his arms. "What a nice surprise. You know Gretchen, of course."

"Celeste," Gretchen said, holding out her hand.

"Well, of course I know Gretchen," Celeste agreed. "She's been out to Big Sky to question me. I understand she's extremely good at her job. I have no doubt at all that the two of you will be finding who's responsible for all the upheaval in the town. Do you think you'll find the person soon? Are you close?"

She opened her eyes wider and glanced at both her nephew and Gretchen.

"It's an old case. Could take time," David said, smiling at his aunt. "Come in. Sit down and rest."

"No, no, that's fine. I'll just be in and out. So you still don't know what happened? You don't really think it was Jeremiah, do you, David?" She let go of her purse with one hand and grasped a bunch of her skirt, twisting the fabric in her fingers.

"Mrs. Monroe," Gretchen began gently, "I know this must be difficult for you, but truly this case is still open. We can't make assumptions."

"Come on, Aunt Celeste," David said, taking her by the elbow. "Let me give you a lift home." He glanced over his shoulder at Gretchen and she nodded back at him as he gently led his aunt out of the office.

"I'm—really, I'm fine, David," Celeste said as they made it to the sidewalk. "I just wondered. That was all. And, anyway, I do have my car here. Will you be home for dinner?"

"I promise we'll all be together tonight, Celeste. I'll even dress for dinner and come prepared to entertain mother's guests. Maybe I'll even bring a guest." He nodded pointedly toward the building they'd just vacated.

Celeste's dark eyes softened just a bit. "That would be nice, David. She's very pretty, isn't she?"

"She's lovely *and* accomplished, too, Aunt Celeste."

"Well, of course she is. Rafe told me so himself when I saw him right after he put her in charge of this investigation. Besides, your mother will approve."

David leaned back and looked his aunt straight in the eye.

"Well, we never get to meet the women you're involved with," she said.

He chuckled at that. "Don't use the word 'involved' in front of Gretchen. I'm afraid she'll walk out the door."

"Well, of course. You're her…"

"I believe the word you're looking for is 'partner,' Aunt Celeste. As in business associate."

"Partner, yes."

"Yes, exactly," he said to himself as she walked away. Partner. He'd better remember the word if he didn't want Gretchen to run.

"You've invited me to dinner at the Big Sky?" Gretchen asked a few minutes later.

David grinned. "At the Big Sky. And don't look so suspicious. We're just going to feed you. I can guarantee that I won't try slipping you into bed under the watchful eyes of my mother. Not that she'd object.''

Gretchen's eyes opened wide. "You've done that before?''

His grin gave way to low, sexy laughter. "No, and that's why she wouldn't object. My mother would assume that if I was serious enough about a woman that I would risk sneaking her into a guest bedroom when there are so many other more obviously private places, that I would be making a more or less public declaration of my intentions.''

"Your intentions being…''

"Taking a wife, making babies, shooting for forever.''

Gretchen drank in a long breath of air. "I see.''

"Yes, I guess you do. So we're just talking dinner tonight. We'll save our private moments for a private place.''

"David?''

He looked down at her, giving her his full attention.

"Has any woman ever told you that you are absolutely shameless?''

"Yes, I believe they have. A few teachers. My aunt. My mother.''

"Not the women you date?''

He shrugged. "I wouldn't call most of what I do dating. In my line of work I do a lot of things…on the run, so to speak.''

The slightest pink glow settled on her cheeks. As if she'd felt the heat, Gretchen rubbed one hand over her jaw, then slipped it into her pocket, suddenly standing up straighter.

"So there'll be no settling down for you, either?'' she asked.

"I'm a bit of a loner. Always have been.''

She stared at him for several silent seconds, her lips soft, her eyes even softer—maybe even a tad worried—before she nodded.

"Then I suppose there's no problem with us having dinner," she conceded. "This will simply be a visit between colleagues."

His smile was rueful.

"What?" she asked.

"You were way too happy to find out that I live my life on the solitary side," he pointed out.

She shrugged one shoulder. "Well, it just makes things easier knowing that you don't get involved. You already know that I don't. Not that being a loner is an essential part of my nature. I have a world of friends and relations so there's always company when I want some, and I want that company frequently, but I choose to *live* alone. So, yes, it's nice to know that we see eye-to-eye on this issue, and, yes, dinner with your family will be lovely. I've missed seeing them. I suppose being involved in this investigation has made me pull back just a bit. In a town this size, the professional and personal often overlap and sometimes I walk a fine line. You don't think anyone will feel uncomfortable having me there, given the circumstances?"

"Well, if they do, then I suppose they'd feel uncomfortable having me there, too. We're in this case together, Gretchen. And besides, my family understands that this case isn't about you or me. It's about justice. My parents instilled the need for justice in me at an early age. I suppose that's part of the reason I elected to get involved in the type of work I'm in."

"Your parents have always struck me as very fair people," she agreed. "Do you think Frannie and Austin will be there? I haven't seen your sister much lately. I like her.''

Her voice sounded so eager, he couldn't help holding out one hand as if he wanted to capture that eagerness, brush his fingers over the softness of her lips in a long, slow caress.

He caught himself just in time.

''Sorry, partner,'' he said, lowering his hand to his side again. ''I'll try to behave in public tonight, and I'll make a point of calling Frannie. Cleo, too. We'll make it a special occasion.''

''The traveler finally comes home to the heart of his family?''

''And he brings a date,'' he said with a wicked grin.

She raised her brows. ''Is that what I am?''

''No, but I thought I'd gone too long without getting a rise out of you.''

She chuckled. ''I'm wise to you, Hannon. I'm learning how you think. You're going to find it harder and harder to get a reaction from me.''

But as she pulled back to walk away from him, he did raise his hand. He let his fingers trail down her cheek. And then he bent and placed his lips just where his fingers had been.

''Tonight,'' he promised her. And though he'd meant to prove something to her, that he could indeed get a reaction from her—and judging by the dusky pink of skin, he definitely had—the jolt of pure desire that skimmed through him proved something even more to himself. His reaction to Gretchen Neal was getting stronger. He was going to have to either back away or else move forward and move on. There was, after all, no other choice but to sit and simmer and hunger for the lady's touch.

And that was a dangerous combination. A man—or a woman—who was spending all his or her time steeped in desire wasn't thinking about the business at hand. And in his and Gretchen's business, that kind of preoccupation could be deadly.

"David? You there?" David was almost ready to step out the door on his way to pick up Gretchen for the evening when Sascha's call came through.

"Sasch? What's wrong?" Hearing the slur in his friend's voice, David gripped the phone so hard he thought the plastic might bend.

"What could be wrong, my friend? I'm fine, very fine. It's you I'm worried about," Sascha said, his voice dipping down low and sad.

"Nothing to worry about here, Sasch," David said quietly. "Everything's fine."

"No. It's not. I heard it in your voice the other day. You're getting tangled up with your Detective Neal."

"We're working together, Sascha. Why are you worried? Have you heard something about Gretchen that I should know?"

Sascha's laugh was low and harsh. "Who needs to hear anything? She's a woman, isn't she?"

Ah, so now they were getting to the point. "Sascha, has something happened between you and Bridget?"

Silence. Complete and utter silence.

"Sasch? Answer me."

More silence, then a muffled curse. "What could happen? I told her I wanted to marry her, she decided she loved her ex-husband more. As if I didn't know better. Hell, I've been married, David. I've been up that mountain, and it was an awful, unpredictable and ultimately disappointing climb. Why did I think I wanted to risk that again?''

"I'm so sorry, Sascha. You're sure she's gone for good?"

"She ran like a rabbit caught in the crossfire of two hunters. And what's more, you know Ted Cosgrove?"

"Sure. Nice guy."

"Nice divorced guy. Or almost divorced. His wife left him just last week. She wanted to be free and now Ted can barely see how to tie his shoes in the morning. He looks awful. He feels awful," Sascha said, clearly equipped with firsthand knowledge of what the man was going through.

A long sigh slipped through David. He wanted to take his friend's pain. Damn, he wanted to be there to help Sascha, but that wasn't possible. "Sasch, I wish—"

"Don't wish. I didn't call to talk to you about Bridget or even about Ted, Dave. Not really. I just called to tell you to stay the same as you always have been. Be careful if a woman makes your clothes fit too tight and your head swim and your heart bang around inside your body like an atomic Ping-Pong ball. You know that feeling, David?"

He wasn't sure if he knew that feeling exactly, but he had a pretty good idea what his friend was referring to. And he was also pretty sure Sascha was right. About being careful.

"I won't do anything impetuous, Sascha," he promised.

A low groan followed. "David, your middle name is impetuous."

David felt his smile forming. If his friend could tease him just a little, Sascha's world still held a bit of brightness.

"Yeah, but I have a good friend who keeps the reins on me. Thanks, Sascha," he said.

"No. Thank you," Sascha told him. "I really did call to talk about Bridget, I guess. It's helped to hear your voice."

And it had helped to hear his friend's voice, too, David realized. Sascha had sprinkled in that tinge of reality he'd been grasping for and missing these past few days with Gretchen. Now maybe he could get on with things, with work, and just leave the lady alone, the way she wanted to be left alone.

But first, he was taking her to a family dinner. He had a pretty good feeling that Sascha would have begged him not to do this.

It wouldn't have worked. This far, at least, he was committed.

"But this is where we hit the end of the line, Hannon," David reminded himself. "That's the way the lady wants things and the way you have to want them, too."

"It's so very good to see you here, my dear," Edward Hannon was saying just a short time later, taking Gretchen's hand in his own. "You don't need to be a stranger, does she, Yvette?"

Yvette smiled and let out a low laugh. "As if you and I had ever met a stranger, Edward. But you know what he means, don't you, Gretchen? Or maybe you don't. Edward and I tend to follow a different drummer, as they say. I think we may have been a sore trial to our strait-laced little Frannie."

Little Frannie, a grown and very married woman, smiled and pressed a kiss to her mother's cheek. "And you know I love you for being just who you are."

"Yes, but I sometimes think you felt a bit uncomfortable. Perhaps you would have liked a few more rules. Perhaps you should have had them if you needed them. Anyway, Gretchen, dear, please don't be a stranger anymore. We like seeing you. We're glad to have you here tonight. You did well, David,'' she said, as if he'd just gotten an A on his report card.

He gave his mother a lazy, indulgent smile and Gretchen suspected he was used to his mother praising him as if he were still unable to tie his shoes without help.

''David climbed a tree yesterday to retrieve a lost kitten. He didn't even wait for the cherry picker to come,'' she volunteered before she realized just how juvenile her own words sounded.

''Of course,'' Edward said. ''He wouldn't. David always did do things his own way. We worried about him a bit as a child, but really, there wasn't any reason to worry. David was just David. Rules never seemed to apply to him.''

''Yes, he broke every one and somehow managed to get away with it, too,'' Frannie said with a laugh. ''I was always in awe of how he did it. But I suppose you're a bit of a rule breaker, too, Gretchen. It takes a rather adventurous sort to go into law enforcement.''

''Maybe,'' Gretchen agreed. ''For me it was just a natural progression. I'd grown up taking care of all my brothers and sisters, helping them fight their battles and making sure their rights weren't violated. I fell in love with law enforcement right from the start.''

''I hear you got Wayne Sadine to go for counseling and to try joining AA,'' Cleo said. ''That's quite an accomplishment. Wayne was always pigheaded.''

Gretchen shrugged. ''I think his willingness to try had more to do with the fact that the powerful Hannons have taken Peggy under their wings. For the first time someone gave him a reason to want to change. How is Peggy, by the way?''

"She's a delight," Yvette said. "I feel so very sorry that I never thought to interfere enough to offer to take her in."

But David had. His first thought had been to get Peggy out of harm's way.

"Don't worry, my dear," Edward said. "She'll have a place here for as long as she wishes. And it won't be charity, either. She's a bright young lady, one who insists on pitching in to help out in whatever way she can. If she wants a job here, there's always plenty to do. If not, we'll help her find work elsewhere and get back on her feet. She won't have to be dependent on a man if she doesn't want to be."

His kind stare told her that he understood that not being dependent was an important issue for her. She smiled her gratitude.

"Why don't you take Gretchen for a tour of the Big Sky, David?" he offered. "I'm not sure she's ever seen the place by moonlight."

"Yes, Gretchen, it's really quite beautiful at night," Celeste said.

"Rather romantic," Yvette agreed.

"How could I turn down such a lovely offer?" Gretchen asked, rising from the table. The black silk of her short dress swished against the tablecloth as David slid her chair back and held out his hand.

"My family's pretty smooth, aren't they?" he asked with a twinkle in his eye as they moved out onto the moonlit terrace. "I'm sure they think I was being a bit slow about luring you out here."

Gretchen couldn't help laughing as she looked up into

his dark eyes. The man was sinfully handsome in formal black and white. And she knew from experience that there wasn't anything the slightest bit slow about him.

"I think your family is delightful. Your parents move together as if they're a single unit. It's obvious that they adore each other. I can see why the Big Sky attracts so many people to come here and then to come back again. Who could resist such a warm, caring atmosphere?"

"Ah, then, you're saying that you find us irresistible, are you, Ms. Neal? In that case, let me pull you farther into the shadows."

He slid his hand up her bare arm to the naked skin of her back. "Mmm, you should dress this way around the office," he told her.

"It's not very practical," she said suddenly. "I wasn't quite sure what to wear for a meal at the Big Sky."

"Anything," he told her. "Denim. Silk. Nothing. But this is nice. Very nice."

"David," she said, placing her hand on his chest as he leaned closer. "Your family—they don't think—"

"That we're lovers? I'm not privy to their thoughts, Gretchen."

"But you know them so well."

Yes, he did, and he knew that his parents, liberal as they were, would like him to settle down closer to home.

"You're not in danger with me, Gretchen. I promise you that."

"I wasn't afraid of that. You don't frighten me, David."

"What does frighten you? Anything?"

She studied his question for long minutes. "Commitment. Boredom. Being tied to someone so that their life has too great an effect on mine. That was my mother. Always following my father around. Always raising babies. And because I was the oldest, it was my life, too. I don't want that, David.''

He rested his forehead on hers, looked down into her moonlit, worried eyes. ''Then you're safe, Gretchen. In spite of my warm, loving family, they were very busy people when I was growing up, and I was a somewhat sickly kid. I didn't fit in with other kids and I learned to like my own company, my own way of doing things. After years of forging a solitary path, I'm not a good candidate for marriage, I'm afraid. You've seen how pigheaded and stubborn and pushy I can be. I'm not likely to change or to want to change. So you're safe from me in that sense.''

''In that sense?''

He nodded, grazing her jaw with his lips. ''But not any other. Because I *am* pushy and pigheaded and stubborn, Gretchen. That said, I'd still leave you alone if you weren't attracted to me. You're not attracted?''

''I'm not blind to your charms, Hannon. I'm a woman, after all.''

His lips rose in a smile against the bare skin of her throat and he kissed his way up to her lips. He touched his mouth to hers, then pulled away just a breath.

''And I'm a man, Gretchen. Neither of us may want marriage, but I want you in every other way a man can want a woman.''

''And you're a stubborn man, I've heard. Someone seems to have told me that.''

''I wonder who,'' he said, kissing her again.

''Some silly man, no doubt. Should we go back inside?'' she asked, her head falling back as he found the soft curve of her breast with his teeth and nipped slightly.

''No.''

''No,'' she agreed.

And he slid his hands up her body and placed a chaste kiss on the top of her head.

"No?" she asked.

"Not yet. Not until we have a proper bed and not until we're away from a roomful of people speculating on what we're doing."

"Mmm, they might make me marry you if I ravished you," she agreed.

"Indeed," he agreed. "My family looks out for those who try to take advantage of other people."

"I want to take advantage of you, David."

He slid his arm along hers and found her hand. "I know. And the fact that you've said that leads me to the truth."

"The truth? As in, who killed Raven Hunter?"

"Exactly. And, also, who filled Gretchen Neal's wineglass one too many times?"

She stared up at him. "I'm not drunk, David."

"No, but you're happy enough to lose all those prickly inhibitions that usually inhabit your body. When I have you—and I mean to—I want you inhibitions and all."

"I see," she said, leaning close to kiss him on the shoulder right through the black linen of his suit. "I wonder who did fill up my wineglass too many times."

He groaned low in his throat and led her to his car. "The same fool who's going to drive you home right now. The man who doesn't intend to make that same mistake again."

"The next time will be different? Will there be a next time?"

"I guarantee there'll be a next time, Gretchen. And maybe even a next and a next. I have the feeling that you and I are going to need a few 'next times' to get each other out of our systems."

She leaned back against the seat as he handed her into the car and fastened her seat belt against her hips.

"I'd like that, David. To get you out of my system. It's very difficult getting my job done when I'm always looking up into your eyes."

"Gretchen?"

"Yes?" Her voice was dreamy and soft and sleepy.

"Don't say another word," he said as he joined her in the car. "And just be grateful that my family instilled in me a certain amount of fortitude. It's that and only that that's saving us both from behaving very foolishly tonight."

But when he looked over, he found that Gretchen had gone limp with sleep. He lifted her hand and kissed her slender fingers before starting the car.

"Let's get you home, partner. Tomorrow you have to be tough and in charge again. Tomorrow we take things a step further."

Six

Gretchen held the sea-green breath of a dress up in front of her the next day. Except for the jacket, meant to be worn during the church service for Pamela's wedding, the gown was simplicity itself. With spaghetti straps and a neckline that dipped in a simple low scoop, the pale clingy material hugged the body in a long straight line to the floor.

"No wonder Pamela wanted to make sure it fit," Gretchen said to a curious Goliath as she slipped into the gown one more time just to make sure. "One extra spoonful of chocolate ice cream could mean disaster with a gown like this." As it was, the dress smoothed over her curves like a caress. It was perfect, except…she looked like a woman in search of a man.

"Which only means one thing, Goliath. My family will be on the prowl, out scouring the streets and parking lots looking for a man for me. They'll consider this dress a slap in the face, a reminder that once again I'm all dressed up without a proper husband to take me home and impregnate me. And then they'll start looking for a husband for me. Again."

She must have said that last word just a little too firmly. There must have been just a bit too much tension in her voice, because Goliath tilted his head and backed away a step or two.

She chuckled softly. "Don't worry, Goliath. I'm not

mad at all males. I just don't see why everyone thinks I absolutely must have one to take home and keep forever. And you know, there's only one way to fight the inevitable, don't you? I'll just have to keep dancing all night. A different man for every song. Otherwise, my best friends and family are going to do their darnedest to pick out a suitable mate to claim my time and my attention. The evening will be long and slow and painful.''

A short, sharp bark signaled her doggy buddy's agreement.

"You know what I mean, don't you, Goliath? I know how you like to play the field. The truth is that someday, somehow, I'm just going to have to make the truth clear to them. I'm not a marrying kind of woman. And that's final. When I wear this dress, I'm going to have the time of my life, and I'm going to go home alone at the end of the night.''

It appeared that Jackson Hawk had finally located Storm, but there was still a question mark as to when the man was going to show up. That fact didn't sit well with David. Another day had passed, they were no closer to a break, and he wanted this case solved. His aunt was clearly being affected much too much by all the upheaval, and he himself couldn't stay away from his work too long. Phil had been indulgent and understanding about his need to—finally—take some time for himself, but his time, after all, belonged to the government, something Gretchen had been asking him about just that morning. Trying to get rid of him more quickly, David suspected with a frown.

"He did say that he was coming in for questioning, though, didn't he?" David had prompted.

Jackson had sighed. "Storm's always been a very private person," he'd admitted. "He's not exactly one for allowing himself to be pinned down easily or for declaring himself, but—"

"But?" Gretchen had coaxed.

"I can guarantee that he'll be here—and that he'll be angry when he arrives," Jackson had promised.

Her shrug had been resigned. "It's to be expected," she'd said.

But after Jackson had gone, David hadn't missed the worried look in her eyes. "You're worried about Storm?"

She shook her head. "He's a man who lost his brother many years ago. And now he's had to face that loss all over again. The families are always angry. Why shouldn't they be?"

And David knew just how much this lady had gone through back on those streets of Miami. She'd seen more than her share of the tough stuff.

"Whitehorn shouldn't be this way," he said, wishing they were in a more private place than the station so he could risk placing a soothing arm around her shoulder or even pulling her in close against his side, dropping a kiss on the flowery fragrance of her silky hair.

She surprised him with the small smile that turned her light green eyes bright. "It usually isn't this way," she promised. "Your hometown is a wonderful place, David. Don't think it isn't just because a few bad things happen now and then. And don't go getting that let's-take-care-of-Gretchen light in your eyes. I'm a very resilient individual."

"A woman who handles things."

She shrugged. "Aren't you a man who handles things? Whatever led you into the Bureau in the first place?"

He laughed out loud at that. "Stubbornness, I'm sure

my family would tell you. I was a puny, sickly kid and when I hit college and started bulking up, I was determined to prove that I could play hardball. Purely pig-headed.''

''Hmm. I can believe that, but I doubt that was the only reason you went into your line of work. Plenty of other opportunities elsewhere to prove yourself. Admit it, Hannon, you're a sucker for truth and justice. You like to make sure that the good guys win.''

She stood in front of him, her hands firmly planted on her hips, her chin thrust out in challenge. An immovable wall, sure that she was right.

He lifted one shoulder. ''I like to even the odds,'' he admitted. ''I like to make sure things are done fairly.''

Gretchen noted that David, who smiled so wickedly and so well, wasn't smiling now. She guessed that he'd seen his share of injustice as a kid. If he'd truly been scrawny and sickly as he'd said, she could well imagine what he'd had to put up with, even if he did have the Hannon name behind him. Maybe *because* he bore the Hannon name. He would have been a target now and then. But no more. He'd grown up. He'd grown gorgeous and tall and strong. He'd found his place, his self-confidence, and he attracted people, especially women, like roses attracted helpless bumblebees. He did it with that sense of justice, that humor, those eyes, and that wicked, wicked smile that promised pleasure beyond belief.

She was no different. She was susceptible. The temptation to rise up on her toes and feel those lips against hers again was almost overwhelming. And that was why she'd spent the morning drowning in paperwork. If there was anything destined to drown out desire, it was paperwork.

* * *

"Gretchen—Officer Neal, do you think you could do something about my next door neighbor? I mean, I don't want you to arrest him or hit him with your club or anything. Not yet, anyway. I just want you to kind of shake him up a little bit."

Uh-oh. Here we go again, David thought, raising one brow as Gretchen slowed to let the spindly man walking behind her have time to catch up. She steered him toward the sensible, neighborly way to handle his sticky problem of his neighbor cutting across his yard on his way to work. This kind of question-and-answer session seemed to follow the lady like shadows trailing sunlight. In the past week and a half since he'd become Gretchen's almost constant companion, David had come to realize that while the lady was fully competent in her role as law enforcer, she spent a substantial amount of her time soothing and mothering the citizens of the town who depended on her.

They'd almost made it all the way to the Hip Hop Café, David noted. Lunch was only a few steps away, and Gretchen very much needed her lunch. First thing this morning there'd been the news from Jackson, which had been less than they'd hoped for. And then she'd spent the rest of the morning wrestling with paperwork, which he knew she hated. Heck, everyone in law enforcement hated paperwork and there only seemed to be more and more of it as the years went on. So it had been a crummy morning. A draining morning. A give-me-sustenance kind of morning. Did the lady really need any more of this nonsense?

No, she didn't, but David was absolutely, completely positive she wouldn't appreciate him butting into her business, either. And so he settled for giving the man disgruntled looks.

When she'd finally soothed Harve's nerves and joined David, walking beside him into the café, she lightly nudged him in the ribs with her elbow.

"You weren't very subtle," she said. "You were all but growling. Poor Harve probably thinks the feds are going to raid his house at midnight just because he asked for a little help."

David raised his brows. "He didn't ask for a little help. He asked you to act like his mother, to act as a mediator between his neighbor and him. A grown man like that, he should be ashamed throwing his petty problems off on you."

He lightly touched the small of her back, motioning her toward a booth in the rear.

"They're my problems, too," she insisted.

David snorted. "You can't baby the whole world, lady."

Gretchen stopped in her tracks. She turned and looked right up into his eyes. Close. She was very close. Near enough for him to catch her to him, to slide his palms around her waist. The thought sent his blood sizzling through his veins.

"I don't baby them, Hannon."

The defensiveness of her tone told him all he wanted to know. She *did* baby the citizens of this town and she darn well knew it. She just didn't want to admit it.

David grinned. "All right, Gretchen, you don't go above and beyond the call of duty. Ever. You're tough as hardtack, cool as ice cream."

Finally, she looked up from beneath her lashes and smiled at him as he urged her to sit in the booth they were standing next to.

She sat. She played with the saltshaker, rolling it between her palms.

"Okay, I do have a tiny tendency to be just a tad proprietary with the people of Whitehorn. I like them to feel that they can talk to me about anything that's bothering them."

"Nothing wrong with that, Gretchen," David said, leaning close. "Except—"

That warning light switched on in her eyes. It occurred to David that he was playing her along in the very hope of seeing that hot green light, that fire that shot through her and right into him.

"Except?" she coaxed.

"Except when people take advantage of your willingness to listen. Except when they become so dependent on you that they don't tend to their own backyards themselves. Except when you don't seem to be able to say no."

Gretchen leaned in close, her face mere inches from David's. "Are you implying that I'm a bit spineless, David?"

Her voice was a dangerous, low whisper. He loved it, longed to lean forward those few inches and cover her lips with his own, drink in those low, seductive syllables that rolled off her tongue and engage in a sensual battle of tongues and teeth and will. He wanted to absorb the lady right into his skin.

Instead, he took a slow, unsteady breath. He held out his palms in surrender. "Any man who called you spineless would have to be blind, sweetheart."

She looked quickly around the room. To see if anyone had heard the endearment, he was sure.

"Sorry," he said, but of course he wasn't sorry at all and both of them knew it.

"All right, then," she agreed, pulling back, picking up her menu and appearing to study it.

"I could say no," she said quietly, as if she had just told him that she was going to order the meat loaf special.

He chuckled and picked up his own menu. "Bet you couldn't. Not in this lifetime, Gretchen."

"I could." She sat up straighter and fiddled with the plain gold band of her watch. "Tell him, Em."

Emma Harper stood beside the table, ready to take their order. "Tell him what, Gretchen?"

"That I'm not a total pushover when someone asks for my help with their…their community problems."

David smiled up at Emma. "Harve Dibbons wants her to help him with his neighbor who keeps cutting across his lawn."

Emma's light laughter lit up her eyes.

"Oh, that. Sure, Gretchen, face it. You're a pushover. That is, I'll bet you steered him in the right direction, but you listened to him tell the whole long, drawn-out story first, didn't you?"

Gretchen opened her mouth, her green eyes irritated. "Okay, maybe at times I let people go on, but that's my choice. I could walk away if I wanted to."

"The way you could say no to all those requests to stand up at everyone's wedding?" Emma asked.

"Hey," Gretchen protested. "The world needs its bridesmaids. They keep everyone feeling good, and they take care of the brides of the world. Besides, I only do that for people I'm close to," she insisted.

"You're right. You do, and people ask you because they love you," her friend agreed, and David could hear the sincerity in her voice. "But then they take it too far. Every wedding you stand up at, people are always trying to fix you up with someone when I know you've asked them not to."

Gretchen blew out a breath. She nodded. "I know, and

I know they do it because they care, but I am absolutely not looking forward to my part in Pamela's wedding. I adore Pamela, I want to be there, but as for the rest, no, thank you.''

But her words and the topic had flipped a switch in David's consciousness.

''I'll bet you can't say no to the next person in town who asks you a foolish question any more than you can turn down one of your friends when they ask you to take part in their weddings.''

Gretchen stared him in the eye.

''You're pushing it, Hannon.''

''I know. You want to take that bet?''

Gretchen looked up at her friend who was clearly interested in this topic. A man in the corner was holding up his coffee cup, but Emma was watching Gretchen's lips. Gretchen nodded toward the man and she and David gave the waitress their orders.

''I want to know how this ends,'' Emma said, her voice a low hiss as she moved away. ''You tell me later, Gretchen.''

But Gretchen had turned back to David.

''Why would I want to take your bet?''

David slid his palms across the table, his fingertips touching hers. ''Because you're a proud, stubborn woman who doesn't want anyone to think that she has an Achilles' heel.''

''I don't have one.''

He widened his grin, covered her hands with his own. ''Well, then?''

''What are the terms?''

He tilted his head. ''I win, you invite me to your friend's wedding.''

''You don't even know Pamela.''

"I know you. And I go with you. We tell everyone I'm your fiancé."

Her eyes widened.

"Why would we do that?"

"So that you can actually enjoy the day. So that you can show everyone you don't need them to find you a man. You don't, of course, but this will simply let everyone relax a bit."

"Except for us."

He shook his head. "Oh, I intend to be very relaxed, Detective Neal, and to enjoy myself. You like to dance?"

She took a deep and visible breath. "Sometimes."

"All right, then."

Gretchen pulled her hands from beneath his. She placed her long, narrow palms over his hands this time. "What happens if I win?"

He studied the room for a moment, tried to think of something that would fly. "I walk your pretend dog for a week."

"Two weeks."

"Done."

She smiled up at him as Emma placed her food in front of her. "Don't think this is going to be an easy bet to win, David," she said.

He grinned at Emma. "What do you think, Emma? A diamond ring or— No, something out of the ordinary. An emerald for her eyes."

Emma shook her head. "What are you talking about, David, you devilish man?"

"Rings, Emma. Rings. Gretchen and I are on the verge of becoming engaged."

"It's not going to happen," Gretchen said.

He reached across the table and brushed her nose with

the tip of one finger. "Okay, whatever you say, Gretchen."

"I'm glad you're finally acting more like a true partner," she said with a sarcastic laugh, but her tone was a bit grumpy and uncertain.

It was grumpy and uncertain all day. When he walked her to her car that night, she turned to face him as she put the key in the lock.

"It won't happen, David. Don't look so smug."

He lifted one hand and touched her cheek. "Good night, Detective Neal. Sleep tight."

And he walked away whistling. Who would have thought that coming to town to solve a murder could have resulted in this much enjoyment?

Lyle Brooks leaned back against the wall of the Whitehorn movie theater and watched David Hannon lean forward and touch Gretchen Neal.

Interesting. His family and Hannon's had never been close, even though they were distantly related. Who would have thought that David would come back to town and snag the attention of his greatest enemy and threat right now? How convenient of the man to do so.

And how interesting that not only were these two working together, they were obviously doing a lot more. They were getting pretty tight.

"Good job, cousin," he muttered. If the two chief investigators were keeping each other company in their spare time, they might be looking the other way now and then. They might be easily distracted, or even better, easily manipulated.

"Oh, I like that," Lyle whispered. "I really do like that. If I need to, I could make use of that little bit of knowledge."

Seven

There were times when a person simply had to admit that she needed a life jacket, Gretchen told herself several days later as she pulled up in the middle of town. This was one of those times. Ever since she'd been thrown together with David Hannon, she'd been struggling to breathe in deep water. The man obviously had way too much experience where women were concerned. She'd seen it that night when she'd had dinner at the Big Sky. He'd been aware of every lady at the table—his sister, his cousins, his aunt, his mother and, oh, yes, herself, as well. He'd been the most gracious of hosts, a man who could make a woman swoon, if women still did that sort of thing.

"But that's not you, Gretchen," she told herself firmly, turning her car off. "You've been courted by men before." And she had. Quite a few men, for that matter. None of them had made a dent in her armor.

So why did she keep finding herself shivering whenever David came into the room?

"Because I'm dealing with a pro, of course," she reminded herself. That was it. Absolutely. The man knew all the right moves, and he had that devilish smile, that long, strong frame, and a look in his eye that made a woman sure that he knew his way around a bedroom way too well.

What's more, ever since they'd made that darn bet,

he'd had a lazy, cat-in-the-cream look about him. She was beginning to feel like a very small and tasty mouse whenever David glanced her way.

But not this morning. This morning he'd had calls to make from home. Apparently the government's business didn't stop just because one of their best agents decided to take a few weeks off.

And so she was on her own. She should feel good about that. Back to normal. Free, so to speak.

She should.

"I do," she insisted, slipping through the door of the Hip Hop. This morning for the first time in a while, she'd been on her own. She'd traversed the town alone, made a few calls trying to locate Storm and get him to come in before she had to take stronger measures. And now here she was heading in to lunch all on her own.

"Gretchen?"

The querulous voice came from the first booth, the one she'd just passed.

Gretchen turned to see Lily Mae Wheeler waving her over.

"Gretchen, I just had to see you. That man—o-oh, that man. I just can't even say his name."

Immediately the word "David" appeared in Gretchen's thoughts. For a second she was almost afraid she'd whispered it out loud.

But apparently she was mistaken. "Him and that darned thick silver hair that covers that equally thick skull," Lily Mae was saying. Her bracelets jangled on her shaking wrist and her beaded earrings swung in fierce opposition as she bobbed her head, trying to force the traitorous name from her lips. "O-oh, that man," Lily Mae said again.

"What man?" Gretchen found her voice long enough to ask the obvious question.

"That man who keeps letting his crabgrass grow over into my yard, that's the one. Do you know what he did yesterday?"

Gretchen was pretty sure she was about to hear.

"Lily Mae…" she began.

But Lily Mae's voice was breaking. "If I had a man living with me, he wouldn't treat me this way. If I weren't alone—"

Immediately Gretchen's heart tipped over. "Lily Mae, I'm sure he doesn't even realize he's upset you. Mr. Vernor is really a very nice man," she said, realizing that Lily Mae was referring to her newest neighbor. "He's kind. If you'd only talk to him."

But the woman was apparently too upset to think about talking to anyone but Gretchen right now. It was a full fifteen minutes before Gretchen could convince the woman that her best course of action was to invite Mr. Vernor over for lemonade and a friendly "chat."

It was well past the time she should have been picking up her menu when she actually did so. She'd barely flipped open the laminated booklet when a shadow fell over her table.

"Hi, sweetheart," David said in that slow, sexy drawl of his. He leaned forward, resting his palms on the table, his lips a breath away from her ear. "How's my sweetest fiancée today?"

She looked up, her eyes wide. She opened her mouth but saw he was nodding toward Lily Mae. "I'm sure you were a help to her, darling Gretchen," he said. "And you've made me the happiest of men."

He took her hand in his own as he sat across from her.

Emma came up, a big smile on her face. "Anything I can do for you two?"

But Gretchen simply sighed. She rested her chin on her fist and stared at David as she shook her head. "I think I've done enough for myself today, Emma."

"You're not a happy woman, Gretchen?"

Gretchen looked at the innocent expression on David's face. "I'm feeling a bit foolish, but I'm okay. You won fair and square," she told the man who had known her better than she'd apparently known herself.

"And I intend to hold up my end of the bargain, sweet lady," he said. "We're going to enjoy ourselves at that wedding. We're going to make people talk. You can bet on that."

Gretchen couldn't hold back a small chuckle. "I think I've bet enough lately, David, so I'll take you at your word."

"You don't want me with you at the wedding?"

She looked across at the mischievous gleam in his eyes, at that bold I-dare-you-to-be-wild-and-crazy expression on his face, at the stunning magnificence of the man, and she shook her head.

"I'm beginning to think maybe I do want you at the wedding."

"We'll have fun, Gretchen."

And suddenly she was looking forward to the day she'd dreaded up until now. She had the feeling that David Hannon could turn any dull occasion into something special.

"Then I'll look forward to it," she agreed. "Partner."

He shook his head as Emma wandered off. "Not this time. This time we go as ourselves. A man and a woman."

And suddenly Gretchen felt as if everyone in the room

faded away, as if she and David were alone. A man and a woman.

That feeling tagged after her all day as she and David returned to the office, made calls, and talked with each other and Rafe about Storm's likely whereabouts.

It was still with her when she wandered out onto the street at the end of the day, as she walked to her car, David at her side.

She reached down for the handle and suddenly his hand was over hers.

''Gretchen?''

She turned to look into his eyes, but he'd come up behind her and when she turned, she was almost up against him, her eyes just beneath his chin, her lips just a finger's breadth from his throat.

David groaned low.

''Come here,'' he said, slipping his arms around her. And it was as if she had been waiting for this for hours. She leaned nearer, went the extra distance to shape her lips to his own. She felt the world dissolve in heat and need as David moved in close and claimed her mouth again and again.

''I haven't kissed you in days,'' he whispered.

She nodded, kissing him again.

''We decided we shouldn't,'' she said, the words barely out of her mouth before she was crushed to his chest again.

''I know, but we weren't engaged then.''

She smiled against his lips and placed her palms against the warmth of his chest. ''David, we aren't engaged now,'' she said, finally pulling back slightly.

He smiled, snagging her for one more kiss. ''Gretchen, you know that and I know that, but the world?'' He brushed her jawline with his strong, gentle fingers. "What do you think the world thinks?"

Gretchen didn't know. Right this second she wasn't sure she cared. But she did know one thing. She and David were playing a game, and games always came to an end.

That was good, she reminded herself. That was the way she wanted things. Still…

"We're supposed to be pretending at the wedding, not here in town," she reminded him, disentangling herself from the warmth of his arms when what she wanted to do was to open his shirt, lean in and bury her face against the muscles of his bare chest. She wanted to breathe in the seductive male scent of him.

"I know that, love," he told her. "But I thought maybe we should practice."

A thought occurred to her. A niggling uncomfortable thought. "Not used to being without a woman for any length of time, David?"

His laugh was automatic. It rumbled through his body to her fingertips where her hand rested against his chest. "You think I have no self-control, Gretchen?"

She tilted up her chin. Green eyes met green eyes.

"I think you're a man who's used to getting his own way, David."

He sobered instantly. He took her hand in his own and kissed the pads of her fingertips. "I'm sorry I pushed myself on you on this case, Gretchen, but that has nothing to do with this."

She knew that. Deep inside she knew that. But she also knew that he was a man who was made to have his way with women, and she was a woman who was wary of getting too close to any one man. She would have to be very careful around David, she thought.

Gretchen wondered just how many women had thought that same thought over the years.

But she refused to guess at the number. This time with David could be simple if she made it that way. She could compartmentalize things. There was work with David and there was the David she was going to have a lark with at the wedding. That was all there was or ever would be for her and David Hannon.

And now that she'd set it out for herself so clearly, she could simply go home and forget about the man for the night.

The slight knock at her door that night startled Gretchen. She was just about to take Goliath for his evening walk. But when she pulled open the door, David was standing there.

He held out his hand.

She frowned. "David?"

He held out his hand farther. "The leash, Gretchen. The men are going for a walk. You stay here and rest."

Gretchen crossed her arms. "David, you won the bet."

Shaking his head, he gently pried the leash from her fingers. Goliath must have heard the noise of the door opening. He came running into the room, dancing and jumping and turning around in quick, chasing circles.

"Come on, boy, just you and me tonight," David said, lowering himself to one knee.

Gretchen knelt beside them. She placed her hand over David's and tried to ignore the warmth that cascaded through her in great gushing streams the way it always did.

"David, why are you doing this? I conceded. You won."

But he placed two fingers over her lips to shush her, a barely there touch that still left her longing for more.

"Not really a fair bet," he said quietly. "Anyone could have won it. Any man could see that a woman like you couldn't just leave Lily Mae sitting there babbling on."

Gretchen smiled against his fingertips.

"Are you telling me that you're not going through with things?" She wondered at the sudden plummeting of her good mood.

He gave her a lopsided, maddeningly sexy grin. "I said it was too easy, sweetheart. I didn't say I'd gone suddenly crazy and stupid. When a man wins first rights to spend an evening touching a woman like you and whirling around a dance floor with you next to his heart, he'd have to have misplaced his brain to give that up. Oh, no, no way am I giving up my winnings. I'm just making things a bit more fair."

Darn. She wished he wouldn't do that. He was hard enough to resist as it was.

"That doesn't seem half fair to you," she suggested. "No matter what you say, the bet was made, witnessed and won. And Goliath's *my* pet."

Of course, the darn animal was licking David's fingers like crazy right now. The man was letting him, only stopping now and then to scratch Goliath's side.

"Well, maybe Goliath and I just need to spend some time together then. It's a guy thing," he told her. "This mutt definitely needs some male companionship. We won't be long, love," he told her. "You just get some rest."

And with that, he clipped the leash on and rose, swinging out the door and up the street.

They were gone for maybe twenty minutes, but

Gretchen didn't rest. She paced. She cursed David for taking over her every thought. She blessed him for being so giving. She was just swishing past the window on her two hundredth pass when she saw him striding up her walk.

Gretchen pulled the door open wide. David didn't step inside. Instead he silently handed her the leash, said goodbye to Goliath, and gave her a slow smile.

That was all it took. One look. One smile. She opened her mouth, on the verge of inviting him in, of giving him coffee and anything else he should care to want, when he curled his palm around her jaw and gently brushed her lips with his thumb.

"See you in the morning, Gretchen," he said softly, thickly. "I'll be dreaming about you in my bed tonight."

And with those maddening words, the darn man left her standing there. Wanting. Hot and empty-handed and as far away from sleep as a woman could get. She'd just bet that he knew it, too.

Why, oh, why, had David Hannon come back home and walked into her police department and into the middle of her case?

Gretchen didn't know, but she knew one thing. She was for darn sure going to be glad when he went back into his world and left hers behind, glad when she could get back to the life where she was a lot more in control than she ever was here. Until then, she was just going to—well, heck, she was just going to enjoy her time with the man, wasn't she? And there was no use lying to herself about it. He was, after all, exactly what she was always saying she wanted. A man who knew when to have fun and when to disappear into the mists of history.

Four days later David was on the phone in the station trying to keep his hand in on one of his own federal cases when he heard the commotion at the front door. "I want to see Detective Neal." A man's low voice echoed throughout the office. It wasn't a happy voice. One might even say it sounded a bit threatening.

Immediately David looked to his right to where Gretchen was scratching away on paper. Her hand still, she looked up and rose to her feet, just as if some candy-voiced grandmother was sweetly requesting her presence.

"Royston, got an unexpected emergency here. I'll call you back ASAP," David said quietly into the phone, not waiting for his contact's reply as he placed the receiver back in its cradle.

Carefully and deliberately, he rose from his desk and proceeded into the other room.

"You Detective Neal?" a tall, brown-eyed man was demanding. His long, black hair was graying slightly at the temples, slicked back in magazine-model style, his Native American ancestry evident in the chiseled cheek-bones. His navy pin-striped suit was expensive and it fit his broad-shouldered, narrow-hipped frame well. He was obviously at home in a three-piece, and David didn't have to ask who the man was. He was the very image of what Raven Hunter would have looked like had he lived, and the word "attorney" was practically stamped on the guy's forehead.

David leaned back against the nearest bank of file cabinets, his arms crossed at his chest. Storm Hunter might have come in full courtroom battle dress, but he hadn't matched wits with Gretchen Neal before. A small smile lifted David's lips as Gretchen stepped forward.

"I'm Detective Neal," she said, holding out her hand.

The man simply thinned his lips and took a step forward into her space. He didn't take the hand she offered.

"I want to know what's going on regarding the murder of my brother, Raven Hunter," he said.

"The case is being investigated," Gretchen said calmly. "Why don't you step into my office?"

"Why don't you explain why you haven't already reached some conclusion considering the circumstances?"

She raised one brow. "The circumstances being?"

"It's been quite a while since the remains were found. It's no secret to anyone in this town that Jeremiah Kincaid hated the fact that my brother, a member of a race he despised, was fooling around with Kincaid's sister. Nor is it a secret that he had words with Raven just before my brother disappeared. And yet I understand you're no closer to the truth than you were when you started."

"It's an old case with all the complications of an old case," Gretchen said, stepping forward herself. "Convictions can't be made on hearsay, Mr. Hunter, as you well know. We need hard evidence. More evidence than we have. I understand your concern, but—"

"You understand nothing. It's clear to me that you're *doing* nothing. In fact, it's come to my attention today that you may be in collusion with the nephew of the man suspected of killing my brother."

David's arms came uncrossed. He straightened. Only Gretchen's brief shake of her head in his direction kept him from stepping in to open his mouth.

"The case is proceeding," Gretchen said, swigging in a deep breath of air and pulling herself up to her full five feet, nine inches. "And it's being given my full attention. We're looking for new evidence all the time. The department is doing everything it can to discover the truth here, Mr. Hunter, as expediently as possible."

The man was shaking his head, slowly, deliberately.

"Not good enough, Neal. If Raven had been white, you would have moved faster. You would have been working on this thing 'round the clock. Your prejudices are showing. Alarmingly so, Ms. Neal."

"I'm sorry you feel that way, but you're wrong, Mr. Hunter."

"You're a disgrace."

The man's words hung in the silent air that had suddenly dropped over the station. All eyes were turned toward Gretchen and Storm.

"I want answers, Neal," the man continued. "And I want them now. If I don't get them in a timely fashion, then I want your badge. And I'll have it."

Gretchen raised her chin, her breath coming more quickly though her expression was one of calm determination. She opened her mouth, but David had had enough.

"You've taken this a notch too far, Hunter. You don't know what you're talking about here," he said, his voice a low, quiet command in the silent room. David ignored the halting look in Gretchen's eyes. He moved into the arena.

"Ah, the good detective's boyfriend speaks." Storm sneered the words. Ice hung in the air around him. "You like Kincaids, Detective Neal?" he continued. "That's what Agent Hannon is, after all, isn't he? I've only been in town a few minutes, just stopped by the café for coffee, but already I've heard that the two of you are pretty tight and hot. Well, no surprise. The Kincaids have always had favored status in this town. Not like the Hunters. Oh, no. It was your uncle that threatened my brother, Hannon, and now I'm going to threaten your woman. I don't particularly care what she does in your bed at night, but she does her job or she loses it."

A flashfire of darkness spiraled through David. He'd been good too long. He'd held back to keep from causing Gretchen any distress. He knew from experience that she could kick the life out of this man—and that she wouldn't. Of course she wouldn't. Because she had no right to touch him in that way just to defend her honor. And because that was just the kind of woman she was. Right now she was probably imagining all the horrible things Storm had probably gone through that had turned him into this bitter, insulting human. She was probably right. David was damn sure she was right.

"My uncle was a sorry excuse for a human being, Hunter, and yes, there've been times when I hated to admit that I was related to him, but you're out of line insulting Detective Neal. She's a fine detective and a wonderful human being. Now why don't you get smart and take back all the insulting things you just said about her, because her hands may be tied by her office, but mine are free. And I happen to be off duty."

"That's good, Kincaid. Very good," Storm said, yanking on his tie. "Because I'm in just the right mood to match my fists against that pretty face of yours."

And in the next split second, he doubled up his fist and aimed.

David dodged, the air buckling next to his jaw as the man's blow barely missed. He tried to quell the roar of anger and to remember all the things that Gretchen would have said about Storm Hunter; that he had a right to be angry, that they had a duty to let him say his piece. But David had lived on the edge for a long time. He'd been in more fights for his life than he cared to count, and his fingers curled easily and eagerly into fists as Storm recovered and prepared to strike again.

"Hunter, stop right there or you'll find yourself in

lockup overnight.'' Rafe Rawlings's voice carried through the panting stillness.

The world froze for five whole seconds. The fire still burned, but the flames died down slightly. Counting to ten, to twenty, to thirty, David finally, slowly, unfurled his fists.

Storm pulled back. He gave David a disgusted look. ''Later,'' he mouthed.

David raised one brow. ''Your call, buddy,'' he said.

''Hannon, you're here on my recognizance. I'd appreciate it if you'd remember that,'' Rafe said quietly.

David remembered, and he remembered the debt of gratitude he owed Rafe and also Phil for looking the other way to let him be here. Nor did he forget that Gretchen would be humiliated if he got into a fight over her in her very own station.

Slowly, he relaxed his muscles and backed away a step or two.

''Storm, you're out of line,'' Rafe said, stepping in to take over. ''You have every right to ask questions, but this is going too far.''

''You're going to deny that this investigation is at a virtual standstill?''

''Absolutely not. As I'm sure Gretchen told you, the investigation is continuing, but we don't have much to go on.''

''You've got my brother's remains and the knowledge that there was a lot going on between him and Blanche Kincaid just before Raven disappeared.''

''We have that,'' Gretchen said, giving Rafe an apologetic look. She was grateful to him for his presence that had somewhat diffused the situation. But Raven Hunter was her case, and it was up to her to deal with Storm. ''And we've interviewed what witnesses we can find to tell us about what was going on at that time. Yes, Raven and Jeremiah were at odds. Yes, Raven disappeared. Yes, Blanche gave birth to your niece, Summer. And yes, there's a possibility that the murder weapon could have come from Jeremiah's collection, but we don't have conclusive evidence. As an attorney, I'm sure you understand the importance of gathering accurate information."

"We were hoping you could provide more details, Storm," Rafe said lazily. "We've been waiting for you to get your tail back here so we could ask you a few things. I understand Jackson contacted you three weeks ago."

A dark rash of color climbed Storm's face. "I've had cases pending in New Mexico. It was difficult to get away."

Gretchen raised one brow. She glanced toward the phone. "You could have called," she said, her tone somewhat lazy and accusatory. "But then, maybe you wanted to be here in person. Maybe you had a lot you needed to get off your chest. A man's brother goes missing and everyone thinks he ran away, it would raise a lot of anger to find out that man had actually been murdered. Probably dredge up a lot of pain he'd already gone through once before and thought he'd put behind him, as well."

"Don't be patronizing, Detective Neal."

She shook her head. "Believe me, I'm not being patronizing, Mr. Hunter. I'm just stating the truth. Maybe you had your own reasons for waiting to speak to us in person."

Storm took a deep breath and eyed her somewhat suspiciously. Then the smallest light of respect edged into his eyes. "All right. We'll talk. I'll tell you what little I know," he agreed.

David stepped forward, prepared to demand that the man apologize to Gretchen, but she stopped him dead with that "Don't even think of it," look she managed so well.

Shrugging, David grinned. He trailed the two of them into Gretchen's office.

"He have to be here?" Storm demanded.

"He's on the case," Gretchen answered quietly. "What I know and Rafe knows, he knows."

Storm held out his hands in sullen surrender. He shot David one last accusatory look. Then he began to talk.

All right, so reality was finally beginning to sink in, Gretchen realized, curling her trembling hand more tightly around her coffee cup, then quickly glancing David's way to make sure he hadn't noticed.

His eyes flashed dark green sparks. "Let's get out of here," he growled, reaching for her as he climbed to his feet. "The day's gone on too long, and in the end, Storm Hunter really didn't tell us anything we didn't already know."

"Except that he's one very angry man," Gretchen said flippantly, stepping out into the aisle herself. She purposely held her hand at her side.

He stared pointedly at where she'd folded her closed fingers against the dark cloth of her pants.

"Lots of officers would have quaked under that kind of abuse," he said quietly.

She gave a small laugh. "You don't have to pat me on the head, David. I'm sure you've had more than your share of people spitting into your face. That comes with the badge."

"Maybe so, but no one ever said it was one of the more pleasant aspects of the law enforcement business."

He waited for her to gather her gear, then strolled out of the office beside her.

It pleased her that he didn't try to baby her as they left the station. He didn't treat her as if she were some fragile female, even though he'd obviously wanted to give Storm a body slam earlier today. He'd wanted to, but he hadn't.

"Thanks," she said quietly as they climbed into the car.

He raised both brows, but didn't ask what she meant.

"You know what I'm talking about, Hannon. You grew up in a house filled with ladies who probably loved having you play the perfect gentleman. Your mother is a wonderful woman, a strong woman, and an absolute sweetheart, but don't tell me that those traditional male and female roles didn't exist in your household. You were born opening doors for women and kissing their hands. I'm sure it took a lot to keep you from defending my honor today."

He gave a harsh laugh. "Don't thank me. Thank Rafe. I was ready to deck Hunter and you know it."

She smiled. "Yes, but you were mulling the situation over. I could see it in the tense cords in your neck. You could have easily flattened him by the time Rafe entered the room, but something held you back. I suspect it was concern for my position."

He turned to the side, but she didn't miss the slow smile that eased onto his lips. "You think you know me, do you?"

She shook her head. "No, but I'm beginning to. Your natural inclination is to come to a lady's rescue. You've done it any number of times with me, but today, when it counted, when my ability to handle my job was in question, you held back. I'd like to think it was because you respected me."

"Don't ever think I don't." The smile had disappeared when he swung back around. "But don't make the mistake of thinking that it was easy, either. Nothing's easy with you, Gretchen. I wanted that guy's blood."

"I could see that, and I can see that it cost you to back away. You've still got some of that residual anger bottled up inside you. Well, if it makes you feel any better, you did come to my rescue today. Just knowing that I wasn't alone made it easier than it's ever been before."

He closed his eyes. "Don't. Don't tell me about the times you've had maniacs waving fists or guns or knives in your face. Working where you have, doing what you do, I'm sure it's happened, but today...just don't, because yes, I'm still angry and frustrated and— Damn it, Gretchen."

David reached across the seat, looped his hands around her waist and lifted her up and over onto his lap. His fingers speared through her hair, his seeking mouth found hers. He wrapped her around him and held her tightly as he plunged them both into sudden and reckless sensation.

The heat of his touch seared her, and Gretchen struggled to get closer. She squirmed against his hard chest, bringing her hands up to wrap around his neck and bind him to her. Seated in the tight confines of the car, she nevertheless felt as if she were falling off a high tower.

Exhilaration flooded her soul as David pulled back for air and then swooped her hard against him again and kissed her over and over.

"You make me crazy," he whispered.

"You make me shiver," she whispered back, and some small part of her realized it was true. She was shaking, literally shaking, in David's arms. His kisses had done what all of Storm's gibes hadn't done. Made her quake. With desire. With need. And with the fear of the unknown.

Someday soon, she was going to be on her own again, as she'd known she would be all her life. As she wanted to be.

She hoped, really hoped, that David's touch hadn't spoiled her for life. And once again, as she finally pulled away from the embrace, she wondered just what kind of trouble she was getting into with David. For delicious as it was, she was sure it was trouble. And it was obviously trouble she wasn't resisting very well. Tomorrow she and David were going to pretend to get engaged. She must have been completely out of control when she agreed to that bet, but she *had* agreed and all she could do now was simply plunge in.

Eight

He'd done some outrageous things in his time, but this probably qualified as one of the more outrageous situations he'd engineered, David admitted to himself the next day. He threw his clothes into a bag, preparing for the wedding in Helena he and Gretchen would be driving to after work. Not that he'd ever followed the crowd in the usual way of things. His parents had been too much the free spirits and he'd been forced into that loner pathway much too early to have ever become a slave to convention, but...there was something about Gretchen that just made him act wilder than usual.

He was obviously not in control of his reactions where the woman was concerned. He couldn't seem to keep his hands off her—or his thoughts from her. She made him want things, things he didn't even want to think about, given the circumstances. He had to be careful with her. She was more vulnerable than she wanted to let on and she was prickly about getting involved. If he pushed, he could do her damage and there were already more than enough people taking advantage of her, even some who might want to hurt her.

Storm Hunter's angry face slipped into his mind, but it wasn't really Storm he was angry with. It was himself he wanted to beat up on. He was, after all, the one who had made her a target of Storm Hunter's ire both because of his Kincaid connections and because of his having kissed her in public.

"And yet you did it again not four hours after Hunter left the office," he chastised himself. "And here you are luring the woman into this fake fiancé charade. Don't you feel guilty, bud?"

He let up on himself, relaxed into the truth. And the truth was…? He grinned. No, he didn't have an iota of guilt about going off with Gretchen to pretend he was more involved with her than he was. Because this weekend he was going to have Gretchen in his arms for hours. At least on the dance floor. Later, maybe, he'd feel guilty about his tendency to publicly plaster his body to hers.

"You ready for this weekend?" he asked her as he breezed into the station and plopped down into the chair beside her desk.

Her smile was slightly taut. "I think it's finally sinking in just what we're planning to do. You should probably be aware, David, that I'm not particularly gifted in the field of acting."

"You don't have to be. Just follow my lead. I'm willing to shoulder the responsibility. All you have to do is give me the occasional adoring look. Think you can manage that?"

He grinned and winked at her, and she rolled her eyes, grinning back. "I'm not sure. How does this look?" And she framed her face with both hands, opened her sea-green eyes wide and parted her lips slightly, leaning forward in his direction.

His own grin faded. He swallowed hard. "That'll do, Gretchen," he whispered, rising to lean over her desk. "That'll do very nicely."

He bent over slightly, looked straight into those beautiful eyes, lifted his hand with every intention of cupping the soft skin of her cheek.

"Oh, excuse me. I just keep managing to come in at the oddest moments, don't I?" Celeste's nervous voice filled the small space of the office.

David quickly rose to his full height. He stepped in front of Gretchen to give her a chance to put her detective persona back in place.

"Don't worry, Aunt Celeste. Gretchen and I were just doing a little role-playing. It comes in handy now and then."

His aunt blinked, then smiled brightly. "Well, of course it does. I suppose law enforcement people have to go undercover now and then, don't they? I knew that. Everyone knows that, don't they?"

David wanted to laugh at the way his aunt was trying to be so accommodating. He wondered if she really believed his story about role-playing.

He couldn't tell, but he knew he had to be more careful around Gretchen. At least at work. He didn't really care what people said or thought, but he had the distinct feeling that she did. He'd do his best not to bring her any grief.

"You're still leaving for the weekend, David?" Celeste asked with a smile, moving forward into the room. "Gretchen's wedding, isn't it?" She waited, her eyes wide and expectant.

"A friend of hers, yes."

"Well, you two just have a lot of fun there," she ordered. "Not that I think you won't. I'm sure it'll be nice to get away from all this trouble for a bit."

He grinned at his aunt. "I remember you once telling me that I seemed to court trouble, one long ago day when I got into some sort of mischief."

Celeste smiled. "Well, yes, but this is different. I know it's the work you've both chosen, but hunting for murderers just can't be as much fun as going to a celebration. You just don't even think about anything except for that wedding while you're there. I want you to have fun, to just be free," she commanded.

She looked at him pointedly.

He grinned. "Yes, ma'am," he answered in the way he had once been wont to do as a child.

She sighed. "I guess you're right. You're too old to have me ordering you around. And anyway, that's not really what I came to talk to you about. I'm…well, I'm just on my way out to the reservation, dear. You know that I sometimes volunteer at the youth center there, and this summer they're having a special program on careers. I'm helping out a bit with some of the research, locating materials and so forth. I was thinking…well, I was thinking of approaching Mr. Hunter. He's an attorney doing some special work in civil liberties, you know. He's been gone all those years. I hear he was in here yesterday. I was wondering what your impression of him might be. Maybe you could tell me something about him."

David frowned, shaking his head in confusion. "I think that while Storm Hunter might be a font of information on the topic you're researching, you would be the wrong person to ask him for help. He has an aversion to anyone associated with the Kincaids."

Celeste took in a long breath. She folded her hands tightly around each other. "He said things to you, then? What did he say?"

David shook his head. "You know that I can't discuss a case with you, Aunt Celeste. But just be warned, this is the wrong time to go asking Storm Hunter for a favor.

If you need his help for the school, get Jackson to approach him.''

"He didn't threaten you, did he?" She had asked the question of David, but she was looking at Gretchen as if she hoped she'd get more information there. Gretchen, true to her professionalism, didn't blink an eye.

"Jackson's very approachable, Celeste," she said gently. "You know that. He and his wife, Maggie, are quite involved with the school, I believe?"

Slowly, Celeste nodded and then let out a sigh. "All right. Of course, you're right. I just thought that if Mr. Hunter is only going to be in town a short while, that maybe we shouldn't waste the opportunity, but of course, Jackson would be the logical person for me to talk to about this. I'll just talk to him. You two enjoy the wedding. And don't let anything stop you from going."

And she squared her shoulders and walked out the door.

Gretchen watched her go, wondering at that strange last comment. Celeste had certainly seemed happy to see them going off for the weekend together, but of course that was probably just her imagination going wild, she told herself. Celeste couldn't know about the pretend engagement and she wasn't the type to push two people together who didn't want to be pushed. She was just a kind woman, a caring aunt. And Gretchen had to admire the woman's strength and determination. "Your aunt's been involved with events on the reservation for a long while, hasn't she?"

David shrugged. "She's always said that she was fortunate to have such access to two cultures. She and my mother raised my cousin, Summer, Blanche's and Raven's daughter, and Summer spent every summer break on the reservation. Those of us who know and love

Summer and have the good fortune to be related to her have been blessed to have been able to walk between both worlds more than most of the people in the town. Still, it's a bit worrisome to have Aunt Celeste asking about Storm. I have the feeling that she's worrying about my safety. Even if Jeremiah isn't proven to be Raven's murderer, there's definitely a lot to be accounted for there. No matter how angry I was with Storm yesterday, the man does have every reason to be bitter.''

"David, you can't be responsible for your uncle's character.''

He held out his hands in a gesture of defeat. "I know that. If I were responsible for all the misery Jeremiah caused, I would have had to go into therapy the moment I came out of the womb. Jeremiah left illegitimate children, unhappy women and so much dirt in his wake, that I'd never be able to atone for all his sins. The Kincaids may be proud, but we've always known that there are plenty of people who have reason to resent our name.''

"But not you."

"I hope not, Gretchen. I do my best to walk a straight line and not cause the same kinds of trouble Jeremiah caused.''

Ah, so he was worrying if all his teasing and flirting was going a bit too far. She wasn't sure. She knew that he was just kidding with her, that he desired her, but that there were limits. Heaven knew she had loads of limits of her own. She didn't want him worrying about her.

"You're interested only in protecting your good name? So that's why you rescue women in distress?'' she teased.

He gave her a lazy grin, settled one hip on the edge of her desk and leaned over her.

"I do that just because it's so much fun. You going to stir up some trouble on the streets today so I can watch you work? I get excited just thinking about you kicking some guy up alongside his head. You could have made some football team very happy.''

She rose up and met him eye-to-eye. "Maybe I did. My brothers regularly called me in as a kicker when they played with their friends. And if watching me work makes your heart sit up and smile, then prepare yourself, Hannon, because I have a treat coming up for you in a few days. Rafe just gave me this assignment this morning.''

He looked down at the paper she was holding out to him.

Long seconds ticked by as he read what was written there. And then read it again.

"Excuse me,'' he finally said. "Maybe I misunderstood this directive. We're giving a talk at the school? You and me?''

"I know,'' she said with a teasing whisper. "Kind of makes you shiver with anticipation, doesn't it?''

He laughed out loud. "I'm not so sure about that.''

She chuckled right back. "Well, I'm looking forward to watching you charm the hearts of a squirming roomful of ten-year-olds, David. I've watched you turn women into melted butter, coax cats out of trees, and make grown men rethink their position on crime. I can't wait to see you interact with the peanut-butter-and-jelly crowd.''

David raised both brows. "Somehow I have the feeling you've done this before.''

She nodded slowly, her eyes wide.

"So you know what I'm in for?''

Gretchen shrugged. "Every year is different. Different crop of kids, different situations.''

He studied her carefully. "You know what I told you about just following my lead this weekend?''

She nodded. "Yes. Why?"

"Just remember that when we get to that school. You lead. I'll follow."

A slow smile formed on her face. "That's the sexiest thing you've ever said to me, Hannon."

He gave her another wink. "Just wait until we get to this wedding. I intend to say a few more sexy things to you. Get ready."

Celeste sat in her car on the shoulder of the highway after her meeting with David and Gretchen. In a minute she would get going. She couldn't sit here much longer. If she did, someone would come along and ask her if she needed help.

She did need help, but she'd learned long ago that the only kind of help that would ever save her was the divine kind. In time, someday, maybe someday soon, there would be a spiritual reckoning for her, a day when she could finally, really, find out what had happened that long-ago night and what was in store for her for eternity. In the meantime, all she could do was try her best to go on and to look out for those she loved.

"David is trying to open up the past, figure out what happened? And what *did* happen? What is he going to dig up? And how is that going to affect all of us?" she whispered out loud.

"I just wish I could do something. I wish I could somehow protect all of them."

She had the horrid, sinking feeling that her children, Cleo and Jasmine, were going to be hurt by whatever news was found. And David, too. If he found anything that would damage his family, what would it do to him? Jeremiah was being blamed and Jeremiah had been a miserable human being, but had he really been a murderer?

She was afraid to find out the answer to that question and afraid not to.

Her niece, Summer, had lived a life without a father because of what had happened so long ago. Storm Hunter had lost a brother, and someone should have to pay for that. The killer should be discovered and revealed to the world.

But the thought of that nearly made Celeste double over with pain.

Someone had a lot to answer for. And somewhere in the darkness of those dreams that haunted her, the answers to who that someone was waited.

But those answers were closed to her. She had to keep searching. In the meantime, all she could do was try to shield those closest to her from the truth and to pray that Storm Hunter found some happiness in his life someday.

"Gretchen!" The curvy brunette standing in the hotel lobby came running across the floor not five minutes after David and Gretchen had arrived. She held out her arms and Gretchen gave her a big hug.

"Karen. It's so good to see you. We've had so little time to talk lately, between your job and mine." Gretchen turned to David, inviting him into the circle with her friend. "David, this is Karen Warren, my very good friend from Miami and another one of Pamela's bridesmaids. Karen, this is David Hannon, my—my fiancé."

Karen let out a scream that could probably be heard all the way back in Whitehorn. "Gretchen, you're engaged! Finally? Why didn't you tell anyone? You didn't tell anyone, did you? I'm not the last to know?"

Gretchen shook her head as David chuckled and took

Karen's hand. "It's very nice to meet someone from Gretchen's other life. I suppose you're the journalist?"

The woman nodded with a huge smile. "She told you about me? Oh, Gretchen, that's sweet."

"Of course I told him about you, Karen. You're one of my very closest friends and David is, as I said, my..."

"Fiancé, love," David supplied when she faltered. "I'm afraid our engagement has taken Gretchen a bit by surprise," he said apologetically. "It's pretty new to both of us. In fact, you're probably the first to know."

"Oh, David, allow me to congratulate you for doing what no man has ever done before," Karen said, rising on her toes to kiss his cheek. "You've managed to win our Gretchen's heart. I hope you appreciate the magnitude of what you've accomplished and the gift that she's given you."

"She's an absolute treasure," he said, pulling Gretchen's hand beneath his arm. "I thank the heavens every day for dropping me into her life and giving me this rare opportunity."

He smiled down at Gretchen and her breath caught in her throat. Horrid man. If only Karen knew that this rare opportunity referred to his chance to play this charade with her and not to the fact that they were engaged. She was grateful, of course. It was already obvious that this wedding was going to be more fun and much less tension-filled than those in recent memory, but she really shouldn't let David carry this too far.

Karen almost sighed and Gretchen felt a small moment's irritation at the dreamlike way her friend was looking at David.

"How did he propose? Come on now, you can tell me," Karen prompted.

David opened his mouth to speak, but Gretchen placed

her hand gently on his cheek. "Let me relive it, darling," she coaxed.

He raised one brow. "You don't know how much I'd love that," he whispered back.

Gretchen looked around to see if anyone else was listening even though she knew that the story would be retold many times. Karen was a hopeless romantic and an equally hopeless gossip.

She looked up at him and hoped she wasn't blushing. Then she lifted one shoulder and plunged ahead.

"David knows how much I love white roses. He filled my room with them when I was away and then, when we went back to my apartment later, he went down on one knee and presented me with another rose. Red. He kissed it and gave it to me. My ring was enclosed in the petals."

Looking up at David, Gretchen saw that he was grinning broadly. Had she taken this too far? She knew she had agreed to let him lead. Indeed, she'd even wanted him to a few days ago, but there was just something about this strange relationship they had, this constant tussle to figure out who was leading and who was following, that made it impossible for her to simply remain a spectator at her own pretend engagement. It was generous of David to offer to help her, but darn it, she was no coward. She had to jump right into the thick of the action, just as she always had. She couldn't let someone else call all the shots.

"Isn't that the way you remember it, David?" she asked tentatively.

"Mmm. I remember it just like that," he said in that low, sexy voice. "Except in my memory you were wearing nothing but rose petals and I kissed you deeply just before I gave you the ring."

She gave him a laser-eyed look that said, "Freeze, buddy."

"David, you're wicked. You'll embarrass Karen," she said in reality.

But Karen was beyond being embarrassed. The lady closed her eyes and let out such a long sigh that for a moment Gretchen was afraid she was going to faint. Then her friend looked down.

"That's so-oo-o romantic, Gretchen. But where's your ring?"

Oh, darn it. She'd gotten so caught up in trying to one-up David that she had embellished this tale just a bit too much. Gretchen looked at her hand as if it belonged to another woman. "I—"

"I have it right here, love," David said, reaching into his pocket. "Gretchen doesn't wear her ring at work. It might get caught on something and be a danger to her."

"Of course," Karen agreed immediately, "but you're not on duty now, Gretchen."

Gretchen smiled wanly at her friend. Oh, no, now what was David going to say? He didn't really have a ring in his pocket.

But the darn man came up from the depths of his pocket with a slender, diamond-and-emerald-studded band. Taking her cold hand in his own, he slipped the ring possessively on her finger, then kissed her palm.

Hot flames shot up through her body.

"So nice to meet you, Karen," he said softly, "We'll see you later, after Gretchen and I have time to settle in and get comfortable. Shall we?"

Karen smiled knowingly. "By all means, you two just go on up to your rooms. I'll see you at the rehearsal dinner and at the wedding. And don't worry, Gretchen.

You know me. I won't tell a soul about your engagement."

Gretchen gave her friend another hug and watched her walk away. "I feel rather guilty. Karen's always loved romance. She's been engaged and had her heart broken several times. How's she going to feel when she finds out I'm not really engaged? She's my friend."

"Yes, she's your friend and she wants you to be happy," David said gently. "And it's obvious that to Karen, being happy means being in love. So she'll understand that you just wanted to experience that glow for a short time, even if you tell her that it wasn't real. She may not believe that it's pretend, even if you tell her the truth. Some people just want to see what makes them happy. Your friends want to see you happy. So be happy. Let them enjoy this brief time. We *are* engaged, as far as I'm concerned. We're simply engaged for the duration of this trip."

She chuckled. "That sounds devious, but I like it. It works for me. If I could have gotten engaged for a mere weekend before, I might have already done so."

He widened his eyes and tilted his head. "Gretchen, are you telling me you would agree to marry another man when I've just now slipped my ring on your finger?" He took her hand into his own and slowly kissed the pads of each finger.

Gretchen dragged in a long breath, curving her fingers closed lightly. She hazarded a hesitant smile his way. "No, David," she said softly. "I can guarantee that this weekend is all there'll ever be. You're the only man whose ring I'll ever wear."

He nodded, a slight frown forming between his eyes. "Come on, love."

"Where are we going?"

"To your room."

He tugged on her hand, but she pulled back. If she allowed David to come to her room, a regular hotel room with not much more than a bed in it, she wasn't sure if she'd be able to keep from letting the inevitable happen this time.

"Why my room?" She still hadn't moved.

He gave a harder tug and she came up against his chest. He kissed her gently. "Because Karen has already told a large group of people that we're engaged and some of them are looking somewhat skeptical," he whispered against her mouth, tensing a shoulder in the direction her friend had wandered off to. "No, don't look unless you want them to realize we're putting on a show."

She kissed him back. "So we're running away to hide in my room, David?"

He laughed against her lips, his breath a warm caress. "We're going to let them wonder what we're doing up there."

"I don't think they'll be doing much wondering. All of them will be sure we're making love."

He raised one brow. "Do you really think so? How shocking."

"Yes, isn't it?" she said, placing her hands on his chest and smiling up at him.

"You wouldn't be in the mood to add a little shocking fuel to the fire, would you? To seal our fate, to make everyone truly believe that the elusive Gretchen Neal has finally been captured?"

She rose up on her toes and kissed his lips. "You want to go to our room, David?" she said loudly enough for those nearby to hear. "That's a wonderful idea, my love."

Allowing him to lead her toward the elevators, she

pretended she didn't know that the mother of the bride was on the way over to talk to her. The idea had been to enjoy themselves, to let everyone think that this time it would be a mistake for anyone to try to fix her up with a man.

But moving ever closer to her room with David, Gretchen wondered if she wasn't making an even bigger mistake.

Nine

He had to be certifiably insane to think he could get away with this, David thought, entering Gretchen's room. The masquerade had been his idea, simply a way to give Gretchen a break from all the matchmaking her well-meaning family and friends would have provided had she come alone.

But that wasn't exactly the complete truth, he admitted for the first time. The truth was that he wasn't sure he could have dealt with sitting back in Whitehorn while good-looking men were marched out for Gretchen's perusal. He'd had her in his sights for weeks now. He wanted her in his bed before he went back to Atlanta, and now that he was alone with her in a room with a king-size bed there was no denying the fact that he wanted very badly to touch her in the most intimate of ways. Immediately.

"They didn't have any doubles by the time I booked," she explained as if he'd asked a question. "I—I didn't request this."

He almost groaned out loud. Just thinking of Gretchen naked and alone in a bed big enough for two to roll around in comfortably was making him a little crazy. He took a step in her direction.

She stood her ground, but she crossed her arms over her chest. "I can't believe you bought a ring."

"It was nothing."

"A diamond engagement ring isn't nothing."

"A necessity then," he conceded. "Adds a touch of reality."

She raised one delicately arched brow. "Just how far are you willing to go to add a touch of reality?"

"You don't like pretending, do you, Gretchen?"

A long sigh slipped through her lips. "It's not that. This could be fun, but—"

"But?"

She leaned back on the long bureau that ran the length of the room. "You and I— There's clearly…something between us."

"Salsa. Steam baths. Molten lava," he agreed.

"Things do tend to heat up when I'm with you," she conceded, "and that's a problem. It complicates the issues, the case."

"You think that maybe Storm is right, that I'm trying to influence you?"

She shook her head. "Actually, I don't, but I'm not so positive that I won't be influenced. I'm very loyal to my friends. That's why I never mix business and pleasure."

He fixed his dark green feral gaze on her. "And yet we're here. Together."

"I know. This probably wasn't very wise."

"You want out? We could tell everyone the truth."

A long, slow smile lifted her lips. "Over my dead body, Hannon. I intend to have fun this weekend. This is the first time in a long time I'll be able to attend a wedding without the vultures circling. If you think I'm going to give that up so easily, you're wrong."

He waited. She clearly had more to say.

"But this unexpected good fortune of mine *was* just the result of a simple bet," she said carefully. "We pretend. We let everyone else believe we're engaged, but we don't take it any further than we need to.''

"You can't pretend away the mutual attraction, Gretchen.'' The darn man's smile was deep and lazy.

"I'm not trying to.''

"What are you trying to do?''

A slight hesitation. "I'm trying to wait it out.''

"You're uncomfortable.''

"Of course I'm uncomfortable. It's bad enough that you and I are collaborating on a murder investigation where your uncle is the prime suspect. Complicating that with sex only makes things that much worse.''

"Or better.''

She sucked in a deep breath. Her hands shook slightly. And it was that little detail that made him swear at himself beneath his breath.

"Sit down, Gretchen. We'll make it right.'' He motioned toward the bed.

"I don't think—''

"I won't touch you,'' he promised. "Unless you ask me to. For now we'll just talk until enough time has passed and it won't look strange if I go back to my room alone.''

"Talk about what?''

"Not about how I'd like to slowly slip open every tiny button on that dress you're wearing,'' he said. "Or how I'm dying to taste the softest part of your inner thigh.''

She clenched her hands at her waist as her color rose.

"What, then?''

He sat on the bed, at the farthest end, and waited for her to join him there. "For now we'll just stick to the basics. Tell me about all the places you traveled to as a child. Tell me what you were like and who your friends were and what you did. Tell me what you were like as a teenager.''

"I was busy.''

"I'm sure you were. Your parents must have gone mad trying to keep the guys away. Mace. Sledgehammers. I'll bet your father had a whole arsenal of weapons to make sure your boyfriends brought you home on time and untouched.''

She wrinkled her nose. "I really didn't get out all that much.''

Something about the way she said that caught David square in the chest. "Maybe you should clarify that, love. You *did* get out? Group dates? Movies? Letting the boy next to you steal your popcorn?''

"David,'' she said sternly. "Don't sound so worried. It wasn't that my parents kept me locked up or anything like that. Or that I was some sort of prude. There just wasn't all that much time.''

"Ah,'' he said gently. "All the brothers and sisters. That nurturing side of you.''

She shrugged. "My parents weren't trying to deprive me. They were just overwhelmed themselves a lot of the time, I think. It takes a lot of time and work and money to raise a big family. My help was appreciated. It was welcome, and really, things got easier as the kids got older. I dated plenty once I went away to college.''

"I'm sure you made up for lost time,'' he agreed, giving her the simple answer he figured she wanted to hear. He wasn't really sure he should have gone down this road in the first place. Now that he'd started, he figured it wouldn't be all that smart for him to hear the details of Gretchen's sexual awakening.

She must have known what he was thinking. She leveled a long, sexy, assessing glance at him, then raised one delicate brow. "Oh, yes, I made up for lost time. In fact, I was practically an animal, David. My studies suffered. Men were like sinful chocolate for me. I couldn't get enough."

"That bad?" he asked with a lazy smile.

She laughed and threw a pillow at him. "No, not that bad at all. I was very studious, but I dated some. And no, I'm not going into details."

"Probably just as well. I'd hate to have to go out looking for some guy you dated ten years ago with the aim of moving his nose from one side of his face to the other. Might be embarrassing. Maybe you'd better skip the dating years and just tell me about your childhood."

She edged nearer to the bed and settled herself against the headboard, looking down at him with an indulgent smile. "All right, then. I'll tell you. Will it surprise you to learn that I was a bossy child?"

He chuckled. "It would absolutely astound me."

She chuckled back. "And were you always as persuasive as you are now? I can't believe you talked me into telling you anything at all about my awkward social debut."

"Persuasive? Mmm, I suppose so. I talked my third grade teacher into letting me lead the investigation of who was stealing the lunches from everyone's lockers."

"Impressive. Did you solve the crime?"

"The case is still on the elementary school's books." His smile didn't tell her anything, at least not too much.

"You solved it, but you didn't turn the culprit in," she guessed.

He shrugged. "Extenuating circumstances. He needed the food. I merely made a deal. I brought an extra lunch for him for a while and he swept floors at the Big Sky until he made enough money to slip some pennies back into the lockers of the kids he'd stolen from. Not exactly the usual way of doing things, but a lot more rewarding and fun.''

She nodded her agreement. "Too bad more crimes can't be atoned for that way."

He frowned. "Yes, it is too bad. No way we can bring back Raven Hunter. Storm's lost his brother. Summer's lost her father. And the killer may well be a dead man."

"But at least Storm and Summer will have some sort of closure."

His laugh was harsh. "When she was growing up, Summer wanted a father, not closure. But yes, I know you're right. Closure is the best we can hope for in this case. For Storm and Summer. For Celeste. For all of us. Not quite as satisfying as taking some drug-runners out of commission, but I guess it'll have to do."

"And we'll do it," she promised him. "Celeste and Summer and Storm will at least have knowledge, David."

"Mmm. They'll have that. And so will I. About you. Now tell me again, how bossy were you when you were a child?"

Gretchen grinned. "You'll meet my younger brother, Vince, tomorrow. I'll let him tell you how I ordered him around mercilessly when he was eight years old. He absolutely insisted that baths were dangerous to his social standing, but the threat of never seeing dessert in this lifetime convinced him that he could somehow survive a touch of soap and water."

David twisted his lips up in a bemused smile. "You withheld dessert from a boy of eight? Gutsy woman."

"Yes. Vince had lungs of steel and real staying power when he howled. I'm prepared to wade into treacherous waters when I have to."

David raised one brow.

"But I'm not stupid, David," she added quickly. "I don't take unnecessary risks."

"I'll remember that, Gretchen," he said as he stood and moved toward the door, obviously on his way back to his room. "When you and I meet on a bed next time, I'll make sure that any risks we take are very necessary ones."

The man was turning her into a feverish woman, Gretchen admitted as she slipped into the body-hugging pale sea-green dress and tugged the jacket over her shoulders late the next afternoon. One minute she was sauna-hot, the next slush-cold as she realized just how close she was getting to the edge with David.

"If it was just the sex thing, I'd be okay," she muttered. "Or even the fact that he respects me professionally." But when those two aspects of their relationship were combined with the way he seemed to almost sense her needs and her fears, and responded with caring and more restraint than any man she knew... Well, darn it, the man just scared her more than a bank robber with a wildly waving gun.

He treated her like a person who needed caring for in ways she didn't even know she needed caring for. And that affected her much too much, even though she knew it was just his way, with everyone, with every woman. Still, it touched her, made her want him in ways she didn't understand or welcome. She couldn't get away from these longings he called forth in her. The fact that he'd held back because she wanted him to, when he knew he could make her ignite with the slightest touch, confused her. He made her hurt to be with him even though she knew the danger of getting too entangled. And by danger, she was not talking about her professional standing. She just didn't want to start letting this man get too close. She *never* wanted to long for any man so much that she would give up all the things that mattered the most to her, the way her mother had done over and over.

"And there's no need to worry about that, is there?" she whispered. "He wants you. You want him, but he's been reasonable. There's no reason to think he won't play fair the rest of the time." She would get to call the shots, and she'd already made her stance clear.

Gretchen tried out a smile in the mirror and found that she looked relatively calm.

Good. She could enjoy herself as much as she wanted today without having to worry about anything else.

Gretchen's dress looked tissue-thin, her elegant shoulders were bare. When she turned and her blond hair brushed her naked flesh, David couldn't help imagining his own fingers doing the same. And right now, smiling though he might be, he was ready to arrest the next guy who looked at Gretchen as if he knew what was beneath that scrap of silk she was wearing.

The fact that he himself didn't know and might never know in spite of the comment he'd made to her upon leaving her room last night, left him raw and aching. The truth was, he wasn't going to force anything on her that she didn't feel right about. He might want to seduce her badly, he might even know that she was ready to tumble with just the slightest push, but he also knew that she was hoping against hope that she wouldn't have to deal with the complications of a physical relationship with him. Knowing that, he couldn't press her. She was right about this situation being a bit delicate and she had every right to back away if she wanted to.

That didn't mean he had to feel good about it. It only meant he had to endure. And if that was the case, he might as well endure with grace. Might as well enjoy as much of the lady's company as the situation allowed.

"You look stunningly beautiful," he whispered, brushing back her hair with his thumb and dropping a kiss on the pulse point just beneath her ear. It was early evening. For the past two hours he'd watched Gretchen walk down the aisle, stand patiently for photo after photo, assist the bride. She'd glowed and smiled, making David ache to touch her. Now he was passing through the receiving line at the reception and he'd had to watch man after man kiss Gretchen. On her cool, soft cheek. On her warm red lips. Meaningless kisses if you didn't know how men operated. David happened to know a lot about how men operated.

She smiled up at him. "The wedding went well, didn't it? Pamela was lovely."

"I'm sure she was. I didn't notice."

Staring into her eyes, his meaning was obvious. Gretchen dragged in a deep breath and continued to just stand there looking lovely. A full-bodied, chortling laugh sounded nearby.

"Looks like my big sister has finally found a man who knows how to stun her into silence."

The voice broke the spell she appeared to be under. She smiled up at David and turned to the man standing at his shoulder. "David, this is my baby brother, Vince. He's the only Neal other than me who could make it in today. Vince, this is David Hannon, my fiancé," she managed to say quite smoothly.

David turned to a handsome young man not much younger than himself. "You must be the brother

Gretchen told me about. The one she threatened to withhold dessert from when he was eight?''

Vince grinned. ''She's a tyrant, Hannon. I hope you can handle her. Gretch very seldom listens to anyone else's side of things.''

''Humph,'' she said, crossing her slender arms. ''I listened to you whenever that bully next door threatened you.''

Vince shifted uncomfortably. ''Don't remind me.'' He looked at David. ''She's unstoppable when someone she loves is threatened, Hannon. You should know it. I distinctly remember my sister sporting a black eye for my sake that time.''

Gretchen looked suddenly sad. ''I'm sorry, Vince. I didn't mean to make you feel uncomfortable. I'd forgotten about the black eye. I only remembered that he was twice as tall as you and a total jerk. He stole your bicycle, if I recall.''

Her brother shifted his head. He turned to David. ''What's a guy to do? She forgot the black eye but remembered that Thad was twice my size. I remember that I had some real growing up to do back then. Fast, if I didn't want my sister getting beat up for my sake every other week. Having a sister like Gretch, you learned to fight your own battles or she'd get in the thick of things for you.''

''Hey, he looked worse than I did when it was over,'' Gretchen protested.

David couldn't help chuckling at her indignant response. ''I'm sure you worked him over and he got his just deserts, love. And don't worry, Vince,'' he told the young man. ''I'm watching out for her these days.''

She gave David a deadly glance.

Vince laughed. "Careful, Hannon. Her pride bruises easily."

David looked down into Gretchen's sparkling green eyes. "I'm watching out for that, too. You're lucky to have her for a sister, Vince."

"Just as long as you know how lucky you are, as well," Vince warned.

"The luckiest," David agreed. "You won't mind if I pull her out of here and keep her to myself for a few minutes before the bridal party drags her away from me, will you?"

"I was wondering if you were being a bit slow, Hannon. You seem like good prospective brother-in-law material. You chose well, Gretch. Be happy, sweetheart." He gave his sister a kiss on the cheek.

"I *am* happy, Vince. Please, don't worry about me."

But as David slipped her arm through his and escorted her away, she looked up at him. "I guess you passed. Vince seemed to relax. He's always been a little worried where I was concerned. Even though he's younger than me, he feels like I'm the headstrong one. Can you imagine?"

David laughed and lifted her up into his arms, kissing her full on the lips for everyone to see before he let her down. "I can't imagine why anyone would consider you headstrong, Gretchen. A black eye. Imagine that."

"The kid deserved it." Her tone was calm, matter-of-fact.

"I'm sure he did, but, Gretchen—"

She looked up, a question in her eyes.

"I'm sure it's a bit sexist of me, but if you ever feel like giving someone a black eye for my sake, do you think you could let me try my luck at him first?"

She smiled and patted his hand. "Of course, David,

dear. Male pride. It's such a delicate thing. I'll try to be kind.''

"You do that."

"As long as you don't try to fight my battles for me."

He opened his mouth to protest, then decided it would be best to not say anything. The thought of anyone touching Gretchen with the intent of hurting her filled him with such anger that he knew he couldn't promise any such thing. It wasn't because he doubted her ability. It wasn't because he really was a sexist. In fact, he was pretty sure he didn't want to know why he felt that way and pretty sure that Gretchen wouldn't want to know, either. Perhaps tonight, they shouldn't think—at all.

And so he kept her close at his side as they moved around the room and she introduced him to all the friends he hadn't yet met. He wondered what fates had linked him to this woman, this wonderful, glorious, infuriatingly self-sufficient woman.

"God, he's gorgeous, Gretchen," Pamela said for perhaps the fourth time that day. "Almost as good-looking as my Raymond. I can't believe it. Oh, you've made me so happy, sweetie. Thinking of you finally bringing home a man and to my wedding, too. It's the best present ever."

Twin tears streaked down the bride's cheeks as she hugged her friend close.

"The day's perfect now. Perfect," Pamela added. "Isn't it, Raymond?"

"The very best day of my life, love," her husband answered. "Thank you," he whispered to Gretchen and David when Pamela went to fix her makeup for the tenth time that day. "She's been worrying about you for weeks. Now she can relax and not feel guilty about get-

ting married and 'deserting you,' as she's been saying,''
he admitted.

"Oh, Raymond, you should have told me she was worrying so much.''

He shrugged. "What could you do to make her happy,
short of getting engaged? And heaven knows, no one
would get engaged for such a frivolous reason.''

"I see what you mean,'' Gretchen said weakly as Pamela returned and her husband spirited her away.

"Relax, sweetheart,'' David whispered. "She's
happy.''

"She is, isn't she?'' Gretchen agreed, smiling up at
him. "And so am I. For the first time in a long time, I'm
at a wedding where no one is giving me worried glances
or trying to make sure I'm not alone too much. Everyone
is able to relax and simply enjoy themselves, and I intend
to do the same thing.''

"You're a very wise and adaptable woman, Gretchen
Neal,'' David whispered. "Have I told you that today?''

"You've never told me that,'' she said indignantly.

"Hmm, that can't be right. I must have. Aren't you
the woman who agreed to put up with a pushy FBI agent
who wormed his way onto your case?''

"I seem to remember something like that. Yes.''

"And aren't you the woman who had to patiently remind me repeatedly that I couldn't play top banana all
the time?''

She shook her head. "You were a fast learner.''

He looked contrite. "But I'm sure you're the one who
got suckered into a bet and then gamely agreed to go
along with the consequences, even though she really
didn't want to.''

"What could I do? Fair is fair.''

"And you're more than fair, Gretchen. Now, go on

and do whatever it is that bridesmaids have to do at receptions and then enjoy yourself when the dancing starts. Save a slow one for me.''

She touched his cheek gently. "Oh, more than one, I think. Many more.'' And then, as if she realized that her touch was sapping all his self-control, she blushed the palest of pinks. Her eyelids fluttered down in a way that would most certainly have surprised all those male detectives who were so used to seeing her manage dangerous situations with ease. "That is, I—we're supposed to be engaged,'' she ended feebly. "We would dance, wouldn't we?''

"Oh, yes, love, we would definitely dance. And more,'' he said, snagging her close and bending her backward over his arm as he touched his lips to hers in a brief, hard kiss. "Just in case anyone should forget that you're wearing my ring tonight,'' he told her.

She nodded slightly, her lips parted, her expression slightly dazed.

"Enjoy the dancing, Gretchen,'' he said, releasing her completely.

And she apparently did. For the next few hours Gretchen twirled. She swayed. She danced with every male that asked her. She glowed with delight, and David delighted in her unfettered enthusiasm. How could he not when the lady was in his own arms every few dances?

"For appearance's sake,'' she said the first time as he twirled her into the dance and later accepted a glass of wine from him to cool her off.

"Just in case anyone has any doubts,'' he agreed the next time she was in his arms.

"To keep everyone happy,'' she whispered softly the next time he fit his hand to her waist and pulled her close against his heart. Only Gretchen wasn't sure whose happiness she was worried about this time. As a bridesmaid, she'd felt obligated to dance with the guests, but her eyes had kept returning to David. It was his arms and his hands she wanted around her, his heart she wanted beating against her own. Her head was swirling. She'd probably had more wine than she should, but for now she was with David and she just didn't care.

"Let's walk outside," she said when the dance was over and she saw another young man headed her way. "I need some air and some rest. It's so warm in here."

David signaled a passing waiter to bring her another glass of wine and then thought better of it, asking the man for water instead. He'd probably had more to drink than he should. The wine had gone down too easily, unheeded as his gaze had followed her around the floor all night.

"You've been very busy," he said as they walked out into the softly lit gardens and along the length of a long blue pool with a fountain in the center.

"It's been fun," she agreed as she stopped and turned to face him. He held her glass up and she sipped the cool water, her lips brushing his fingers slightly where he grasped the delicate crystal.

His hand shook and she swayed against him.

Somehow he got rid of the glass. Somehow she was up against his heart.

"Do you have anything else you need to do tonight?" he asked.

She shook her head. "There's the bouquet, but then I don't need to be there for that this time. And anyway, Pamela will understand if I'm gone. She probably won't even notice. Her eyes haven't left Raymond all night long."

"If we leave, Gretchen," David whispered, his voice

thick as he dipped the fingers of one hand into her hair, "I can't make any promises to behave like a gentleman."

He leaned and dropped a kiss on the bare skin of her shoulder. His fingers grazed the gentle slope of her breast above her dress.

She swallowed hard. "If we don't leave David, I can't promise that we won't both embarrass all the other guests."

And so he swept her close. Somehow they crossed the ballroom, the lobby, found the elevator and closed themselves in together.

The door closed and he tugged her close, claimed her lips.

She placed her palms against his chest and pulled herself closer.

"I want us to make love," she managed to get out.

"I don't think there's any doubt that we're going to," he said as the door started to open and he glanced up, his lips still fastened to Gretchen's, just in time to see an elderly couple waiting to get in.

David reached out and pressed the Close Door button. He snatched Gretchen closer and heard the couple's soft laughter, saw the man's thumbs-up as the door locked them in again.

"Are they gone?" Gretchen whispered.

"Mmm," he agreed.

"Good." She wrenched her lips from his and began to rain kisses over his face, his chin. She touched her lips to his Adam's apple and busied her fingers with tugging open his tie.

When the door of the elevator opened this time, David scooped Gretchen into his arms and carried her down the hall. He could feel the lovely curves of her legs beneath the thin, slippery cloth of her dress.

"What are you wearing beneath this, love?" he asked, stopping long enough to kiss her lips once more, to savor the feel of her slender fingers against his scalp.

"Not much," she whispered. "Hurry, David."

He was, as she'd said, a fast learner. In a matter of seconds, David was at her door, she was leaning over in his arms to insert the key card and then, at last, they were alone in her room.

Letting her slide down the length of him, he waited until her feet found the floor. Then he reached behind her, gently gathered her wrists in his own and walked her slowly backward until her legs hit the side of the big bed. He swept his hands up her sides, his fingers resting on the low-slung straps that grazed her arms.

"Are you sure, Gretchen? Be very sure you know what you're doing. I'd do my best to turn back if we took this over the edge, but it would be much easier to do so now."

And yet his fingers shook against her skin. She closed her eyes and let the essence of him surround her. The gentle flexing of his fingertips on the straps, the knowledge that he was going to touch her at last, the fear that he would not touch her, filled her.

She opened her eyes, reached up as she gazed into the fiery depths of his green eyes. She grasped the lapels of the black suit that sat so well on his broad shoulders and she opened his jacket, shoving it off his shoulders. She slipped off the tie she'd unfastened earlier. She grasped the crisp white front of his shirt.

"David?"

"Yes, love?" Being a somewhat tall woman, there weren't many men who towered over her and made her feel small, or feminine. But when she looked up at that stunningly handsome face, she did feel feminine. The thought that countless other women had no doubt stood just this way with him rankled. He really was too good-looking for any woman's good. But she wasn't just any woman. She was herself, Gretchen Neal, and she wasn't going to wait for what she wanted.

She rose up on her toes, parted her lips and slid them across David's. Slowly. Once. Twice. Again.

He groaned, but still he didn't claim her with his arms. Her head was spinning, her breasts were aching where she'd pressed herself close against him.

"David," she whispered again.

"You know I want you, love," he said with a low moan against her lips. She could hear the slightest hesitation in his voice. And suddenly she was tired of all the questions, all the hesitation, all the good intentions and wise words she'd spoken these past couple of weeks.

The swirling longing that David called up in her was dangerous. The man himself was dangerous, and right now danger was just what she wanted. Mostly, though, she wanted David. His touch, his skin beneath her fingers, his length and weight pressing her into the depths of the bed, covering her.

"I want you, too, David. Please. Have me," she said in a frantic whisper, and with a quick wrench, she pulled on the shirt she was still holding clenched between her fingers. Buttons flew, and suddenly all that was between David's chest and her breasts was one small bit of silk that covered her.

He tightened his fingers on the slim straps of her gown and gently pulled downward, sliding her dress over her breasts and past her hips, letting the thin material slither to the ground. Only the slightest touch of silk panties covered her now.

David stared at her for long seconds. Her nipples stiffened beneath his gaze and he cupped one breast in his hand, lifted the soft round swell and kissed the sensitive bud.

She was going to faint. The sensation was simply too great as David kissed and suckled her, tugging gently on the turgid tip. When he moved to the other breast, she grasped his shoulders, digging in her fingers to keep from falling.

But he was there. Lifting her onto the bed, David shrugged out of what was left of his shirt. He lowered himself over her and claimed her lips again.

His hand stroked downward, outlining her from shoulder to breast to hip to knee. When he tugged his lips from her own, she surged upward. Nothing mattered at this moment but the magic of David's touch, and he was taking it away.

"Don't leave," she whispered, lacing her arms around him, urging him back to her.

"Not a chance," he whispered, his voice strained as he reached for his belt buckle. She stopped him with her touch, rising to her knees, rolling her head forward languorously as she freed him, exposed him and he peeled away the last layers that shielded him from her gaze.

She'd seen plenty of naked men before, of course. She was not untried, and besides, she operated daily in a man's world, a rough world. But she had never seen a man so clearly made for giving pleasure to a woman.

He was magnificently formed, his long, thick shaft standing proudly from his body.

She reached for him without thought and he surged into her hand then backed away.

"No. It has to be good. For you."

"It will be," she promised, reaching for him again.

"It will be," he promised as well, urging her back onto

the bed. He removed the tiny patch of silk that still covered her and pulled her into his arms, breast to chest, thigh to thigh. Framing her face with his hands, he pleasured her with deep, long kisses.

He slid his body down the length of hers, kissing her shoulder, suckling at the tip of her breast, feathering his fingers down the inside of her thigh and then placing his lips there lightly, as well.

Pressure built within her, making her weak and helpless with longing and need.

"David, please," she said on a gasp, digging her fingers into his shoulders. "Be with me."

And he rose up above her. He gazed down at her, naked want in his eyes, and she opened to him. She welcomed him as he took care that she was safe and then entered her fully.

The feel of him filling her, joined to her, thick and long and strong, was exquisite, an ecstasy almost beyond bearing. His body came into hers, touching her over and over in the most pleasurable places.

She arched to meet him, rocked with him. Her muscles tightened around him. She grasped his biceps, shifting her hips, bringing him in deeper, and she felt the tension in his skin beneath her fingertips.

"Not yet." David choked out the words as she pulled him deeper still. "Not yet. Not alone."

And he slowed his movements, gasping for breath as he fought for control. He gained a small measure, gazing down into her eyes, his own dark with barely caged desire.

Her own need spilled over.

"Please," she whispered again. "Yes. Yes, now."

He tumbled her back. He took her down, took charge as he braced himself above her. He slid into her depths again and began the final movement. He held her gently by her wrists just above her head and thrust into her. Slowly, slowly, caressing her inside and out, turning her to melted butter. Making her hot beyond belief.

Craving climbed within her, building as he moved in her. Slow and then fast. He played her body, and she wanted—she needed—to reach the pinnacle he was urging her to. Too slowly.

"You're making me crazy," she said, biting her lip, her head lolling softly on the pillow.

"I'm past crazy, love. I'm barely hanging on." And then he reached down, just barely, expertly brushing one finger over that part of her where her body was joined to his, and she couldn't stop herself from spinning out of her body and into the sun. Hot pleasure flooded her. She heard David shout her name as he drove thick and hard into her one last time.

She fell back against the pillows and wondered if she'd ever be able to move again. And then she stopped wondering as she relaxed into drowsiness and let her suddenly leaden limbs rest.

The clock ticked. The time passed.

After long moments of simply waiting for thought and steady heartbeat and even breathing to return, David gathered her close in his arms. He touched his lips to her hair.

She remembered wishing that she could always feel this wonderful, this glowing. She had never lost herself so completely. She had felt so storm-tossed and yet still safe. Surely she had been right to give in to this.

Ten

"No." The word sounded in her head so clearly that Gretchen could almost have sworn that she had spoken it out loud. This morning her head was only slightly fuzzy, slightly pained, but the sense that something was very wrong was excessively strong. And she knew just what that something wrong was. She'd thrown common sense out the window last night.

Turning her head to the side, she looked right into David's eyes. He wasn't smiling.

She sat bolt upright in bed, clutching the sheet to her.

"It seems—" She couldn't quite get the words out of her mouth without needing to close her eyes, without stumbling.

"Gretchen." One word, a deep command in his voice. "Look at me."

She did. His eyes were dark green, worried.

"It seems we made a mistake," she finished.

"Like hell we did."

"I probably had too much to drink. Maybe you did, too," she whispered. "Otherwise—"

"We didn't have too much to drink. And we knew this was going to happen someday, Gretchen. We were going to make love one way or another."

She froze, spearing him with a look. "You would have forced me?"

Dark anger flooded his eyes. He sat up and reached out for her. She scooted back against the headboard.

"Damn it, Gretchen. You know there would have been no force."

"You're right." She couldn't keep the coldness from her voice. "I seem to have a surprising lack of control where you're concerned."

"Which really ticks you off, doesn't it?"

She blew out a long breath. "You don't understand, David." Her voice softened.

He rose up on his palms, leaning over her. "I understand. You value your privacy. You don't want anyone breaking down those barriers you put up, and you don't trust me to honor those barriers. You don't trust me not to push."

She opened her mouth to answer, then closed it again. Because the truth was much more frightening than that, as far as she was concerned. It wasn't that she didn't trust him not to push. She didn't trust herself not to give in. This man had the power to make her feel too much. And feeling more than she should could only lead her down paths she would regret and down paths he would regret, as well. David wanted her, but he was a man who chose to be a loner and who was here on a temporary assignment. In no time at all, he would be returning to his own world and she would stay in hers.

"We can't do this again, David," she whispered. "It was a mistake."

"All right, then," he suddenly agreed, his voice low and calm. "It was a mistake."

He meant that, David thought as they both went about the business of getting ready to leave. Making love to Gretchen *had* been a mistake, because back in his room, imagining her in the shower with warm fingers of water caressing her body, he already wanted her again. He was losing control where this woman was concerned. He wanted her way too much, too often. She seldom left his thoughts for long. And yet there was no future here. She wanted a life alone. He could understand that. He'd been a loner too long not to know the lure of that life. She was a woman who had given and given all her life, a woman who'd grown up in a big family and had had responsibility thrust on her all during the years when she should have been carefree and unencumbered by burdens.

He wanted to tell her that he would never take advantage of her that way and yet, he couldn't promise that. Because right now he wanted to ask a great deal of her. At this point in time, he couldn't be trusted from one minute to the next. Not where Gretchen was concerned. His feelings were intensifying and that was dangerous. To her and to him. Growing up sickly, cut off from children his own age, he'd wanted so much. Too much. That need to belong, that longing to be a part of a world that was closed to him, had nearly driven him mad as a child. Until he'd learned to submerge those needs, to depend only on himself. And now he was starting to feel that intense longing again.

Gretchen was right. Getting too involved with her would be a mistake. He'd do his best to keep things light and easy from now on. As for desire, that could be managed, too. He'd always been able to handle it before.

The only thing he couldn't manage was returning things to the way they'd been before they'd made love. No matter how much they both wanted to deny it, that intimacy couldn't be forgotten. It would change things. He wasn't sure how or by how much, but there would definitely be a difference. There was just no road back to yesterday.

* * *

"Okay, next verse," Gretchen said with a laugh the following Monday. David watched her as she sat cross-legged and hugging a guitar in the center of a circle of giggling children, leading them through a song she had made up to teach them safety rules. The song was silly, but the rules were very real and David was sure that the children would remember them much better than they would have if Gretchen had simply written a list on the chalkboard.

At a pause in the song, a solemn little red-haired girl tugged on Gretchen's sleeve and when Gretchen smiled down at her, the little girl leaned close. "Agent Hannon isn't singing," the child whispered a bit too loudly. "He looks mad."

Gretchen looked up from her position on the floor to where David was lounging easily against the wall, his arms crossed.

"He does look a bit...tense," she teased.

David couldn't help smiling then. And why not? Gretchen, after all, had been treating him to her own smile all morning, convinced that she had finally tamed him by bringing him in as a "classroom exhibit." She was looking absolutely beautiful in pale gray, her hair slightly mussed after a long session with the children. And yes, David acknowledged, he supposed he had looked a bit angry just a moment ago. He had been frowning, at least.

Because that smile of Gretchen's was so damned tempting. And also because the lady was clearly, totally in her element with these children and yet he knew she had decided not to get married and have any of her own. It was a crime, if anything was. He'd been mulling over that fact, and regretting it.

But then, who was he to challenge the lady's choices

when she'd obviously made them carefully? She didn't think she was up to making the sacrifices that marriage would entail. Well, who was he to talk when he was pretty darn sure that he wasn't a prime choice for marriage, either?

And why was he frowning and upsetting innocent children when absolutely none of this was their fault?

David gave a deep inner sigh. He pulled his thoughts back into place, back where they should be. He turned to the little girl and gave her a wink and a grin.

"Sorry for looking like a thundercloud. I was just sulking because you weren't paying any attention to me," he teased. "Detective Neal looks like she's having all the fun."

The little girl giggled as Gretchen rolled her eyes.

"Well, then, Agent Hannon," Gretchen said, patting the floor beside her. "Why don't you come over here and help us out? We could use a baritone."

"She only keeps me around for my voice," he said in a mock sorrowful tone as he took a place in the circle of children.

"And so you can help her fight the bad guys," one little boy said. "That's what you do, isn't it?"

David turned to the wide gray eyes of the little boy who was looking right and left, first at Gretchen, then at himself. He was rocking and fidgeting, clearly excited. "I'd like to fight those guys, too," he confided.

David knew just how the skinny little guy who was way too small to fight anyone bigger than a watermelon felt. He'd been that child once a long time ago. But he also knew things he hadn't known then.

"My job is to protect, yes, but it's more important to prevent," he confided. "Listen to the words of the song Gretchen is singing. All those things are designed to keep you as safe as possible so the bad guys won't have a chance. That's fighting them in your own way."

The little boy narrowed his eyes and shook his head. "Aw, we hear those rules all the time. They don't do anything. And it's the same old stuff every year."

"Jamie," Gretchen drawled, her voice soft. "I'm sorry you feel that way, hon, but—" David reached out and touched her hand, almost imperceptibly, stopping her midword.

"Same old stuff," he agreed gruffly, trying not to notice the quick wounded look in Gretchen's eyes. "Wonder why we keep nagging you about the same old things all the time. Day in. Day out. Year in. Year out." David gave a loud yawn, covering his hand and pretended to fall asleep slumping down sideways against Gretchen.

"David," she yelped as the children laughed.

He opened his eyes and gave her a big grin as he sat up. "Why *do* we keep coming here with the same thing year after year?" he asked. "Is it because we've forgotten what we said the year before? Is it because we just don't know any better?"

"But Gretchen does it differently every time she comes here," another little boy said, bunching his forehead and his fists. "Last visit she put on a play and before that we went on a field trip around town looking for all the ways we could make ourselves safer. She doesn't make it all the same even if the rules don't change." And he would clearly like to punch David in the nose for seemingly criticizing his beloved Gretchen. David could have hugged the boy just for that.

"Do you think that's maybe because she knows that it's not always the same? Ever. The rules don't change, but the situations do. Like the rules about strangers. We ask you not to talk to strangers and sometimes we give examples.''

''Like a man offers you candy,'' the little red-haired girl said.

''Exactly, sweet stuff,'' David said. ''But what if the stranger told you that he needed you to come help him find his lost puppy?''

''You run away just the same as the man with the candy,'' she said firmly.

''I love the fact that you know that,'' he confided. ''Or what if he told you his little girl was sick and he needed your help.''

''Oh,'' a little girl with big blue eyes said. ''We could help then, couldn't we?''

A freckle-faced boy groaned. ''Elly, no. If his little girl was sick, he should be getting a grown-up to help.''

The little girl turned pink and tried to slide backward. David smiled at her. ''You've got a heart that glows with goodness, Elly. I'm glad you'd want to help, but the point is, and the rule is, that if a stranger needs help, he goes to the nearest grown-up. And if someone asks you for help, you run away to the nearest grown-up. If the person really needs help, they'll get it that way. And if they were just trying to harm you in some way, an adult can help keep you safe.''

He smiled at the little girl again.

''He looks very nice when he smiles, doesn't he, Gretchen?'' the little red-haired girl asked.

David raised one brow and grinned at Gretchen who was looking slightly flustered. Then Gretchen obviously collected herself. She raised one delicate brow and smiled teasingly.

''He's a looker, all right, Mary Kate.''

All the boys groaned.

The little boy who'd wanted to fight the bad guys stared at David. "So that's why she keeps repeating the same rules every year. So we see that they stay the same even if everything else changes?"

"That's part of the reason," David agreed. "And also just so you don't forget. So you know them so well that you can remember them without thinking. For those times when your brain short-circuits."

The little boy looked confused. "I don't get it."

Elly gave him a patient, motherly look. "You know, Jamie, like when you know you're not supposed to pet a strange dog but then one comes up to you and it's just so-oo happy to see you. Don't you remember when you and I saw that lady walking her dog this summer and you—"

Jamie slumped down a bit lower. "Okay, I remember. I get it now. Sometimes we do get so excited we forget the rules."

The little boy looked slightly defeated. He had obviously wanted, maybe even needed, to win something, David decided.

"We all forget sometimes, Jamie," he confided. "Even grown-ups. Even grown-ups who aren't ever supposed to make mistakes make them."

The boy looked up. "Not you?" he asked incredulously.

David tried to look abashed. "Me, too," he said. "Especially where dogs are concerned. You can ask Detective Neal."

The lady nodded sadly. "He has a weakness," she confessed.

"I'm working on it," David said, knowing that he really did have a weakness, but it wasn't just for exuberant, irresistible puppies. He seemed to have developed an even greater weakness, for one lovely, courageous female detective who had a soft spot for kids.

"You come back next year," the little red-haired girl told him, patting him on the hand with her own small one. "Gretchen will keep reminding you and one day you'll get past your weakness."

He hoped so, David thought as he and Gretchen said goodbye to the children later and left the school behind. He hoped he would be able to get past this abominable weakness. He'd gotten past his physical weakness as a child. Surely he'd be able to overcome his weakness for this woman, as well.

"I don't know how I missed this, Gretch," the young woman at the lab was saying the next afternoon. "That shirt was gone over very thoroughly. Or so I thought."

Gretchen stared down at the small slip of paper Reba Peyton was indicating.

"It was in his pocket?"

"Wadded up tiny and shoved down deep," Reba replied. "That's the only excuse I can give. That it was overlooked and once it had been overlooked, the shirt hadn't been moved."

Nodding, Gretchen studied the cryptic note. Very short. Very simple. Not much to it at all, and yet...

"Thanks, Reba. This changes a few things. Maybe."

And maybe it changed nothing, she conceded as she drove away. But at least it gave her some direction, something to do. At least she wasn't just twiddling her fingers and thinking of David Hannon, acting like a woman without a brain.

She considered heading back to the station, but that would have been out of the way, and besides, David had mentioned that he had a few calls to make regarding a case he still had open in Atlanta. Surely he wouldn't want her to interrupt him. This was, after all, just a preliminary questioning. Nothing too involved. Nothing she needed to consult with anyone on.

"Should be a piece of cake compared to some things I've done lately," she conceded, but she refused to dwell on what those things had been. Instead she concentrated on making sure that Lyle Brooks's car was in the parking lot outside the expensive boxy condos where he lived.

The car was there.

Good. Finally something positive was happening.

The housekeeper that had led her into Lyle's office quietly slipped away, clicking the door shut behind her.

Lyle looked up from some scribbling he was doing.

"Detective Neal?" he said with some surprise. "Esther told me it was you, but I thought maybe she'd got it wrong."

"No, she wasn't wrong," Gretchen said in an even tone. Brooks was a small man, with dark hair and dark vacant eyes. His expensive suit fit him well but didn't enhance his image. It was more like a costly wrapping on a slightly used present. The thought rose up. She brushed it aside. No fair prejudging the man even though he always made her uncomfortable and slightly tense.

"Mr. Brooks," she said as he tried out a smile that moved his mouth but otherwise made no difference in his appearance. "I have a few questions about Peter Cook and I'd like to ask your cooperation on several matters."

"Of course, Ms. Neal," he said, leaving off her title. "What can I do for you?"

"You can tell me why you wrote Peter Cook a note asking him to meet you at the site at ten o'clock the night he fell."

He shrugged. "No mystery here, Ms. Neal. Peter and I were close. He wanted to see this project finished as much as I do. I often included him in my planning sessions, and I often made my plans for the next day after hours. It simplifies things, ensures that all of the day's problems have been put away before we move on to the next day's concerns. Anything else?"

"Yes, Mr. Brooks. How long exactly did you and Peter spend together that night?"

She gazed down at him unblinkingly. He still smiled up at her, but she noticed that he'd flattened the fingers of one hand against the desk's edge. As if he wanted to keep from making a fist. Or curling his fingers around her neck. Not exactly a novel response. She'd seen it before, from the guilty and from the innocent. There were plenty of people, herself included, who didn't enjoy having their actions questioned. She tried to remind herself that this wasn't something she hadn't experienced before, although it did feel different somehow. Off kilter. But then, she had been rather off kilter lately and her reactions hadn't had much to do with her work.

"Mr. Brooks?" she prompted.

He shook his head. "It was a very brief meeting. We were simply discussing the next day's continued excavation. We went over the plans and then I left to go to the country club. I assure you Peter was alive and happy when last I saw him. The work was going well. I'm afraid I don't know anything about what happened to him after I departed, Ms. Neal. I'm sorry."

Yes, she was, too.

"I understand that you can only tell me what you know, Mr. Brooks," she agreed. "I hope that *you'll* understand when I tell you that we'd like to obtain some hair, skin and blood samples from you."

The silence was enormous. Then the man slowly smiled. "Of course, Ms. Neal. I want to find out what happened and to help all of us to move on in time."

She tilted her head in agreement. "Then we have the same goals, Mr. Brooks."

"And what would life be like without goals?" he said with a cheerful smile. "Don't worry, Ms. Neal. You'll have your samples. I know you're just doing your job."

He rose as she thanked him. He held out his hand, and she had no choice but to take it. Truthfully, she wasn't sure why she would want to hesitate. His explanation seemed plausible, given the situation. She was probably just a bit jumpy. She'd been much too jumpy lately. That really wasn't Lyle Brooks's fault.

But as she left Lyle's condo, she had an itchy need to look back over her shoulder.

The lady cop had very bad timing, Lyle Brooks thought after she left. His day had not gone well. He'd spent long hours trying to convince the leaders at the reservation that the Kincaid property that had been set aside for the resort/casino was the wrong piece of property. Two bodies. The land was undoubtedly bad luck. Cursed, one might even say, if a person believed in such things.

He believed in curses, although not this one that he'd conveniently invented. His whole life he'd been cursed, but now he had a chance. All he had to do was convince those people, those undeserving partners of his, to use *his* property that skirted the reservation in lieu of the current tract of land they'd chosen. They'd be happy, he'd still be in charge, and no one would go nosing around those sapphires.

Except for him, of course. He was the only one who

even knew they existed now that Peter was gone. Convincing the Cheyenne to move to a different location was the perfect solution.

If only they'd listen.

But they weren't listening. Something about destiny and dreams and this land being the perfect land.

Lyle Brooks let out a growl. His fist came down hard on the desk, sending paper clips and pens and an expensive ashtray flying.

He was just going to have to convince them. He didn't want anyone nosing around that land and discovering those sapphires that, right now, were his for the taking.

And he didn't want Detective Neal nosing around his business, either. Not that she could prove a thing. He'd been careful. No prints. Not even much of a touch to send Cook over the edge. Peter hadn't expected to be pushed. It had been easy to remove him as an obstacle.

He intended for it to be easy to remove every other obstacle or anyone who tried to cross him, as well. Lyle flicked a paper clip with his finger. A short, simple painless movement, but the paper clip flew through the air and fell to the ground. If it had been something breakable, it would have broken.

His laugh was low and strong as he thought how easy things were going to be.

Eleven

Gretchen opened the door a few hours later and unfastened the chain when she saw that it was David standing there. She gave him a smile.

"You don't have to keep coming to walk Goliath," she said when the little dog came running.

David absentmindedly reached down and gave the dog a quick pat, but he turned his attention back to Gretchen immediately. He wasn't smiling.

"I didn't come to see Goliath," he said.

He still wasn't smiling. His eyes were dark green and fierce. His face was set in sharp lines. He rested one hand on the door frame, making him seem even taller and broader of shoulder than usual.

Gretchen looked up at him and she wanted nothing more than to slide her hands up to frame that starkly handsome face of his and to brush her thumbs across his lips. She wanted to press her lips to his and see if the light came back into his eyes. A slight tremor ran through her at just the thought, at just how much this man made her lose every drop of common sense she possessed.

"Come inside, anyway," she said softly, stepping back to let him in.

He stepped in, letting the door fall shut behind him and then he kept coming.

"Gretchen," he said on a growl, moving into her space, gripping her arms lightly but firmly so that she was forced to look up at him. "What in hell were you doing today, lady?"

She looked down at where he held her, trying to make her eyes disdainful and cool, to ignore the fact that his touch fired through her and made her want to move closer.

"I was working," she said, her voice coming out too soft for her own satisfaction. "I was doing my job. What are you talking about?"

He shuffled forward one step, bringing his chest almost up against her own, moving his hands up to her shoulders, crowding her, a pained look on his face.

"You know what I'm talking about."

She did.

"I was doing my job, Hannon."

"You went to see Lyle Brooks. You went alone."

She placed her hands on his chest and pushed lightly. He backed off.

"I wasn't making an arrest, David. I was only asking a few questions. Standard stuff. Nothing to get excited about. I've done it a million times."

"Not with Lyle Brooks. I don't like the man."

"Neither do I, and he's being way too complacent for a man who has a reputation for impatience. The excavation of his resort has been held up and he's not screaming loudly enough, I think."

"I think you're right. And when a man starts acting out of character, he isn't a safe prospect."

He stared at her pointedly, the heat and frustration and anger rolling off him in long, slow waves. His jaw was like cold steel, his eyes like twin green flames.

Gretchen let out a sigh. She gave a gentle shrug, shaking her head. "David, I didn't need to tell you," she emphasized. "You were otherwise occupied. Don't try to tell me I wasn't doing my job right."

"You weren't."

Her chin came up. "That's unfair. Furthermore, it's not true. If you're going to make those kinds of accusations, Hannon, you'd darn well better have a good reason for making them. I followed the letter of the law."

"I'm not talking about the law this time, Gretchen. I'm talking about common sense. You know that guy is slime. Even if he didn't commit a crime here, he's not the kind of man you go up to alone and ask for evidence that indicates you might be suspicious of him."

"I do."

"Not when you have a partner, you don't. Let's try for a little trust here."

"All right, let's try for a little trust," she agreed. "If you had trusted me to do my job, you wouldn't have insisted on being allowed on this case. So who doesn't trust whom now? And for the record, David, my actions today had nothing to do with my lack of trust in you. You were working on something else. And it seems to me that I've trusted you quite a bit. I've shared my work with you. I've taken you to meet my friends when I've never done that with anyone else. But you just keep—"

She took a long deep breath and closed her eyes.

"But what, Gretchen? What is it I've done to upset you?"

Gretchen leaned back and looked up into his eyes. "You keep pushing. You keep making me uncomfortable." She breathed in again and the small action brought her chest up against his.

His eyes turned dark and slumberous. "I make you uncomfortable, do I? In what way would that be?"

But her eyelids drifted down. She didn't want to give

him his answer, and besides, darn it, he knew what way he made her uncomfortable. He knew it too well, she could tell, by the way his thumbs were rubbing slow circles upon the skin of her upper arms.

He leaned in closer, dragging her against him. "In this way?" he whispered, covering her lips with his own, sweeping her against him, her hips against his so that she could feel every angry inch of him. So that she could know that she made him uncomfortable, as well.

"No. In this way," she said when they came back up for air, and she plunged her fingers into his hair. She rose on her toes and molded her body to his, sliding up against him as she took the heat of his mouth.

Her lips chained him to her, held him still, made him moan. He was hers for the moment. He stood there and let her kiss him, his body tense and taut.

And then he moved. His mouth roved over hers, lightly at first, exploring. He shifted, lingering longer over each taste of her. The kiss turned dark and deep and hungry. He fed on her, taking her under time and time again. His hands claimed her shoulders, his fingertips teased her breasts.

She arched into him and pushed against his touch.

"Do that again. Please," she said, and he popped the top three buttons of her blouse, freeing the lace and pale skin that lay beneath.

"Touch me," he whispered, his voice ragged as his lips came down on hers once more and his fingers found the clasp of her bra and released her.

When his thumb grazed her nipple, she tore her lips from his, grasped the collar of his shirt and pulled on the cloth in one quick, jagged move, baring the golden muscles that lay beneath. Her palms came up against his chest and she lightly pushed, waltzing him backward across the carpeting toward the couch.

"No," he said, covering both her hands with one of his own to stop her. He only waited for her to pause before he scooped her into his arms.

"No?" Gretchen looked into his eyes, her own vision dull and glazed.

"Not the couch. We need room," he whispered, whisking her into the bedroom, striding the width of the floor and falling with her onto the bed.

"Room. Yes," she agreed, rolling from beneath him as she climbed to her knees and slid his shirt off his shoulders. She pushed, and he lay back against the pillows. Her lips found the small male nipple she was seeking.

A long, low breath slid from between David's lips as he let her lead the way. Gretchen leaned over him, her blouse curtaining his torso as she rose up to study him. He was beautiful, golden and hers for the moment, and she intended to feast.

Her tongue swirled against his skin. The flavor of him was a joy to the senses. She kissed her way over the tight muscles in his chest, dipping down to savor that washboard stomach. Finding his belt with her hand, she quickly flicked open the buckle and reached for the snap on his jeans. Her fingers slid beneath the waistband and she heard the slow hiss of his breath.

"Better to wait on that, love," he said on a gasp. "I want to make this last. At least a little bit longer." And without knowing exactly how he did it, Gretchen found herself in David's arms, sliding beneath him. With a few efficient movements, he tossed away her blouse, sent her bra sailing and removed her slacks, leaving only her ice-blue satin panties.

His smile was wolfish as he reclaimed the dominant role. "You are the most delicious, beautiful thing I've ever seen," he whispered, his warm breath teasing her skin as he nuzzled her hair aside and began to lightly nibble his way beneath her ear, down the exquisitely sensitive column of her neck.

"Soft," he murmured, dropping the lightest of kisses on the rounded slope of her breast.

"Firm," he whispered, his lips just catching the tip of her breast, tugging, tightening, then taking her into his mouth when she cried out at the heavenly sensation.

She thought she would go mad when he pulled away and gazed down at her. But he only paused to brush her lips lightly with his own before he turned his attention to her other breast, rolling the nipple between his lips, then suckling her gently.

A burgeoning need heated her, as sensation spiraled in her breasts and between her legs. She pressed her thighs together as David stroked her body, leading her, lifting her to heights of want she had never known.

"Gretchen, love." The words were strained with tension and Gretchen opened her eyes to look up at the man who controlled her every reaction at this moment. His eyes were dark with need and wonder and reverence. The fingers he touched to her lips shook. She knew that he was holding back everything that was coiled tightly within him. A light sheen of perspiration covered his magnificent chest. He needed her touch, needed release and yet when she reached for him again, to free him from the constraints of his remaining clothing, he closed his eyes and shook his head.

"David?"

He took a deep breath, opened his eyes and smiled at her slightly as he kissed his fingers, dampening them and then lightly touching the tip of her breast again. His light touch against her distended nipple sent her whole body bowing upward.

She called out his name again and he slid his hand down her body, parting her thighs as he reached beneath that scrap of silk and found the center of her, his fingers slipping in deep to stroke and tease.

And she flew apart on a broken cry. She lost herself to immeasurable pleasure. She touched the sun, the edge of the rainbow, and the deepest depths of the ocean in the same moment.

And David held her as she gave in to ecstasy.

When the tremors had finally subsided just slightly, she opened her eyes and looked up into his. He cupped her jaw, caressed her cheek.

"Well, I see I'm still here on earth, after all," she said, her voice weakened but still filled with the glow of satisfaction.

"Not for long," he whispered with a smile. "We're only halfway to heaven, angel."

"I was sure I was almost there."

"Soon," he promised, sitting up to skim his jeans down his legs and stepping out of his briefs. His body was long and lean and fully aroused.

Gretchen trembled as he moved back to the bed and gazed down at her, impatient desire written in every detail of his body.

"Maybe I was only halfway to heaven," she agreed brokenly, pushing up on her elbows, rising to her knees.

"Gretchen," he warned as she reached out for him, her small slender fingertips lightly tracking down his body from shoulder to waist to hips.

"This time I lead, partner," she whispered, kissing his beautiful chest, sliding her fingers over his warm male skin, lightly stroking all of him. He was hard and long and strong and she wanted him.

"A trip to heaven for two," she whispered. "Now."

And she pushed him back and slid onto the length of him.

"Now, sweetheart," he said with a low growl as she mated her body to his.

Rising and falling, she pleasured them both, loving the feel of his skin beneath her fingers, of her own body closing around his over and over again.

"Gretchen, come here," he said as he rolled over and took control again. He took her hands lightly in his own, holding them gently over her head as he thrust into her slowly. So slowly, pulling himself out and then slipping in deep. Touching her in places she had never been touched.

Her pleasure rose and rose. David slid into her depths again and again. The corded muscles on his arms stood out as he held back.

"Heaven." He choked the words out.

"David. Oh, yes. Heaven." The words flew from her as she reached the peak and he tumbled after her with a satisfied groan.

The world went silent except for the sound of their breathing. Gretchen lay beneath the man who had stolen her will, sapped her strength and shared her soul for the last length of time. He shifted, taking the weight of his body away and she felt the loss.

The very thought sent a tiny shaft of fear echoing through her. The need to pull him close again, to fold herself into the haven of his body was almost overwhelming. And not just for the pleasure he could provide her, she knew all too well. It was the man himself who pulled at her emotions so deeply. The yearning to reach out for him nearly cut her breath off. The thought that she could ever want that badly was like a straitjacket, binding her, cutting off her choices and the freedom she'd worked for all her life. Especially since this man wasn't known for staying in one place with one woman for very long. How could she have allowed this to happen? She couldn't, Gretchen told herself. With the greatest effort, she edged away from the sensation, pushing it into the deepest recesses of her mind.

Groggily, she pushed up to her knees, brushing her hair from her eyes.

Deep emerald eyes studied her. A mouth that could kill a woman with pleasure lifted into a smile. She reached out to touch, then pulled her hand back.

"Hi, angel," he said, rising to join her, his height bringing him up above her. He reached out, cupped her cheek and gently kissed her before she had time to think or to stop him. "Thank you for the sweetest hour I think I've ever spent."

For just a second her eyes softened, but David didn't miss the shades that slipped over those sea-green windows immediately after. She was already distancing herself from him, already pulling away. The thought made him angry, and he didn't want to be angry with her anymore today. True, it was his anger that had made him reckless and blind and brought him here with her to the edge of bliss, but it wasn't anger they'd shared here on this bed.

And he knew now that he wanted to share something very special with Gretchen Neal. For however far it went, he wanted them to go together. He wanted her to trust him for more than a few minutes of ultimate ecstasy.

"Don't do that," he whispered, holding her still when she started to pull away, to slip backward off the bed, out of his arms, and, he was sure, as far away from him emotionally and physically as she could go.

"Don't do what?" She tossed her chin up, halting her backward movement, halting her physical retreat but not coming closer in any emotional sense.

"Damn it, Gretchen," he said, his voice hoarse and a bit hard. "Don't act as if you don't want to be near me when we just shared something pretty spectacular. Don't pretend it didn't happen."

She took a deep breath, licked her lips nervously. And that slight vulnerable motion, the scared-puppy look in her eyes nearly did him in.

"I'm not. I won't. It was beyond pretty spectacular," she said, her voice so low he could barely hear her. "It was totally spectacular. Wonderful, in fact." Her lashes dipped low, hiding her lovely eyes from him.

"It wasn't just sex," he insisted, curving his palm around her arm, stroking lightly with his thumb. "It went beyond the moment."

She didn't answer, but he felt the tension in her body, as though she was holding in her breath, trying not to feel or react.

"Gretchen? Don't tell me you're regretting this time with me."

She breathed in deeply. "No," she said slowly, firmly, placing her hands lightly on his chest, looking him full in the eyes. "I don't regret making love with you, David."

"You're afraid I'll ask for more."

"Do you have more to give?"

He studied her for long seconds, wanting to say yes but having no basis for those words.

"I don't know how much I have to give," he finally

admitted, "but I know we can share more than a few hours of passion. I want more than that with you."

She opened her mouth as if to speak and leaned in close. Then she tamed her parted lips. She kissed him softly on the mouth.

"I can't think beyond the day, David. I don't want to think of the future. Just today. Just now."

And though her words were as soft as her body, they sliced right through him, wounding him in ways he hadn't realized he could be wounded. But her eyes…oh, her eyes were large and wide and completely vulnerable. Because he was pushing her when he had no right to push, asking for answers he'd learned in the past he couldn't give himself.

David pulled her close. He pressed her head to his chest, running his palm over the silk of her hair.

"You're right, Gretchen, sweetheart. Just today. Just now."

And she twined her arms around him.

He entered her slowly. He savored the moment as the world fell away and the lady gave him her all, her body, her pleasure, her world. Her today.

And he took.

Because today was all that either of them could promise.

The workday had barely begun when Gretchen looked up to see Storm Hunter talking to Rafe Rawlings two days later. It wasn't the only time since that first fateful day that he'd come into the station. He seemed to have a need to check up on the progress of the investigation— or a desire to make a point. He wasn't going to simply sit around with his thumbs in his belt loops while the law took its sweet time on this case.

At that moment he turned to the side and caught sight of her. His dark eyes narrowed. He raised his proud chin and for a second Gretchen thought she knew what Raven must have looked like when Jeremiah had insulted him by insinuating that he wasn't good enough for his sister.

But she wasn't Jeremiah, Gretchen reminded herself, and there was no question that Storm was here to ask about her case. She rose and headed his way. She was just a few feet away from him when his lips turned up just slightly in a cold, knowing smile.

She turned to see what he was looking at and gazed straight into David's eyes as he came in the door.

"Your boyfriend's here, Detective," Storm said softly. She wanted to squirm. She wanted to deny. She wanted to proudly proclaim that it was true. Instead she did none of those things. She simply raised one brow.

"That's old territory, and we've already covered it, Storm," she said quietly.

"You deny that the Neal–Kincaid ties are growing tighter? You've been seen together after hours. A great deal," he said with a slow nod of his head.

"What can I do for you, Storm?" she asked, her voice calm and devoid of the emotion that churned inside of her.

He shook his head. "I don't think you can do a thing for me, Detective. If you could, you already would have."

"We'll do all we can to solve Raven's case," she said once again.

"Or I'll solve it myself," he said quietly, stepping around her and moving down the aisle, headed toward the door.

"What was that all about?" David asked as he reached her elbow. "You okay?" he asked.

She nodded and turned to Rafe. "As to what it's all about, I can't completely say. What did he come for, Rafe?"

The man shook his head. "Same thing he always does, Gretchen. Information. I've told him a thousand times that the case is yours."

"He doesn't want to hear that," she told Rafe and David. "He wants to hear that we have some answers. Unfortunately, we don't have any yet. There's just not enough hard evidence. I hope we find something soon."

"So do I," David said. "I just talked to Phil. I have a case that looks like it may need my attention real soon, and it seems my time here is running out. I'm expected back in Atlanta in a week."

Gretchen knew that she should have felt glad to hear that news. When he'd first arrived she would have cheered at the prospect of getting rid of him. Now all she could think was that a week wasn't nearly enough time. Not for this case, and not for herself. The fact that she felt that way was enough to prove to her that it was, in fact, a good thing that David was going back home. A very good thing.

If she didn't get in any deeper, she'd be just fine.

Twelve

It was the next evening and Gretchen was trying very hard to convince herself that the book on her lap interested her. It should have, but she was preoccupied, too conscious of the passing of time, too aware of the man sitting beside her on her old blue-and-white-plaid sofa. And that just wouldn't do. She had to stay focused on what really mattered, on the things she could control. On her work.

She intended to do that even though up until this moment she and David had simply been sharing each other's company. They hadn't engaged in work at all. How had that happened? Why had she invited him to dinner?

Gretchen didn't know—or maybe she just didn't want to examine those motives too closely. Instead she cleared her throat and looked up at the man who raised his beautiful eyes from the newspaper he'd been studying.

"What would you do if you were in love with a woman who also happened to be carrying your child and her brother tried to do everything in his power to get you to leave her?" she suddenly said.

David sucked in a breath, and she wished that she hadn't used the word "love."

"You're trying to retrace Raven's last day again?" he finally asked.

She felt her muscles relaxing, glad that they were back

to the clear-cut parameters of work. "What else is there to do? We've got nothing else to go on."

"I know. I've been doing the same thing, and I'll tell you what I'd do. If I loved a woman, truly, desperately loved her, and someone was effectively trying to keep her from me, I might do anything."

The words were forced from David's lips as though he struggled with the very concept of love. Gretchen knew how he felt. She definitely didn't want to think about love—or to think about David loving one particular woman.

"Maybe I'd just pace and snarl at everyone," he continued. "I've talked to people who saw Raven in those last few days, and he apparently did a lot of that. I might get in a few arguments. He did that, too. And yes, most likely I'd confront the man who was hiding her from me. That's the one thing we don't know about. There's no record of Jeremiah and Raven meeting after Jeremiah gave Raven the money." He stared at her long and hard. "But that doesn't mean it didn't happen. Those two men were first-class enemies. Raven had good reason to hate Jeremiah and anything could have happened between them."

Gretchen let out a sigh. "And maybe nothing did. Maybe Raven, in his anger and grief, picked a fight with someone who decided to shoot him. Maybe there were other circumstances we don't know anything about. We just don't know enough."

"We know that Jeremiah had several guns that could have been the murder weapon, but then, we haven't been able to conclusively link those weapons to that bullet."

"So we're just going around in circles again, David," she said, rising to her feet.

"Not exactly," he said with a soft murmur, standing

and taking her hands in his own. "We've talked to a lot of people in the past few weeks. We've learned something of both of these men. We know that there was a lot of powerful emotion between these men, and those kinds of things get noted, get stored away in people's memory banks along with other snippets of information that seemed to be lost over time. Maybe in time if we keep hammering away, those events will resurface in someone's memory and we'll know a little more about what happened between Jeremiah and Raven."

She tried out a smile. "Maybe in time?"

He pulled her to him with a gentle tug. "I was... presumptuous in coming here to help you with your investigation. You never really needed my help, after all. You'll find your answers."

Gretchen dredged up a smile from somewhere. "Don't underestimate yourself, Hannon. You have a way of getting people to open up. Women, especially, seem to remember things, little bits of conversations, that they had forgotten until you start jogging their memory. Wasn't it Lily Mae who, when you were questioning her the other day, finally remembered Raven telling her that he never gave up what was his?"

David smiled. "I believe the lady was trying to make a point. She was digging for information on you and me, trying to see if I felt the same way about what was mine."

Gretchen's eyes widened. She sucked in her breath. "Well, nevertheless, I—"

"I'll miss you when we're done," he said, pulling her to him, kissing her lips. "We're not done yet, Gretchen."

She let out the air she'd been holding in, studied the man in front of her, and realized just how lucky she'd been to have him show up in this town. Professionally and personally. "No, we're not done yet," she whispered, feathering her lips across his, opening to invite him inside.

But apparently they were done for now. The doorbell rang at that instant, and David growled low in his throat as he let her go.

When she opened the door, her friend Karen was standing there. The woman let out a squeal.

"Gretch," she said, throwing her arms around Gretchen. "Guess what? I was on my way to Helena to visit my mother and my car nearly ran out of gas just outside Whitehorn. I figured it had to be fate, and besides, I don't see you nearly enough. It seemed like too good an opportunity to stop and say hello in person. I tried to call you earlier but you must have been out on a case or something. So, here I am."

The words came out on a long breathless rush the way they always did with Karen. Her face was glowing and pretty with enthusiasm and Gretchen couldn't keep from smiling in spite of her disappointment at having her time with David cut short. She hugged her friend and stepped back from the doorway.

"Come on in," she said. "You remember David?"

Karen's eyes were like blue stars. "Gretch, how could any woman with eyeballs in her head forget David? The man is better than double chocolate pudding topped with whipped cream and sprinkles," she said, giving David a sisterly hug. "I just got finished telling his aunt so myself. I'm staying at the Big Sky for the night," she explained. "I must say everyone at the B and B was full of talk when I mentioned your engagement. They seem very enthusiastic about getting you into the family, Gretch. In fact, no one could talk about anything else. You're creating quite a stir."

Gretchen's heart plummeted through her body, knowing that this was the first anyone at the Big Sky had heard about the engagement. She hazarded a tentative look at David who was grinning broadly. Wicked man. How were they going to explain their way out of this one?

"It's the badge," he conceded solemnly. "And the attitude. My mother is just happy that I'm settling down with a woman who can protect me from potential villains."

For a moment Karen looked startled. Then her eyes twinkled. "Gretchen really is going to have to put a leash on you," she said. "A man who can grin and tease and look like you do is almost too much man to handle. How are you going to deal with him, Gretch?"

Gretchen smiled sweetly. "Handcuffs," she said calmly.

David raised one brow. "For you or for me?"

Karen chuckled. "This is going to be one interesting marriage. I can't wait for the ceremony itself. Have you set the date?"

Gretchen's heart began to hammer. This bet had been a bad idea altogether. "Not yet," she said, looking to David for backup.

"We don't want to be rushed," he said, his voice low. "Gretchen and I want to have time to go slowly, to let our relationship simmer…and burn…and bubble over until the time is totally, completely right. Until we just can't wait to be together," he said, gazing directly into Gretchen's eyes, his own expression one of unveiled lust.

For a moment Gretchen felt as if everything in the room had dropped away until there was only this man, this feeling, this moment.

"Whoa," Karen said, fanning herself with her hand. "I can see why you were finally forced to give in and change your mind about marrying, Gretchen. I—I suppose I should have called before I just barged in.''

Her words seemed to serve as an alarm to David. He took in a breath, allowed the desire to drain from his expression and smiled reassuringly at Karen.

"Forgive me," he said. "I'm afraid I tend to forget myself where Gretchen is concerned. And please, don't apologize for anything. You're not barging in. Anyway, I was just on my way to take Goliath for a walk. Why don't the two of you visit while I do that? I'll see both of you later."

He dropped a light kiss on Gretchen's lips before retrieving Goliath's leash and taking him out the door.

"Gretch, how can you stand letting him go for even a few moments?"

It was difficult, Gretchen admitted, watching him go, but she was just going to have to get used to it. In just a few days she was going to have to let him go forever.

"I can't believe the entire town thinks that we're engaged now," Gretchen whispered, her voice worried as she and David left their cars and walked toward the station the next morning.

"Believe it," David said with a slow, lazy smile. "When I went home to change this morning, the entire family was waiting for me, wearing their best smug smiles. My mother has been patting me on the head all morning, as though I'd just told her I'd won the Nobel prize. My sister berated me over the phone before I left for work today for not telling her that I was getting married. Then she told me that she wanted to hug me for choosing you."

"And I finally had to take the phone off the hook last

night," Gretchen said in amazement. "I can't believe how many people care whether or not I get married."

"They love you, sweetheart."

She looked up at him and her heart took a long plunge off a high and rocky peak. He was such a caring man. After Karen had gone last night, he'd made long, slow love to her. He'd made very sure that she'd found pleasure in his arms. He'd taken care of Goliath and brought her breakfast in bed before he'd left her this morning. "I grew up in a house where breakfast was very important," he'd told her. "You need this." And he'd sat there and watched her eat every bite. Like a husband—or maybe a fiancé.

"Admit it," he whispered near her ear, after an elderly couple crossed the street to offer their congratulations. "You're having fun and so is everyone else."

She was. There was something about making everyone so happy with a little news, even erroneous news, that made her feel good. For a split second, she wondered whether she could ever get used to this, if she could ever be a happily married woman. But even the thought sent a thread of panic spiraling through her. She smothered her thoughts.

"Maybe we're having fun and maybe everyone else is, but our engagement is a lie," she said.

"But not a mean-spirited one," he maintained. "No one's being hurt. And when I get ready to leave, we'll tell everyone that we've decided to just remain best friends. They'll spend all their time hoping we'll get back together and even that can be fun for some of them. Lily Mae will eat it up. Until then, let's enjoy our freedom."

And he turned her toward him, slid his arm behind her back and lifted her lips to his in a dipping, searing kiss.

Her feet left the ground, she pressed her palms to his

chest to balance herself, and then she forgot everything except the heat of David's touch, the soap-and-man scent of him, the pleasure of his mouth against hers.

When he finally pulled back slowly and balanced her on unsteady legs, a round of applause could be heard from across the street.

"David, how are you going to keep your mind on the business of keeping the peace if you're thinking about kissing Gretchen all the time?"

David raised his head and grinned. "Kissing Gretchen clears the fog out of my mind," he said in a low teasing voice.

"Then kiss her again," the man called with a whoop of laughter.

But Gretchen, not to be outdone, wasn't about to let David call all the shots. She stood on her toes until she was almost eye-to-eye with David, looped her arm around his neck and slanted her lips to his own.

"Now," she said when her head was spinning and she had pulled back from the temptation of David, "I'm more than ready to face a day's work."

"If you should feel the need to do that again anytime today, love, feel free. Go right ahead and press your body against mine," David said as they entered the station. "Could make for an extremely interesting day."

It had been, as David said, an interesting day. Gretchen had talked to Reba at the lab and been told that since they were almost finished with a backlog of work, she could expect the results on her hair and skin samples very soon. She and David had rescued a woman whose car had rolled over and ended up in a ditch. They'd also taken some good-natured ribbing about their engagement, but it had been fun and freeing to be able to show her attraction to him without worrying about what people would think.

Now they were settling down to a relaxed dinner at the Hip Hop before heading for home.

"Nice ring, Gretchen," Emma said as she came over to the table with her coffeepot. "When are you going to get married?"

David looked at Gretchen's flustered expression. He felt a little bad for having dragged her into this situation, but not too bad.

"We thought...next spring," he said suddenly, delighting in Gretchen's wide-eyed shocked gaze. "I always liked June."

She turned those delicious green eyes on him. "Why wait until June?" she asked in a low, sultry tone. "When May is so much...fresher."

The sound of chairs shifting sounded throughout the diner. David risked a glance away from Gretchen and noticed that they'd snagged the attention of almost everyone in the place. He could tell from the way Gretchen's eyes shifted slightly that she'd noticed the same thing. Dinner had never been conducted so silently at the Hip Hop, he'd just bet.

"May is good," he agreed with a lazy smile. "Even better than June, really."

"Oh, Gretch, look how he went along with you on that. Isn't that sweet? I love a romantic man," one woman in the fourth booth proclaimed. "You'll have the wedding here in Whitehorn, won't you?"

David raised one brow.

"I wouldn't have it any other way," Gretchen agreed, lowering her lashes to hide the amusement he knew he'd find there if he only looked in her eyes. "Karen and

Pamela will come and all my family. And the brides-maids will all wear sea-green. It's my favorite color.''

David grinned at the game she'd entered into so gamely.

"It suits you," he assured her. "Turns your eyes that misty green I can't resist. Those eyes of yours make me feel sort of wild and untamed, Gretchen."

David leaned closer, gazing into those bewitching eyes, and Gretchen parted her lips just a breath. The tea-kettle clock on the wall ticked loudly in the ensuing fas-cinated silence. A robber could have come in and walked off with everyone's dinner right then and no one would have stopped him. Or even noticed that he was there, so intent was every diner on the scenario at Gretchen and David's table.

David finally keyed in on the silence. He shook his head to clear his mind. "As for the wedding day," he continued with some effort, "I have friends with musical backgrounds. We'll hold the ceremony at the Big Sky with dinner and dancing afterward. We'll open up the gardens, set tables up around the lake if you like."

"I like," she answered softly. "And I'll like it even better if you wear a black tux. You look sinfully hand-some in black and white," Gretchen told him in a low, provocative voice.

"Wear something sexy," David whispered, reaching across the table to cup his hand around her neck and pull her closer to him. "I don't care if it's white. Just sexy."

Someone dropped a glass. It shattered, and Gretchen jerked upright.

David drank in a long gulp of air. He shook his head and grinned at the other customers, tossing money down onto the table to pay for their meal.

"Well, this has been enjoyable. Great seeing everyone," he said cheerily as he rose and reached for Gretchen's hand. "But now it's time to get the lady back home to her bed. Good night."

She blushed, and it was a precious sight even though he knew the heat in her cheeks would embarrass her. Gretchen prided herself on being strong and tough.

"Good night," she said to Emma and to those who were calling their farewells. David held open the door and she stepped outside.

The door had barely floated shut behind them when she looked up at him, both brows raised.

"Well," she said, "that was certainly entertaining for everyone, wasn't it?"

David laughed and then he indulged himself by doing exactly what he wanted to do and what everyone else wanted him to do, too. He picked Gretchen up, swung her around and kissed her.

Her mouth was cool and sweet. She kissed him back.

"It was certainly entertaining for me," he agreed.

"But now it *is* time to go home," she whispered, her breath feathering over his lips in a honeyed caress. "The day is over."

"And the night is beginning."

She didn't answer, and that in itself was the answer. The one he wanted. All in all, it had been a wonderful day, and there was only more to come.

Gretchen listened to the comfortable sound of her steps and David's clicking together against the sidewalk. It was late as they made their way back to the station so that she could pick up some paperwork she'd left there. It was later still as they stepped back through the doorway onto the sidewalk. They'd spent much of their day piecing together the testimonies of all the people they'd interviewed about Raven, rearranging the information, jotting down scenarios they might have missed. Something just didn't quite fit and she meant to find what it was. But for now, they'd put that behind them for the day. David was heading for his car and she was heading to hers. As if they were going to their separate homes. And they were.

But in a little more than an hour he'd be with her again. He'd claim that he'd come to walk Goliath, and he would do that, but then he'd also come to her bed.

Gretchen shivered at the thought, vaguely uneasy at how deeply David always seemed to affect her. She'd enjoyed that scene at the Hip Hop way too much. It had been fun and fast and wild and so very David. She hoped that she'd get over him easily when he left.

I will, she promised herself. She'd always done whatever she'd had to do. This time would be no different.

"Goodbye, Gretchen," he said, drawing out her name in that slightly sensual way he had as he kissed her once, hard, and moved away, stepping off the sidewalk.

"Goodbye," she said softly, barely resisting the urge to touch her lips.

He had turned away, she was pulling her keys from her pocket, ready to step off the sidewalk just as he had, when he turned to smile at her once more.

A scraping sound came from above and David looked up. Instead of the smile she saw his eyes turn dark and dangerous.

"Gretchen, move!" he yelled, and then before she could act, he launched himself at her, snagged her around the waist and rolled with her to the ground, cushioning her fall with his body. As her teeth clamped together in a sharp clack inside her head, she heard a loud crack.

She looked to where she had been standing and saw a large rock smashed in two on the concrete.

"Go back inside," David whispered, whisking her off him as he leaped to his feet and raced for the back of the building where the fire escape was located.

She struggled to stand and ran for the fire escape herself, keeping David in her sights.

David threw himself up the metal stairs and scrambled to the top, not worrying about the noise he was making. At other times he could run as silently as a cat, but here he had a need for speed and no time to worry about being careful.

Someone had tried to hurt Gretchen, damn it, and that someone was going to pay.

He cleared the fire escape, swinging onto the tar-papered roof. In the distance, he could see someone—a small adult or a kid—scurrying over the rooftops. David threw on some speed, leaped the few feet from one roof to the other and cut the distance in two.

The noise of his footsteps getting closer had the man turning to look over his shoulder, stumbling, scrambling to get back up, and taking off again, swinging over the side of a roof.

In the short time he had, David skidded on the tar paper, made it to the spot where the guy had disappeared and vaulted over the side himself. Sliding down one railing and then the next, he made it to the first floor platform, jumped over the side and dropped lightly to the ground. The mop-topped, black-haired man jumped on him. David tossed him over his shoulder but the wild-eyed heavily muscled attacker landed on his feet. Butting David with his head, he knocked him off-balance, pulled out a knife, and slid the blade into his hand, aiming to throw it. David feinted, and the knife missed, but his move was enough to give the man some time. Snatching up the knife and sliding into the street, the thug threw himself into a car and took off.

David could only watch the car skid away.

A clicking behind him caught his attention and he turned to see Gretchen clearing the last steps of the fire escape.

He frowned and she put her hands on her hips. "Don't even mention the fact that I didn't hide in the station, David, if you know what's good for you. You know I couldn't do that."

He dragged in air, and nodded curtly. "Did you recognize him?"

She shook her head. "Never saw him, and that car he took belongs to Joe, one of the ushers at the movie theater. I try to tell people to lock their cars, but this is Whitehorn."

"Might as well tell them to fly without wings," he agreed. "Come on, let's go see if we can get a composite photo out and start a hunt for this guy."

"I was just going to say that," she said.

"I know you were," he said in a gruff whisper, suddenly dragging her against him and holding her to his heart. "I know just what you were going to say. Gretchen, I know something else, too. You're not going to like it."

She looked up at him, her eyes wide. "If you're going to point out that I'm trembling, then don't. I wasn't scared for myself. I never saw the rock until it hit the ground. I was halfway down the stairs when he went for you. That knife he tossed your way could have ended it for you, David."

"It didn't," was all he said. "And that wasn't what I was going to say."

"Tell me, then," she whispered, moving closer against him.

"I just wanted you to know that I intend to stick close to you for the next few days. Don't argue with me."

She didn't answer, but her lips were cool and giving when he pulled her against him. She knew that he needed to be macho about this, and for his sake, she was going to let him, it seemed. For a few days, at least.

Thank goodness for a woman who knew when to talk and when to kiss. For a few days, at least, he could still have her for his own.

And heaven help any man who tried to take her from him.

Thirteen

With not much to go on, they hadn't identified her assailant. But that wasn't exactly surprising, Gretchen thought two days later. The fact that he had tried to attack her didn't necessarily mean that he was someone she would know or remember. The fact was that she wore a badge. She'd been in law enforcement for years, and that meant making enemies at times. She'd made more than her share in Miami and a few in Elk Springs and even Whitehorn, as well. He could be someone she'd once put in jail, someone who knew someone she'd put in jail, or he could be a man who just didn't like cops, or women, or blondes, for that matter. The newspapers were filled with people who hated for a living, and trying to make rhyme or reason out of such things could make a person crazy.

That didn't mean they hadn't tried to connect the man in some way to the work she was doing at the moment, but the truth was that thinking that way could lead a person down a lot of wrong alleys. She and David now had another investigation on their hands, they'd sent out a drawing of the man and as much information as they had. They'd asked for witnesses or information, but so far they had nothing. And while she was being careful, Gretchen wasn't losing sleep over this incident.

"I couldn't live that way," she told David. "Neither could you. Looking over your shoulder is part of what we do, but looking over your shoulder all the time and never looking forward means you've become ineffective at your work.''

"Sweet lady, I love it when you're logical," he said, dropping a kiss on her bare breast and then moving his mouth up to cover her lips.

She chuckled against his lips. "You know darn well I haven't needed to look over my shoulder anyway. You've been watching me like an overprotective bear."

"You don't like the way I've been treating you?" he asked, sweeping his hand down between their bodies and driving all thought from her mind for several seconds.

When she was able to control herself at all, she took long deep breaths, shuddering at his touch.

"I love the way you treat me," she confessed. And barely brushing his skin, she slowly walked her fingers down his chest and lower. Lower still. She gently closed her fingertips around the tip of his shaft.

He stopped breathing, she was sure of it, though his heart slammed against his chest and echoed into her own. He endured the exquisite torture of her barely there touch until he was shuddering deep inside. Then he lifted her leg, parted her and drove deep into her depths. He shattered her, destroyed her, and had her asking for more.

When they finally came up for breath, he smoothed the hair back from her forehead and kissed the damp skin there. "I love the way you treat me," he said, repeating her words. "And I thank you for letting me fuss. I have nightmares about that moment when that rock nearly fell on you. I'm not going to let anything happen to you as long as I can prevent it. And when I go—"

"When you go, I'll be fine." She grabbed the hand he was caressing her with, took it between both of her palms and kissed it. "I'm a big girl, David, and anyway, everyone in the department is looking out for everyone else since that incident. No one's taking any chances. I won't take any chances,'' she promised.

''Then we'll be okay,'' he finally said as he eased into her again.

''We'll be wonderful,'' she whispered as they traveled to a world scattered with bright stars. She smiled against his skin and he smiled against hers and they waited for the morning together.

Lyle Brooks crushed a cigarette under his shoe as if it gave him great pleasure to extinguish the life of something.

He bit off a harsh expletive.

The Cheyenne were still not cooperating. He'd given them his best smooth talk, his clearest arguments. They didn't want his arguments. They wanted what they'd agreed to in the first place. They pointed out that they were old hands at the bait-and-switch game. He had to give them credit. They were no fools, even if he did hate every last sorry one of them.

And as for the real fools—or rather, fool, there was no question who that was. The idiot had made a mess of things. He'd been told to make things look like an accident. Who would believe that a rock falling from the sky was an accident?

''Nobody,'' he whispered, his voice a thin rasp of sound squeezed from a mouth thinned by rage.

Now he'd have to handle things himself. He'd already taken care of the fool. Only one more to go. Or maybe two.

He had to get the man out of the way and that wouldn't be easy. It hadn't been easy. David Hannon was like water running along the ground, impossible to separate from the sand it flowed into. He took his watchdog duties with Gretchen Neal very seriously. Still, sooner or later the guy had to let down his guard. They always let down their guard, didn't they?

Then, he thought calmly, then he would finish his business with the woman. Eventually he'd convince the leaders of the Laughing Horse Reservation to make the trade of the land.

And the sapphires would be his and only his. He would finally have the last word and the last laugh and the money.

He was going to be the greatest Kincaid ever known.

David rubbed the frown from between his brows and tried not to think of Gretchen. The woman had been too much a part of his thoughts from the very start, but now since that time three days ago when he'd seen that rock hurtling down toward her, he'd been unable to dislodge her from his mind for even the shortest period of time. He was, quite simply, besotted with her. And he was pretty darn sure he was in love with her. It was a damned shame, because she'd made it clearer than clear that she only wanted a short, mad fling.

Oh, they were having that, all right. Every time he plunged into her body, he went mad for her. He wasn't so humble that he didn't know that she reacted the same way to him, but that was all it was for her. She was happy with this. True, she might miss him for a few days when he was gone, but she was the type of woman who would prefer missing him over complicating her life with visions of things that would only be a prison for her. And he couldn't, he absolutely couldn't, try to force his feelings on her. If he ever damaged her spirit, her heart, or her pride, there'd be no way around the fact that he deserved a strong, solid kick in the pants. It just wasn't going to happen.

And so, he'd been hovering. Caring. Wanting. He'd been going damned near insane. It had to stop. Now.

The phone rang beside him.

"Hannon," he said, practically barking into the receiver.

"Whoa, buddy. What have you been eating for breakfast that's turned you into a ticked-off grizzly?" Sascha's voice was laced with humor, but also a familiar trace of concern.

"Rocks," David said, knowing someday he'd tell his friend just how close that answer was to the truth. But not today. He couldn't talk about Gretchen today. And maybe not anytime in the near future.

"What can I do for you, Sasch?" he asked. "You need an ear to listen? Bridget still on your mind?"

"Bridget's yesterday," his friend said. "And you know me, David. I'm on to someone else. A luscious redhead named Terri. You know the rules of the game. Win some, lose some. Always move on. Always enjoy."

David knew the rules of the game or what they were supposed to be. They just didn't apply where Gretchen was concerned. She was special, different. She'd taken the rule book and ripped out the pages.

"What can I do for you, Sasch?" he asked again.

"Not for me. For Phil," Sascha said. "He's in D.C., but I got a call from him. There's new info on the Tedrin case that might finally make a difference and break things open for someone who knows the particulars. That would be you, bud, as well you know. Time to give up this life with the locals and get back to the federal world. Phil asked me to fax the papers to you in the Billings office so you could make a determination of what the next step should be. It's confidential stuff, of course. You'll be all right picking it up there?''

''Sure.'' Of course he'd be all right. His work had always had his heart, and this was probably just what he needed to get his life back where it belonged. Action. Results. Something to occupy his thoughts and his time. ''You fax it. I'll deal with it,'' he promised. ''Thanks for the message, Sasch. I needed this.''

''David? You okay?''

''Yeah. I'm okay. Just needed something to do with my time, I guess,'' he said. ''You know how it is when you're sitting on your hands.''

''Don't I? Yeah.'' He paused a moment, then, ''You're not getting in over your head in the heart department, are you? Not losing it over that lady cop of yours? Not doing anything stupid?''

David hesitated for half a second. Of course he was doing something stupid. He'd been making mistakes with Gretchen from day one. It was time to stop.

''David?''

''Not doing anything stupid, Sasch,'' David managed to say smoothly. ''Do I ever?''

Sascha's chuckle was low. ''You're right. What was I thinking of? This is David I'm talking about. The guy who never commits. All right, buddy. I'm glad things are good with you. See you in a few days. Take care.''

And the line went dead.

David waited for Gretchen to emerge from Rafe's office. When she did, he gave her a smile. ''You'll be happy to know that your shadow has to leave for a short while. Business in Billings.''

''Your business or mine?''

He grinned. ''You think I'd keep you in the dark about your own work?''

She studied him for a minute, then shook her head. "No. You're a bit overprotective," she said, smoothing his collar and then kissing him, "but you're fair. You want to swing by the house when you're done?"

"Ah, I see," he said, teasing her with his lips. "You're just afraid I won't be back in time to walk Goliath. You only want me for my skill with animals."

She smiled against his lips. "I adore your skill with animals, and your skill with…other things. Maybe there's a little animal in you. Maybe Goliath recognizes a kindred spirit—or at least a kindred male."

"He still mooning over that little Pomeranian?"

Gretchen nodded and the lemony scent of her went through him. Her hair brushed against his skin and his senses. "She's a tease, I think. He's frantic to have her."

"I'm frantic to have you, too," he whispered, pulling her closer, pulling her around the corner of the file cabinet so no one could hear and no one could see.

"Then come by my house when you're done. Will it be long?"

He shook his head. "I can be there and back in just a few hours."

"I'll meet you at home when I get off work," she promised.

"If you leave here for any reason other than to go home, you take a partner," he warned.

She frowned. "David, I know the rules. If it's something that warrants extra muscle or extra care, I take a partner. I'll be careful," she promised.

He caught her to him for one last kiss before he marched out the door on the way back to his future.

The information from the lab came in just as Gretchen was getting ready to go out the door for the day.

And there were no real surprises, but there was, at last, hard evidence. She still didn't know why she'd been hearing rumors that Lyle Brooks had been hounding the Cheyenne to make a land switch that just didn't make sense. But she knew enough to take the next step. Some of the puzzle pieces had finally stopped spinning around and locked into place.

Now she had proof. A man's life had been taken. It had been stolen, not by an accident but by an intentional act. And so she finally had room to move, to act, to do what she had been trained to do, Gretchen thought.

She sat for a few seconds concentrating on the information she'd been given, realizing that at last one criminal at least would be taken off the streets.

It wouldn't bring back the life of an innocent man or help his family deal with their pain and grief. Those kinds of miracles didn't happen, but she could at least make sure that no one else suffered at the hands of that scumbag. As always, it had to be enough. It was the nature of the job.

"So let's take care of business," she whispered as she picked up the phone. Punching in the number of the cellular in David's car, she listened through the rings and hoped he had taken care of his own business. If she had to, she would take another officer, but after all his time and effort, David deserved to be the one to partner her on this arrest.

The ringing came to an abrupt halt.

"Hannon." David's deep strong voice washed over her, even distance and the slight haziness of the connection not dulling the reaction she had yet to get accustomed to.

"David, it's Gretchen. I just got word from Reba. Hair and skin were found under Peter Cook's fingernails that matched the samples I took from Lyle. How far away are you?''

"Fifteen minutes tops," he said.

"Good. I'll meet you at the house and save you the trouble of driving all the way into the center of town and back out again. We'll hook up and make the arrest from there."

"On my way," he confirmed as she said goodbye and hung up the phone.

There was a sense of rightness in going to meet David, Gretchen thought as she climbed into her car and started the ignition, and a sense of relief. And it went beyond what she felt in his arms or how she felt about him as a man. She'd learned to trust him in these past few weeks. He'd learned to trust her. In spite of all her initial reservations about the man, his family, and the unusual nature of his request to be in on her cases, they'd worked well together. Arresting Lyle would be like adding sprinkles to the ice cream. A sweet bonus.

She drove the short distance to her house. No sign of David yet, but then, she hadn't expected it.

Turning her key and clicking open the door to the cottage, she waited for Goliath to greet her with his usual patter and gleeful bark. The patter never materialized. The bark was loud and clear and distressed. She noticed for the first time that the bedroom door was closed.

"Goliath?"

Her answer was a frustrated and frantic whining.

She moved to the door, pushed it back.

The wildly rolling eyes of her dog met her own gaze as Goliath barked and scuffled over the floor, jumping up on her, clearly anxious.

"What's wrong, boy? I didn't lock you in there somehow this morning, did I? I'm sorry. No wonder you're so upset.''

Gretchen knelt to soothe her hand over Goliath's head, but his barking didn't stop. He flung his head around, looking behind him.

She turned to see what he was looking at and an arm hauled her up, a gloved hand clamping over her mouth. The taste of old leather and the scent of sweat and heavy cologne assaulted her. She was dragged backward against an unyielding body.

Her fingers automatically went for her gun. Too late. They slid away as the gun was dragged from its holster and tossed aside.

The cold and oily smell of steel drifted to her as the hard snub of her assailant's revolver was shoved right under her chin.

"Don't worry about your little dog, Neal," a low, unpleasant and all too familiar voice told her. "He's just a tad upset that you weren't here to greet a visitor. He had to handle all the duties of hosting by himself. Can you blame him?"

Sheer panic rose up in her and she fought to calm herself.

Think, Gretchen, think! Don't fight. He'll be expecting that. He'll be prepared for that, so don't fight. At least not yet.

Yet as Goliath lunged at Lyle, the urge to fight was there. Goliath was trying to nip at Lyle and she wanted to do the same.

"Call him off," Lyle said, kicking out at the little dog as Goliath took a nip again.

She held her tongue.

Lyle shoved the hard butt of the gun harder against her throat. He pulled back his foot to kick just as Goliath recovered from the roll he'd taken and headed in to try again.

"Goliath, sit," she ordered.

The little dog ignored her. She remembered what she'd told David about him, how he'd been considered untrainable. But he'd always obeyed her since she'd worked with him. Until now.

The gun bit into her flesh harder. Gretchen nearly choked as the press of steel nudged at her windpipe.

She swallowed hard, opening her mouth. The pressure of the gun let up just a touch.

"Sit, Goliath," she said again, aiming for a calm tone, fearful for both the little dog's life as well as her own. Reluctantly, Goliath did as he was told. His little body wiggled, he whimpered, but he obeyed.

And now the reality of the situation shoved in on her. David wasn't that far away. He was barreling toward her. And he didn't know there was an ambush waiting behind her door.

She had to disarm Lyle, trip him up somehow. But how?

"Why did you come here?" she managed to say in spite of the press of metal to flesh. "What is it you want?"

An eerie chuckle rolled through Lyle's wiry body and the sound echoed through the arm he was crushing against her.

"Oh, I think you know," he said. "You see, I'm a businessman and I don't exactly like anyone interfering in my business interests. I especially don't like it when someone keeps pushing me, when someone all but accuses me of something. And I really don't like it when anybody repeatedly comes between me and what I want. Now, Ms. Neal, you've closed down the excavation of my resort, you've insinuated that I might have something to do with the death of one of my employees. How do you think all of this is going to affect future business developments? People don't want to conduct transactions with a man who can't control his business."

"And what would that business be, Lyle?" She spat out the words. "What did Peter Cook do that caused you to kill him?"

The arm that was holding her jerked and tightened. Gretchen struggled for breath. She worked to maintain her control. She did her best to not think of David. If she did, she would panic. She would lose.

"You killed him, didn't you?" she said, her voice as cool as she could make it.

His chilling laughter sent shivers slipping down her spine.

"Neal, haven't I told you it was an accident? And yet, you've never believed me. Not like everyone else. I have to say I admire you for sticking it out and not following the crowd. It's amazing what people will believe if you set the scene just right."

"Why?" She forced herself to not react or move, forced her mind to think about what she could do to warn David rather than what this dirtbag was saying. Maybe if she could keep him talking, she would have time to plan, to ready herself.

"Why?" he echoed. "You mean, why did I kill Cook? He did something stupid. Just like you, Neal. If you hadn't pushed me, you'd be just fine. Now you're dead. Let's go." He pulled the gun from her throat and shoved it into her back.

She considered not moving for just a second, but if she couldn't outwit Brooks and he killed her here, David would come in and find them—and then he'd be dead, too.

Fear and pain and distress reared up in her. She fought to shove them aside.

She had to stay alert and alive, to give herself time to think. Time was what she needed the most. Time and luck. But she would have neither if she broke down. And she would have nothing if David died, if she let him walk in on this, if she didn't move now.

Gretchen moved.

Lyle slithered in closer behind her, like a guard—or a lover. One arm was looped over her shoulder in what might be presumed to be a friendly embrace. His jacket hung open slightly, enclosing her. His gun was concealed between his body and hers.

"This is cozy, isn't it, Detective?" he asked in a harsh, laughing whisper. "Your car, please. I'm afraid mine isn't here. I guess I left it in my driveway where everyone could see it."

That laugh again. Gretchen wondered if anyone had ever actually smiled at this man's laughter.

"Sorry, you'll have to drive," he said as he edged her in the passenger door and followed her inside. "I seem to need my hands," he said, wiggling the gun just a bit.

She slid over the gearshift to the driver's seat, the gun following her, low on the seat, pointing up at her.

"Don't move more than you need to in order to drive the car. Don't make any wrong turns. Don't act like a dumb cop, Neal," Lyle said quietly as he gestured for her to start the car. "If you follow directions, your boyfriend might survive. I understand he's leaving town soon. He's not a danger to me. So just be a good girl and follow the rules. I know you know how to do that. Isn't that what they teach you about in cop school?

He laughed again as if he'd said something funny and Gretchen pulled out onto the street. She could, as he said, swerve the car, but she'd be dead long before the car crashed—and Lyle might survive.

"Where are we going?" she asked.

"Nowhere anyone will find you real soon, Neal. You'll simply disappear. No body to trace. We'll find a good place to stash you. Make no mistake about that."

"How did you know I was on my way to arrest you?"

A long silence filled the car. When Gretchen turned to look at Lyle, he was grinning, his eyes narrowed in glee.

"You were coming to arrest me? Now that makes this so much better. Not that I didn't think you'd do just that in time, but actually I had no idea. I've been following you for days now. Only problem is you never seem to be alone. Today I saw your guard dog ride out and I took my opportunity the way I always do. It's one of my most endearing qualities, I'm sure. But as for your coming to arrest me, well, Neal, I'm flattered that you would come alone. Maybe you really do care."

And maybe she'd better shut her mouth, Gretchen thought, before Lyle figured out that someone else would be looking for him really soon.

Lyle wouldn't be happy to see another cop. He'd be angry, desperate, and desperate men tended to shoot wildly and repeatedly.

A trickle of fear found its way in. It drizzled right through her. This morning the world had seemed bright. Now her life was at stake. And the life of the man she loved hung in the balance, as well.

Gretchen didn't take the time to refute the fact that she loved David or that the thought of anything happening to him filled her with anguish right now. When a madman was holding a gun against you, there was no point in lying to yourself.

The fact was that she loved David desperately.

The fact was that if she didn't survive, she'd never see him again.

Gretchen drove, mindful of the turns she was making, up the mountain pathways that normally looked so beautiful, around steep turns heavily packaged in lodgepole pines that hid the curling road behind her from view.

In a matter of minutes they had left civilization and all hope of rescue behind.

She was on her own. Just her, her training, and a man who had nothing to lose by killing her.

Fourteen

David rounded the last turn leading to Gretchen's house. He was still two blocks away, but on the deserted street he was close enough to see her car pull out of the driveway.

His first thought was that she had tired of waiting for him and was moving off to arrest Lyle Brooks alone.

"No," he decided. She was brave but also bright and she was honorable. She'd said she'd meet him here. If she was leaving, there was a reason. A good reason. Something important enough to have her leaving when she knew he'd be arriving any moment.

David maintained a distance, but he slid right past her drive, moving off in the direction she had gone.

He leaned forward, straining to see her. Two heads visible. Could be anyone. A tall woman, a small man. Her friend Karen, his sister, or someone else, he thought as she took a turn leading out of town.

Something didn't feel right here.

An emergency call? Maybe, but then she would have radioed for assistance. Maybe she had. If so, there was no problem. He'd find out when they got there.

And if the other person in the car was a man?

"Then she'll know you for the jealous fool you are when this is over, Hannon," he muttered. And there would be hell to pay all around.

But this soul-deep fear that was growing within him

with every passing curve of the road didn't feel like jealousy, and anyway, Gretchen had been very open about her involvement with him. There was no one else for her at this point in time. He knew that. He was just reaching for logical solutions, grasping, hoping that there was some ordinary reason Gretchen was headed out of town without him in the opposite direction from the one they would have taken to go to arrest Lyle Brooks.

And as she turned onto a dirt road that led to nowhere, stark fear rushed through David. Gretchen was in that car. There was someone with her, and he was almost dead sure he knew who it was.

The urge to speed up was so great, he could feel his foot pressing the accelerator closer to the floor without any conscious intention of doing so.

He muttered a foul curse and forced himself to ease up a bit. In spite of the twists and turns of this road, he couldn't risk following too closely. If he drove up to Gretchen while Brooks had her in his grasp, it was anyone's guess what the man would do. Whatever the answer was, it wouldn't be good.

"If anything happens to her, Hannon…" He couldn't finish the sentence. Letting his mind go down that road was unacceptable. He'd flay the man alive and feed his body to the nearest bear if he so much as broke one of Gretchen's fingernails.

That was his last thought before he rounded a turn and saw a quick flash of white and chrome. Gretchen's car pulling into a deeply forested part of the woods.

"Nowhere to go here," he muttered. Once the car was in the trees, it would be hidden from view of the road, which was most likely all that Brooks was looking for. A good hiding place for a body.

David sucked in a breath. He rolled his own car to a

stop and got out, leaving the door ajar as he slipped onto the grass and began to follow.

"Stop here. Get out slowly." Lyle fired commands like bullets from a semiautomatic.

Gretchen edged her way out of the car. All the way here she'd done her best to talk Lyle into letting her go without revealing that she had hard evidence against him. If he knew that, then he'd realize that David wasn't just going to go away. He'd consider him a threat, as well— and he'd go after him.

Now she was running out of things to say to Lyle and running out of time. A thread of terror slipped in.

"No time for that."

"What?" Brooks practically shouted the word and Gretchen realized that she'd actually spoken out loud, her nervousness getting the best of her.

In spite of her complete aversion to the man, she stayed as close to him as he would allow. If she got the chance, now that her hands were free of the steering wheel, she'd go for the gun or whatever else she could grab to throw him off balance.

Nothing, she thought, her eyes quickly taking in her surroundings, the small clearing up ahead where he was leading her. He'd chosen well. There was nothing in this clearing for her to latch on to, nowhere to hide for the first twenty or thirty feet if she ran, but there was plenty of cover to hide a body once the deed was done. Acres and acres of trees well away from any inhabited territory. He'd been right when he said that no one would ever find her here.

But he was wrong if he thought that no one would at least look. Reba knew about the matching hair and skin samples. And David knew. He'd look. If there was any

way of finding her, any evidence at all of where she'd
been taken, he'd dig it out. But not in time. Not nearly
in time. And maybe he'd lose his life, too. She fought
the pain, but couldn't keep from closing her eyes for a
second in a last failed attempt to blot it out.

"Over here," Lyle ordered, wrestling her to a large
flat rock. "Kneel. I have a tremendous urge to see you
at my feet begging."

She wondered if she would do that when it came to
the end. She hoped not, especially since there was no
way it would do any good. This was a man without feeling, without a conscience.

Gretchen couldn't help but move when he shoved, but
she did her best to keep her feet. If he was going to kill
her, if there was no way she could make an escape, she
wouldn't give him the pleasure of letting him shoot her
execution style, or of watching her run so that he could
put a bullet in her back.

I'm sorry, David, she thought. Sorry for what, she
didn't know. She'd been going to meet him. She hadn't
planned on going it alone this time. But this would hurt
him. She knew that, and she wished she could change
that.

Brooks narrowed his eyes at her stubborn struggle to
stay upright. He caressed his gun against her cheek and
started to pull it back into position for firing.

A slight movement against brush sounded in the trees.
Like a squirrel or a chipmunk tripping over a twig.
Gretchen moved just a touch.

Lyle laughed and grabbed her, holding the gun to her
temple.

"I don't think our furry friend is going to save you,
beautiful," he whispered.

"Move your finger one hundredth of a centimeter on

that trigger and I'll donate your internal organs to the vultures, Brooks.''

David's voice was like the inside of a butcher's freezer, icy, crisp and deadly to those who didn't recognize the danger.

Gretchen felt the tremor—of fear or anger—go through Lyle as he swung her around to face his attacker, never letting the gun drop from its deadly position, planting her body firmly between himself and David.

''Well, well, look here, Neal, your boyfriend's come calling, after all. What could be more perfect? Here I thought I wouldn't have to bother with him, but now this works out so much better. With everyone well aware that the two of you are engaged, I won't have to plant much information at all to make them think you've eloped and left town together.''

''You won't have to do anything at all, Brooks. You'll be dead.''

The gun jostled against Gretchen's temple as Lyle shook his head.

''Sorry, you'll be the one dead, Hannon.''

Gretchen didn't need to see the man's face to know that he was smiling, and she knew then that in spite of the gun, it wasn't her life that was in the most immediate danger right now. It was David's. If Brooks shot her, David would kill him before he'd finished squeezing the trigger. But with her as a shield, David couldn't shoot to protect himself right now. Time enough to kill her after David was gone. Time had run out.

Almost.

She had to act now and she knew exactly what she had to do. Looking straight into the eyes of the man she loved, she opened her mouth.

''They'll find you after we're gone, Lyle,'' she said

quietly, never taking her eyes off David, trying her darnedest to send him a message he could read. "I was coming to arrest you, because those hair and skin samples I took from you matched what was found beneath Peter's fingernails. He didn't die from an accidental fall. You pushed him, and it's no secret anymore. Don't think you're safe."

She blinked her eyes and David blinked back. He didn't even nod, but she had to believe that he knew what she intended. She needed to believe that they had, indeed, become partners in the closest sense.

"He fell," Lyle said, his voice agitated. "I just tried to save him. He clutched at me. That's why my skin's underneath his nails."

"That's not what you said," she said, her voice sinking even lower, growing even more accusing. "When your original testimony was taken, you stated that Peter was alive when you left him."

She forced herself not to tense up. She only had time to blink her eyes firmly once more, but as the last word left her mouth, Gretchen dropped bonelessly. She brought her leg up in as smooth an arc as she could manage, aiming for Lyle's chin.

The blow knocked him sideways, but he recovered quickly, swearing as he latched back onto the gun he had nearly dropped. He turned in a wild swoop, firing at David.

But David had dropped low just as Gretchen had moved, as she'd hoped he would. He dodged Brooks's bullet and fired in one rolling movement. One clean shot, but one was all that was necessary. Lyle staggered back and fell.

His gun clattered to the rock. His body relaxed into total stillness.

Gretchen took one look. She didn't need to take a pulse to know that he was dead, but she did it anyway. This man had given Peter Cook no chance. He'd given David and her no chance, but she would give him what little chance she could if it existed. She wouldn't become an animal like him.

But when she touched the skin of the man who would have taken her life without one regret, she found not even the faintest hint of a heart doing its job.

And so she rose—and stepped right into David's arms as he barreled toward her. She looked up into eyes that were still bright and fierce and angry.

"Don't," she said, pushing as close as she could get. "Don't be angry with me right now. You can yell and lecture tomorrow. For today, just kiss me. Hold me."

And he held her as close as two bodies could get without becoming one. He cupped the back of her head in his hand and covered her mouth with his own in a long, desperate, seeking kiss.

"I thought you were gone, Gretchen," he choked. "I thought— I almost wasn't quick enough. I damned near lost you."

"Not yet," she whispered, her voice as desperate as his kiss. His legs gave out and so did hers, and they dropped to the ground beneath them. "Not yet," she repeated, and she twined her arms around his neck. She gave in to the joy creeping up within her. She rained quick, whispery kisses over every inch of David that she could get near.

He ran his palms over every available centimeter of her skin.

Together they reclaimed the day, reclaimed each other. They reclaimed life as they fed each other with kisses and caresses and all the emotion they'd been forced to hold inside during those last few terrible moments.

"How did you know?" she finally asked, pulling back from him long enough to look up into his eyes.

His slow, shaky smile was a relief to see. "I know you," he whispered. "That's what partners do, after all, isn't it? They get to know each other well, well enough to anticipate each other's moves."

He found her lips again, anticipating just what she wanted him to do.

"Come on," he said, pulling her to her feet and into his arms. "Let's get you home. I'll have Rafe send someone back for the body. But for now, you need some time to recover."

She did, and she wanted to do it in David's arms. She wanted to make him forget that he had been forced to kill and she wanted them both to drive away the threat of death that had stared them straight in the face that day.

Then she could face the rest.

She and David weren't over. They were both alive and well and they would survive. But their days as partners were coming to a close.

She would regret that. But for tonight she would have as much of him as she ever could have.

And it would have to be suffice. In two days' time all she would have of David would be achingly sweet and distant memories.

David lay in the dark with Gretchen draped over his chest. He kissed the top of her hair and she snuggled closer in sleep, soothing the rage that still lay banked deep within him.

He'd work through it in time, but it would be a long, slow process to put this day behind him, and he would never, he knew, forget the sight of this lady, a gun pressed to her head, silently telling him that she was about to make a move.

A long, deep river of emotion ran through him. He wondered if he would ever stop loving Gretchen or if he would ever stop wanting to love Gretchen.

He would live without her, because she wanted things that way. He wouldn't intrude on her space because he knew after today that he would do anything, give anything, to see her happy and safe and contented for all eternity.

And contented for Gretchen meant living a single life.

But she couldn't keep him from caring, and neither could he. No matter what he'd done or thought to prevent it, he hadn't been able to back away from what he felt about this slender, strong-willed woman.

She was what made life special. He would have lived in hell forever if she'd died today.

But she'd lived, and it was only right that she be allowed to live on her own terms, in her own way.

He could watch from the sidelines, but he couldn't let himself force his heart on her any more than he could have allowed Lyle Brooks to hurt her and survive.

That was just the way things were.

"So deal with it, buddy," he whispered to himself.

He would. Somehow. But he shook his head as he tried once more to settle down to sleep. How ironic that he'd finally found one woman who could make him want to settle down and make a home, and she happened to be a woman who had absolutely no interest in such things.

Leave it to Gretchen to do things a little differently.

But why not? She was a woman who went along with a ridiculous scheme to pretend she was engaged to him. She was a detective who took the time to listen to people even when she didn't have the time or the ability to solve their problems, just because it made one person's day a little easier to bear. She was a woman who faced the ultimate terror and still managed to keep her thoughts clear enough to stay alive until help could be arranged.

She was, quite simply, he thought, the heart that beat within him.

He shifted and snuggled her just a little closer to him and that small movement jostled her just enough to have her blinking those wide green eyes at him and propping herself up on his chest.

A slow, sweet, sleepy smile lifted her lips. "I'm so glad you're alive, David," she whispered, her voice groggy with sleep. And then she laid her head back on his chest, touched her lips to his skin, making every cell in his body snap to attention as she drifted back into sleep.

As he lay there, smiling into her hair, fighting the instant desire that she had awakened and was now no longer awake to assuage, David felt his heart lurch just slightly.

Tomorrow he was leaving, but there was absolutely no doubt in his mind that Gretchen Neal was going to haunt his sleepless nights for the rest of his life.

And there wasn't a damn thing he could do to fight it.

He settled her closer, kissed her once more and realized that he had no urge to fight anything that had to do with Gretchen.

If he loved her forever—and he would, even if it was to no avail—at least she would be with him in the only way he could have her. In his soul.

Fifteen

She'd been trying her best to keep her mind on work all morning, but Gretchen just couldn't keep her gaze from straying to David again and again. This was his last day. He'd been given his orders and he had to get on a plane back to Atlanta tomorrow. The fact that he'd come in to work at all today amazed her. She knew that yesterday had been hard on both of them, but she suspected that it had been harder on David than herself.

She'd been so busy trying to think her way out of the situation that she hadn't had time to give in to the natural terror that any sane person would feel.

But David—he'd had to watch her life being threatened while his hands were effectively tied. She had a hint of what that must be like, because in those moments when she'd feared David would barge in on her and Lyle and be gunned down, she'd barely beaten back the panic.

And David had been the one who'd had to take a life. No matter that it hadn't been the life of a good man, and no matter that he'd done it before. He'd confessed that much to her when she'd asked, trying to make sure that he was all right. She'd seen officers who'd been forced to kill before. There was always a bit of fallout. No one came out completely unscathed. And the few who did seem to have no reaction whatsoever were the ones who had to be watched most closely.

David had not been unaffected. She'd seen the acceptance in his eyes and the regret that a life had had to be given for justice to prevail.

But he was here, finishing up the paperwork with her, and mostly—she knew the man too well—offering her his presence. He wanted to make sure that she was past her own reactions to yesterday's bad experience.

Without thought, without the time to prepare herself, her heart overflowed. She had to fight a teary feeling deep inside, and that made her so angry that she slammed the folder she was holding down onto the desk.

David looked up from the scratching of his pen on paper.

"You okay?" he asked.

No, she was not okay. She hadn't been okay since the day she'd met David Hannon.

"I'm perfectly fine," she lied with a smile. Except this man had flipped her world like a top spinning off its string. He had her thinking about her mother and herself and all those years when she'd sworn she'd never follow in her parents' footsteps. He had her wondering if her mother really had regretted all those moves, or if the regrets had only been her own imaginings, her own grumblings. She knew for a fact that her father had regretted having to uproot his family, that her mother had always smiled and reassured him as best she could.

"I wish I could stay and help you work out things on Raven's case," he said, reaching for her hand.

Without thought, she pulled away. Her emotions were much too close to the surface. She had a feeling that tears weren't far behind, and she *never* cried. She made a point of not crying. It was bad for business, especially if you were a female detective. It was unacceptable and left you open to criticism, made people think you couldn't take whatever was dished out. Worst of all, it left you vulnerable. If she let David see she was upset, he would know what she didn't want him to ever know.

She loved him. Completely. Devastatingly. And it just wouldn't do.

Somehow she dredged up a smile. Phony, but it would have to do.

"We'll get through on the case. And I'll be protected," she assured him. "Haven't you noticed all the eyes that have been following my every move today?"

He smiled slightly. "Everyone feels guilty that you were abducted yesterday while the world and the White-horn force went on."

She shrugged. "How could they know?"

He frowned. "Exactly."

She leveled a stare at him. "It won't happen again. Rafe's set shadows on me. And, anyway, the danger is past."

"Yes," he said solemnly. But she still heard the doubt in his voice. Both of them knew that in their line of work the danger was never past.

She felt the catch in her throat. David was going away. He would no doubt put his life on the line over and over and she would never know. She knew now why her mother had calmly packed up her household time and time again. It had been important to her to be with the man she loved beyond life, to see him every day, to know that he was alive and with her, day and night. Her father had, she realized, been her mother's world. Their life had been complicated by her father's work and responsibilities and their constant moves from one place to another, but they'd loved, and they'd raised a houseful of children whom they'd taught how to love.

She didn't regret her childhood, just as David didn't regret what he'd gone through as a child. Her struggles had made her stronger. They'd made her who she was, just as his challenges had made him what he was.

The man she loved. The man who was leaving just when she'd realized she wanted him to stay with her forever. The man she couldn't reach out and latch onto because she knew he had a path of his own to follow. And because he hadn't asked her to share his life. He wouldn't. David Hannon loved women, but he didn't stay with just one.

"Atlanta must be pretty at this time of year," she couldn't help saying, although she wished she could shove the words back into her mouth.

He gave her a deep, lazy smile. He rose and dropped a kiss on her lips. "I'll show you sometime," he whispered.

But he wouldn't, she knew. Because she didn't think she could bear to visit him and go through a goodbye all over again.

"Hey, Hannon," a voice called at that moment, and Gretchen turned to look toward the door. "Your aunt's here to see you."

"Come on," David said, giving her hand a tug. "Come with me. Aunt Celeste came in, I'm sure, to see you alive and in person. Ten to one she brought you comfort food. She needs to know you're all right. And who can blame her?"

"I'm going to get spoiled by all this attention," Gretchen said softly and with a laugh. "Detectives are supposed to face danger, David. They're not supposed to be fussed over."

He stopped midstride and looked over his shoulder. "Baloney, Gretchen. You don't have anything to prove. People love you. Let them fuss. And let yourself enjoy."

She placed her hand on his sleeve. "I do," she assured him. "I will."

The words that were so close to the kinds of vows lovers made as they joined their hands in marriage fell from her lips too easily. She removed her fingers from his arm, wishing she could hold his warmth next to her forever. And she turned to Celeste who wrapped her in a warm hug.

"You should be in bed, sweetie," the older woman ordered. "But David told me I might as well suggest you hang from the ceiling naked, so I brought you brownies instead. Caramel and fudge."

Gretchen grinned at Celeste and hugged her again. "If I were in bed, I'd miss all your good cooking, Celeste. Pretty clever of me to come in and claim all this attention, wasn't it?" she asked with a grin as she bit into a heavenly brownie oozing with melted fudge.

Celeste laughed out loud. She turned to her nephew and opened her mouth to make a comment.

Her mouth opened wider. Her eyes widened like a gaping door. She brought both hands up to cover her mouth.

"Oh, no," she whispered through the tunnel of her fingers.

Gretchen spun around to see what had distressed Celeste so. Her gaze swept across Storm Hunter who was on the other side of the room deep in conversation with Rafe. Storm's eyes were dark and tired and leveled on David, Celeste and herself. He looked slightly stooped and bleary, as if weariness had left him sleepless of late. But as Gretchen made eye contact with the man, she saw his attention sharpen, she saw him blink. She felt a swoosh of movement at her side.

And she turned to see David catching his aunt in his arms as Celeste slumped toward the floor.

* * *

The day had slipped away, David thought as he walked Gretchen to her car that evening. Celeste had been taken home, apologizing to everyone for behaving so foolishly in fainting, in not realizing how closely Storm resembled his brother, Raven. She apologized for thinking even for a second that she'd seen a ghost.

The excitement was over.

And the torture was about to begin.

His bags were packed. He had to say goodbye to Gretchen. How was he ever going to do it and survive? He wanted to kiss her, needed to kiss her, but if he did that now, he was afraid he wouldn't be able to let go.

She solved the problem by holding out her hand.

"Well," she said, her voice the barest trace of shaky sound, "I guess this is where we say goodbye. I wanted—"

She took a deep breath. She bit down on her lip.

He swayed toward her.

"I wanted to thank you," she said, forestalling his movement. "For being such a good partner. A detective couldn't ask for better backup. A woman couldn't ask for a better fiancé."

Her voice shook on those last words. Her fingers were ice-cold when he took them in his own.

And David knew in that moment that he had to warm her. He had to take the risk, he had to do what he'd promised himself he wouldn't do for her sake.

He lifted her hand to his lips, turned it over and kissed the palm deeply, savoring the way her skin warmed beneath his.

"I wanted to make it that easy for you, sweetheart, but I'm afraid it isn't going to be that simple."

She looked up at him. She opened her eyes wide, shaking her head in a mute question. But she didn't retrieve her hand, he noted. She didn't step back from him.

"I don't understand," she finally said.

"You want me to just walk away, but when have I ever just walked away when you wanted me to, Gretchen?"

And her fingers curled closed slightly. She raised her hand as if to touch his cheek, then held her hand there in midair as if uncertain what to do.

"You've never been a very conformable man, David," she agreed in a husky whisper. "You were pushy right from the start."

"So you think you'll get rid of me just by saying good-bye?"

"I don't know. Won't I?"

He shook his head. She wrapped her palm around his jaw. "I won't?"

"Do you want to? Get rid of me, I mean?"

And then a terrible thing happened. A mist of tears filled her beautiful green eyes.

And he couldn't help himself. He tugged her close and kissed her eyelids shut as a tear trickled down. She opened her eyes again.

"I'm sorry," she said with another gentle shake of her head. "I know this is a game we're playing, and I—I seem to have forgotten the rules."

"No rules. No game." His voice was a harsh, choked whisper. He thumbed away the dampness from her cheeks.

"It never was a game with us, really. Was it?" she asked.

He shook his head slowly, leaned forward and brushed her forehead with his lips. "I wanted it to be. I suspect we both wanted it to be, but no, it never was a game. What went on between us was as real as it gets, angel.''

She pulled back, touched her fingertips to his lips, staring earnestly into his eyes. ''I don't want to distress you, David. I promised I wouldn't be this way, but I don't want it to end. I don't want you to go.''

''Try and make me leave you. I couldn't,'' he whispered against her fingertips, biting softly on the flesh.

The softest of smiles brightened her eyes. Her lips curved upward, giving him the response he needed and was desperate to have.

''I can give Rafe my notice,'' she offered.

''Too late. When I was in the Billings office, I saw that there was a position opening. It can be mine. I've grown to realize how much I love this place where I grew up. I thought about it on the ride back to White horn yesterday. I half considered applying for it, but—''

''You've changed your mind?'' Confusion colored her expression.

''I've made up my mind,'' he confessed. ''Gretchen, you've taught me a few things since I've been here. You've made me see that I've always pushed away the things I really wanted because I grew up knowing I couldn't have so many of my heart's desires. Denying those things has become a bad habit, a protective armor...

''You've changed things, though. I don't want to deny those wants and needs anymore, and what I really want is you. Day and night, in every way that counts. I know the thought of teaming up with any man permanently isn't your idea of heaven, but I'll do my best to make it work for you. I can't promise not to invade your space from time to time, but I'll try hard not to. I'm sure you'll remind me when you need time alone, and I'll do my best to protect you from people who ask too much from you. But I just can't imagine my world without you anymore, love. Do you think you could ever love me in the same way?''

Gretchen felt her heart filling up, her throat closing.

''Who gets to lead and who follows?'' she asked with a teary smile.

He smiled back and she knew that look in his eyes was the love she wanted to see.

''We'll take turns,'' he promised.

She rose up on her toes and kissed him. Once. Twice. Too many times to count.

''I wonder if that will work,'' she whispered.

He slanted his lips over hers in one quick, hard, answering kiss. ''You know that it will, lady. It's what we've been doing all along. Besides, you have to marry me now.''

She grinned and looked down at her stomach. ''I have to marry you? I'm not pregnant.''

He chuckled and the sound thrilled her completely. ''I hope you will be very soon. Besides, you have to marry me for one other reason, Gretchen. We've already planned our wedding.''

She smiled up at him and watched his dark emerald eyes grow warm in that way that she knew she would always love. ''I guess we have planned our wedding, but even if we hadn't, it wouldn't matter, David, my heart. I love you beyond belief. I'll marry you whenever you say.''

''Today?''

''Or maybe yesterday,'' she agreed.

He grinned and pulled her in close for a kiss. ''Your call this time,'' he said.

And she raised her lips to meet his. She claimed the man who owned her heart.

"Welcome to Whitehorn, love," she finally whispered. "I think this forever partnership is a wonderful idea."

And he folded her close and showed her just how very much in tune their thoughts were and would always be.

*   *   *   *   *

Storming Whitehorn
Christine Scott

To Bill, a great brother and a cowboy at heart.

One

"She's never been this late before." Jasmine Kincaid Monroe crossed her arms at her waist and stared out the large front window of the Big Sky Bed & Breakfast.

Jasmine's aunt, Yvette Hannon, joined her at the window. A tall, striking woman with classic features and graying hair, she exuded an enviable grace and confidence. Her smile reassuring, she placed a warm hand on Jasmine's slender shoulder. "Knowing your mother, she probably bumped into an old friend in town and has lost all track of time. I'm sure Celeste is all right."

"My mother hasn't been all right in a long time. Not since—" Jasmine stopped, frowning as she averted her gaze.

"Not since they found Raven Hunter's remains," Yvette finished with a sigh.

Raven Hunter was a name from the past, which had only recently resurfaced with a vengeance. Thirty years ago, Raven and Jasmine's aunt, Blanche Kincaid, had been illicit lovers. When it had been discovered that Blanche was pregnant, their affair had caused a scandal in the Kincaid family, as well as in the town of Whitehorn. Blanche's brother, Jeremiah, had vehemently opposed any suggestion of his sister marrying a member of the Cheyenne. It hadn't been long after Blanche's pregnancy was revealed that Raven disappeared. Some say Jeremiah had paid him off, that Raven had taken what

money he could get and run. Others say he'd loved
Blanche too much, that he wouldn't have abandoned her.
They believed Raven was dead, most likely at the hand
of Jeremiah Kincaid.

Apparently, the latter was true.

For, at the construction site of the new casino/resort
that straddled the Laughing Horse Reservation and the
Kincaid ranch, Raven's remains had been recently uncovered. A bullet lodged in the rib cage confirmed Raven
had died a violent death. The discovery set into motion
a chain of events that had led to two more deaths, the
most recent of which had hit too close to home. Jasmine's
family was still reeling with the news of their cousin Lyle
Brooks's death.

"This investigation into Raven Hunter's murder is
wearing on Mother. Why won't she talk to us? If she'd
just tell us what's wrong…" Jasmine let the words drift
into a frustrated silence.

Choosing her words carefully, Yvette said, "Darling,
you have to understand what this must mean to your
mother. I was at school in Bozeman when Raven disappeared, but Celeste was still there at the ranch. Despite
Jeremiah's opposition, she stood by Blanche during her
pregnancy and when she gave birth to your cousin, Summer. She was also with Blanche when she died. It was a
very trying time for everyone, but most of the burden fell
on Celeste. Discovering Raven's body has dredged up a
lot of painful memories. Is it any wonder that your
mother might be upset?"

"No, I suppose not. But she isn't sleeping, Aunt
Yvette. I hear her up at night, pacing. Last night, at two
o'clock in the morning, I found her sitting cross-legged
on the floor in the middle of her bedroom, surrounded
by candles, burning incense and chanting." She shook

her head at the thought. "When she turns to the spiritual world, there has to be something more than just memories troubling her."

"She was chanting?" Yvette's brow furrowed. "Celeste does have a strong belief in the spiritual hereafter. Perhaps she was calling upon the spirits to help Raven find peace at last."

"It isn't Raven Hunter who needs to find peace, it's my mother," Jasmine said, her voice sharper than she'd intended. She sighed. "I'm sorry, Aunt Yvette. I didn't mean to snap."

"It's all right, dear," she said gently. "I know you're worried."

Absently, Jasmine touched the gold-plated compass hanging by a chain around her neck, and felt her heart catch with emotion. The compass had been a gift from her mother when she'd turned twenty-one and had returned home after finishing her training at the culinary school. Because of Jasmine's love for hiking in the mountains, Celeste had told her it was her reassurance that Jasmine would always find her way home.

With the memory strengthening her resolve, Jasmine strode to the front desk and snagged her purse from behind the counter. "She should have been home hours ago. I'm not waiting any longer. I'm going to Whitehorn to look for her."

Yvette followed her to the desk. "Perhaps you're right. I'll take care of things here at the B and B while you're gone. You will call, won't you? If you find anything...anything at all."

At the sound of her troubled voice, Jasmine squeezed Yvette's arm. "I'll call."

Releasing her aunt, Jasmine strode to the front door. The heels of her cowboy boots tapped against the lobby's pinewood floor, matching the nervous beat of her heart. She wiped a clammy hand down the length of her short pleated skirt. Despite late August's cooling temperatures, she felt hot and sticky. Her eyelet shirt clung uncomfortably to the curves of her body. Pushing aside her discomfort, she stepped outside onto the large, open porch that ran the length of the front of the house.

By the time she reached the first step of the wooden stairs, however, she noticed a cloud of dust being kicked up on the lane that led into town. Jasmine stopped, squinting at the rapidly approaching car. From what she could see, the luxury car was a silvery gray, one that she didn't recognize. An unexpected guest for the B and B, she supposed. With an impatient scowl, she reminded herself that she didn't have time to greet a visitor. Yvette would have to handle this new arrival.

Gravel crunched beneath its tires as the car slid to a quick stop in front of the manor house. Coughing, Jasmine waved a hand in a vain attempt to clear the air of the dust whipped up by the skid. A fine layer of grit floated over her like a powdery blanket. Once the dust settled, the driver's door opened and a tall, dark, handsome Native American man stepped out onto the driveway.

He was muscular, with broad shoulders and narrow hips. His hair was straight and black, with touches of gray at the temples. He wore it long, to the collar of his buttoned-down shirt, and all one length. Lifting his sunglasses from the bridge of his nose, his dark brown eyes glimmered in the sunlight as he fastened a gaze upon her.

Jasmine froze, unable to move as he slowly raked his eyes up and down the length of her body. Never before had she been subjected to such a blatantly assessing stare.

She nearly trembled beneath its weight. It felt as though he were undressing her with his gaze.

Despite the differences in their ages—his she guessed to be late thirties, or early forties; hers a mere twenty-three—she felt an instant stirring of awareness deep in the pit of her belly. A sensual heat warmed her blood. She was surprised by her strong reaction to this total stranger, but not intimidated by him. Instead, she returned his stare with a curious gaze of her own.

The stranger was the first to break the spell that seemed to hold them both. His deep voice rumbled in her ears as he asked, "Is this the Big Sky Bed & Breakfast?"

"Y-yes, it is," she said, stumbling over an assent. Rolling her eyes at her clumsiness, she cleared her throat and began again. "I'm Jasmine…Jasmine Monroe. My family owns the B and B. May I help you?"

"My name's Storm Hunter," he said, his eyes never leaving her face, as though testing for her reaction. He stepped toward her, closing the distance between them. "And I believe that I'm the one who can help you."

Hunter? Jasmine's heart skipped a beat at the name. Storm Hunter, Raven Hunter's brother. She'd heard he was back in town. Her cousin David Hannon, a special agent for the FBI who'd been on a leave of absence since shortly after the remains of Raven Hunter had been found, had mentioned Storm's tempestuous arrival in Whitehorn. The two men had nearly come to blows when Storm had refused to accept the lack of progress in the investigation of his brother's murder. Apparently he bore a personal grudge against anyone with a connection to the Kincaid family.

Goodness only knew why this forceful man was now standing on the driveway of her family's bed-and-breakfast.

"I don't understand," she said, unable to hide the skepticism from her voice. "*You* want to help *me?*"

A corner of his mouth lifted in a semblance of a polite smile. "Perhaps I should clarify. What I meant was, I believe I have something that belongs to you." With a sweep of his hand, he gestured toward the front seat of his car.

For the first time Jasmine noticed another person inside. There, slumped against the passenger door, was Celeste Monroe, Jasmine's mother.

"Mother!" Jasmine gasped in alarm. She turned, calling over her shoulder for her aunt's support. "Aunt Yvette, come quick. It's Mother."

Not bothering to wait for her aunt, she pushed past the disturbing Storm Hunter and hurried to her mother's side. Wrenching open the car door, she was stunned by her mother's pallid complexion. Her short, russet hair looked disheveled. A fine layer of perspiration dampened her skin.

Gravel crunched beneath his shoes as Storm joined her. She glanced up at him, her gaze accusing. "What have you done to her?"

He flinched at her bitter words. A reaction that he quickly hid behind a stony mask of indifference. His expression cool, he said, "I haven't done a thing to your mother. She fainted at the sheriff's office in Whitehorn. I was there when it happened. I offered to drive her home. She accepted. That's the extent of my involvement."

Jasmine's face grew hot with embarrassment as she realized how unjust her accusation must have sounded. "I'm sorry, I didn't mean to—"

The skin around his finely sculpted cheekbones grew taut. His jaw stiffened, his strong chin lifting in defiance. "There's no need to apologize, Ms. Monroe. I assure you, I'm used to the white man thinking the worst of me merely because of the color of my skin.''

Jasmine felt as though she'd been struck by the words. ''The color of your skin? Don't be ridiculous. I never—''

''Jasmine…'' Celeste's fragile voice interrupted.

Forgetting all else, Jasmine leaned forward, reaching for her mother's hand. ''Mother, are you all right?''

''Take me inside,'' she whispered.

''Of course,'' Jasmine murmured.

''Jasmine?'' Yvette's breathless voice caught her attention. Her aunt's cheeks were flushed from hurrying. Worry lines creased her careworn face. ''What's happened? What's wrong with Celeste?''

''She fainted in town,'' Jasmine said quickly. She glanced at Storm. ''Mr. Hunter brought her home.''

''Mr. Hunter?'' Yvette's troubled gaze traveled to Storm.

''Yes, *Storm* Hunter. Mr. Hunter, this is my aunt, Yvette Hannon. I believe you've already met her son, David?''

The reminder of his and David's ill-fated meeting, the one that had nearly ended in a fistfight, was uncalled for. But so was his accusation that she would judge another man by the color of his skin. When she saw Storm's eyes narrow in irritation, she couldn't help but feel a bittersweet sense of satisfaction.

Now they were even.

Gracious as always, Yvette extended a hand in greeting. ''Thank you for your help, Mr. Hunter. It's, uh, good to finally meet you.''

If Storm seemed surprised by this show of cordiality, he didn't show it. Instead he accepted Yvette's proffered hand with a smooth smile. ''You're welcome, Mrs. Hannon. I hope your sister will soon feel better.''

"Celeste, right." Yvette gave a quick nod, as though gathering herself to take control of the situation. "Jasmine, help me please. Let's get your mother inside."

Together, the two of them half lifted Celeste from the car. Celeste's white cotton, Gypsy-style shirt had come untucked from the waistband of her long broomstick skirt. The gauzy fabric sagged against her shapely curves. As was her mother's habit, somewhere along the way, she'd kicked off her sandals and was barefoot. Jasmine plucked the wayward shoes from the floor of the front seat to carry inside.

Flanking her mother on both sides, Yvette and Jasmine each held her by one arm. Slowly the three women headed for the front porch. As they neared the top step, Jasmine turned, glancing over her shoulder at the quiet figure still standing beside the silver car. "Mr. Hunter," she said, "if you wouldn't mind waiting, there's something I'd like to tell you."

Not bothering to wait for his answer, Jasmine turned away and led her mother inside.

Storm Hunter didn't like being told what to do. Not by anyone. But most especially not by an outspoken young woman who was nearly half his age.

A part of him wanted to get into his rented car and leave this place, this home of the Kincaid family, and never look back. The other part, the impulsive, illogical part, was curious as to what Jasmine might have to say.

"Jasmine," he murmured her name out loud, savoring the sound of it as it tripped over his tongue. An exotic name for an exotic beauty, he mused silently as he stood beneath the glaring sun on the white rock-covered driveway of the B and B, with his hands on his hips, staring at the door through which she had disappeared. Her image was as fresh in his mind as though she were still present.

Jasmine the woman, he decided, was a contradiction in terms. A delicate flower, as her name might suggest, though one who'd found roots and strength in the wild, untamed lands of Montana. With her black hair cut short in a pixie style, she seemed so young and innocent. The cut and color emphasized the paleness of her skin, the smooth perfection of her complexion and the classic lines of her features. Yet, at the same time, he saw the wisdom of an older woman in her eyes, one who'd experienced much of life. She was tall and slender, but with enough womanly curves to make any man stand up and take notice. Her eccentric way of dressing—black cowboy boots, a red pleated skirt and a white eyelet blouse—certainly made him wonder. Yet, the outfit hinted at a personality that was free-spirited and vivacious. Traits that he envied. Traits that he'd lost over the years, somewhere along the way.

Storm blew out an irritated breath. What was wrong with him? He was spending entirely too much time speculating about a young woman who was destined to play nothing more than a fleeting role in his life. She was a Kincaid. He was a Hunter. As history had already proven, the two did not mix. If it hadn't been for her mother and his misguided sense of chivalry, their paths would never have crossed.

Earlier, when he'd stopped by the sheriff's office on yet another fruitless call upon the investigator in charge of his brother's murder case, he'd happened to bump into Celeste Monroe. To say her reaction to his appearance had been strong would be an understatement. One fearful look at his face and the woman had collapsed in a dead faint. She'd looked as though she'd seen a ghost.

It wasn't until after she'd reluctantly accepted his offer of a ride home that he'd realized who Celeste Monroe really was. Celeste *Kincaid* Monroe, sister to Blanche and Jeremiah Kincaid, the very people he'd blamed all these years for the loss of his brother. The family who'd been at the very heart of his troubled life.

And now he was being unwise enough to let his hormones blur his judgment. He'd allowed himself to become intrigued by a Kincaid—a family he'd sworn to hate. Jasmine...

Though she'd never invited him inside, curiosity got the better of him. Quietly, Storm crossed the gravel driveway and climbed the steps of the large front porch. The double doors stood wide open, allowing anyone to enter.

Even an unwanted Cheyenne, he told himself, allowing his rancor to fester.

The floors were of polished pine. The rooms were large and spacious. The ceilings were high, measuring at least ten feet; rough-hewn beams graced the dining room ceiling. Natural wood trim stretched as far as the eye could see. The house itself was mostly furnished with the clean lines of the mission-style decor, but there were enough chaise longues and overstuffed club chairs to make a guest comfortable.

Storm stepped through one of the living room's set of French doors and onto a wide screened-in porch. The porch ran the length of the back of the house. From here, the view of Blue Mirror Lake was spectacular. Its flat, shiny surface, indeed, looked like polished glass. A dense forest of pine trees surrounded the property, and the air was thick with their pungent scent. In the distance, he saw the mountains of the Laughing Horse Reservation.

His breath caught painfully at the sight. Though he'd traveled many miles to escape from his past on the reservation, he could never completely leave behind its harsh memories. He glanced around the bed-and-breakfast, at the casual display of Kincaid wealth, and felt a bitter taste rise in his throat. No matter how many college degrees he might acquire, or how much money he made in his law practice in New Mexico, he would never forget his troubled past, his poor, hand-to-mouth upbringing. He would never be able to stand tall in a world that included the Kincaid family.

With the ghosts of the past chasing him, Storm whirled away from the sight of the reservation and strode back into the house. The heels of his shoes pounded against the pine floor as he made his way to the front door. But he didn't care about the noise. He didn't care about anything but escaping.

"Mr. Hunter…Storm." There was a note of desperation in Jasmine's sweet melodic voice.

Storm clenched his jaw in annoyance and told himself to keep walking. Don't look back. Don't stop, no matter how great the temptation might be.

Her boots tapped an urgent beat against the wood floor as she hurried toward him. Guiltily, he heard the breathless quality of her voice as she called, "Please wait. I'd like to talk to you."

A heavy hand of frustration pressed against his shoulders, slowing his pace. Though he was only a few steps from a clean getaway, he couldn't find the strength to abandon her. He chided himself for being so weak-willed and wondered what it was about this woman that, when she was near, made him lose all sense of judgment.

Wheeling to face her, he didn't bother to hide his annoyance. "Ms. Monroe, I'm very busy. I don't have time—"

"This won't take long," she assured him. Her cheeks

were flushed from exertion. Her chest rose as she took in a steadying breath. "I—I just wanted to thank you."

He raised a brow in disbelief. "*You* want to thank *me?*"

She nodded. "That, and to apologize."

He didn't respond. Instead he waited for her to continue, purposefully schooling his face to be void of expression, uncertain whether to trust her unexpected change of heart.

"Earlier I jumped to the wrong conclusion. When you brought my mother home, she looked so weak and helpless, I—I was shocked. I said the first thing that popped into my mind. I accused you of hurting her, without knowing the facts. For that I'm truly sorry. Please don't think that I would judge you, or anyone else, for that matter, solely on the color of their skin. Because it just isn't true."

He believed her.

During her plea for understanding, Jasmine had looked him straight in the eye. Her gaze had never wavered, not once. Either she was the coolest liar he'd ever met, or she was telling the truth.

He'd bet the house on the latter.

Grudgingly he asked, "Your mother, is she all right?"

"She's fine," she said, striving for a lighthearted tone, and failed. Blushing, she gave a self-deprecating smile and added, "Or at least she will be, now that she's home. Thank you, once again, for taking care of her."

Then, with the impetuousness of the young, she reached out and enfolded him in an innocent hug of gratitude.

While he told himself the gesture was probably not unusual for this woman who seemed so open with her own feelings, he wasn't prepared for such a free-spirited reaction. To his chagrin, his body reacted in a most uncordial manner.

With her soft curves pressed against him, he felt himself harden in response. His hands caught her waist with the intention of pushing her away. Instead he found himself pulling her closer.

As though she sensed a shift in the mood, Jasmine pulled back. With her hands still linked behind his neck, she lifted her eyes to his. A slight frown wrinkled her brow. Her look was not one of alarm, but rather of curiosity.

Her face was turned upward to his. Her lips, so soft and full and inviting, proved too much of a temptation. Once again, he lost his battle with willpower.

Knowing full well all the reasons why he shouldn't be doing this, Storm was unable to stop himself. Slowly, his eyes never leaving her face, he lowered his head and brushed his lips against hers.

He heard the quick inhalation of her breath, felt the rise and fall of her breasts against his chest, and waited for her to resist. But she didn't. Instead she leaned forward, tilted her head in a more accommodating position and silently encouraged him to deepen the kiss.

Logic and reason escaping him, he brushed his tongue against her lips and felt them open to him. Gently he explored the moist heat of her mouth, savoring its sweet taste.

Closing her eyes, she collapsed against him, letting her softness mold his body. She clung to him, burying her fingers in the hair at the back of his neck, bringing a delicious shiver coursing down his spine.

A low moan of desire escaped his throat as he tightened his grip on her waist and let the kiss deepen. Storm had never felt this way before, this recklessness, this intense yearning for more. Proof was in the fire in his belly, as well as in his heart. This was different. Jasmine was different. After a lifetime of loneliness, it had taken him only a moment to realize what had been missing.

She was the one.

He had finally found his soul mate.

The unexpected thought came from out of nowhere, chilling him. Abruptly he ended the kiss. Winded, he sucked in deep drafts of air as he stared down at her flushed face. Her lips were swollen from his caress, and her eyes sparkled with an excitement that he had ignited. He felt another surge of desire for this woman deep in his loins.

He tore his gaze from her face and forced himself to look at the pale, white arm that rested against his own coppery skin. Once again, the differences in their lives came crashing down upon him, screaming out to him what a fool he'd been.

Jasmine Kincaid Monroe would never be his soul mate. The only thing they shared was a star-crossed history. What he felt for her was lust, plain and simple.

As his brother before him, he wanted what he could not have. The sooner he realized that, the better.

With the harsh reminder echoing in his mind, he pushed himself from the tempting warmth of her embrace and turned away. He hurried outside. Rocks crunched beneath his shoes as he strode to the car. He slung himself into the front seat, gunned the engine to life and shifted the car into gear. Gravel and dust spewed from beneath the tires as he spun out onto the driveway.

Midway down the lane into town, he allowed himself to glance into the rearview mirror. Like a dream that had disappeared upon waking, Jasmine was no longer there.

Two

Jasmine felt numb the next morning as she stared across the rolling green slopes of the Whitehorn Cemetery. The sky was overcast, the sun hidden behind a bank of storm clouds, making the white marble headstones and the simple limestone crosses appear almost luminescent in the false twilight. A cool breeze swept the grounds, carrying with it the promise of the long winter ahead. She shivered in her simple black dress, wishing she'd remembered to bring a sweater.

Moodily, she blamed her lack of forethought on Storm Hunter. Him, and his damned kiss. Since yesterday she'd been unable to think of little else. Thoughts of Storm and their encounter had left her restless and preoccupied. He'd come and gone in a blink of an eye like a fast-moving tornado, but the damage he'd left behind had been devastating.

Her womanly pride had been shattered.

Pushing the troubling thought from her mind, she concentrated on the ceremony taking place. Along with a small gathering of the Kincaid clan, Jasmine had come to pay her respects to a cousin she barely knew. For this was the day that Lyle Brooks was being laid to rest.

While they'd been close in age, only a year apart, Lyle had spent most of his life in Elk Springs. It wasn't until recently that he'd made his presence known in Whitehorn. A presence that had spelled trouble from the start.

Though the details were still sketchy, Lyle's fateful business dealings had rocked the small town of Whitehorn. He'd been a major player in the planning of the casino/resort that would encompass both the Kincaid property and the Laughing Horse Reservation. His grandfather, Garrett Kincaid, had entrusted him to oversee the family interest in the project. A decision that an obviously distraught Garrett now regretted.

For reasons unknown, Lyle had killed one of the construction workers at the building site by pushing him off of a forty-five-foot ledge. When Gretchen Neal, the lead detective on the case, uncovered his culpability in the crime, Lyle had tried to kill her to silence her. Before he could carry out his plan, Jasmine's cousin, David Hannon, had shot and killed him in a gun battle.

Construction on the new casino/resort had been halted, its future in limbo. The business deal, which would have been profitable for both the town of Whitehorn as well as the members of the Laughing Horse Reservation, had been dealt a lethal blow. One from which no one was certain it would recover.

Now they were gathered here to pay their respects to a man who hardly deserved them. Even before they'd discovered the extent of Lyle's evil, Jasmine had never felt comfortable around her cousin. He'd had such a dark aura, and there were always too many bad vibrations emanating from him.

Jasmine frowned. Dark aura? Bad vibrations? Good grief, she was starting to sound like her mother. She sighed. Mystical nonsense, or not, Lyle Brooks was one man whose spirit she wanted to see settled, not roaming free to cause more heartache.

She scanned the group, looking for familiar faces. Her mother and her sister, Cleo, were nearby. As well as Aunt

Yvette and Uncle Edward, with their daughter, Frannie, and her husband Austin, at their side. Noticeably absent, however, was their son, David, the man responsible for Lyle's death, and his fiancée, Gretchen Neal, whom he intended to marry come spring.

Garrett Kincaid, with his distinctive head of silver hair, stood tall and straight at the front of the group, supporting his grief-stricken daughter, Alice Brooks, Lyle's mother. Alice's husband, Henry, hovered at his wife's side, helplessly patting her arm, trying to ease her sorrow. Henry looked pale and hollow-eyed, devastated by the loss of his only son.

Across the way, Jasmine spotted her cousin, Summer Kincaid Nighthawk. When Summer's mother, Blanche Kincaid, had died, Yvette and Celeste had taken her under their wing, raising her as their own daughter. Inseparable since childhood, Jasmine and Summer were like sisters. Now, though Summer wore a somber expression and her long dark hair was gathered into a severe bun at the back of her head, Summer glowed with an internal happiness that couldn't be dimmed even in the darkness that surrounded this day. Obviously marriage to Gavin Nighthawk agreed with her.

Some of the new cousins were in attendance also. These were the illegitimate sons of Larry Kincaid, Garrett's only son, who'd recently been united on the Kincaid ranch. While Jasmine barely knew this new batch of relatives, it felt good to have them gathered around her. It gave her hope for a new beginning, the possibility of a familial closeness yet to come.

The minister's final blessing rose above the cry of the wind and Alice Brooks's sobs of grief, signaling an end to the service. With a nod toward Garrett, the minister picked up a handful of newly spaded dirt and tossed it onto the bronze casket as it was lowered into the ground. In turn, Garrett and Henry Brooks followed suit, letting a fistful of dirt sift through each of their hands.

When it was Alice Brooks's turn to perform the ritual, she stood beside the gravesite, shaking uncontrollably. Then, with an ear-piercing scream of anguish, she threw herself onto the casket, wailing inconsolably. The winches holding the coffin shuddered at the added weight. The groundskeeper operating the lift fumbled with the switch, cutting the power. A communal gasp of surprise arose from the crowd.

"For God's sake, Alice. What are you doing?" Garrett called, reaching for his daughter.

At first Henry Brooks stood frozen to the spot, his eyes wide, his mouth dropping open in surprise. At the sound of his father-in-law's gruff voice, he gave a visible shake, ridding himself of his stupor. Quickly he grabbed for his wife.

Alice clung to the casket, stubbornly refusing to relinquish her death grip. Jasmine's heart went out to the woman. Though Alice had a reputation for being shrewish, no one deserved to suffer such grief. After a few agonizingly discomfitting moments, the two men finally coaxed her to loosen her hold. They pulled her away, half carrying, half leading her from the gravesite.

The crowd dispersed amid murmurs of shock at the dramatic scene they had just witnessed.

Shaken by the unexpected events, Jasmine turned to leave. As she did so, she spotted a tall figure at the fringe of the gathering. He stood apart from the group, almost hidden beneath the shading branches of one of the many pine trees that stood sentry over the hallowed grounds. But she had no trouble recognizing him.

It was Storm Hunter.

Her heart skipped a beat as she stopped and stared at him, wondering why he'd come. Though he saw her, he didn't move, nor did he look away. Instead he held her gaze without flinching.

In deference to the day's event, he wore a black, double-breasted suit. His starched-white shirt complemented the darkness of his skin. His long hair was slicked back *GQ*-style, emphasizing his high cheekbones and the sculpted line of his jaw. Despite his grim expression, he looked breath-stealingly handsome.

Memories of the kiss they'd shared flooded her mind, warming her skin with a sensual flush of heat. She could still feel the pressure of his mouth against hers, could still taste his lips. Desire still pulsed through her body.

Though her pride had taken a blow when he'd left her without a word of explanation, she found herself drawn to him like a willow branch to water. She stepped toward him, her mouth curving into a tentative smile of greeting.

But the cold, prohibitive look in his eyes stopped her. Jasmine stumbled to a halt, shivering beneath his frosty glare. Holding her gaze for just a moment longer, he turned away, spurning her once again.

She couldn't move, couldn't think what to do next. An unfamiliar chill of rejection enveloped her, stiffening her limbs, numbing her mind. Never before had she been rebuffed by a man twice in as many days. The experience was as humiliating as it was crushing to her ego.

Until now she'd thought of herself as a desirable woman. At least, the men in town had certainly made her feel that way. She'd never wanted for a date, not since she'd turned a sweet sixteen. But with all their clumsy attempts to woo her, none of the local men had ever come close to arousing in her the earth-shattering sensations she'd experienced with Storm's single kiss. What made his rejection even harder to understand was that she could have sworn Storm had felt the same way.

"Jasmine?" Summer's soft voice interrupted her pensive thoughts. She linked arms, pulling Jasmine close to her side. "You're trembling. Are you all right?"

Jasmine watched Storm's departure through the cemetery while trying to focus on her cousin's words. "It's just the wind, the cold. I'm fine, really."

Summer frowned. "You don't look fine. You look as though you've lost your best friend."

No, just a chance at something wonderful.

Summer followed the direction of her distracted gaze, her frown deepening. "Do you know that man?"

Jasmine bit her lip, hesitating before answering, uncertain what to say. Storm Hunter was Summer's uncle. Though Storm had left Whitehorn long before her birth, and had never bothered to contact her since, he was still her closest living relative on her father's side. She wasn't sure what Summer's reaction might be to his appearance.

Unable to lie to her cousin, Jasmine said, "That man was Storm Hunter, your uncle."

Summer flinched at the words. Her gaze startled, she looked across the cemetery grounds to the chapel's parking lot where Storm was climbing into his car. Pain and confusion filled her eyes. And Jasmine realized she wasn't the only woman feeling rejected.

Jasmine muttered an oath beneath her breath. Damn the man. Since arriving in Whitehorn, Storm Hunter had caused nothing but trouble for every single person his presence had touched.

Hadn't he done enough damage?

For her sake, as well as her family's, perhaps it would be best if he returned to where he'd come.

* * *

One hand clenching the steering wheel, Storm put the cemetery far behind him. With his free hand, he loosened his tie and wrenched it from the collar of his shirt. Fumbling blindly with the top button, he breathed a sigh of relief as it popped open. A suit and tie were his daily lawyer's uniform, but today the outfit felt as though it were choking him.

At least, that was the excuse he allowed himself for his agitated state. He refused to blame his foul mood on his reaction to seeing Jasmine again. He told himself that the white-hot flash of desire he'd felt had nothing to do with his quick departure from the cemetery. Nor did it have anything to do with the lingering conviction that somehow he and Jasmine were fated to be together. No, he wasn't running away. He'd merely accomplished what he'd set out to do—see for himself the family that had destroyed his life. The Kincaids.

Only, until he saw her standing alone amid the mourners, he'd forgotten that one of the Kincaids included a member of his own family. Summer Kincaid, his brother's only child.

Storm drove slowly through Whitehorn's downtown area, passing the police station and the movie theater. Down the street from the courthouse, he spotted the Hip Hop Café. Though it was too early for lunch, he didn't think he could face the four silent walls of his hotel room. He needed a place where he could go to unwind and not have to listen to the sound of his own guilty conscience.

He pulled into a space and parked the car. Tossing his suit coat into the back seat, he headed inside the café. A country tune by Garth Brooks greeted him at the door. A handful of patrons were scattered around the café, some at the counter, others in booths. Heads turned at his entrance. Curious glances followed him as he made his way to a booth in the back. Whether they were staring at him because he was a Native American or because he was overdressed for the lunchtime crowd, he wasn't sure.

Since arriving in Whitehorn, he hadn't felt an open hostility from any of its residents. Though he couldn't say he felt welcomed, either. Bigotry was alive and well across the country. Whitehorn was no worse or no better than any other town. No matter how much he'd like for it to be different, he would never be able to convert everyone to a world of complete acceptance.

A waitress with a bright smile and long blond hair pulled back into a ponytail, joined him at his booth. She plunked a menu down onto the Formica-topped table and set a coffee mug next to it. Without asking, she filled his cup to the brim with the steaming brew. "If you're looking for breakfast, you're half an hour too late. We've already got the grill set up for lunch."

Storm shook his head. "That's okay. Coffee's fine for now."

"Sure thing," she said with a nod. "My name's Janie. If you need anything else, just holler."

Storm watched as Janie made her way to the front counter. His mind drifted back to the haunting scene he'd witnessed at the cemetery. Other than Alice Brooks's histrionics, he had to admit the Kincaid family had seemed normal. They weren't the monsters he'd remembered them to be as a child.

For years he'd clung to his hatred of the Kincaid family like a lifeline, finding solace and strength in bitterness. He'd blamed them for Raven's unexplained disappearance, not wanting to believe that his brother would have abandoned him unless he'd felt he'd had no other choice. While Raven had talked little of his affair with Blanche Kincaid, Storm knew he'd been disturbed by Blanche's older brother, Jeremiah. Jeremiah had been the devil incarnate. He'd belittled Raven in public and had threatened him in private. There was little doubt in Storm's mind that Jeremiah Kincaid had played a role in Raven's death.

If only he could get the police to agree.

Storm picked up his mug, blew the steam off the top and took a sip of the hot coffee. Once the mystery behind his brother's death had been officially solved, he intended to be on the first plane back to Albuquerque. There was nothing here to keep him in Whitehorn.

Nothing but a family he'd turned his back on.

And a niece he did not know.

Storm set the mug back on the table. He stared at the clouds swirling across its cooling surface, as though searching for a way to soothe his guilt. In the days since he'd returned to Whitehorn, he'd seen Summer a handful of times. Always from a distance, never face-to-face.

He'd told himself he was waiting for the right moment to approach her. Only that moment had yet to come. Today he'd been just a few feet from finally meeting her. But as was too often the case, when it came to facing up to his personal responsibilities, he'd chosen the easy way out. He'd run.

Storm closed his eyes and took in a painful breath. For thirty years he'd lived with the thought that his brother had abandoned him. Wounded and betrayed, he'd purposefully distanced himself from the town and the people that had reminded him of his loss.

But now he knew the truth. Raven had died all those years ago.

Storm had run out of excuses to hide. His brother was gone for good. But Raven's daughter was still alive and

well. And she was his last link to the only person he'd
ever loved.

With a deep sigh, he opened his eyes. Glancing around
the café, he caught the eye of the blond-haired waitress.

Smiling, she strolled over to his booth. "Did you
change your mind about lunch?"

"No," he said, shaking his head. "I'd just like to pay
the bill."

"That's too bad," she said, tearing a page from her
receipt book and placing it on the table in front of him.
"Fried chicken's the special today. The cook fixes a
mean bird."

Storm gave a polite smile. "Thanks, but I'm not really
hungry. Maybe you could help me with something,
though. I'm looking for someone. Summer Kincaid. Do
you know her? Or where I might find her?"

"Summer? Sure, I know her. She's a doctor. Your best
bet at finding her would be at the Whitehorn Memorial
Hospital, or the clinic she runs at the Laughing Horse
Reservation. If you can't find her at either of those two
places, she's probably at home taking care of her baby
stepdaughter, Alyssa. Her number's in the phone book.
Only look under the name Nighthawk." The waitress
winked as she turned to leave. "She's a married lady
now."

Nighthawk. So Summer had married a Cheyenne. Despite being raised by the Kincaids, she'd chosen to live
her life with a Native American. He felt vindicated by
the thought.

He knew her name and how to reach her. Now all he
needed was the courage to call her.

Slowly, Jasmine replaced the receiver in its cradle.
Frowning, she stared at the phone. Summer had just

called. Shortly after Lyle Brooks's funeral, she'd received an unexpected call from her uncle, Storm Hunter.

He'd asked to meet with her. Summer had agreed.

Only, Gavin was busy and unable to be with her. Summer felt the need for family support at this initial meeting with her long lost uncle and had asked Jasmine to join her.

Jasmine bit her lip. She'd do anything for her cousin, and she'd felt honored that Summer had turned to her in her time of need. As the baby of the family, Jasmine had spent most of her life being taken care of, not caring for others. She'd longed for the chance to prove herself to be mature and responsible in her family's eyes. Finally she'd been given that chance.

If only Storm Hunter wasn't a part of the picture.

She dreaded the thought of seeing him again. She didn't know how much more humiliation she could take in one day. Even if he was Summer's uncle, the man was unforgivably rude.

"Jasmine, who was on the phone?"

She looked up to see her mother approaching the front desk. This afternoon Celeste looked more like her old self. A healthy flush colored her cheeks and dressed in a tea-colored tunic and loose-fitting pants, she looked relaxed and at ease for the first time in days. Jasmine hated the idea of disrupting her fleeting moment of peace. "It was Summer," she admitted.

"Summer? Is everything all right? The baby isn't sick, is she?"

"No, nothing like that…it's just—" She stopped, struggling to find the right words. Knowing there was no easy way to break the news, she said, "Storm Hunter called. He wants to meet with her."

The healthy color drained from Celeste's face. She sat

heavily on a tapestry-covered chair. "Oh, my. I knew it was only a matter of time before he'd seek her out. I suppose there's no avoiding it."

"He is her uncle," she reminded her mother.

"I know. Believe me, I know." Her hands shook as she brushed a strand of russet hair from her face. She took in a deep, cleansing breath, in through the nose, out through the mouth. "I only wish Summer didn't have to face him alone."

"She's not," Jasmine said carefully. "I'm going over to her house now. She's asked me to be with her when he arrives."

Her mother surged to her feet. "Absolutely not. I don't want you anywhere near that man."

Jasmine blinked, stunned by the outburst. "Mother, you can't be serious."

"I'm deadly serious. The man's a Hunter. He belongs to a family that has brought us nothing but heartache. I forbid you to see him."

"You forbid me?" Jasmine's voice rose in self-righteous indignation. Since she had returned to the B and B and had taken over all of the kitchen duties, her mother had been treating her as an adult, with respect and admiration. Having Celeste now treat her like a strong-willed teenager was devastating to her ego. "Mother, I'm not a child. I'm twenty-three years old. You can't send me to my room if I don't want to do what you tell me."

"Believe me, if I thought it would do any good, I'd try," her mother said, releasing an exasperated breath. "When it comes to men, you haven't paid attention to me in years. Not since you filled out your first training bra."

Jasmine rolled her eyes. "Mother, really, would you

listen to yourself? Since when have you been distrustful? Storm may be a Hunter, but so is Summer. Are we supposed to abandon her, just because you don't approve of the other half of her family?''

Celeste took in a sharp breath, seemingly shocked by the question. ''You know I'd never abandon Summer. I've raised her since she was just a baby. I love her as much as I love you and Cleo.'' She heaved a resigned sigh. ''If Summer needs our support, then we will give it to her.''

Jasmine felt the tension ease from her muscles. Finally, she told herself, they were making progress.

The thought had no more than surfaced when her mother threw another curve at her self-esteem. With her brow furrowed into a tight frown, Celeste said, ''But that doesn't mean it has to be you, Jasmine. Surely David or Cleo could be with Summer.''

''Mother,'' she said, her tone a warning note. ''I'm going to pretend you didn't suggest that.''

Jasmine was confused and hurt by her mother's sudden lack of confidence. She didn't understand what was wrong. Normally a very liberal, open-minded person, Celeste had raised her daughters to be free-spirited and independent. It wasn't like her to be so overly protective. But then again, Celeste hadn't been acting normal since the Hunter family had resurfaced in their lives. Jasmine truly doubted that, if she were to meet anyone but Storm Hunter, her mother would care.

''Mother, I love you,'' she said, struggling to remain calm, ''and I will always respect your concern and advice. But this time you're wrong. Summer needs me. And I'm going to help her, whether you approve or not.''

Without waiting for a reply, she gave her mother a quick hug goodbye and hurried out the door. Midway to her Jeep Wrangler, her heart was still pounding and the muscles in her legs felt like jelly. She'd never felt so awful. This was the first major disagreement she'd ever had with her mother. A disagreement over a man, of all things.

But not just any man, she told herself as she rested her hand on the door of her Jeep. A man whose mutual history had had such a devastating affect upon their family. Storm Hunter.

Three

"Are you sure you want to do this?" Jasmine asked. She studied the delicate lines of her cousin's pensive face as she rocked her stepdaughter, Alyssa, in her arms.

Summer didn't answer right away. Instead she glanced down at the sleeping child, her gaze softening. Jasmine envied the look of maternal pride shimmering in her dark brown eyes. Quietly Summer said, "Storm is the last of my father's family. It's time we finally met."

"Right," Jasmine said, not bothering to hide the doubtfulness from her tone. She glanced at her wristwatch for the second time in as many minutes. "If and when he shows up, that is."

Storm was late. He should have arrived thirty minutes ago. Jasmine wished she didn't have to voice the concern she knew Summer shared. That Storm had changed his mind. That he wasn't going to come, after all.

"He'll be here," Summer said, her voice firm with conviction.

Jasmine sighed. "I wish I could be as certain of this meeting as you are. I'm not sure I'd be quite as forgiving of an uncle who'd ignored my existence for twenty-nine years."

"I'm sure he had his reasons, Jasmine. What matters is that he's making the effort now," Summer murmured. She stood, gathering Alyssa close. "I need to put Alyssa in bed for her nap. I won't be long."

Jasmine nodded, resisting the urge to sigh again. Instead she rose to her feet and began pacing the floor. Her protective instincts billowed inside her. She swore, if Storm Hunter didn't show up after putting her cousin through all this turmoil, the man would have to answer to her.

She stopped, frowning as she reconsidered the threat. For some reason she didn't picture Storm as a man who answered to anyone, let alone an irate woman who barely stood higher than his chin.

The doorbell rang, jarring her out of her skeptical thoughts. Jasmine jumped at the sound, her stomach knotting with unwanted tension. She took in a quick breath and released it with a whoosh, trying to relieve some of her pent-up anxiety. She was being ridiculous, she chided herself. Summer was the one who should be nervous, not her.

Speaking of whom…where was Summer? Jasmine glanced down the hall and saw no sign of her cousin. Swallowing hard at the lump of trepidation that had stuck in her throat, she forced herself to move. Her hand shook as she reached for the knob. Pasting a polite smile on her face, she opened the door to greet the newcomer.

Storm's brooding scowl stopped her. With a quick glance that grazed her from head to toe, he demanded, "Where's Summer? I was expecting your cousin, not you."

Jasmine's smile faded to a grimace. Through clenched teeth, she said, "Hello to you, too, Mr. Hunter. Your presence is as pleasant as usual."

The sarcasm was lost on this stony-faced man. He half turned from the door, looking ready to escape. Given the choice, Jasmine had no doubt that he wouldn't want to find himself alone with her. If he were, he just might have to explain his own imprudent behavior. As in, why he had kissed her, then run the day before.

Swinging his gaze back to her, he said impatiently, "Is Summer here or not?"

"Yes, she's here. She's putting the baby down for a nap." Jasmine stepped away from the door, motioning for him to enter. "Won't you come in, Mr. Hunter? I'm feeling a bit of a chill in the air."

He ignored the jab. Instead he strode past her, without a second glance, leaving behind a familiar whiff of musky cologne. The scent triggered a sensory overload in Jasmine's fickle mind, setting her nerve endings on instant alert, reminding her just how good it had felt to be held close in his arms. Oblivious to her wavering thoughts, he let his gaze travel around the living room, taking in the carpet, the painted stucco walls, and the framed photos of family scattered around. Wryly, she noted that he looked everywhere, but at her.

The silence lengthened between them, the tension in the room growing thicker by the second.

Jasmine crossed her arms at her waist, sent him an impudent glance and did nothing to lessen his unease. Admittedly she took an undeniably wicked pleasure in his discomfort. Considering his own rude behavior, she told herself, Storm was one man who deserved to squirm under pressure.

Summer breezed into the room. "Jasmine, I thought I heard the doorbell. Who was—" She stopped to stare at Storm, the look in her eye one of surprised uncertainty.

Jasmine felt a new surge of protectiveness at Summer's presence. No matter how angry she might be at Storm, she refused to let her own feelings cause her cousin any awkwardness. She stumbled over an attempt to ease the situation. "Summer, this is your uncle...Storm Hunter. Storm, this is Summer."

For a long moment neither Storm nor Summer spoke. They simply looked at each other, their gazes frank and assessing. There was no denying a resemblance. They shared the same high cheekbones, the large, dark brown eyes and the sculpted features. Summer had definitely inherited her dark beauty from the Hunter side of the family.

Summer was the first to find her voice. She gave her uncle a heartwarming smile. "Welcome to my home, Storm."

He gave a genuine smile in return. The transformation was remarkable, surprising Jasmine. The grim set of his face was softened by a tenderness she had no idea he was capable of showing. Grudgingly she acknowledged that perhaps there was reason to hope a caring man lived beneath that gruff exterior, after all.

"Won't you sit down?" Summer asked, motioning in the direction of the couch.

"Yes, thank you," Storm said. He took a seat. Then, frowning, he glanced meaningfully from his niece to Jasmine.

Taking the obvious hint, sensing that it was time for the two of them to be alone, Jasmine searched her mind for an excuse. "Why don't I make us some tea?"

Summer turned a startled look her way.

Reaching out and squeezing her cousin's arm, she murmured a brief reassurance before leaving the room. "I won't be long. I'll be in the kitchen if you need me."

Summer nodded, still looking uncertain.

Jasmine lingered in the doorway. She waited long enough to see Summer take her seat next to her uncle on the couch. The smiles on both of their faces and the soft murmur of their voices eased her qualms. She had no reason to fear leaving Summer alone with Storm. He appeared as anxious as her cousin to make this initial meeting as comfortable as possible.

In the kitchen, she put the teakettle on a low heat, giving it ample time to boil. Gathering cups and saucers, she arranged a tray that would have made her mother proud. For good measure, she even threw in a plate of cookies that she'd found in the cupboard.

After several long minutes had passed, she returned to the living room to rejoin her cousin. From the expression on Summer's face, the meeting was a success. She wore a look of utter joy, and her dark eyes glimmered with unshed tears of emotion.

Even Storm appeared moved by the encounter. His intense gaze never left Summer's face. He seemed fascinated by everything she had to say. At the moment she was talking fondly of her husband, Gavin Nighthawk.

"Gavin was so disappointed that he was unable to be here today. He's anxious to meet you."

Jasmine set the tray on the coffee table and began to fill the cups with tea.

"I'd like to meet him also," Storm said, an undeniable ring of sincerity in his deep voice. "Perhaps we should arrange another meeting soon?"

"Why not tonight?" Summer suggested, her enthusiasm bubbling. "I'm sure I could find a baby-sitter. We can go out for dinner. Give ourselves a chance to relax and talk without worrying about Alyssa interrupting us." A worried frown touched her brow as she glanced anxiously at Storm. "That is, unless you have other plans."

His smile was one of patient indulgence. "No, not at all. Dinner tonight sounds like a wonderful idea. I'll look forward to it."

Summer's own smile returned. She glanced at Jasmine. "And, of course, Jasmine will have to join us. Then we'll be an even four for dinner."

"D-dinner…tonight?" Jasmine stammered. She nearly dropped the teacup in surprise. Her gaze flew to Storm's stunned face. He appeared almost as pleased as she was by the unexpected invitation. Obviously he wanted her to say no. "I—I don't know, Summer."

"Jasmine, please," Summer persisted, a silent plea in her eyes. "I won't take no for an answer."

"It is late notice, Summer. I'm sure Jasmine has made other plans," Storm said, smoothly providing her with a way out.

Jasmine glanced at him sharply, wary of any sort of helpful overture on his part. His expression had shifted from one of surprise to one of complacent smugness. He looked so damned certain that she was going to refuse Summer's invitation.

If she had half a brain, that was exactly what she should do. After all, what woman in her right mind would want to spend any more time than necessary with a man who was rude, overbearing and impossible to deal with?

But no one ever said Jasmine was smart when it came to dealing with men. Instead, as was too often the case, she let her emotions override her good judgment. Before she had a chance to reconsider, she smiled brightly and blurted, "Dinner tonight? Sounds good to me. Just tell me when and where."

For that one moment in time, Jasmine decided, the vexed look on Storm's face was almost worth the misery she'd surely suffer tonight. If only she knew how she'd explain to her mother that her dinner partner was to be Storm Hunter.

* * *

Later that evening, feeling the need to vent some pent-up tension, Storm decided to walk to the restaurant. Neela's, the restaurant, was only a few blocks from his hotel room. A short distance, one that would only take minutes to accomplish. Besides, he could use the exercise. The last few days he'd spent too many hours cooped up in his hotel room on the phone, handling his law practice in New Mexico via long distance.

With the sun down, a chill had settled over the town. The cool night air felt invigorating. He breathed deeply, welcoming its mind-clearing embrace. The longer he was in Whitehorn, the more confused he seemed to become. He didn't understand what was happening to him.

Normally he was a man who prided himself on complete control of his emotions. But now, if he wasn't losing his temper at some incompetent police officer involved in his brother's murder investigation, he was mooning over a woman. One particular woman, that is. Jasmine Monroe.

She was driving him crazy. No matter how hard he tried to avoid her, she kept popping up wherever he went. If he were a superstitious man, he'd say it was fate's way of telling him they were meant to be together. An idea that, considering the troubled history their families shared, was utterly ridiculous.

Even worse, he seemed to be enjoying their chance encounters. Whenever she was near, he felt energized. She challenged him on a level that went beyond a mere physical attraction. Despite her youthfulness, she was smart, witty and totally unpredictable. No woman had ever made him feel the way she did. Whether it was trading barbs, or simply staring into her large, doelike green eyes, he looked forward to being with her.

Before he was ready, he arrived at his destination. Reluctantly, he stepped out of the night's soothing darkness and into the harsh lights of the restaurant. Neela's, as Summer had explained to him, was a cut above the Hip Hop Café. Owned and operated by a fellow Cheyenne, Neela Tallbear, it was comfortable yet classy, boasting a rough-hewn plank flooring and polished wood tables. As a French-trained chef, Neela had made locally grown beef her specialty. The restaurant had quickly grown in popularity, often becoming crowded.

Storm, as he soon realized, was the last of his party to arrive.

Seated at the table was his niece, Summer, and a fit-looking Native American man, whom he presumed to be her husband, Gavin Nighthawk. And last, but not least, was his dinner partner for the evening, Jasmine.

Dressed in a simple, sleeveless burgundy dress that emphasized the darkness of her hair and the paleness of her skin, she took his breath away. No matter how hard he'd tried to fight it, the pull of attraction was just as strong now as it had been the first moment he'd met her.

Storm felt as though he were fighting a losing battle.

Gratefully, he hid his unease behind the polite motions of an introduction to the man who had married his niece. He studied Gavin Nighthawk as they shook hands. Gavin's grip was strong, self-assured. He wore his hair short, anglo-style. His taste in clothes was casual yet expensive. From what Summer had told him, he was a surgeon who split his time between work at the Whitehorn hospital and the clinic on Laughing Horse Reservation. While his features were that of a Cheyenne, he appeared to be a man comfortable with the white man's ways.

Frowning thoughtfully, Storm took his seat as he realized that he and Gavin Nighthawk had much in common.

As he settled himself at the table, his knees bumped against a pair of smooth, silky legs. An electrical shock of awareness traveled up his thigh. He glanced at Jasmine as she sucked in a sharp breath and shifted in her seat, her actions telling him what he already knew. She'd been the owner of those slender legs.

"Summer tells me you're a lawyer," Gavin said, unaware of the sensual undercurrents traveling between Storm and Jasmine.

"That's right, I've set up a practice in Albuquerque."

Gavin nodded. "That's quite a way from home."

Storm's muscles tensed defensively at the remark. "New Mexico is my home. I've lived there for almost thirty years."

"I meant, from your family here in Whitehorn, those still living on the Laughing Horse Reservation," Gavin said. He placed a protective hand over Summer's, his meaning clear, his expression unapologetic.

Storm hesitated before answering. Obviously he'd misjudged Gavin. His ties to life on the reservation were still strong. His loyalty to Summer, unquestionable.

He didn't blame Gavin for being protective of Summer. If the roles were reversed and someone he cared for was faced with a relative who, after almost three decades, decided he wanted to establish a newfound relationship, he'd question the man's motives, also.

Aware of Jasmine sitting next to him, her gaze curious, Storm quietly said, "I was thirteen when I left Whitehorn. At the time the reasons for going seemed compelling. There have been many times that I wished I had reconsidered my decision. But, as we all know, what is done is done. No man can change the past."

"No, but they can change the future," Gavin murmured, lacing his fingers with Summer's. "I'm curious.

Why did you choose New Mexico to work, instead of Montana?"

Because New Mexico was as far as he could run away from Whitehorn without leaving the country in which he'd been born, he admitted to himself. Out loud, however, he said, "There were many more opportunities in New Mexico. I was able to put myself through school and earn my law degree. Even now I find the work in Albuquerque challenging."

"That's too bad," Gavin said with an even smile. "We could use a good lawyer here on the reservation. Jackson Hawk is the tribal attorney at Laughing Horse. Now that he's assumed the duties of tribal leader, he's having a hard time juggling both jobs."

Again, Storm hesitated. He'd heard of the tribal leader's burdensome schedule firsthand, from Jackson Hawk himself. Jackson had been a childhood friend. Recently they'd reconnected when he'd tracked down Storm to tell him of the discovery of Raven's remains. Since his arrival in Whitehorn, Jackson had already made a play to convince Storm to return to Laughing Horse, using guilt as his tool of choice.

Now, in the presence of his last remaining family, Storm had no intention of showing any false interest in returning to a life that had caused him nothing but pain. He'd made his choice to leave the reservation many years before. He saw no reason to change his mind now.

As though sensing his growing discomfort, Summer released an impatient breath. "Gavin, please. Just because you've returned to the reservation and have accepted the ways of our people, that doesn't mean you need to pressure everyone else into doing the same." Her eyes twinkled with undisguised mischief. "Give Storm some time. Perhaps he'll change his mind on his own."

Gavin laughed, a deep hearty laugh that chased away any tension that remained between the men. "Forgive me, Storm. I've become something of a zealot, when it comes to talking about the res. Summer tells me you've done pro bono work for the Navajos in New Mexico. And that you've taken on some civil liberty cases. Tell me about them."

For the next hour, between ordering their dinners and tackling their food, Storm, Gavin and Summer embarked on a lively discussion on the right and wrong ways to help their people. A conversation that revolved totally upon the world of the Native American.

During this time, Jasmine remained noticeably silent.

Storm tried not to feel guilty. While he hadn't set out to exclude her from the conversation, he hadn't made an effort to include her, either. Though she seemed to listen with polite interest, he wondered if she felt bored, or uncomfortable. He almost wished she did.

It would reinforce what he'd known all along. That they were from two entirely different worlds. Jasmine from the privileged world of the white man. Himself from the hard, struggling life of a Native American. It wasn't surprising that they would be unable to relate to each other on an everyday basis.

Just as they'd finished ordering dessert, Gavin's pager went off. Unclipping it from his belt, he held it up to the light and glanced at the number. "It's the clinic."

Before the words were out of his mouth, Summer's pager chirped a warning beat. Frowning, she said, "The clinic's paging me, also. If they want us both, there must be an emergency." She sighed as she rose to her feet and joined her husband, looking from Storm to Jasmine for understanding. "I'm sorry for leaving so early. But we really must go."

"Don't be silly, Summer," Jasmine assured her, breaking her silence. "Of course, you have to leave."

"I enjoyed the dinner, and our discussion. I hope we'll be able to spend more time together before I return to New Mexico," Storm said, surprised to realize he'd meant the polite words. He scooted his chair back and started to rise to his feet, preparing to leave.

"Stay," Summer insisted, shooing him back to his seat. "Just because Gavin and I have to miss dessert, that doesn't mean you must, too. Finish your coffee, eat your apple pie. Enjoy yourselves. There's no need to rush off."

Slowly, Storm returned to his seat. He glanced at Jasmine, sitting next to him. If she felt uncomfortable at the prospect of being alone with him, she gave no outward sign.

Instead she focused her attention on saying goodbye to her cousin. It wasn't until they were finally alone that she turned her head to look at him. If he thought she would remain the shy, retiring woman who'd said little for the past hour, he'd been wrong. Her cool, confident gaze sent a shiver of trepidation down his spine.

Leaning an elbow on the table, her chin resting on the palm of her hand, she looked him in the eye and said, "So, tell me, Mr. Hunter, what sort of game do you think you're playing?"

"Game?" Storm sat back in his chair and studied her carefully. "I assure you, Ms. Monroe, I don't know what you're talking about."

She raised a finely sculpted brow. "Don't you?"

Not trusting himself to answer, he raised his hands in mock surrender, feigning a confusion he did not possess. "Really, I haven't a clue."

She ran a slender finger over the rim of her water glass

as she considered his response, the action catching his attention. Finally, without so much as a blink of an eye, she said, "You kissed me yesterday. An unexpected experience, yes, but special, nonetheless. Both of us seemed to have enjoyed ourselves. Since that time, however, you've been avoiding me. I'd like to know why."

Storm's breath caught at her bluntness. Taken aback, once again, by her penchant for complete honesty, he was at a loss as to how to answer. The truth was, she scared the hell out of him. The kiss they'd shared had been more than special. It had been magical. An experience he'd like to sample again and again. But he'd be damned if he was going to admit that much to her.

Buying himself time while he thought of a way out of this tenuous situation, he lifted a hand and motioned for the waitress. When the heavy, round-faced Cheyenne woman arrived at their table, he said curtly, "We're finished. I'd like the check."

The waitress blinked in surprise. "But what about dessert? I was just about ready to bring out the pies—"

"We've changed our mind," he said, refusing to look at Jasmine for her reaction. "You can add the cost to the bill, but we won't be staying to eat them."

The waitress heaved a tired sigh and shook her head. "Yes, sir, whatever you want."

Flipping through her receipt book, she totaled up the cost of dinner and handed him the check. Without looking at the amount, Storm handed her his credit card, not wishing to delay his departure a minute longer than necessary.

Raising a brow, the waitress said, "I'll run this through the machine. Be back in a jiffy."

With that, he was alone once again with Jasmine. And he realized he could no longer avoid what must be done.

Once and for all he must make it clear to her that there was no possibility of a relationship between them. There were too many obstacles standing in their way.

Whatever means he must take, it was Jasmine's turn to be scared away.

Leaning forward in his chair, keeping his tone confidential, he said, "I'd be careful what I ask for if I were you. You might not want to know the answer."

A slow smile stole across her beautiful, exotic face. "And what is that supposed to mean?"

"It means, my dear Jasmine, that you are just a child," he said, keeping his voice smooth and silky, like a caress. "And I am a man of many, many experiences. The kiss that we shared was nothing compared to the things I know to please a woman. And you, little one, are nowhere near ready to handle what I can do for you."

The smile faded. Her lips parted in a silent gasp of surprise. She looked...stunned.

Satisfied, Storm rose to his feet. Tipping his hand in mock salute, he turned and left, not daring to glance back at the woman he was leaving behind, lest he changed his mind.

Her mouth still drooping in surprise, Jasmine stared after Storm's departing figure. He moved through the crowded restaurant with the primal grace of a predator. With his wide shoulders and narrow hips, he reminded her of a sleek mountain cat, coiled and ready to spring into attack.

Suddenly the room felt as though the heat had been cranked up by at least twenty degrees. Feeling flushed, on a shaky breath, she murmured, "Oh, my."

The waitress chose that moment to return. She glanced at Storm's empty chair. "What happened to tall, dark and in-a-hurry?"

Jasmine's face warmed with embarrassment. "He had to leave."

"What am I supposed to do with his credit card?" She held up the gold card for Jasmine's inspection. Its shiny surface glittered beneath the muted lights of the restaurant.

The slow smile returned. Jasmine told herself he may be cool and collected on the outside, but Storm Hunter wasn't as in control of his emotions as he'd like for her to believe. She held out a hand for the forgotten card. "I'll take that."

The waitress frowned, looking uncertain. "I don't know. The restaurant policy is—"

"Mr. Hunter and I are close friends, practically family," she assured her, giving the woman what she hoped was a most sincere look. "His niece is my cousin."

"Family, huh?" the waitress asked, her gaze skeptical.

Jasmine nodded. "Family."

"Well, okay." Reluctantly, she handed Jasmine the card. "The bill's still going on his account, with or without his signature."

"I'll be sure to tell him that. Just as soon as I see him again."

Anxious to leave, Jasmine scooted her chair back. Her legs felt wobbly as she stood. The sound of her heart pounded so hard in her ears, she could barely hear the voices of the restaurant patrons around her. Gathering her sweater, she hurried for the exit.

Storm was a man who obviously had pressing things weighing on his mind, proof of which was resting in her hand. She hadn't bought his Casanova routine. Beneath that cool exterior, she sensed there was a man with deep emotions just waiting to be tapped.

It was time she found out if she was right.

Four

Jasmine's heels clicked against the concrete floor, echoing in the quiet night, sounding much too loud in the walkway of the dimly lit hotel. Her stomach fluttered with a mixture of anticipation and trepidation. Thanks to the help of a former classmate working the front desk, she'd learned the room where Storm was staying. Now she just needed the courage to follow through with her decision to find him.

Shakily she inhaled a calming breath. Never before had she had the nerve to follow a man to his hotel room. Especially not a man as overwhelming as Storm Hunter. Defiance, pure and simple, had brought her here. Earlier, before abandoning her at the restaurant, Storm had told her in no uncertain terms that she was a child. And that he was too much man for her to handle. She was determined to prove him wrong.

Only, what if she was the one who was wrong? If sitting next to him in a crowded restaurant had the power to set her pulse racing and her blood warming, goodness only knew what would happen when they were alone. Especially with no one but herself to save her from his obvious charms. A tiny sliver of excitement traveled down her spine, setting second thoughts tumbling around in her confused mind.

Too soon, Room 147 came into sight. Jasmine slowed her pace. She swallowed hard at the lump in her throat as she studied the black numbers on the faded gray door. Gathering her flagging courage, forcing herself to move, she lifted a trembling hand to knock.

Seconds seemed like hours before Storm answered the door. The shocked look on his face was almost worth the butterflies dancing in her stomach. Taking advantage of his stunned state, she eyed him from head to toe. Sans jacket, he still wore the lightweight black sweater and the pleated charcoal gray pants from dinner, both of which emphasized his dark coloring, the width of his shoulders and the slenderness of his hips.

He looked dangerously handsome.

Storm's expression slowly changed. Impatience replaced his surprise. He glared at her, his face darkening with ill-temper. "What are you doing here?"

Jasmine winced inwardly. Not quite the welcome greeting she'd hoped for.

"What I'm doing is a favor for you. Though I doubt if you'll be grateful," she said, her calm voice belying her jittery nerves. The gold credit card glittered in the light streaming out from the door of his room as she held it up for his inspection. "Remember this?"

Recognition flickered in his dark eyes.

A satisfied smile stole across her face. "It would seem this time *I've* got something that belongs to *you.*"

With an irritated breath, he reached for the card.

Jasmine sidestepped his attempt to reclaim his property. Instead she brushed past him into the room, her body sizzling wherever they touched. The musky scent of his cologne filled her nostrils, making her light-headed. Second thoughts pushed their way into her mind, forcing her to reconsider her actions.

What in the world was she thinking? Did she have any idea what she was getting herself into?

Ignoring the nagging voice of reason, she continued her single-minded trek until she stood in the middle of the room, inches from the king-size bed. Only then did she turn to look at him.

His hands on his hips, he stared at her in disbelief. His big body dwarfed the small room, making him appear even more formidable. The scowl on his face did little to settle her qualms of uncertainty. Finally, his voice deep and forbidding, he said, "There must be a misunderstanding. I don't recall inviting you inside."

She forced a smile. "Well, now that I'm here, I think it'd be a perfect time for us to continue our discussion."

"There's nothing more we have to say to each other, Ms. Monroe."

"Wrong again, Mr. Hunter." Her attempt at a light-hearted chuckle sounded strained even to her own ears. "You do have a tendency to jump to the wrong conclusions, don't you?"

His eyes narrowed. "When have I been wrong?"

"Lots of times. This evening, for one. You said you were a man of many…" Her voice caught beneath the strain of his unwavering gaze. Nervously, she licked her lips, then plunged on. "Of many experiences. And that I wasn't old enough to handle someone like you. Well, I beg to differ. I may look young, but I assure you, I'm old enough. I'm not scared of you, Mr. Hunter. No matter how hard you try to frighten me away."

He raised one dark brow. "Are you sure you're not scared?"

She shook her head, not trusting herself to answer.

With exaggerated care, he closed the door. His eyes never leaving her face, he stepped toward her. "I want you to be absolutely certain, Jasmine."

He spoke her name slowly, softly, drawing it out like

a caress. She shivered, feeling as though he'd physically touched her.

"Because in another moment," he said as he narrowed the distance between them, "it'll be too late to change your mind."

The hairs on the back of her neck lifted. Goose bumps speckled her skin, her body's way of warning her what her heart didn't want to accept. Despite all of her blustering to the contrary, she knew she wasn't ready to deal with someone as sensuous and as strong-willed as Storm Hunter.

Before she could give voice to her second thoughts, he was standing in front of her. She felt frozen to the spot, unable to move, watching him. Gently he lifted a hand and stroked her face with the knuckles of his fingers, letting them travel down her cheek, her chin, stopping only to settle at the slender column of her throat.

Shockwaves of desire coursed through her body. She closed her eyes and gasped at the shuddering impact of his soft touch.

The sound shattered the strained silence.

Suddenly the mood shifted, letting the pent-up gates of tension explode wide open. A primal growl of frustration sounded low in Storm's throat. With a ragged breath, he slipped his fingers behind her neck and pulled her roughly toward him.

Her hands were caught between them, pinned against the solid strength of his body. She felt winded, her breath stolen by the quickness of his actions.

Before she could protest, he took her mouth with a savageness that both scared and aroused her. His kiss was hot, possessive. Impatiently he stroked her lips with his tongue, forcing her to open to his demands. She was unable to stop him. He plundered and took with a fierceness that sent heat and awareness throbbing through her.

His big hands slid up and down the length of her body, grazing her breasts, cupping her derriere. Her sweater slid from her shoulders, falling in a silken puddle to the floor. Pulling her snug against him, she felt the hardness of his body, the strength of his arousal. His touch was intimate, turning her muscles to jelly and setting her blood on fire. She clung to him, feeling weak with undeniable desire.

But this wasn't what she'd intended.

She'd thought her first time with Storm, with any man for that matter, would be different. She had wanted it to be special, not a groping match in a hotel room. The embrace felt wrong, sullied in its intent.

"No," she whispered, dragging her mouth from his. Knowing she'd been the catalyst to this onslaught of passion, she turned her head, unable to meet his gaze. Greedily, he took advantage. His lips brushed her neck, nibbling the sensitive spot behind her ear. His breath felt hot against her skin, his tongue warm and moist. Her body trembled at his probing caress.

Shamed by her lack of willpower, she tried to push him away. But she couldn't find the strength to accomplish the task.

He seemed unaware of her change of heart, holding her tighter, his hands growing even bolder. He fumbled with the top snap of her dress.

Desire and fear rose up inside her as she heard the rasp of her zipper. She felt torn by the clashing emotions, weakened by her own inability to think, or to act. Finally, a whimper of a plea escaped her lips. "Storm, stop... please, stop."

* * *

Through the firestorm of passion crackling in his ears, he barely heard the soft whisper of her voice.

"No, Storm. Not now, not like this."

As if drugged by the intoxicating lure of her body, he struggled with his own desires. He forced himself to pull away, to put an unwanted distance between them. His body burned, aching with a need for release. With the loss of her body heat, cool air slapped against his hot skin, chilling him, making him realize just how close he'd come to losing complete control.

Even now, as he stared down at her and saw the evidence of his mindless assault, he knew he still teetered on the edge of repeating his lapse in judgment. Her lips were red and swollen, her hair and makeup mussed, her clothes rumpled. She was trembling. Self-consciously she wrapped her arms around her waist and held herself tightly. She looked so young, so far out of her element.

Jasmine had taken him up on his challenge. Wisely or not, she'd come here to prove herself mature enough to handle him. He'd intended to teach her a lesson. To show her that there was a difference between tempting a man and a boy. Only the lesson had backfired. He'd been the one to be seduced. Holding her in his arms, he'd lost all sense of restraint. If she hadn't stopped him...

Storm clenched his jaw against the anger rising up inside him. Anger directed more at himself than at her. No matter how bold she'd been in coming here, he should have known she wasn't prepared for what had happened. She was just a child, a scared, frightened child. And instead of sending her packing out the door, he'd taken advantage of her naiveté.

"I warned you," he said, unable to keep the accusation from his voice. Remorse made his tone bitter. "I told you you weren't ready."

"Not for this. I didn't know—" Her voice broke as she looked up at him. Moist tears filled her big green eyes. Her chin trembled as she struggled for composure. "I hadn't expected—"

"To be treated like a woman?" The corner of his mouth lifted into a sardonic grin. "What did you expect when you came here to my hotel room, Jasmine? That I'd be a gentleman? That I'd treat you like a prom queen? With kid gloves and genteel manners?"

Her face flushed a deep rosy hue.

"I'm not one of your wet-behind-the-ear suitors." His cynical smile faded. "Or did you forget? I'm an Indian. Honor isn't supposed to be high on my list of qualities, is it?"

Before she could answer, he moved to step around her, heading for the door. As he brushed past, she flinched, shrinking away from him. Storm's heart tightened at the fear he saw in her eyes.

Not allowing himself to reconsider, he threw open the door and turned to face her. "I warned you I wasn't to be trusted," he said, the words harsh even to his own ears. "Now run, Jasmine. Run before I change my mind and take what you were so willing to offer."

Blinking back tears of shame and embarrassment, she refused to look at him. Instead, with her eyes downcast, she stumbled to the door and escaped into the night.

For a long moment he stood in the doorway and listened to the rapid click of her heels as she ran down the walkway from his room. He listened until the distant taps faded to a dull and painful memory. Then he closed the door and leaned against its solid strength.

Shutting his eyes, he sighed wearily. He'd made such a mess of things. From the very beginning, Jasmine had been nothing but honest about her feelings toward him.

Instead of returning the favor, he'd used those feelings against her. He'd been too afraid to face his own emotions. Too afraid to admit that he might be attracted to her.

Like a bully, he'd used his size and brute strength to frighten her. As a result, he'd destroyed the self-confidence of a woman who'd shown him nothing but respect. Ironically, Jasmine was the only person in town who hadn't treated him like a specter from the past.

His heart thumped a hollow beat against his chest. Opening his eyes, he glanced around the room, forcing himself to face the scene of his own crime. He frowned as he spotted something white on the floor in the middle of the mauve carpeting. He pushed himself away from the door.

It was Jasmine's sweater.

Reluctantly, he picked it up and held it in his hands. The delicate material felt silky, cool to his touch, reminding him of Jasmine's smooth skin. Burying his face in the sweater's softness, he inhaled its sweet floral scent and felt as though he were still holding her close in his arms.

A sharp and jagged pain jigsawed through his heart as he realized what a fool he had been. Even now he couldn't admit the truth, just how much he had wanted her to stay.

He hadn't wanted to let her go.

Gravel spewed from the tires of Jasmine's Jeep as she made the turn too quickly into the long driveway of the Big Sky Bed & Breakfast. Easing up on the gas pedal, she told herself to slow down. That no matter how much she wanted to she couldn't run away from what had just happened.

Her headlights cut a narrow beam through the thick darkness. She shivered as cool, crisp air poured in through the open window. A complete and utter stillness filled the night, doing little to quiet the troubling thoughts echoing in her head.

There was no denying she'd made a fool of herself over a man. Not just any man, but Storm Hunter. A man who held her entire family in such disdain.

She gave a bittersweet smile. Well, she'd certainly done little to change his opinion of her. Or the Kincaid clan, for that matter. If anything, she'd given him even more reason to believe the worst of them. He'd made her feel like a spoiled child who couldn't handle not getting her own way.

Once again Jasmine felt the tears well up in her eyes. She pounded a fist against the steering wheel, refusing to give them release. Her feminine pride wouldn't allow the show of weakness.

Silently she vowed no man would ever make her cry.

A light shone from the front porch of the B and B. Upstairs, the guest rooms were dark, their occupants asleep for the night. Navigating her Jeep around to the side of the house, she parked and let herself in the back door.

Thankfully, the kitchen was empty. At the moment she didn't think she could face her mother. She was in no mood for another lecture. Slipping off her heels, she tip-toed through the dark and silent house. Midway up the stairs to the third floor, a loose board creaked beneath her weight. She froze, straining her ears for signs of life.

The house remained quiet.

Relieved, she continued upstairs, longing for a soak in a hot tub. After her encounter with Storm, she felt dirty, soiled. Disappointment rested heavily against her heart, making it hard to draw a breath. Disappointment not because of what had happened, but because of what hadn't.

Despite everything, she couldn't shake the feeling that she and Storm had missed a chance at something special. Perhaps it was just wishful thinking on her part, but she still believed they were meant to be together.

Wearily, she moved past her sister Cleo's empty bedroom. The light shining from beneath her mother's door told her she wasn't asleep. Guiltily, instead of stopping to say good-night, she continued on. Jasmine took only two steps past before her mother's door swung open, startling her. In the swath of light coming from the room, her mother stood in the doorway, wrapped in a cream-colored dressing gown.

"Jasmine, it's late." Concern laced her mother's voice. "Where have you been?"

Instinctively, Jasmine backed away from the light, unwilling to let her mother see her disheveled appearance. "Dinner, Mother. I told you I was going to meet Summer—"

"Summer called nearly an hour ago. She wanted to make sure you'd gotten home all right. And to apologize for having to cut dinner short."

Jasmine nearly moaned in dismay. Earlier this evening she'd told her mother she'd be dining with Summer and Gavin. Not wanting to upset her mother further, she hadn't mentioned her other dinner companion, Storm. Now, barring another lie of omission, she had no excuse for her tardiness.

"Is anything wrong, Jasmine? Why are you hovering in the dark? Come closer, where I can see you."

Reluctantly, Jasmine stepped forward.

Her mother's sharp gaze scanned her from head to toe, lingering on her mussed hair, her swollen lips and rum-

pled dress. With a tsk, she shook her head. "You've been
with that man, haven't you?"

"'That man'?" Used to her open-mindedness and free
thinking, Jasmine was stunned by the condemnation in
her mother's tone. "He has a name, Mother. It's Storm
Hunter."

"I know his name. I know all about him and his fam-
ily," she said, her voice quavering, her expression hard.
"I told you to stay away from him. He's too old for you,
Jasmine."

"Too old? Mother, I can't believe you'd mean that."

"I refuse to argue with you." Celeste turned from the
doorway. In a flurry of cotton and lace, she swept across
the carpeted length of her bedroom floor.

Reluctantly, Jasmine followed her inside.

Candles lined the fireplace, setting shadows dancing
against the floral-and-striped wallpaper. The pungent
scent of incense spiced the air, telling her that her mother
had once again been calling upon the spiritual world for
guidance.

"Why can't you understand?" Celeste demanded, calling her attention. "It would never work between the two
of you. You and Storm come from two entirely different
worlds."

"Surely you don't mean because he's a Native American?"

"No, of course not," Celeste said impatiently. She
stopped, narrowing a gaze to study her. "I'm talking
about life experiences. You're so young, Jasmine. He's
nearly twice your age. Is it any wonder that I'd be concerned?"

"Mother, really." Jasmine sighed. First Storm. Now
her mother. When would everyone stop bringing up her
age as though it were a handicap? "I'm not a child. Nor

am I completely inexperienced. You know as well as I do that I've been dating since I was sixteen.''

"You've dated men your own age. That isn't the same as seeing a man as old as Storm Hunter.''

"No, it isn't. It's better.'' Ignoring her mother's shocked expression, she added, "Mother, I've never felt the way I do when I'm with Storm. Not with any other man. You're right. He is different. But not in a bad way.''

Her mother's hand shook as she raised it to her throat. She looked stricken. "I don't want to hear this. How can you even consider a relationship with him? There's too dark a history between the Hunters and the Kincaids. It wasn't all that long ago that his brother's affair with my sister nearly destroyed my family. I lost my sister because of Raven Hunter. I won't stand by and let it happen again.''

"Mother, that was another time, and another place. Prejudices of the past stood in Raven and Blanche's way, not their love for each other. Blanche died from complications of childbirth. There wasn't anything anyone could have done. It wasn't Storm's fault. Nor was it Raven's—''

"Stop!'' Celeste's eyes took on a wide-eyed fearfulness that Jasmine had never seen before. "I don't want to talk about Raven. I just want you to promise me that you'll never see Storm again.''

Jasmine stared at her, too stunned to speak. Finally, after a long moment, she shook her head and said, "It's too late, Mother. You don't need to worry. None of this really matters, anyway.''

Celeste frowned. "What are you talking about?''

"I'm talking about Storm...and me.'' The ever-present tears filled her eyes. With a humorless laugh, she raked a hand through her short, cropped hair. "You're too late with your advice, Mother. Storm has made it perfectly clear that he isn't interested in me. In fact after tonight I doubt if he'll ever want to see me again.''

Her mother took a step toward her. "Jasmine, I'm sorry—"

"No, Mother." Jasmine held up a hand, stopping her. "I don't want to hear any words of sympathy. I wouldn't believe them, anyway."

Celeste blinked, looking wounded by the accusation. "Jasmine, you're not being fair."

"No, I suppose I'm not," Jasmine said, choking back a sob. "Pardon me, but I'm not feeling very gracious at the moment."

"I love you, darling," Celeste said, wringing her fingers. "You know I care—"

"Sometimes you care too much. You worry too much about me, Mother. It's time you let me make my own decisions…and my own mistakes. It's time you let me go."

With that, she turned from her mother's room. Refusing to look back, she escaped down the night-darkened hall. She felt weary beyond words, her feet leadened as she strode to her bedroom. Her heart throbbed painfully in her chest.

Tears blurred her vision as she fumbled with the knob. Thankfully the door finally opened and she hurried inside. Closing it behind her, she bolted the lock, in no mood to risk any more company.

With only the moonlight to guide her, she stumbled to the window seat that overlooked Blue Mirror Lake. A silvery glow lit the surface of the lake, shimmering like diamonds in the soft, cloudless night. In the distance she saw the outline of the mountains of Laughing Horse Reservation.

Once again, she was reminded of Storm Hunter.

She felt his presence as though he were in the room with her at that very moment. It would take a long time, perhaps forever, before she could forget the chiseled angles of his handsome face, the dark and penetrating beauty of his eyes, or the determined set of his strong chin.

A tear slid down her cheek, followed closely by another, then another. Unable to help herself, Jasmine did what she swore she would never allow. Hugging a chintz pillow to her chest, she gave in to a much-needed bout of tears.

In the safety of the empty room, she mourned the loss of a man she'd never even had the right to call her own.

Five

At nine o'clock the next morning Storm paced the floor of his hotel room. The floral-papered walls were beginning to close in around him. He felt as restless as a caged animal. He'd been up and prowling for so long his footsteps were permanently imprinted on the mauve carpeting.

"Dammit, what am I supposed to do now?" he growled, his deep voice echoing hollowly in the empty room. Frustrated, he plowed long fingers through his hair, raking the dark strands from his face. Instead of focusing on what he'd come to Whitehorn to accomplish, uncovering the truth behind his brother's murder, he'd been distracted by thoughts of a woman. Since sending Jasmine fleeing into the night, he'd been unable to relax, to sleep, to do anything but think about what a complete and utter fool he'd been. In his attempt to discourage her interest in him, he'd frightened and shamed her. While his intentions may have been honest, his delivery had been cruel.

Now guilt rested uneasily upon his shoulders.

Storm reluctantly forced his gaze to the phone. He had no choice, he realized. He had to speak to her again. He had to apologize for his behavior. If he didn't, he would forever be haunted by the hurt, disillusioned look in her eyes.

Sighing, he glanced at the bedside clock and decided

now was as good a time as any to call. Jasmine lived and worked at the B and B. Surely she'd be up and about, seeing to the needs of her guests.

His stomach tightened as he crossed the room to the nightstand. He sat down heavily on the edge of the unmade bed, with its mauve and blue print bedcovers. Picking up the phone, he sucked in a breath of courage, then punched in the number for the Big Sky Bed & Breakfast.

Listening to the phone ring, once, twice, three times, it suddenly occurred to him that Jasmine might not be the one to pick up the receiver. After all, she wasn't the only member of her family working at the bed-and-breakfast. Storm tensed, unnerved by the thought. What was he supposed to say if her mother answered? Remembering Celeste's skittish reaction to his appearance at the sheriff's office, fainting dead in David Hannon's arms, he doubted she would be overjoyed by his early morning call.

Before he could reconsider, the phone was picked up. "Big Sky Bed & Breakfast," a familiar voice chimed.

Relief eased the tension from his muscles. "Jasmine?"

Deafening silence was his only response.

Undaunted, he said, "Jasmine, it's Storm Hunter."

"I know."

The two simple words spoke volumes as to her frame of mind. Obviously she had not forgotten, nor forgiven, what had happened between them last night.

Refusing to be discouraged, he tried again. "I'd like to talk to you."

"I'm listening."

He hesitated. Considering the coolness of her tone, he knew in his heart this was one apology he must make in person. "If you don't mind, I'd rather meet with you."

Once again silence stretched across the phone line. For

a heart-stopping moment, Storm thought she'd hung up on him. "Jasmine?" he said, unable to hide the fear from his tone. "Are you still there?"

"Yes, I'm still here." Her soft whisper of a sigh set his senses prickling with awareness. "I'm just not sure if it would be wise for us to have any more contact, Mr. Hunter."

Mr. Hunter. He winced at the formal use of his name. Last night, she'd called him Storm. It would seem they'd taken one step forward, two steps back. She wasn't going to make this easy for him. Not that he deserved otherwise.

"I don't see that we have much of a choice. I have your sweater. You left it here last night," he countered, using any excuse within his means to see her again. He hoped he didn't sound as anxious as he felt. "I feel I should return it to you. If you want, I could stop by the B and B—"

"No, I'll meet you," she said quickly. Too quickly, leaving little doubt of his welcome at her home.

But her family's feelings toward him didn't matter, he told himself, almost smiling his relief. What mattered was that Jasmine had finally relented; she had agreed to see him. "Just tell me when and where."

"In an hour. There's a lookout in the mountains overlooking Crazy Peak. It's a popular spot with the locals. But I doubt if anyone will be there this morning."

No, they wouldn't. The lookout would be busy after nightfall. If memory served, it was popular with young lovers—Native American and Anglo alike—looking for a place to be alone, he mused silently. Frowning, he wondered which of her young suitors had taken her to this notorious makeout point.

Out loud, he said, "I know the place. I'll be there in an hour."

Without another word, Jasmine hung up the phone.

For a long moment Storm didn't move. He listened to the tinny silence humming in his ear, until the warning beep of a disconnected phone line sounded. Only then did he return the receiver to its cradle.

Obviously, Jasmine was still upset. Rightly so.

It would take more than a simple apology to convince her of his remorse. A task that shouldn't be hard, considering his life's work as a lawyer hinged on his power of persuasion. Storm's frown deepened. So, why did it feel as though he'd just taken on the toughest case of his life?

Why did he feel as though his last chance of finding peace and contentment rested on the outcome of his meeting with Jasmine?

One hour later, her heart heavy with regret, Jasmine drove her Jeep into the foothills of the Crazy Mountains. With the top down on the Wrangler, a brisk wind buffeted her skin, bringing tears to her eyes. At least that was the only excuse she allowed herself for the show of emotion. For the first time in her life, she had lied to her mother. Instead of being honest and telling her she was going to meet Storm, she had used an errand as an excuse to leave the B and B.

Lying and deceiving didn't come easily to her. By her mother's example, she'd been taught to live her life honestly, openly. At times, perhaps, too openly. There were those in Whitehorn who believed her family to be eccentric. The reminder brought on a familiar burr of irritation, which Jasmine forced aside. She didn't care what others thought. She'd rather be considered odd than live her life in the rigid confines of closed-minded conformity.

The road narrowed, demanding her attention. With the ease of experience, she negotiated the steep curves. The air felt cool, thick with the scent of the pine trees that lined the road. Ever since she'd been a child, the Crazies had been her favorite place to visit. Even now, when things got too hectic in real life, she escaped to the mountains, finding peace and solace in their rugged peaks. Her mother's explanation for her beguilement was that she'd lived a past life in the mountains, perhaps as a goatherder or a trapper.

The thought brought a reluctant smile as she considered her mother's off-centered influence upon her life. The first year of their marriage, her parents lived in Baton Rouge. Then Celeste had convinced Ty to return to Whitehorn to raise Summer. From then on, even after Ty's death, Celeste uniquely shaped all of their lives—hers, Cleo's and Summer's—by stressing the importance of free-spirited independence.

When they were old enough to toddle off on their own, Celeste had pushed them out the door to experience all the world had to offer. She'd encouraged them to think for themselves and to voice their own opinions. A philosophy that, to the chagrin of others in the community, Jasmine had embraced wholeheartedly.

In first grade, wanting to be like the cowboys she'd seen on her uncle Jeremiah's ranch, Jasmine had refused to give up her boots for a more appropriate pair of Mary Jane shoes. Only Celeste's promise to host a class field trip on the grounds of the Blue Mirror Lake had convinced the principle to bend the rules of the dress code.

During her sophomore year in high school, the dissection of a frog had been a requirement for biology class.

Appalled at the idea of such inhumane treatment of a helpless creature, Jasmine had refused to do anything so cruel. Not only had her mother applauded her decision, but Celeste and her aunt Yvette had joined her protest by holding a sit-in on the school steps. Despite their help, she'd failed the lab section of the class, ending up with C for the course. But together they had scored a victory in the name of family solidarity.

When Jasmine had blossomed into womanhood, her mother had gone beyond the usual birds-and-the-bees speech. When other mothers were blushing at the mention of sex, Celeste had left no doubt in her young daughter's mind what a healthy relationship between a man and woman ought to be. Not only that, but she'd made sure Jasmine was aware of the methods of birth control available to her should she decide the time was right.

Instead of encouraging her to be promiscuous, her mother's openness had left Jasmine with an overwhelming sense of responsibility. She'd taken to heart the trust she'd been given, by deciding to remain a virgin until she met the man she intended to marry.

Now, at the age of twenty-three, she was still waiting for the right man.

Unbidden, Storm Hunter's handsome image cropped up in her mind's eye. The thought of seeing him again left her confused and uncertain. In Storm she thought she'd found that perfect man, that she was ready to take that giant step of trust. But last night in his hotel room Storm had proven to her that she wasn't nearly as worldly as she'd like for him to believe. Nor as brave as she would have liked to have believed for herself.

He'd hurt her deeply.

Not physically so much as emotionally.

Rejection was painful, but most especially at the hands

of someone such as Storm, a man with whom she'd felt
such an instant and strong connection. Fresh tears pressed
against her eyes. Jasmine blinked hard, fighting their release. She wasn't sure of the reason behind Storm's unexpected request to see her again. But one thing was for
certain, her pride would never allow him to see just how
much he had wounded her.

Cornering the next curve too sharply, Jasmine's tires
squealed in protest. Shifting to a lower gear, she slowed
the Jeep to a more manageable speed, concentrating on
the road ahead. Too soon, she arrived at her destination.
Her heart thumped painfully against her breast as she
pulled into the lookout's parking lot.

Storm was waiting for her.

He stood outside his car, leaning against its silver finish. This morning he'd dressed in a pair of casual but
expensively labeled jeans and a polo shirt. He wore loaf-
ers with no socks and looked as though he'd stepped off
the cover of a *GQ* magazine. He was the perfect adver-
tisement for the professional man at ease.

Kicking up a cloud of dust in her wake, Jasmine
parked her Jeep next to his car. Letting the dust settle,
she slowly unhooked her seat belt. Turning his head, he
watched as she stepped down onto the graveled lot. A
light wind ruffled his long hair. Mirrored sunglasses hid
his expressive dark eyes from view. His chiseled face
remained somber, revealing none of his emotions.

Daunted, she stopped short of joining him, leaving a
small but safe distance between them. But even with that,
he was so blatantly male, she couldn't help but feel a
primal pull of attraction.

For a long moment they stood staring at each other,
neither seeming to know what to say. With each passing

second, awareness grew inside her, until she thought she might explode with the unwanted tension.

Storm was the first to break the spell of silence. His deep voice startled her when he finally said, "Thank you for coming."

He sounded so frank, so earnest. She almost believed he meant it…almost. His harsh rejection still echoed in her mind. Forgetting her resolve to remain aloof, she blurted, "Why did you call? After last night I thought I'd be the last person you'd want to see."

"Last night was a mistake," he said, slipping the sunglasses from the bridge of his nose. He tossed them through the car's open window onto the dashboard, then pushed himself away from the door. Taking a step toward her, he held her in his gaze. "I'm not in the habit of ravishing young women. Things got out of hand. My behavior was uncalled for. I hope you'll accept my apology. I assure you it won't happen again."

Jasmine felt a confusing mix of relief and disappointment. Standing here, close enough that she could almost touch him, she couldn't deny that she was still deeply attracted to him. Yet, looking into his expressive eyes, she saw nothing but sincerity in their depths. She believed him when he said things had gotten out of hand. Unfortunately, she also believed him when he said it wouldn't happen again.

Still, a part of her wasn't ready to settle for just an apology. Last night he'd acted as though he'd wanted to punish her, to punish himself for wanting her. Once and for all she needed to know why.

"Why are you so determined to dislike me?"

Emotion flickered in his eyes. Averting his gaze, he stared out at the scenic mountain view, watching as clouds scudded past the white-tipped peaks. He remained silent for so long, she thought he'd decided not to answer. Until he inhaled a deep breath, then released it with a whistling sigh. "It's not that I dislike you. It's that—" He stopped, his jaw clenching reflexively. A tiny vein pulsed at his temple. Still unable to face her, he continued, "Too much has happened between our families. Our pasts are connected in a way that makes it impossible for us to do anything but remain on opposite sides. I'm sure you must realize this."

Jasmine's breath caught painfully in her throat. She wanted to argue, but couldn't find the words. Perhaps he was right. Theirs was a dark history, one that couldn't easily be forgotten. Making amends now, after all that had happened, seemed too little, too late.

Unwilling to give up, she said, "We weren't the ones to start the feud between our families. Why should we keep it alive after all this time?"

He looked at her, his gaze so direct, so penetrating, she felt as though he could see inside to her very soul. "My brother died because he fell in love with the wrong woman, a white woman. I'm not going to make the same mistake."

Jasmine met his gaze, unable to look away. She considered his answer, deciding if they'd come this far, she couldn't turn back now. Steeling herself for his condemnation, she stated the obvious. "You blame me and my family for your brother's death."

She saw the flash of pain in his eyes. Lying badly, he said, "I don't know who's responsible for Raven's death. Because of the circumstances surrounding his murder, we may never know the truth. And for that reason, I'm afraid my brother's soul will never find peace."

"Circumstances? You mean justice won't be served because there may be a Kincaid involved?"

Storm's lips formed a thin, tight line. He refused to answer.

But he didn't have to. They both knew the truth. The Kincaid name was a powerful influence in this area. Powerful enough to put a murder investigation into permanent limbo, if the motivation was great enough. No matter how much wealth he may have acquired since leaving town, or how many connections he might have made as a lawyer in New Mexico, they both knew Storm's reputation meant nothing here in Whitehorn.

"I can't tell you who is or who's not involved," he said, his tone sounding defeated. "I can't get close enough to the investigation to find out the truth."

Jasmine felt his frustration as though it were her own. Her heart swelled with compassion for the pain she saw in his eyes. She blamed herself and her family for putting him through this turmoil. There was only one solution. One way to end his suffering, once and for all.

Surprising them both, she made her offer, "I'm going to help you, Storm. We're going to uncover the identity of your brother's murderer together."

"Do you have any idea what you're proposing?" Storm asked, his voice sharper than he'd intended.

"I'm proposing an alliance," she said. The calmness with which she spoke clashed against turbulent emotions churning inside him. "I think if we tried, we could work together as a team."

"A team?" He stared at her, unable to believe his ears.

Despite the obvious reason why an alliance between them would not work—namely, the unwanted attraction that sprung up whenever they were near—there was an even more compelling reason to refuse. She was a Kincaid, offering to help him find out the truth behind his brother's murder. There was obviously a conflict of interest.

He didn't know whether to trust her or to suspect her motives, as he'd learned to suspect all white men's motives.

But then again, this was Jasmine. A woman who, as he was quickly finding out, was nothing if not painfully honest. From their few encounters, she didn't appear able to lie, even if she'd wanted to.

"The whole idea is ridiculous," he said in a dismissive tone. Gravel crunched beneath his shoes as he turned on his heel and spun away from her, eager to leave and put a much-needed distance between himself and temptation.

"Please hear me out, Storm," she said, reaching a hand to stop him.

Her palm felt warm, soft, as she wrapped her fingers around his wrist. Arrows of heat and awareness darted up his forearm. He flinched at the unexpected contact. Slowly his gaze traveled from her hand up to her face. There, in the depths of her green eyes, he saw an innocence that nearly took his breath away.

It wasn't an act. Her proposition, as impossible as it might be, was for real. She really wanted to help him.

"What's wrong with my wanting to help you?" she asked, echoing his own thoughts.

He tightened his jaw against his weakening resolve. "I don't need your help, Jasmine. I don't need anyone's help. Whatever I've achieved in my life, I've done it on my own terms. The last thing I want is someone else poking their nose into my business out of a sense of pity."

"That's what you think I'm feeling? Pity? How dare you presume to know my own thoughts!" Anger flashed in her eyes. She released his hand, growling her frustration. "At this moment I don't know who to be more angry with—the legal system for refusing to treat you fairly, or you for being so stubborn."

He felt winded, stung by her unfair reprimand. He was the wounded party, not her. Yet, standing awkwardly by the car, he wondered how she'd accomplished the feat. Somehow, once again, she'd made him feel guilty, as though he were the one in the wrong.

"I don't want to argue with you, Jasmine. Arguing is pointless. We both know who killed my brother."

"You mean, Jeremiah Kincaid…my uncle."

"Your *deceased* uncle," he corrected, surprised by her admission. "Jeremiah has been long buried, and his secrets along with him."

"Maybe, maybe not," she countered. "There's only one way to find out for sure. Listen to me, Storm. My cousin, David, is the FBI agent helping with the investigation. We've always been close. If there's any information that the police aren't telling, I'm sure I could find a way for him to confide in me."

Reluctantly, Storm acknowledged what she had to say was the truth. His previous encounters with David Hannon had been strained at best. Frustrated by the investigation's lack of progress, he'd allowed his temper to get the better of him. He'd argued with the man, almost coming to blows over the disagreement.

Oblivious to his wavering thoughts, Jasmine continued, her voice gentle, her tone a plea for reason. "Your brother was last seen alive at the Kincaid ranch. A ranch that now belongs to my cousin, Garrett Kincaid. Alone, you can't get anywhere near that ranch. But as a member of the Kincaids, who would think it odd if I wished to visit the family homestead and bring along a guest?"

Storm released a growl of impatience. "Jasmine—"

"No, wait, there's more. I have an intimate connection to the only surviving person known to be in the house on the night of your brother's murder—my mother." She hesitated, a flush of color stealing across her face. Then, with an honesty to which he'd grown accustomed, she said, "My mother doesn't want me anywhere near you. Just how far do you think you'll get if you try to question her on your own?"

Nowhere fast, he admitted to himself. Since his return to Whitehorn, he'd been stonewalled by the police department. No one seemed to care about him, or his brother's death. Why should they? He was just another annoying Indian. Storm fought the rising tide of bitterness. Jasmine was right. The investigation into Raven's murder was at a virtual standstill.

For years he had lived without knowing what had happened to Raven. His life had been put in limbo. Not knowing whether to be angry and hurt by his brother's abandonment, or to grieve over Raven's death.

Now that he knew what had happened to his brother, he couldn't allow the questions to go unanswered. He could not rest until he uncovered the truth. He had to know why Raven had died, and who was responsible.

"What about last night?" he asked abruptly. "What happened in my hotel room...do you think you could trust me enough to work with me?"

She shrugged, giving an unconvincing attempt at nonchalance. "Like you said, last night was a mistake. We both allowed our emotions to overrule our judgment. It won't happen again."

He raised a brow. "You're sure about that?"

"Positive, because I won't allow it." She raised her chin in a show of feminine pride. "Trust me, Storm. I'm not a glutton for punishment. I'm simply not interested in a man who isn't interested in me.''

Not interested was hardly the way he felt. He studied her for a long moment, debating the wisdom of telling her just how wrong her assumption really was. Deciding that some things were best kept to himself, he gave a resigned sigh and said, ''If I were to agree—''

A smile blossomed on her beautiful face. Storm's heart pounded a warning beat in his chest.

''I said *if* I were to agree,'' he repeated firmly. ''You would have to promise me that you wouldn't risk putting yourself into any danger.''

''Danger?'' The sculpted line of her brow furrowed. ''What danger could there be after all these years? Those who were involved are long gone. They can't hurt us now.''

It had been his experience that people would go to great lengths to cover up a family scandal, especially those that had been long buried. ''I just want you to be careful.''

She gave a dismissive shake of the head. ''I will.''

Storm frowned, agitated by her apparent lack of concern. ''When do you want to start?''

Her face brightened. ''How about tomorrow?''

He nodded. ''Tomorrow, it is.''

''I feel like we should celebrate. We've finally agreed on something.'' Jasmine laughed, her eyes sparkling with mischief. She glanced at her wristwatch and sighed. Her tone shifted from playful to business-like. ''Unfortunately I don't have the time. I took an early lunch to meet with you. My mother's waiting for me. I've got to get back to the B and B. I have to make breakfast tomorrow morning for our guests. After that, I should be able to get the rest of the day off. There's no use in both of us driving tomorrow. Why don't I pick you up at your hotel, say around eleven o'clock?''

Second thoughts worked their way into his mind, setting his nerves on edge. Instead of giving in to his doubts, he nodded. ''I'll be ready.''

With a smile that set fire racing through his veins, she bid him goodbye and strode to her Jeep. Today her long legs were hidden beneath a pair of blue jeans. But that didn't spoil the view. The faded denim clung to her legs and backside like a second skin. His body ached with awareness as he studied the gentle sway of her hips.

Swinging herself up into the driver's seat, she fastened her seatbelt and gunned the motor to life. With one last wave goodbye, she threw the gear into reverse and backed out of the parking space. Spewing dust and rocks, she shifted forward and peeled out, leaving him to stand alone in the middle of the empty lot. He felt her absence like a hollow place in his heart.

At that moment Storm knew, with this new alliance of theirs, he was courting trouble.

He had never met a more beautiful woman. The longer he was with her, the greater his desire for her grew. But even more disturbing than desire, what he felt for her was respect.

As everyone else in town, including the members of her own family, Jasmine could have gone out of her way to avoid him. After all, Raven's death was his problem, not hers. She was under no obligation to help him.

But instead of running away, she'd taken on the responsibility of seeking the truth. She was risking the wrath of her own family to help him. He had never known a woman quite like her.

Desire and respect, Storm mused. In his opinion, the two were a dangerous combination.

Six

Jasmine tugged at the bedcovers, feeling restless and out of sorts. It was late, after two o'clock in the morning, and she hadn't yet been able to relax enough to sleep. Knowing that she'd be up in less than four hours to start breakfast for the B and B's guests made the late hour seem even more daunting.

Each wrinkle in the bed, imagined or otherwise, irritated her. Despite the open windows, there was no cooling breeze filtering inside. The room felt hot and stuffy. Her skin was damp with perspiration. Her head ached with fatigue. She wanted to blame her insomnia on the unusually warm night. But the truth was a guilty conscience had kept her awake.

Sighing, Jasmine sat up in bed. She snapped on the lamp at her bedside table. A soft light washed over her, bringing into focus the room that had been hers since childhood. The dusky green-and-cream striped paper she'd picked out when she was ten years old still hung on the walls. Her grandmother's handmade patchwork quilt covered the dark mission-style bed. Chintz curtains framed the large windows. Matching pillows and a collection of stuffed animals were arranged on the window seat beneath.

The room was as familiar as the back of her hand, as soothing as a hug from an old friend. Yet tonight she could find no comfort in its embrace. Tonight, she felt as

though she were a stranger in its midst, as though she
didn't belong. Since agreeing to help Storm with his
search for the truth behind his brother's death, she felt
oddly detached from her home as well as from her own
family.

Her eyes burned from lack of sleep. Rubbing them,
she leaned back against the pillows and considered the
consequences of her decision. In her heart, she knew
helping Storm was the right thing to do. No one should
have to endure the pain he was suffering. For almost
thirty years he'd lived without knowing what had happened to his brother. If she'd lost Cleo or Summer in that
way, she'd didn't know if she could survive.

Storm had survived the ordeal.

But not without a price.

This morning she'd heard the bitterness in his voice
when he'd told her that he didn't need her help, that he
didn't need anyone's help. She had seen the suspicious
look in his eyes when she'd pledged her support. Through
the years of struggle Storm had learned not to trust anyone. She had to prove her sincerity. No matter how hard
he tried to push her way, she couldn't abandon him.

She had to help him.

Even if it meant doing so behind her family's back.

Giving up on sleep, Jasmine pushed aside the sheets
and climbed out of bed. Crossing the room to the window
seat, she picked up a favorite stuffed animal from her
past, Mr. Truckles, a well-loved bunny with lopsided
ears, patchy fur and a nose that was almost completely
worn off. She hugged the stuffed rabbit to her chest and
sat on the cushioned seat. Tucking her long legs beneath
her, she peered outside into the dark night.

Clouds blocked the moon's shimmering light, casting
the lake into a murky darkness. The night seemed too

black, too forbidding, putting her nerves even further on edge. She didn't know how she was going to get through the next few days, helping Storm without telling her mother the truth. Now that Cleo and Summer were married, her mother had come to rely upon her even more. Jasmine felt a keen sense of responsibility for her mother's well-being. It wasn't any wonder that telling lies didn't sit well with her conscience.

An ear-piercing scream shattered the silence, jolting her out of her troubled thoughts.

In her haste to stand, Jasmine nearly tumbled from her seat at the window. Catching herself, she scrambled to her feet and stood frozen in the middle of the room, with her heart pounding and her ears straining to listen to the sudden quiet that surrounded her. For a moment she thought she must have heard the screech of an owl, or had even imagined the cry.

Then it sounded again.

This time she knew it was from inside the house. The scream had come from her mother's bedroom.

She dropped Mr. Truckles back onto the window seat and in two quick steps was at the door. Fumbling with the knob, she tore it open and ran blindly down the night-darkened hall. Her mother's bedroom door was closed, but, thankfully, not locked. The bedside lamp was still on, guiding her. An opened book, with her mother's reading glasses beside it, had been placed on the bedside table. A white candle was lit, softly shimmering in the dim light beside her. Her mother was propped up in bed against a cushion of pillows, looking as though she'd fallen asleep while reading.

But her expression was anything but restful.

Agony twisted the beautiful, care-worn features of her face. Her complexion was ashen, her russet hair tousled.

With her eyes still tightly closed, she thrashed her head from side to side, as though trying to rid herself of a nightmare.

Celeste was dreaming, Jasmine realized.

Her step faltering, she hesitated, not sure whether to wake her mother. Afraid that she'd scare her more if she did. But another cry of alarm settled her indecision. Jasmine hurried to her mother's side. She placed a hand on Celeste's shoulder and shook her gently.

Celeste woke with a start. Her eyes wild and frightened, she stared at Jasmine, as though she were looking through her, not at her. Her body trembled with fear. Her chest rose sharply, as she sucked in a shuddering breath.

"Mother, are you all right?" Jasmine asked, unable to keep the tremor of fear from her own voice.

Celeste opened and closed her mouth, but no sound was emitted. Looking as though she were seeing a ghost, she stared at her daughter. Finally, her voice sounding as hoarse and dry as the wind on the plains, she whispered, "Blanche?"

Jasmine's heart stuttered. "No, Mother. It's me—"

"Blanche, it's been so long." Celeste reached out a shaky hand and touched Jasmine's cheek. Tears welled up in her eyes. Her breath catching on a sob, she said, "Oh, Blanche…don't be angry. I'm so sorry, so very sorry. I never meant for it to happen. Please…please forgive me."

"Forgive you?" Jasmine frowned, her concern growing. "For what, Mother?"

Celeste closed her eyes and shook her head. "No, I— I can't talk about it. I won't. Do you hear me? I won't."

Jasmine's heart slammed against her chest. A lump of dread lodged in her throat. Desperate, she gathered her mother's hands in hers and said, "Mother, look at me. Open your eyes and look at me."

Celeste's eyes slowly opened, though the wild, frightened look still remained.

"Can you see me, Mother? It's Jasmine, not Blanche. Jasmine, your daughter."

Celeste's expression shifted. The terror burning in her eyes dimmed. She blinked, quick rapid blinks, as though trying to bring the room into focus. "Jasmine?"

Relief surged through her body. "Yes, it's Jasmine."

"W-what happened? What's wrong?" Celeste struggled to sit up.

Jasmine placed a hand on her mother's shoulder, quieting her. "Just lie back and relax for a moment. You were having a nightmare."

"A nightmare," Celeste repeated, frowning in confusion. "I don't remember. I—I couldn't sleep, so I decided to read." Her frown deepened, the pitch of her voice rising anxiously. She pushed the hair from her eyes and searched Jasmine's face. "I must have dozed off, but I just don't remember."

"It's okay, Mother. Everything's all right now. You just scared me for a moment."

Tears slid down Celeste's cheeks. "I'm so sorry, darling. I didn't mean to disturb you."

"Don't be silly. There's no need to be sorry. You've been under such a strain lately. I just wish I could help you."

Celeste didn't answer. Instead, lifting a hand, she wiped the telltale moisture from her face and struggled to compose herself.

"Do you want to talk about your dream?" Jasmine persisted, unwilling to let her mother avoid what had happened. "It might help."

Celeste shook her head. "No, I—I can't."

"Mother, you called me Blanche."

"Blanche?" Her red-rimmed eyes widened in alarm.

Choosing her words carefully, Jasmine explained, "When I woke you, you looked at me so strangely, like you weren't really seeing me. Then you called me Blanche."

Celeste sat up abruptly. She brushed the covers aside and swung her shapely legs off the bed. Rising stiffly to her feet, she waved off Jasmine's offer to help. "I'll be all right, Jasmine. I just need to get up and stretch my legs."

"Mother, you're not all right," Jasmine said, giving an exasperated breath. "You just had a terrible nightmare. Why won't you talk to me about it?"

"It won't do any good to talk about it now. It's over...done with. I just want to forget about it." Celeste crossed the room to the fireplace. There, with a trembling hand, she lit a match and began to light the numerous candles scattered about on the nightstand and mantel.

Jasmine sighed. First the candles, then the oil would be next. Then, as was too often the case, instead of confiding in her daughter, Celeste would turn to the spiritual world for comfort. Though Jasmine knew she was wasting her time, she asked once again, "Mother, are you sure there's nothing I can do to help you?"

From a vial on her nightstand, Celeste poured out a dollop of bergamot oil and rubbed it into her left hand. "Jasmine, there's no need to worry," she said, her voice regaining some of its former confidence, though the dark circles under her eyes and the drawn features of her face did little to allay Jasmine's concerns. "I just need some time alone. I hope you understand."

"Yes, of course," Jasmine said numbly. She understood all too well. As she had done so often these past few weeks, her mother was pushing her away. Celeste was pulling inside herself, struggling alone to find an answer to a problem that Jasmine knew nothing about. Frustration roiled inside her, leaving a bitter taste in her mouth.

As though sensing her distress, Celeste crossed the room and enveloped her in a quick hug. ''Don't look so worried, dear. I'll be fine. Go on back to your room. There's no need for both of us to lose any more sleep.''

Jasmine had no choice but to comply. Slowly she crossed to the door. Her hand lingering on the knob, she hesitated, glancing back at her mother, watching as Celeste placed a thick candle on the braided rug in the middle of the room. Tucking her nightgown around her, she assumed the lotus position, sitting cross-legged in front of the light. Folding her hands in meditation, she closed her eyes and began to chant beneath her breath.

Feeling like an intruder, Jasmine stepped into the hall and closed the door quietly behind her. As she headed back to her room, a renewed sense of resolve grew inside her, quickening her step.

Since the discovery of Raven Hunter's body, her mother's health and stability had been slowly deteriorating in front of her eyes. Something was troubling Celeste. Something that had to do with the murder of her sister's lover.

She had no doubt Celeste knew something that she wasn't sharing. She'd felt this as certainly as she had felt the tremors shaking her mother's body. But without Celeste confiding in her, Jasmine's hands were tied in her attempts to help her mother.

Which left her with only one choice.

Now there were two reasons to help Storm.

First, in the name of the Kincaid family, she would make amends to him for the wrongs committed against him and his brother. Second, for her mother's sake, she would find out the truth—before it was too late.

Somehow she had to help her mother find peace of mind.

Because, if she didn't, she was afraid that she might lose Celeste for good.

At precisely eleven o'clock the next day, a knock sounded at Storm's hotel room door. Half dressed, his hair still wet and only finger-combed from his shower, he glowered at the closed door. Of all days for Jasmine to be prompt, why did it have to be today?

For the first time in weeks he'd been able to sleep the night through. In fact, he'd slept so soundly, he hadn't heard his alarm. When he finally had awoken and had seen the lateness of the hour, he'd been rushing like a madman ever since.

Growling his impatience, he strode to the door and swung it open.

A smile of greeting died on Jasmine's lips as she skimmed the length of his body, taking in his shirtless, shoeless, blue jeans-clad state. Swallowing hard, she stared at the smooth expanse of his bare chest.

"I'm not ready," he said needlessly.

Raising a thin, dark brow, she quipped, "Isn't that supposed to be a woman's line?"

The tension eased from his muscles at her attempt to lighten the situation. "It'll only take me a few minutes to finish dressing. Would you like to come inside?"

"Mmm…" She stole another glance at his naked chest and shook her head. "It's too nice a morning. I'll just wait out here. Take your time."

He nodded, his lips twitching with the urge to smile as he recalled her bravado of the day before. How she'd assured him there would be no problem with their working together, since she was no longer interested in him in a physical way. It assuaged his bruised ego to know that Jasmine wasn't as immune to him as she'd like for him to believe.

He turned, leaving the door open, and strode to the closet. Pulling out a neatly pressed blue chambray shirt, he slipped it on, tucking the ends into his jeans. Fastening the top button of his fly, he looped a woven belt around his narrow waist and stepped into his shoes.

Glancing outside, he saw Jasmine with her back to him, leaning against a concrete pillar, gazing in the direction of the distant mountains. Her black cowboy boots were crossed at her ankles. She wore a pair of snug blue jeans, coupled with a black scoop-neck T-shirt. The outfit emphasized the flatness of her stomach, the gentle curve of her hips and the primal beauty of her body.

Awareness stirred in Storm, warming his blood, making the fit of his jeans even tighter. He stifled a moan. Jasmine wasn't the only one not immune. The day had barely begun and already his libido was working overtime. He inhaled a steadying breath, releasing it through clenched teeth.

It was going to be a long, long day.

With fierce, punishing strokes, he brushed the hair from his face, tucking it behind his ears. Letting the wet strands air dry, he picked up his keys and headed for the door.

At the sound of his approaching footsteps, Jasmine turned to face him. In the revealing rays of sunlight, he saw for the first time the dark smudges beneath her eyes.

He paused in the doorway and frowned his concern. "You look tired."

"I didn't sleep well last night." Self-consciously she raked both hands through her cropped hair. With a quick smile, she said, "It was too warm in the house. I couldn't seem to get comfortable."

Storm didn't believe her for a minute. Jasmine was a terrible liar. There was something she wasn't telling him. He could see that as clearly as the blush of color rising on her cheeks.

He couldn't help but wonder if her restlessness had anything to do with her decision to help him. She had been honest yesterday about her family's wishes for her to not become involved with him. But she'd offered to help him nonetheless. Perhaps the burden of betraying family loyalties was beginning to wear on her.

For his own sake, he hoped not. As hard as it was to admit, he needed her. There was too much depending upon the success of their mission. He owed his brother the truth. And he didn't have a snowball's chance in hell of uncovering that truth without her.

Closing the door behind him, he joined her on the walkway. Standing close, he experienced the first of what he was sure to be many second thoughts of the day. She looked so fresh, so beautiful. His fingers itched to reach out and touch her. Not trusting himself to indulge his hormonal urges, he crammed his hands into the back pockets of his jeans and wondered how he was going to get through the day without giving in to his desires.

"So, where do we begin?" he asked, unable to keep his eyes off the delicate features of her face.

"The Hip Hop Café," she said. At his look of surprise, she gave a self-deprecating smile. "I made breakfast for our guests this morning at the B and B, but I didn't have time to eat my own. I can't think straight on an empty stomach.''

His own smile was obliging. ''I guess I could use a cup of coffee, too.''

''Good,'' she said, giving an audible breath of relief. ''Without food, in another hour, I'd have been a real bear to live with.''

Somehow, he doubted that.

The heel of her boot scraped against the concrete as she turned toward the parking lot. He followed behind her, cutting his long-legged strides to match her smaller steps. But he stayed close enough to be on the receiving end of a heady dose of her sweet-smelling perfume. The scent reminded him of warm, sunny days, of lazing in a meadow surrounded by wildflowers. In the parking lot, she hesitated, glancing between his silver luxury car and her Jeep Wrangler.

''There's no need for both of us to drive,'' she said, her tone matter-of-fact. ''We may be visiting some rugged territory. Four-wheel drive will come in handy. I guess we should take my Jeep.''

''Whatever you say,'' he said, distracted by the way she chewed on her lower lip when trying to work her way through a problem.

Jasmine didn't move. Instead, placing her hands on her hips, she glared at him. ''It's not just my decision, Storm. We're supposed to be partners, remember? If you've got an opinion, say so!''

After a moment's consideration he said, ''In my opinion, we're wasting time standing here in the parking lot. The daylight's burning. Let's go.''

She hesitated. Then, looking as though she'd like to pick up the argument where she'd left off, she gave an impatient humph and strode to her Jeep.

Storm continued at a slower pace. On this warm, cloudless day, she'd driven with the top down. Adjusting the mirrored sunglasses onto the bridge of his nose, he slung himself into the passenger seat and buckled in, adjusting his long legs to the limited space.

Once they were both settled, Jasmine gunned the engine to life. As she popped the car into gear, her long, slender hands caught his eye. Instead of being smooth and manicured, they were red and rough, the nails cut to the quick. They were the hands of a laborer, not of a woman who lived her life at ease.

Curiosity getting the better of him, he asked, "You said you made breakfast this morning?"

"Uh-huh." She turned onto Center Avenue, heading for the café. A brisk wind lifted the short strands of hair from her face. Raising her voice over the noise of the engine, she said, "I make breakfast every day. I'm the chief cook and bottle washer at the B and B. Not too bad at it, either." Her grin was rueful. "At least, that's what I've been told. I guess all that time I spent at culinary school has paid off."

"You're a chef," he said, once again, unable to hide his surprise.

She flashed him an amused glance. "You seem shocked."

"No...well, maybe a little surprised. You don't look—"

"Old enough?" she finished for him. He shifted uncomfortably in his seat as she raised a brow in question. Despite her light tone, he heard the annoyance in her voice when she said, "Don't worry, Storm. Just because I look like a teenybopper, it doesn't mean I live like one."

"That's not what I meant. I—"

"No, I know exactly what you meant. You've got some strange idea in your head that I'm just a kid." Gliding the car into a higher gear, she stomped down on the accelerator. The sudden surge of momentum pushed him back into his seat. She tilted her pert nose skyward, the indignation rising with each word as she said, "Well, you're wrong. I'm twenty-three. Old enough to know what I want to do with my life, and believe it or not, it's being a chef. I've always loved working in the kitchen.

"Learning to hone my skills seemed only logical, since my family owns a bed-and-breakfast." Her brow furrowed. "Actually, I've been trying to talk my mother into expanding the dining room at the B and B, but she's been hesitant about taking on the added responsibility."

She was rambling.

Surprisingly he didn't seem to mind.

Storm normally tuned out the intimate details of the women who'd come and gone in his life. Most of the time he was interested only in surface information such as name, phone number and address. Not to mention how fast he could sneak out once he'd sensed a woman was becoming too interested.

But with Jasmine it was different. He wanted to know all he could about her. Instead of being discomfited by the personal bent of their conversation, he found himself listening carefully, watching the slight pout of her lush lips and the lively sparkle in her eyes as she spoke.

Did she have any idea just how beautiful she really was? She had the finest, most delicate complexion he'd ever seen. Her smooth, flawless skin reminded him of a porcelain doll. But more than just her exotic looks, he was intrigued by what she had to say and how she said it. He'd never met anyone quite like her.

Everything about her seemed to fascinate him.

Braking hard, forcing his thoughts back to the matter at hand, she pulled into the lot of the Hip Hop. Switching off the engine, she turned and looked at him expectantly.

He studied her for a long moment, raising a curious brow. "May I finish what I was about to say now? Or do you have something else to add?"

A flush of pink tinged her cheeks. She waved a dismissive hand. "Go right ahead. Speak your piece."

Biting back an amused smile, he said, "What I was about to say—before I was rudely interrupted—was that I couldn't picture you as a chef because you're so thin. You don't look like a person who spends her time working with food. My surprise had nothing to do with your age, but with your size."

"Oh," she said, her flush deepening. "Sorry, I'm just a little self-conscious about my age. Everyone seems to be pointing out my youthfulness lately. I guess I jumped to the wrong conclusion."

"No apology is necessary," he said, his tone brisk. Reluctantly he glanced at the diner. As usual, it appeared busy. "Should we go inside?"

"Sounds good to me. For once I'd like to put something other than my foot in my mouth."

Storm chuckled. Unbuckling his seat belt, he swung himself out of the Jeep, stepping down onto the paved lot. Still smiling, he held open the door to the café, then stepped inside.

Heads turned, and curious stares bore into them. More than one eyebrow of surprise was raised. Hushed whispers followed their entrance into the restaurant.

And Storm realized their mistake.

Last evening they'd dined at a restaurant owned and operated by a Cheyenne. Not only that, but they'd been accompanied by Gavin and Summer. Their presence together hadn't raised any alarms.

Not so today. Storm wasn't certain if the fact that he was a Native American and Jasmine was white was what had set the town's gossips abuzz. Or if it was the fact that he was a Hunter and she was a Kincaid. Either way, in the town of Whitehorn, the two did not mix.

If Jasmine noticed the extra attention, she gave no outward indication. Instead, with her head held high, her shoulders ramrod straight, she made a beeline for a pair of empty stools at the front counter. Sliding onto one, she glanced at him, waiting for him to join her.

With one last self-conscious glance across the café, he sat on the vinyl stool.

"What are you having, Storm? The Western omelettes are good," Jasmine said, her light tone sounding forced. She picked up a menu and scanned the plastic-covered sheet. Lowering her voice, she whispered, "Ignore them, Storm. Whitehorn's a small town. There's not a lot to do around here. People have to have something to entertain themselves, even if it is just finding something to gossip about."

Obviously he'd been wrong. She was fully aware of the extra attention their entrance had brought.

But she was wrong, too. It did matter what others thought.

The reaction of the citizens of Whitehorn to their being together today was the same reaction Raven and Jasmine's aunt Blanche had received when they were secret lovers nearly thirty years earlier.

The disapproval in the air was palpable.

Storm's chest tightened with an unwanted emotion. He didn't want to admit how much it disappointed him to know that nothing had changed in Whitehorn since he was just a boy.

Janie, the blond-haired waitress who'd waited on him the last time he'd dined at the Hip Hop, joined them at the counter, wearing a contagious grin. "Jasmine Monroe, this certainly is a pleasant surprise. It's been a long time since I've seen you in here."

Jasmine's returning smile was pure mischief. "Just came to check out the competition, that's all."

"Well, I'll be sure to tell the cook to be extra careful with your order." Her gaze moved from Jasmine to Storm. "And you brought a friend. It's good to see you again, Mr. Hunter. What can I get for you today?"

"Just coffee, please," he said, his somber tone spoiling the lighthearted banter.

"Not too hungry, huh?" Janie turned to Jasmine. "How about you, Jasmine? What would you like?"

Sighing, Jasmine placed the menu back in its spot between the sugar and napkin holders. "Coffee, and one of your special cinnamon rolls. Only could you make both of our orders to go. We're running a little late."

"Sure thing." Janie's smile faltered. She glanced around the café, catching the curious stares of the other patrons. With a quick nod of understanding, she said, "It'll only be a moment."

Neither Jasmine nor Storm spoke again until they'd paid for their order and had left the café. Once they were out of earshot of others, only then did he realize just how upset she really was—with him.

She turned on him, anger flashing in her eyes. "Why did you let them bother you? It doesn't matter what they think about our being together. It doesn't matter what anyone else thinks."

"Of course it matters," he said, his voice harsher than

he'd intended. He stopped short, his shoes skidding against a loose rock. The coffee sloshed in his cup, nearly spilling over the brim. Brusquely he added, "You live here, Jasmine. You need these people's approval."

She pointed an accusing finger in his direction. Her voice and hand trembling with barely controlled anger, she said, "Don't you dare tell me what I need. I don't need a watchdog keeping track of my status in the community. I've long given up on the idea of seeking Whitehorn's approval."

Despite her adamant tone, he heard the pain that underlined the words. A pain that he knew only too well. A pain that came only from a lifetime of shame and guilt.

Somehow, Jasmine had been exposed to the prejudices of others.

Perhaps he'd been too hasty in his assumption of her so-called privileged lifestyle. Perhaps they had more in common than he'd first imagined.

"Jasmine, I'm sorry. I didn't mean to overstep—"

"I don't need your sympathy, Storm," she said, cutting off his apology. "Like you said, daylight's burning. It's time to move on." Turning on her heel, she strode to the Jeep.

Reluctantly Storm followed, a burr of discomfort riding low in his chest. The more he was with Jasmine, the more he learned about her. Before, it was easy to discount her as just one of the Kincaids, the family who'd caused so much pain in his life. Now, his hatred was being replaced with a new and even more disturbing emotion.

Empathy.

Not only did he understand her, but he found himself caring for her, too.

Seven

Wind whistled through the open Jeep, blowing the long, dark strands of hair into Storm's face. Dust boiled up from the tires, covering everything—including himself—with a fine layer of grit. The heavy scent of sage peppered the air as they passed over the rolling green hills of the Kincaid ranch. They'd left the main road a few miles back. Now they were traveling on a hard-packed dirt lane, which would lead them to the original casino/resort construction site.

The site where his brother's remains had been found.

Despite the warm, sunlit day, Storm shivered as a cloud of darkness slowly enveloped him. He knew there was much more to this feeling of dread than having to face the spot where Raven had died. Straight ahead, abutting the Kincaid border, stood the mountains marking the Laughing Horse Reservation—the land that had been his home for the first thirteen years of his life.

Since arriving in Whitehorn, Storm had yet to find a reason, or the will, to visit the place of his birth.

"I doubt if anyone will be at the construction site. No one's been working there since my cousin Lyle died," Jasmine said, raising her voice above the wind, pulling Storm back to the present.

Startled, he glanced her way, thankful for the mirrored sunglasses that hid his eyes.

She continued, seemingly oblivious to the strong emotions churning inside him. "As far as I know, the plans for the casino and resort are on hold. At least until someone can decide what to do next."

Giving himself a moment to collect his thoughts, Storm sipped the last bit of his drink. The dregs of lukewarm coffee tasted bitter. Forcing himself to swallow it down, he said, "I've heard a little about what's happened here, but not the whole story. Do you mind my asking exactly what's been going on at this construction site?"

"No, I don't mind. But the truth is, I'm not really sure if I know the whole story." Shaking her head, she said, "Now that Lyle's dead, I doubt if anyone does. I guess it all started in May, when they broke ground on the resort. Everyone was so excited. There were such high hopes of the venture bringing prosperity to both the reservation and to Whitehorn."

Storm bit the inside of his mouth, resisting the urge to contradict Jasmine's rose-colored view of the real world. From his own experience, he'd found that Native Americans earned prosperity only after leaving the reservation and making their way in the white man's world. For those who stayed on the reservation, prosperity remained an unattainable dream. Too many of his people still lived in poverty, losing all hope of bettering their situations. Even when an opportunity to improve their lives came along, somehow fate always found a way to keep it beyond their grasp.

"As you probably already know, that first site was on Kincaid land. Lyle was appointed by his grandfather, my cousin Garrett, to oversee the family's interest." She paused, taking her eyes off the road long enough to send him a hesitant glance. "It wasn't long after they broke ground that they discovered your brother's remains."

Storm schooled himself to show no reaction, unwilling to let her see the depth of his own pain.

Despite his efforts to remain aloof, concern flickered in her eyes. He hadn't fooled her for a moment. Despite her uncertainty, Jasmine continued, "Instead of delaying the construction, they moved the site. All was going well until Peter Cook, one of the workers, was killed. One morning they found his body at the bottom of the construction pit. At first everyone thought it was an accident. But there were signs of a struggle, and it was decided that he'd been murdered. Apparently he'd been pushed to his death." She stopped and shuddered, looking sickened by the horrible events she'd just relayed.

Storm remained silent, not sure how to respond to her obvious distress. Though he wanted to reach out and comfort her, he didn't know if the overture would be welcome, or wise. He'd made that mistake earlier, when he'd tried to convince her that she needed Whitehorn's approval.

Theirs was a temporary relationship of convenience, he reminded himself. As soon as his brother's murder was solved, he'd be on the first flight back to New Mexico. No matter how tempting it might be, for his own sake, as well as hers, it would be best to not become too involved in Jasmine's life.

After a moment she said, "Gretchen Neal—she's the detective handling the case—"

"I've met Ms. Neal," he said, his voice sharper than he'd intended. His dealings with the detective and her FBI partner David Hannon, Jasmine's own cousin, had been frustrating, to say the least. The two had seemed more intent on solving the murder of the white man, Peter Cook, than on finding the truth behind his brother's death.

Not that he should have been surprised. It had been Storm's experience that the concerns of a white man always took priority over those of an Indian's.

Jasmine's gaze lingered on his face, as though she had read his thoughts. Finally she said, "Then you know that Gretchen discovered evidence linking Lyle to Peter Cook's murder."

Storm nodded.

Reluctantly she turned her gaze back to the road. "That's why we think Lyle tried to kill her. To silence her. Thankfully, David was able to stop him before he succeeded."

Storm mulled this over, then asked, "Does anyone know why Lyle murdered Peter Cook?"

"Not that I've heard. His grandfather and his parents were stunned by Lyle's actions. They haven't a clue what could have triggered such bizarre behavior."

He studied her face, seeing the telltale doubts in her expression. "How about you? Do you have any idea why Lyle might have done something like this?"

She hesitated a moment before answering. Grimacing, she said, "Lyle was a distant cousin of mine. He lived in Elk Springs most of his life, so we really didn't see much of each other. But what I did know of him, I didn't like. He was mean-spirited and spoiled, always looking for the easy way to make fast money." The sound of her resigned sigh carried on the wind. "If I had to guess, I'd say that greed motivated him."

"Greed?" Storm frowned. "I don't understand. I thought Garrett Kincaid owned the land the resort's being built on."

"He does," Jasmine said. "That's what makes it all the more confusing. Lyle tried to buy the land from Garrett a few weeks ago. But Garrett refused to sell it, he wanted the land to go to Gabriel Reilly Baxter, his youngest grandson. Now no one can figure out what Lyle hoped to gain by killing Peter Cook. But I'd bet my favorite saucepan there was something he was hiding, something that would have made him a rich man. The problem is, now that both Lyle and Peter Cook are dead, no one ever will know the truth.''

History did have a way of repeating itself, Storm mused with an unexpected tinge of bitterness. In his heart he believed that Jasmine's uncle, Jeremiah Kincaid, was responsible for his brother's death. But both Jeremiah and Raven were now dead. The truth behind what had really happened thirty years ago on the night Raven died may be buried along with them. This trip to uncover the past may just be a waste of their time.

Jasmine shifted gears, slowing the Jeep.

Up ahead was the abandoned construction site. Dust devils danced across the barren landscape. Sunlight shimmered off the surface that had been stripped of its topsoil. Heavy machinery stood in silent testimony to the tragedy that had taken place on this site. Like a dark plague, desolation and despair hovered in the air.

It was the first time Storm had visited the site where his brother had supposedly died. A fist of dread gripped his chest, making it hard for him to breathe. He took a shallow breath, struggling to calm his nerves.

Bypassing the newer construction pit, Jasmine slowly steered the Jeep toward the original site. There in the distance Storm saw the yellow crime scene tape rippling in the wind, marking the spot where Raven's remains had been found. His pulse quickened. He steeled himself against the ribbon of pain that flowed through him.

Before he was ready to face the past, Jasmine coasted the Jeep to a stop.

A stifling blanket of dust caught up with them, rolling over them like a thick, dark cloud. Grit coated his skin, clung to his face, his lashes. His eyes burned in irritation—or with emotion, he wasn't sure which.

Jasmine switched off the engine, but remained in her seat. She turned to look at him, waiting for him to take the first step.

Unable to move, he sat frozen in his seat, staring straight ahead.

"Storm?" she asked, her voice tentative, gentle. "Are you sure you want to do this? You don't have to be here—"

"Yes, I do," Storm said, suddenly finding his voice. "This is where my brother's body lay for thirty years. I owe it to Raven to see where he died."

Taking a deep breath of courage, Storm stepped out of the Jeep. His feet felt leaden as he moved slowly toward the area cordoned off by the yellow tape. Behind him he heard the scrape of a boot against the hard-packed dusty ground. Prickles of awareness feathered his skin, telling him that Jasmine was close.

Encouraged by her presence, he forced himself to continue. He ducked beneath the crime scene tape, holding it up for Jasmine to pass under. Her black T-shirt was covered with a thin layer of dust. Her short hair was mussed by the wind, and by restless fingers plowing through it. Deep lines of tension etched her face. She looked almost as nervous as he felt.

But still she found the strength to give him a smile and an encouraging nod.

The shallow pit of an abandoned foundation lay in the center of the circle of tape. Scrape marks from a hand shovel identified the exact location where his brother's remains had been excavated. Removing his sunglasses,

Storm tucked them into the breast pocket of his shirt and carefully made his way to the spot.

Jasmine stood close at his side as he lowered himself on bent knee. Holding his hand inches above the ground, he let it hover for a moment. Saying a silent prayer for the spirits to guide him in his quest to allow his brother's soul to finally find rest, he closed his eyes and lowered his hand to the ground, raking his fingers through the powdery dust.

And felt nothing but a vast emptiness in his heart.

Storm's brows knitted into a frown. His eyes shot open. He scooped up a handful of dirt, letting it sift slowly through his long fingers. Then, shaking the dust from his hand, he looked up, meeting Jasmine's confused gaze.

"My brother's remains may have been here, but his soul never was. He died elsewhere."

"We need to tell the police," Jasmine insisted, quickening her step to catch up with Storm's long-legged stride to the Jeep, unable to shake the feeling that he was running away.

His strong jaw set in a resolute line, he remained stubbornly silent, refusing to answer.

Frustrated at being ignored, she grabbed his arm.

He stopped, wheeling around to face her. His eyes were dark, his glare forbidding. Beneath her fingers she felt a slight tremor in the powerful, sinewy muscles of his forearm, as though he were struggling for control.

A twinge of unwanted fear riffled through her. She tightened her grip, determined to not back down, or to let him see the effect he had on her. "We should let Gretchen Neal know that Raven was killed elsewhere. It could send the investigation into a more positive direction."

Silently, deliberately, Storm looked down at her hand. Then he raised his eyes to her face. She shivered as he held her in his gaze for a long, discomfiting moment. Finally he said, "We can't do that. We can't go to the police."

"Why not?"

"Because, Jasmine, no matter how good a detective she might be, Ms. Neal won't be willing to change the course of her investigation simply because of a 'feeling.' Especially if she knew that feeling came from someone like me, an Indian."

Disappointment and anger billowed up inside Jasmine at the unjustness of his statement. With an irritated breath, she released him, dropping her hand to her side. In his own way Storm was just as narrow-minded as the rest of the people of Whitehorn. She opened her mouth, ready to argue that his heritage should not stand in the way of Gretchen listening to him.

But something stopped her.

Reason returned.

She, of all people, should understand the prejudices of others. She'd grown up with her mother, Celeste, a woman who'd done nothing to hide her beliefs in the spiritual hereafter. Over the years Jasmine had endured the ridicule of a town that thought of her mother as an oddity. But it had not been easy. Unfortunately she understood Storm's hesitancy in revealing his "feelings" to a complete stranger.

With a resigned sigh, the last of her anger dissolved. "All right, we can't talk to the police...yet. So what should we do next?"

"There's nothing more we can accomplish here," he

said as he glanced around the construction site. His impatient gaze glided over the dusty barren ground, the abandoned machinery and the gaping pit. He shook his head, his frustration obvious. "I just keep wondering if there's a connection between finding Raven's remains and Lyle's unexplained behavior. If only we could talk to someone who knew Lyle best. Someone who might be able to help us understand what he had on his mind before he started his rampage."

Jasmine frowned, considering the problem. "Lyle was closest to his mother. Even if she would talk to us, which I doubt, she's already gone back to Elk Springs."

"What about Lyle's grandfather?"

"Garrett?" She shrugged, considering the possibility. "He did spend a lot of time with Lyle those last few weeks."

"Do you think he would talk to us?"

"He's always seemed like a fair and honest man to me. But there's only one way to find out for sure. Why don't we pay him a visit?"

Storm nodded. "Let's go."

Her step lighter, more purposeful, Jasmine headed for the Jeep, chattering as she did so. "Garrett's been living at the main house since he moved to Whitehorn. Right now we're at the opposite end of the Kincaid ranch. I know of a shortcut, though. It'll be quicker if we go through the reservation to get back onto the main road."

Storm's step faltered.

Jasmine skidded on the sandy soil, forcing herself to stop. She looked at him, unable to hide her concern. "Is something wrong?"

"No, nothing's wrong," he said, his tone curt. Once again a stony mask of indifference slipped into place, hiding the flicker of emotion. "It's just this site... It's giving me the creeps. The sooner we get out of here, the better.''

Jasmine nodded and continued walking, but she didn't believe Storm's explanation for a second. She'd seen the look in his eyes. His sudden wariness had nothing to do with the construction site. He hadn't acted skittish until she'd mentioned the reservation.

Unbidden, she felt a surge of sympathy for him. Storm seemed so lost, reminding her of a drifting soul. Though he'd reached out to Summer, the only other time he'd mentioned his family was in regard to Raven's death. She had no idea if he still had any other ties to Laughing Horse.

If his reaction to going back to the reservation was any indication, she doubted it.

Pushing aside the troubling thought, she climbed into the Jeep and waited for Storm to join her. Once he was settled, she revved the engine to life. Making a quick U-turn, she headed down the gravel road that would take them to the reservation.

The road soon narrowed, rising and falling as they skirted the foothills of the Crazy Mountains. With the aid of the four-wheel drive, Jasmine maneuvered the Jeep through the rugged terrain with ease, seeming to enjoy the bumpy ride.

Storm glanced at her, his brow raised in question as she plowed through a shallow creek bed and sent a spray of water shooting up into the air around them. ''Are you sure you know where you're going?''

She grinned. ''You're not worried, are you?''

''Worried? Of course not. We're only miles from nowhere. No living soul in sight. It's just the spot I'd pick to have a flat tire, or a breakdown.''

"So much for your confidence in my driving abilities," she said, raising her nose in indignation. But he caught the twinkle in her eye and the slight curve of a smile on her lips.

Her lighthearted mood worked to ease some of the tension from his muscles. The truth was, Storm had never intended to return to Laughing Horse. Now that he was on reservation land, he tried to ignore the growing sense of dread.

"I'll have you know I've spent many a summer exploring these mountains," she said, interrupting his pensive thoughts. "I know these peaks like the back of my hand. Besides, we're not that far from civilization."

As though to prove her point, the ground slowly leveled out. The road, while still rugged, straightened, with tall, fragrant stands of pine trees flanking both sides. While he knew the effort was futile, he sat back and tried to not let disturbing memories interfere with his enjoyment of the breathtaking scenery.

He glanced at Jasmine. "Do you mind if I ask you something?"

"Not at all. Ask away," she said, keeping her tone light, though he heard the catch of uncertainty in her voice.

Earlier he'd warned himself to keep a safe distance from her. Now he was breaking his own silent vow to not become personally involved. But he felt the need to find something—anything—to keep his mind off of his own past.

"Back at the construction site, when I told you that Raven died elsewhere, you accepted my feeling without question. I just wondered why."

"Years of experience," Jasmine said with a self-deprecating smile. Then she explained. "I grew up with a mother who places a lot of stock in the power of the spiritual hereafter. Communicating with restless souls from the past is an everyday occurrence in my household.''

''Your mother communicates with the dead?'' Storm frowned, not sure whether to believe her.

''Seances, meditation…you name it, she does it.''

''I see.''

''No, I don't think you do. I know it sounds crazy,'' she said, her tone defensive. ''But I've witnessed too many things to know that not everything my mother believes in can be attributed to what people call 'a high-strung woman's overactive imagination.'''

''I never said I didn't believe you,'' he said, meeting her fiery gaze. ''Respecting your mother's faith in the spiritual world isn't crazy. It only proves that you're wise for someone so young.''

''Here we go again with my age.'' She shook her head and rolled her eyes. ''You know, it's funny, but my mother used to tell me that I was old beyond my years. She called me an 'old soul' and insisted that a part of me lived before in another life.''

Storm didn't laugh at her mother's homegrown explanation. Instead he said, ''The Cheyenne hold similar beliefs and explanations for the unknown. Your mother has good instincts despite…'' He stopped, letting the words drift.

''Despite the way she's behaved since you've arrived in town?'' Jasmine finished for him. Sighing, she said, ''Believe it or not, my mother is one of the most open-minded people I've ever known. Her reaction to you has been unusual. Never before has she allowed the color of a man's skin or his family heritage to influence her judgment of him.''

"I believe you, Jasmine," he said, surprising himself that he really meant the soothing words. "This investigation into my brother's death has been difficult for all of us. I know it's placed a strain on your mother. I, of all people, should know what stress can do to a person."

She looked at him, her gaze questioning.

Knowing he'd said too much, but unable to stop, he purged himself of memories that had been bottled up inside him for too many years. "When I left Laughing Horse I was only thirteen years old."

"You were just a boy."

Storm shook his head. "I hadn't been a boy for many years. I was old enough to fend for myself. For a long time, I wandered until I found a place in New Mexico to settle. I worked during the day on a ranch. At night, I studied to earn my high school degree. From there, I went on to Albuquerque and attended college, then law school."

"You've accomplished a lot in your lifetime," she said, her voice tentative.

"If you mean by accumulating material wealth, yes, I have. Over the years I've worked hard to succeed in the white man's world." He looked out at the beautiful landscape of the Laughing Horse Reservation. "But in the eyes of the Cheyenne, material items aren't what's important. The richest man on the reservation is the man who gives of himself to everyone else. Despite the pro bono work and the civil liberty cases that I've taken on to defend my people, I've traveled among the white man for so long, I've forgotten my own roots. The years have made my heart hard."

"I'm sorry, Storm. I had no idea—"

"I'm not looking for sympathy, Jasmine," he said, cutting her off abruptly. "I only meant to tell you that I understand how your mother must feel. That I know of the burden of responsibility that we place upon ourselves.''

Emotion shimmered in her eyes. Jasmine looked as though she wanted to say something more to ease his turmoil. But she hesitated, looking uncertain. Instead she let the silence lengthen between them and focused her attention on the rugged road.

Soon a homestead came into view. The paint on the white clapboard house was peeling. Chickens roamed the grounds, scratching in the dirt. To one side of the yard, a car was raised on cement blocks, its wheels missing.

Storm replaced his sunglasses and he pressed his lips into a grim line as he fought to control the anxiety mounting inside him. They passed more houses, each in various states of disrepair. As they neared the heart of the reservation, Storm held himself stiffly in his seat. Unable to help himself, he searched the streets for a familiar landmark.

Then suddenly it was there.

''Stop,'' he said, startling Jasmine. He pointed to a small, ramshackle house. ''Pull over there.''

Braking, Jasmine did as he'd asked. She slid the Jeep to a stop at the side of the road, parking next to a thick tangle of weeds and overgrown grass. Turning off the engine, she swiveled around to face him, watching him as he stared at the house.

It looked abandoned, in even worse shape than the others they'd passed. Rusting junk filled the untended yard. The small shack leaned unsteadily on its foundation. The paint was completely worn from its clapboard siding. The collapsed remains of a front porch lay on the ground, as though no one had bothered to pick it up from where it had fallen. Sadly, the neglected house looked beyond repair.

Sliding his sunglasses from the bridge of his nose, Storm studied the abandoned house, his eyes stinging with unwanted emotion. He slung himself out of the Jeep. Unmindful of the brambly weeds that snagged his jeans, he took a step toward the house. Then stopped. Standing frozen in the yard, he stared in silence.

Climbing down from the Jeep, swishing her way through the tall weeds, Jasmine joined him. She stood quietly beside him, waiting for him to speak.

"This was my parents' house," he said, finally finding his voice, though the words sounded flat, hollow of emotion. "This is where I spent the first thirteen years of my life."

Jasmine didn't say a word. Not pushing him, she let him decide how much to reveal.

"My parents were alcoholics," he said, unable to stop the words, needing to share his past with her. "For as long as I remember, my father went from one job to another, never finding anything that would satisfy him. My mother grew tired of complaining. She gave up on changing his ways. Instead of trying to improve their lives, they both turned to alcohol to escape their fate."

He swallowed hard as the bitter taste of self-pity rose in his throat. "My brother, Raven, was older than me. He was more of a father to me than my own father ever was. As long as Raven was here, life was bearable. But when he left…" He shook his head, closing his eyes against the painful memory. "I couldn't stand to live here any longer. When Raven left, I ran away, and I didn't look back."

Her voice gentle, she asked, "You never heard from your parents?"

Opening his eyes, he forced himself to look at the house that still haunted his dreams. His throat tightening, he said, "No, no one ever tried to find me. If they even noticed that I was gone, they were probably relieved that I'd left. It was one less mouth for them to feed."

"Oh, Storm," she murmured, her voice catching with emotion. "I'm so sorry."

Giving a mirthless laugh, he said, "So am I."

Until that moment Jasmine had kept her distance, letting him spill out all of his anger and bitterness. Now she did the one thing he needed the most—she reached out and took him into her arms. With her warm, reassuring body pressed against his, she held him close until the tremors shaking his body were stilled.

Eight

The bond between them was growing stronger.

In front of the deserted home of his youth, Jasmine held Storm in her arms, not afraid to give him the comfort she instinctively knew he needed. He clung to her, his large hands gripping her waist, holding her tight. His strong body trembled, overwhelmed by emotions to which only he was privy. With a sigh, he pressed his smooth cheek against hers. Their bodies melded and she felt his heart pounding in his chest, matching her own erratic pulse beat for beat. Their stolen moment of closeness brought a quivering of awareness deep in the pit of her belly.

She wasn't sure how long they stood that way, entwined in each other's arms. Time seemed to have stopped. It had no meaning, no consequences. All that mattered was holding him, touching him, easing his pain.

His chest rose and fell as he took in a deep breath. Still holding her close, he lifted his head, just far enough to look at her. With her face inches from his, their lips almost touching, the air crackled between them with a sensual spark of awareness. Heat flushed her skin. Her breath caught in her throat. In his dark eyes, she saw the reflection of her own desire.

Slowly, Storm lowered his head, closing the distance between them. He came closer...and closer...until the shadow of a large, dark bird passed overhead, blocking the sun. Swooping low, it landed in a nearby tree, disturbing a squirrel from its branch. The rodent's chattering protest echoed across the yard, spoiling the quiet hush that had surrounded them.

Distracted, Storm glanced up at the tree and frowned.

Jasmine felt a twinge of disappointment at the interruption. Her lips longed for his touch. Her body throbbed with a need only Storm could fulfill. She had never felt this way before, this restless ache deep inside her. It seemed incomprehensible that the world around her had remained unchanged while her life had been turned upside down. In her heart she knew nothing would ever be the same.

But it was more than just lust. Whether Storm wanted to admit it or not, they were connecting on a level that went beyond a mere physical attraction. Though they'd met each other only a short time ago, it seemed as though she'd known him all her life. She shivered, struck once again by a feeling of déjà vu. The ease they felt when they were together, the undeniable attraction that raged just below the surface, it was as though they'd been lovers once before.

That they were meant to be together again.

Curling her fingers into the thick strands of hair at the back of his neck, she forced his attention back to her. Her resolve melted beneath the sudden intensity of his troubled gaze. Gathering her strength, she said, "Storm, I—"

Before she could put into words what she felt in her heart, a truck slowly drove past, its driver staring at them. Jasmine recognized the driver. He was the reservation's new tribal chief, Jackson Hawk.

She wasn't the only one to notice the unexpected attention.

Storm's muscles tensing, he looked across the yard to meet the other man's curious gaze.

Though it was obvious the two men knew each other, instead of stopping, Jackson Hawk continued down the gravel road. Storm's reaction was quick and brutal. He pushed himself from her embrace. With a look of chagrin, he put an unforgivable distance between them.

Jasmine felt a chill that had nothing to do with the warm weather. The coldness came from within, from the icy fear that had enveloped her heart.

"It's getting late," Storm said, his voice as distant as the look now in his eyes. "If we're going to the Kincaid ranch to visit Garrett, we'd better get moving."

Numbly, Jasmine nodded. Her vision blurred with unwanted tears as she waded through the tall weeds. Blinking hard, she refused to let her own disappointment show. She would not allow Storm to see just how much she'd been hurt by his rejection. Obviously she'd been wrong. She'd read more into the embrace than Storm had meant.

The heavier sound of his footsteps followed her to the Jeep. Jasmine's heart thumped so hard against her chest, she thought it might break in two. Never before had she felt such pain.

Over and over again in her mind's eye, she saw the stony expression cross Storm's face when Jackson Hawk had driven by, the quickness with which he'd pushed her away. A part of her couldn't help but wonder if Storm was embarrassed at being caught in an intimate embrace with her because she wasn't a Native American, if in his own way, he held a prejudice against the color of her skin.

Unsettled by the thought, Jasmine climbed into the Jeep and waited for him to join her. She refused to look at him, keeping her gaze focused on her trembling hands that she held fisted in her lap.

Storm approached. He hesitated, standing with one hand braced against the rollover bar, watching her. With a prickling of awareness, she felt the heavy measure of his gaze. He didn't move, or speak, until she raised her eyes to look at him. "Jasmine, I…" He stopped, averted his gaze and swore softly beneath his breath. Then facing her once again, he said, "I just wanted to thank you. Coming here today…it wasn't easy for me. I appreciate not having to be alone."

She nodded, feeling a sudden rush of warmth. The icy lock thawed from around her heart. He'd neither apologized nor explained his behavior. But his gratitude was a step in the right direction. For now it would have to do.

"You're welcome, Storm," she said, hiding her relief behind a crisp, business-like tone. "Now, I'd like to get to the Kincaid ranch before it gets too late."

"Yes, ma'am." The corner of his mouth lifted into a half grin, softening the hard angles of his face. With a mock salute, he climbed aboard, settling his tall frame into the seat next to hers.

Jasmine turned the ignition and revved the motor to life. Pulling away from the grassy roadside, she drove from the house that held so many bittersweet memories for Storm, thankful to be leaving it behind.

The rest of their journey through the Laughing Horse Reservation was accomplished in uneasy silence. Though they received a handful of stares from curious passersby, no one stopped to wave or to make them feel welcome. Glad to escape the unwanted scrutiny, Jasmine turned onto the main road and headed for the Kincaid ranch.

The sun lit the grounds of the ranch house. A cool

breeze swept the manicured yard of the stately surroundings. But there wasn't a single soul in sight. Jasmine
wondered if they should have called before stopping by.
She hoped they hadn't wasted their time, making the long
trip.

Parking in front of the house, Jasmine smoothed a hand
through her wind-tousled hair and stepped out of the
Jeep. She waited for Storm to join her on the front steps.
Standing in front of the house, she felt goose bumps race
across her skin as an omen of dread traveled through her.

If she was this nervous at the thought of entering the
ranch house, she wondered what Storm must be feeling.
After all, this was the house where Storm's brother,
Raven, and her aunt, Blanche, had met and had fallen in
love. Tragically, it was also the last place Raven had been
seen alive.

Despite the dark history the house held for both of their
families, Storm seemed amazingly at ease. He walked
with confidence, his head held high and his wide shoulders straight. It was as though he were trying to prove a
point to anyone who might be watching. That no one
would take away his pride.

Giving Storm a quick smile of encouragement, Jasmine
rang the doorbell.

Garrett Kincaid answered the door himself, much to
her surprise. Tall and rawboned, in his early seventies,
Garrett had a thick head of silvery hair. Standing in the
doorway of the sprawling ranch house, his resemblance
to Jeremiah Kincaid was uncanny. It was as though the
family photos of Jeremiah had come to life. So taken
aback by this unexpected image of her late uncle, Jasmine
found herself speechless.

The similarity ended when, instead of receiving her
uncle's usual scowl, Garrett smiled in greeting. Jeremiah

would never have been quite so civil to an unexpected guest. "Jasmine, this is a surprise. And you've brought a visitor. Please come in, both of you."

Stepping back, he let them enter the large foyer.

The spacious rooms were cool and dark. The furnishings in the house looked well-worn and dated, but still comfortable.

Remembering her manners, Jasmine turned to Garrett, making the proper introductions. "Garrett, I'd like you to meet Storm Hunter. Storm, Garrett Kincaid."

The two men shook hands. Of similar height and build, they stood eye-to-eye, sizing each other up. Unlike her mother, or the townspeople of Whitehorn, Garrett didn't question her being in Storm's company. His instant acceptance shouldn't have surprised her, since he shared Storm's heritage. Cheyenne blood also ran through Garrett's veins.

"Hunter?" Garrett frowned, his gaze thoughtful. "The name sounds familiar. You wouldn't be related to—"

"Raven Hunter," Storm finished for him. "He was my brother."

Garrett nodded, the news bringing a flicker of concern to his eyes. "I see."

"That's why we're here," Jasmine said, hurrying to explain. "The investigation into Raven's death is going nowhere. We're trying to find any new information that might help us figure out what happened on the night he died."

Garrett lifted one silvery brow. "I've already talked to the police when they came to check Jeremiah's old gun collection. I'm not sure what else I can add."

"This ranch, it's where—" Storm stopped, looking frustrated.

"It's where Raven was last seen alive," Jasmine finished for him. "And the construction site for the casino and resort, it's where Raven's remains were found. We know your connection to Raven's death is secondhand, but there's still a connection."

"I guess I see your point." Garrett sighed. "Well, let's not stand here in the foyer. Let's go to the study, where it's more comfortable, and talk about this."

The study was large and roomy, the furniture masculine. Bookcases and faded wallpaper lined the walls. The deep hues of an Oriental rug covered the polished wooden floor. A large desk stood in the center of the room, with a worn leather chair behind it, and a pair of matching wing chairs in front. Garrett stepped behind the desk, taking his place in the leather swivel chair. Jasmine and Storm claimed the wing chairs for themselves.

"Now," Garrett said, the leather creaking as he turned his chair toward them, "how can I help you?"

Jasmine glanced at Storm, looking to him for guidance. Instead of meeting her gaze, he gripped the arms of his chair and stared straight ahead. Since Garrett was her relative, she assumed that he wanted her to do the questioning. Turning to Garrett, she said, "We just came from the construction site for the casino and resort, the place where Raven's remains were found."

Garrett nodded, encouraging her to continue.

Storm remained unusually quiet.

"It's just that, we feel the coincidence is odd. Raven's body being found at the construction site, then Lyle doing what he did. We can't help but wonder if there's a connection between Raven's death and Lyle's—" She stopped, biting her lip. "Well, his unexpected behavior."

"You don't have to sugarcoat it for my sake, Jasmine," Garrett said with a weary sigh. "Lyle went off the deep end. He killed one person and tried to murder another. His behavior was more than unexpected. It was unforgivable.''

Jasmine flushed, feeling as though she were invading Garrett's private grief. "I'm sorry, Garrett. I know how hard this must be. Maybe we shouldn't be here now.''

"No," Garrett said, giving his head a firm shake. "I'm glad you came. Everyone else has been pussyfooting around, treating me like I was as fragile as an eggshell. It feels good to talk about it, to get it out in the open.'' He leaned back in his chair and frowned. "The problem is, I don't see how there could be a connection between Lyle's and Raven's deaths.'' He looked at Storm. "From what I understand, your brother apparently died almost thirty years ago.''

Storm nodded.

Jasmine glanced at him, her concern growing. Something was wrong. Storm was more than just quiet. His face had taken on an unhealthy pallor. Fine droplets of sweat beaded his forehead. His jaw was clenched in a tight line. He looked as though he'd been stricken.

"Well, Lyle was only twenty-two," Garrett continued, oblivious to the undercurrents of tension flowing through the room. "He wasn't even born when Raven died.''

"I know it sounds crazy," Jasmine said, forcing herself to concentrate on the conversation at hand. "But somehow it seems as though finding Raven's remains triggered the events leading to Lyle's death. Did Lyle say anything to you that might have explained his strange behavior?''

"Not to me," Garrett said, his tone regretful. "Other than complaining about the delay in construction, Lyle never talked the discovery of Raven Hunter's remains.''

Jasmine gave a frustrated sigh, unwilling to admit they

were wasting their time. "So what happens next? The construction site looked abandoned. With all the bad luck surrounding the site, I wouldn't blame you if you decided to scrap the plans."

"The plans haven't been scrapped," Garrett said, his voice ringing with determination. "In fact, I've just been talking to the tribal leaders at Laughing Horse. We've decided to go ahead with the casino and resort. But this time I'll be taking over the Kincaid interests. I'm going to make damned sure that a fair arrangement is made with the Cheyenne people."

Jasmine felt a new respect for the older man. She wondered how a man with such strength and morality could have spawned a grandchild as corrupt and evil as Lyle had been. "Will you be starting soon?"

"Just as soon as the engineers pick another site for us to dig on." Shaking his head, he gave a wry grin. "Can you believe it? We hit a stubborn vein of bedrock at the second site. Now we have to move the whole shebang and start all over again."

Jasmine shivered. "More bad luck."

"That's for sure," Garrett said, his sigh wistful. Suddenly he seemed very tired, the years showing on his face.

Sensing that they'd overstayed their welcome, Jasmine stood. Storm followed her lead, rising slowly to his feet, his expression still troubled.

Garrett rounded the desk and escorted them through the house to the front door. Turning to Storm, he extended a hand and said, "Good luck with your search. I hope you'll find what you've been looking for soon."

"Thank you for your help," Storm said, accepting the polite gesture, seeming to have regained some of his composure.

Garrett enveloped Jasmine in a bear hug and murmured, "It's good to see you again, Jasmine. Next time bring the rest of your family along and we'll have a proper visit."

She nodded an assent and smiled. Exchanging their good-byes, Jasmine and Storm returned to the Jeep and left the Kincaid ranch. But before they'd even gotten past the front gates, Storm leaned back in his seat, closed his eyes and took an audible breath.

Jasmine shot him a worried glance and demanded, "What's wrong?"

"Nothing," he said, shaking his head. Slowly he opened his eyes, though he wouldn't meet her gaze. "Just the beginnings of a headache."

She frowned, not sure whether to believe him. Storm didn't look like the type of man who let something as small as a headache stand in the way of his getting what he wanted. "You didn't say much in Garrett's study."

"You were asking all the right questions. I didn't see the need to interfere."

"Interfere? Storm, this is your brother's death we're looking into. You, of all people, should have the right to ask a few simple questions."

He sighed, looking out onto the late day sun along the horizon of the rolling expanse of green pastures. "What Garrett had to say…that wasn't what was most important about our visit to the Kincaid ranch."

"It wasn't?" Her frown deepened. "Then what was this all about? Why did we go out of our way to get here, if it wasn't to talk to Garrett?"

"The house, Jasmine," he said cryptically. "The answer is in the house."

Jasmine gripped the steering wheel, feeling the frustration churning inside her. "I don't understand. What does the house have to do with anything?"

He shook his head. "I'm not sure, yet. But there's something."

"Storm, you're not making any sense."

"I know," he said, rubbing a hand to his temple, looking tired and beaten. "Trust me, Jasmine. I'm just as confused as you are. As soon as I figure it out, you'll be the first person I'll tell."

This time she did believe him. At the moment Storm was being deliberately evasive, but perhaps with good reason. Something obviously had bothered him when he was in the study at the Kincaid ranch. But if he didn't want to share his unease with her, then she must respect his wishes.

Besides, he'd promised to tell her the truth eventually. It was time to prove that she trusted his word.

They drove the rest of the way into town in silence. When they arrived at Storm's hotel, Jasmine parked the Jeep in a slot in front of his room. Delaying his departure, she shifted in her seat to look at him. "That headache of yours any better?"

He grimaced. "Not much."

"It's getting late. Neither of us has had much to eat today. Maybe dinner would help?"

His gaze lingered on her face. He looked tempted by the offer. "Dinner sounds good. Unfortunately, I'm just not up to it right now. Do you mind if I take a rain check?"

"Of course not," she said, averting her gaze, feeling the telltale warmth of embarrassment rise on her face. Being turned down wasn't easy, no matter what the circumstance.

"Jasmine," he said, his voice a hoarse whisper against

the softness of the dusky hour. Before she realized his intentions, Storm reached across the car, crooking his fingers beneath her chin. He lifted her face to look at him. "Thank you for helping me today."

She swallowed hard, not trusting herself to answer.

But she didn't need to speak.

Storm's actions spoke volumes, needing little interpretation. Leaning across the seat, he tenderly captured her mouth with his.

Jasmine's lips trembled beneath his gentle kiss. Closing her eyes, she took in a shuddering breath, savoring the feel of his warm mouth against hers.

Seeming encouraged by her response, Storm slid his hand to the back of her neck, cradling her. Slowly, deliberately, he pulled her closer and deepened the kiss.

She gripped his shoulders, steadying herself, giving in to the sweet sensations that flooded her body. Moist heat pooled in the pit of her stomach, sending out warm tendrils of awareness. Never before had she felt such an intense longing for a man. Yet these new feelings didn't scare her. Touching him, kissing him, wanting him, it all seemed as natural as taking a breath.

Tentatively, his tongue brushed her lips.

Without hesitation, she opened her mouth to his gentle demands. Twining her fingers through his thick strands of hair, she tugged him even closer.

Moaning, he glided his hands down the length of her back. His long fingers spanned her waist, measuring its narrow breadth. The heat of his palms burned through the thin material of her shirt, branding her with his touch.

Her strength abandoned her. Jasmine collapsed against him, losing all sense of caution and reason in the smoky haze of desire.

Impatiently he shifted his long legs, angling for a more

comfortable position. In the process, he knocked his knee against the gearshift. The crack of bone against the metal bar sounded in the Jeep, splintering the intimate mood, bringing them both crashing back to reality.

Reluctantly Jasmine pushed away, giving herself a much-needed moment to cool her passion-heated senses.

What had she been thinking?

They were in the middle of a hotel parking lot, teetering on the verge of making love, their actions exposed for anyone to see. In a town the size of Whitehorn, gossip traveled fast. While she didn't care about what others thought, she did care about her mother. Celeste didn't know Jasmine had spent the day with Storm. All it would take was a simple phone call from a concerned "friend" for Celeste to know her daughter had lied to her once again.

"I need to go," she said, with all the regret she felt in her heart.

Storm nodded, studying her flushed face. "We have a lot to talk about. When can I see you again?"

"Tomorrow," she promised as his words raised the fine hairs on the back of her neck, signaling a reckless thrill of excitement. This time he'd made no pretense of using the hunt for Raven's murderer as an excuse to see her. They were skirting dangerous territory. "Late morning, after breakfast at the B and B."

Storm nodded. With one last lingering look, he climbed out onto the pavement. Standing on the sidewalk, he watched as she started the engine and backed out of the parking lot.

With his gaze following her, Jasmine felt his presence as though he were still sitting next to her. She had never felt this way before, this overwhelmed by a man.

Little by little, Storm was letting down his defenses.

They were getting closer by the minute. While encouraged, she tried not to let her hopes get too high, or to read too much into his actions.

In her heart she knew they were meant to be together. Today they'd taken a giant step toward forging a real relationship. But there were still too many obstacles standing in their way. Only time would tell if they could make this fledgling alliance last.

Storm stood outside his hotel room and watched until the tail lights of the Jeep faded into the dusky twilight. His heart beat so fast against his rib cage it felt as though it were about to explode. His lungs burned in his chest. Slowly he released the breath he hadn't even realized he'd been holding.

She'd gotten to him somehow.

Despite his resolve to keep her at arm's length, Jasmine had done what no other woman had ever accomplished. She'd broken through that protective shell he'd carefully erected around his heart. And she'd made him care.

Care about the future.

Care about her.

He hadn't a clue what to do next.

Storm raked both hands through his hair, tucking the long strands behind his ears. Getting involved with a woman, especially a woman like Jasmine, hadn't been in his plans. He'd come back to Whitehorn for one reason. And one reason alone.

To see that justice was done.

A justice that was thirty years past due.

The thought chilled him, cooling the heat of passion that raced like a fire through his veins. His brother had been murdered. He'd been brutally killed and his body dumped in an abandoned field. That was what had brought him back to Whitehorn.

Not the lure of a beautiful woman.

The fact that Jasmine was a member of the Kincaid family only complicated matters more. What he hadn't been able to tell her on the way back into town was that he'd had another feeling while at the Kincaid ranch house. As soon as he'd walked through the doors of the study, he'd been overcome by the lingering presence of his brother's soul. Storm had no doubt. He knew the study had been the last place his brother had been alive.

Which told him only one thing. A Kincaid had been involved in his brother's murder.

A member of Jasmine's own family.

Storm sucked in a steadying breath and inhaled the delicate scent of wildflowers, Jasmine's scent. He moaned in frustration. Even with Jasmine miles away, his clothes still held the fragrant traces of their embrace. Steeling himself against the memory, he pressed his mouth in a resolute line and tasted the lingering sweetness of her lips.

He couldn't stop thinking about her. Or wanting her.

But he had no choice.

Later, when he had time to sort through his feelings, he would decide what to do about Jasmine. For now there was something else that needed his attention.

He had a long overdue visit to pay.

Nine

With no streetlights to guide him, the rough road leading into the Laughing Horse Reservation demanded all of his attention. The headlights of his car barely penetrated the thick darkness, making the potholes nearly impossible to see. Storm bounced over the ruts, wondering if the rented car's shock absorbers would hold out over the rugged terrain.

His white-knuckled grip tightened around the leather-wrapped steering wheel as he fought to ease the tension that filled him. He'd thought coming back to the reservation would be easier the second time around. But he'd been wrong. The painful memories of his past were just as sharp now as they had been earlier this afternoon.

Even more so, now that Jasmine wasn't beside him to ease the blow.

Being back on the reservation today and seeing the dilapidated house that had been his home, he'd been taken by surprise, rocked by the memories and shaken by unexpected emotions. And Jasmine...

Storm released a long, shaky breath. Jasmine had stood by him, waiting patiently for him to regain his control. Unlike most Anglos that he'd dealt with, she hadn't demanded answers, demanded to know everything he was feeling. Instead she'd listened quietly, letting him be the judge of how much he'd wanted to reveal.

And reveal he had.

He'd spilled out his entire miserable childhood to her. Storm's jaw clenched; his face warmed at the memory. Since leaving Whitehorn, he hadn't spoken of his past to anyone else. Even now he didn't understand why he'd felt the need to share it with Jasmine.

Or did he?

In the darkness the outline of the Tribal Center loomed up ahead, giving him an excuse to push his troubled thoughts aside. Storm slowed his car and eased into the parking lot. Turning off the ignition, he stared at the sprawling building. The huge complex housed the reservation's tribal offices, including those of the tribal leader, Jackson Hawk.

Storm had known Jackson since childhood. Once they'd been friends. Though they'd lost contact over the years, Jackson had been the one to track him down in New Mexico to tell him of the discovery of Raven's remains. Since his arrival in Whitehorn, however, Storm had only brief and impersonal contact with Jackson. His choice, not Jackson's, he admitted, shifting uneasily in his seat. Until now they'd met on neutral ground, never on reservation land. Storm had carefully insulated himself from his past the best he could.

But that was about to change.

Gathering his wavering resolve, he opened the door of the car and stepped out into the night. The air felt cool, bracing. The reservation seemed inordinately quiet, as though the community had drawn a hushed breath at his arrival. Climbing the stairs of the building, he paused to read the black letters painted on the door of the complex. Welcome To The Laughing Horse Tribal Center. Home Of The Northern Cheyenne Western Band.

Home. The cold palm of loneliness pressed its icy fingers against his back, chilling him. Laughing Horse had stopped being his home almost thirty years ago. Since then he'd lived and worked in New Mexico. But there he had no house, only an apartment. No family, since his job was his life. He had made no roots in the community to make it feel as though he truly belonged.

For the first time he realized he had no place to call his home.

Shaking off the bleak thought, Storm yanked open the door and stepped into the dimly lit building. A single light coming from an office down the hall marked his destination. His footsteps sounded too loud in the quiet building, making him feel as though he were an intruder. The weight of uncertainty pressed against his shoulders, slowing his step. Second thoughts eroded his confidence. His decision to come had been impulsive.

Perhaps he'd made a mistake.

Stopping just outside the doorway of the office, he peered inside. Jackson Hawk sat with his back to him, his long legs outstretched, his boot-clad feet propped on the sill of the window that overlooked the reservation grounds. He wore faded jeans and a white T-shirt. Hardly appropriate attire for a tribal official. But as Storm recalled from their youth, Jackson had always been something of a rebel.

Jackson's long black hair was pulled back into braids. From the reflection in the night-darkened window, Storm saw that his eyes were closed, the sharp features of his face relaxed. He hesitated in the doorway, debating whether or not to disturb the new tribal leader.

With his eyes still closed, Jackson murmured, "Well, Storm, my friend, are you staying or not?"

Storm flinched, the unexpectedness of the words startling him.

Smiling, Jackson opened his eyes. His feet hit the floor

with a thud as he swiveled around to face him. "Don't look so surprised. I haven't turned psychic on you. Not yet, anyway." His grin deepening, he motioned to the window. "I happened to be watching when you pulled that fancy car of yours into the lot."

Fancy car. From anyone else it would have been considered just a casual remark. Coming from a fellow Cheyenne, it was a jab at his show of wealth, of his apparent adoption of the white man's ways. Storm stared at Jackson, his defenses on instant alert.

After a long moment Jackson filled the gaping silence. "I'm glad you're here, Storm. I wondered when you would finally come back to the reservation."

At the subtle censure in Jackson's tone, Storm's wariness grew. It took all of his willpower to not turn on his heel and run, to escape from this unsettling meeting. Instead, gathering his courage, he set his jaw in a determined line and said, "I'm here...for now."

Jackson rose to his feet, stretching to his full six-foot-plus height. Rounding the desk, he closed the distance between them. The two men stood eye-to-eye, their gazes guarded.

"So you're a big-shot lawyer in New Mexico," Jackson said, the words sounding like a taunt.

Anger flared inside Storm. Refusing to be baited into an argument, he returned calmly, "I have a practice in Albuquerque."

"A lucrative practice from what I can see." The man who'd once been his friend, raked an assessing glance, taking in his professionally styled haircut, the gold watch on his wrist and his casual yet expensive clothes. The corner of Jackson's mouth lifted into a smirk. "You've learned to blend in well with the white man's world."

"I didn't come to discuss my business practices,"

Storm said, unable to keep the defensive note from his voice.

Crossing his arms against his chest, Jackson sat on the edge of his desk. "Then why did you come?"

"I saw you this afternoon," Storm said.

"Ah, yes." Jackson nodded, his gaze thoughtful. "I wasn't sure if you'd noticed my presence. You were otherwise—" He tapped a finger against his chin, lifting a suggestive brow. "How shall I say it? You were occupied with a beautiful woman. A beautiful *white* woman."

Storm's hands balled into fists of rage at the innuendo. It took all of his strength to hold them stiffly at his sides. "You have no right to judge whom I choose to see."

"Someone has to use good judgment. It's obvious that you're not."

"What are you talking about?" The harsh demand reverberated throughout the small room. The force of the words surprised even himself. Coming here, Storm's intention had been to tell Jackson that he'd misread what he'd seen that afternoon. That there was nothing between him and Jasmine.

Instead he was defending his right to be with her.

Jackson's measuring gaze never wavered. "I'm talking about your involvement with a white woman. A Kincaid, no less."

The sharp reminder struck like a blow, leaving its mark.

"Did you forget? Raven died because he fell in love with a Kincaid," Jackson said, shaking his head and looking disappointed. "Can't you see that you're repeating your brother's mistake? You and I both know you're asking for more trouble than you can handle."

"Stay out of it, Jackson. It's none of your damn business," Storm said, his voice shaking with barely controlled emotion.

"Or what? Are you going to push me away, too, just like you pushed your family away when Raven died? Or have you lived so long in the white man's world that you don't even know when you're turning your back on your people?"

Hot anger flowed through him, setting his blood on fire. Storm's heart pounded in his chest, the sound echoing in his ears. "You don't know what you're talking about, Jackson. My parents pushed me out of their lives long before I left the reservation. They chose to drown themselves in alcohol. I wasn't going to stay and watch them do it. And I haven't forgotten my people. I've done more work for Native Americans than any other attorney—"

"In New Mexico perhaps. But not here in Whitehorn." Jackson stood, a vein pulsing at his temple, his face set in a hard, condemning line. "Why don't you admit it, Storm? You've shunned your life on Laughing Horse and the Cheyenne people. You've even found a white woman, a trophy wife to prove yourself worthy to live in the white man's world."

In a blaze of red heat, something exploded deep inside him. Grabbing a fistful of Jackson's shirt, Storm slammed him against the wall. The impact shook the framed documents hanging nearby. Through clenched teeth, Storm said, "Don't you ever talk about Jasmine in that way. She would never be any man's trophy wife. She's too special to settle for something like that."

To his surprise, instead of continuing the argument, Jackson smiled.

At first Storm didn't understand the other man's reaction. Then, suddenly, the meaning became all too clear.

His heart skipped a beat. His head felt light, as though he were floating above his body, as an observer, not a participant in this farce. He realized that he'd just been coerced into revealing his true feelings for Jasmine.

Slowly he released his old friend. His strength seemed to have seeped away with his anger. Raking his fingers through his hair, Storm sank into a nearby chair.

"I'm sorry, my friend. I never meant to hurt you," Jackson murmured, straightening his shirt as he returned to his seat on the edge of the desk. "But I knew you would never admit to me, or to anyone, just how far your relationship with Jasmine had gone, if I didn't use a little deception. I had to know the truth."

Storm shook his head. "You want to know the truth? The truth is, I don't know what's happening between me and Jasmine."

"But there is something," Jackson said.

Storm fell into an uneasy silence, unable to admit his own feelings, even to himself.

Jackson heaved a strained sigh. "Storm, do you have any idea what you're getting yourself into—"

"I don't need a lecture, Jackson," Storm said, abruptly cutting him off. "I know all the reasons why I should stay away from her."

"Yet, you still see her."

A statement, not a question. Storm felt the unnecessary need to explain. "Jasmine's helping me. We're trying to find out the truth behind Raven's death."

Jackson gave a harsh laugh. "And you trust her? What if she discovers something that will hurt her family? Do you really think she'd betray them in order to help you?"

Struggling to hide his own uncertainty, Storm said, "Jasmine is the most honest woman I have ever met, white or Native American. If she finds something that will answer the questions behind Raven's death, then she will tell me.''

Jackson didn't answer. The skeptical look in his eye spoke volumes.

He was wasting his time. Jackson was almost militant in his jaded opinion of the white man's intentions. Storm would never be able to change his mind. Feeling tired and defeated, more lost and alone than he'd ever felt before, he rose to his feet, unwilling to continue the useless debate.

Storm had returned to Whitehorn with the intention of finding peace, for himself and Raven. So far, all that he had found was bitterness and turmoil.

Without another word, he turned on his heel and headed for the door.

Before he'd gotten far, Jackson said, "It's not too late to come home, Storm. You can still be a part of our people's lives. Here on Laughing Horse you can make a difference.''

Storm's step faltered. Reluctantly he turned to face his old friend.

"I know that I've told you this before, but now that I've taken over the duties of tribal chief, the council could use a new tribal lawyer.'' Jackson smiled, his sharp features softening with amusement. "Especially a lawyer who has had experience handling pro bono civil liberty cases.''

His own words came to haunt him. Having no answer for his friend, Storm turned and left.

Her mother was waiting for her when she returned to the Big Sky Bed & Breakfast. She was outside on the porch, curled up on a wicker chair, sitting alone in the dark. Her quiet voice startled Jasmine as she climbed the front steps. "You're home, Jasmine."

"Mother, I didn't see you," Jasmine said, pressing a hand to her breast, stilling her pounding heart. She glanced through the closed doors into the brightly lit living room. "Where are our guests? And Aunt Yvette? Is anyone else here?"

"The Humphreys went into town for dinner. The Sterlings are taking a walk around the lake before they leave, also. Things have quieted down, so Yvette went home to be with your uncle Edward." Her mother motioned with a beringed hand to a nearby chair. "Sit down and join me."

Jasmine felt a shiver of trepidation at her mother's wooden tone. She knew her mother too well not to know that something was wrong. Reluctantly she did as her mother requested. She took a seat in the wicker rocking chair, sinking into the overstuffed cushion.

Despite the cool night air, Celeste wore only a thin cotton shirt and matching skirt, with no sweater or shawl. Her legs were bare, as were her feet. Her russet hair was unkempt, as though she'd dragged nervous fingers through its carefully coiffed style. The circles beneath her eyes looked even darker in the twilight hour, giving her a haunted expression.

Troubled by her mother's appearance, Jasmine reached out, covering her mother's trembling hand with her own. "What is it, Mother? What's wrong?"

"I've just gotten off the phone with Doris Atkins," Celeste said.

Jasmine's heart sank. Doris Atkins was the owner/manager of the hotel where Storm was staying. She was also a gossip. Mentally, Jasmine prepared herself for what was coming next.

Celeste's disappointed sigh whispered in the quiet night. "Are you going to tell me what you did today? And with whom? Or am I going to have to get my information secondhand from my supposed 'friends' in town?"

"Mother, I'm sorry." Jasmine tightened her hold on her mother's hand. "I should have been honest with you."

"Yes, you should have." Celeste clung to her, her grip desperate. "You were with Storm Hunter today, weren't you?"

Her voice barely a whisper, Jasmine said, "Yes, Mother. I was."

Celeste loosened her grip, then pulled her hand away. Crossing her arms at her waist, she held herself tight, as though she'd been physically wounded by the admission. "Can't you see what you're doing? This relationship with Storm is doomed from the start." She shook her head, looking older than her years. "We may not be the Capulets and the Montagues, but there is bad blood between the Kincaids and the Hunters. Jasmine, I don't want to see you hurt."

Unwanted tears filled Jasmine's eyes, blurring her vision. The rift between her and her mother was growing, and she felt powerless to stop it. Swallowing hard at the lump of emotion that had stuck in her throat, she said, "I know all the reasons why I should stay away from Storm. But I can't, Mother. There's something between us, something I can't ignore. I'm falling in love with him."

Celeste closed her eyes and leaned forward in her chair, giving a low, mewling sound of pain.

Jasmine started to reach out to her, to comfort her, but she stopped, not sure that she could give her mother the solace she needed. Instead she said, "Mother, I don't know what's going to happen between me and Storm. But you've always encouraged me to follow my instincts. Well, my instinct is to listen to my heart. And my heart is telling me I have to see where these feelings for Storm will take me."

Slowly, Celeste straightened. Though pale and shaky, she rose to her feet.

Jasmine stood, facing her mother.

Gathering her daughter into her arms, Celeste held her tightly. "I love you, Jasmine," she whispered, "I just hope you won't be hurt by your decision."

With that, Celeste released her. She whirled and hurried to the front door. Her bare feet padding softly against the wooden floor, she disappeared into the house, leaving Jasmine to stand alone on the front porch.

Her body shaking from the impact of what had just occurred, Jasmine sat down hard, collapsing back into the wicker chair. The night felt colder, darker. She pulled her knees up, tucking them under her chin, hugging her legs with her arms. Around her she heard the sounds of the Montana wildlife, the cracking of a twig underfoot, the quiet scurry of an animal's step and the distant flap of a bird's wing. Around her, the rich scent of the pine trees filled the air.

She took comfort most nights from the rustic charm of her surroundings. Tonight she felt only solitude and loneliness.

Her mother's parting words echoed over and over again in her mind. *I just hope you won't be hurt by your decision.*

Jasmine's dismal mood sank a notch lower as she realized it was as much of a sign of approval as she could hope of getting from her mother.

* * *

Jasmine slept fitfully. The wee hours of the night passed slowly as she listened to her mother's restless pacing in the room down the hall. Though she wanted to go to Celeste, to try to ease her concerns, she knew she couldn't allow herself to do it.

For she knew in her heart she was the cause of her mother's pain and distress.

Finally Jasmine closed her eyes and succumbed to an exhausted sleep. But not for long. Just before dawn, she felt a hand on her shoulder, shaking her. Someone calling her name.

"Jasmine?" It was her mother's voice. Yet it sounded so strange, so flat and emotionless. Jasmine blinked, wincing as the sandy grit of sleeplessness burned her eyes. "Wake up, Jasmine. I need you."

Alarmed, Jasmine sat up. "Mother? What's wrong?"

The table lamp was switched on and she shielded her eyes against the sudden brightness. It took a moment before she could focus on Celeste standing beside her bed, wrapped in a terry-cloth bathrobe. In the dim light, her mother's face was so pale against her russet hair that she looked like a ghost.

Despite her distraught appearance, Celeste's voice remained unnaturally calm. "I can't tell you. Not now, Jasmine. I've called the family. They'll be here soon. As soon as you're ready, come downstairs. I'll explain everything then."

With that ominous bit of information, she turned from the bed and left the room.

Jasmine's heart seemed to have stopped beating. For a long moment she sat frozen in her bed, unable to move. She stared at the empty doorway through which her mother had disappeared, forgetting to breathe. These past few months she'd sensed her mother was deeply troubled, that she was teetering on the edge of some sort of spiritual reckoning.

It would seem the time had finally come.

Her lungs burning in her chest, Jasmine gulped in a cooling draft of air. Her hands trembled as she pushed aside the bedcovers. Swinging her feet to the floor, she stood on unsteady legs.

Forcing herself to move, she hurried to the dresser and pulled out a pair of jeans. She slipped them on beneath her nightshirt. Tying the long ends of her oversize T-shirt at her waist, she left her feet bare and hurried from the room.

Hushed voices sounded from the kitchen as she made her way down the back staircase. Her mouth watered at the welcoming scent of coffee. She would need more than one cupful of the fortifying liquid to wake her groggy senses.

Aunt Yvette and Uncle Edward were seated at the kitchen table. Yvette, with her gray hair and striking features, looked worried. Edward had a hand on his wife's shoulder, absently rubbing it in soothing circles. They glanced up at her when she entered the room. From the troubled expressions on their faces, it was apparent they hadn't a clue what this family meeting was all about.

Before she could greet them, the back door banged open. Bringing with her a draft of cold morning air, her sister, Cleo, entered the kitchen. "I got here as soon as I could," she said in a breathless tone. Her thick russet hair was uncombed and tangled. She wore a beige trench coat over her pajama pants, looking as though she'd just jumped out of bed. "Summer's parking her car. She'll be here in just a minute."

The door opened again. Summer breezed in, bringing David, Yvette and Edward's son, along with her. Her eyes widened in alarm as she glanced around the room, taking in the gathering of familiar faces. A deep frown creased her brow. "I came as soon as I could. Gavin is at home with Alyssa. What's happened? Where's Celeste?"

A cacophony of voices erupted at once, each talking, but no one seeming to know what had brought them together. The one person with all the answers to their questions was nowhere in sight. Worriedly Jasmine paced the room. This couldn't go on, she had to find her mother.

As though she'd read her mind, Celeste entered the kitchen. A hush fell across the room. All eyes were riveted upon the frazzled features of her normally lovely face.

Jasmine's chest tightened with apprehension, making it difficult to breathe.

Still dressed in her terry-cloth robe, Celeste looked numbly from one person to the other. Frowning slightly, she said, "Where's Frannie?"

"With Austin," Yvette said, wringing her hands together in a helpless gesture. "Remember, Celeste? I told you there was a NASCAR event this weekend. She travels with him whenever he's out of town."

"Of course, I forgot," Celeste said, looking chagrined. She sighed, giving a satisfied nod. "Everyone else is here."

"What's this all about, Celeste?" Yvette asked, rising to her feet.

"No, sit down please. Everyone." Celeste motioned to the table, waiting for them to take their seats.

Exchanging nervous glances, Summer and Cleo took a seat at the table. Jasmine remained standing, as did David. He stood next to her at the kitchen counter, an unreadable expression on his lean face.

Celeste seemed oddly calm in the wake of their rising unease. Her voice sounded hollow, almost void of emotion, when she asked, "Would anyone like a cup of coffee before we begin?"

"Celeste," Summer said, her voice filled with uncharacteristic impatience, "this isn't a tea party. You called us here for a reason. I for one am anxious to know that reason."

"Yes, Mother," Cleo said, unbuckling her trench coat and revealing a yellow print pajama top. "What's going on? What couldn't wait until morning for us to hear?"

With shaking hands, Celeste reached into the pocket of her terry-cloth robe and withdrew a gun. Taking a deep breath, she placed it in the center of the table.

Though she knew little about guns, Jasmine saw the markings identifying it as a Colt .45. She felt her heart thud against her chest.

Beside her, David stiffened. He took a step toward the table, then stopped. Standing uneasily, a deep frown of concern furrowed his brow.

Cleo and Summer looked helplessly at each other, confusion obvious in their eyes.

Yvette shrank back in her chair. Edward's arm went around her in a gesture of support. Encouraged, Yvette was the first to speak. "What's this all about, Celeste? This was Jeremiah's gun. What are you doing with it?"

"I've had it for years, thirty years to be exact. I've kept it so well hidden I nearly forgot about it myself." Celeste swayed unsteadily on her feet. Grasping the back of a nearby chair, she closed her eyes, as though trying to gather her strength. Then, opening them, she slowly glanced at each of them, her gaze regretful.

"I've asked each of you to come here to tell you..."

Her voice trembled and broke with emotion. With a sigh she cast her eyes downward. Then, the words so soft they had to strain to hear her, she said, "It was me.... I killed him. I killed Raven Hunter."

Ten

Jasmine stood motionless, feeling as though the bottom had just dropped out of her world. She couldn't believe her own ears. Her kind and gentle mother, a woman who'd lived her life in the pursuit of spiritual peace and harmony, had just confessed to a murder.

It wasn't possible.

The whole idea was absurd.

Despite her own denials, Jasmine's vision blurred as a picture of Storm's pain-lined face cropped up in her mind. She closed her eyes against the sting of tears, unable to bear the image. Her mother's uncharacteristic objections to her seeing Storm echoed in her mind. No wonder Celeste didn't want her to be with him. She'd been afraid of what might be revealed. All this time Jasmine had been helping Storm look for the murderer of his brother and the truth was right in front of her, in the fold of her own family.

No! With a jerk, Jasmine opened her eyes. She forced herself to look at her mother, to see her as she really was, frightened and more fragile than ever before. She shook her head. No, it couldn't be true. Her mother wouldn't have deceived her all this time. She wouldn't have lied to her own daughter.

"Celeste," David said, the first to break the spell of silence that had held the room. His gentle voice jarred Jasmine from her trance of disbelief. "Raven Hunter has been dead for thirty years. If you killed him, why haven't you told anyone before now?''

Celeste looked at him, a plea for understanding in her tired expression. "Because I didn't know for sure."

"But you're sure now," David said, keeping his voice even, with no hint of censure.

"Tonight I had another dream," Celeste said, her voice distant and hollow. She stared straight ahead at a spot on the kitchen wall, her eyes glazed and unfocused. It was as though she were reliving a memory, and not truly aware of what was happening here and now.

"A dream," David coaxed, gently prodding her to continue. "What sort of dream?"

"A dream that isn't really a dream." Blinking away the stupor, Celeste sighed. Wearily she took a seat at the kitchen table. Unable to face them, she studied her hands that she held tightly clasped in her lap. "It was a vision from the past. A memory that I've spent thirty years trying to forget. But now I know the truth. I finally know what happened on the night Raven Hunter died."

Yvette scooted her chair next to Celeste's. Wrapping an arm around her sister's shoulder, she said, "We all love you, Celeste. No matter what, you know that we'll always support you. Please don't be afraid to tell us what happened."

Murmurs of agreement sounded throughout the room.

Still too stunned to speak, Jasmine remained unforgivably silent.

With her eyes still downcast, Celeste began to speak, spilling out the guilty memory that had haunted her dreams for almost thirty years. "It all started when Jeremiah discovered Blanche's pregnancy. When she admitted that Raven Hunter was the father, Jeremiah nearly went insane. I—I'd never seen him so angry before. He looked wild, and filled with hatred. I thought for sure he'd do something to Raven...to hurt him in some way.''

Celeste stopped and shuddered at the thought.

Yvette squeezed her shoulder, silently giving her encouragement.

Celeste covered her sister's hand with hers, clinging to it, then continued, ''Instead of lashing out at him, Jeremiah paid Raven to leave town. No one expected Raven to accept the money. But when he did, Jeremiah made sure everyone knew, including Blanche. It nearly killed Blanche to hear the news. Something died in her after that. The disappointment she must have felt—''

Her voice broke. Tears filled her eyes. Celeste blinked rapidly, allowing a single drop to cascade down her pale cheek. The words thick with emotion, she said, ''I never believed Raven would leave Blanche. I knew he would change his mind. It shouldn't have been a surprise that he'd come back to the ranch.''

Celeste looked directly at Summer, her gaze fierce and determined. ''Raven was a good man. He wouldn't have abandoned Blanche or you, Summer. I'm sure the reason he returned was to give Jeremiah back the money.''

Summer nodded her understanding, her smile hesitant.

Celeste looked at the gun she'd placed on the kitchen table. Her gaze terrified, she said, ''I was in bed, trying to sleep. But there was a terrible thunderstorm that night and I couldn't relax. That was when I heard the shouts, the angry voices coming from the study. I didn't know who was downstairs, or what was happening. I recognized Jeremiah's voice, but no one else's. I was frightened and not sure what to do. I knew Jeremiah kept a gun in his dresser drawer. So I went to his room and got out the Colt.

''When I went downstairs, I only saw the back of a

man's head. He'd pinned Jeremiah to the floor, and he was beating him with his fists.''

Celeste choked back a sob. She lifted a hand to her mouth and closed her eyes, struggling for control.

Yvette and Summer both looked close to tears. Cleo looked shocked, devastated by the events unfolding in front of her. David and Edward wore looks of resignation and utter sympathy.

Pain knifed Jasmine's heart as she shared her mother's distress. She wanted to go to her, to comfort her, to stop this tragic testimony. But something held her back. She needed to know the truth, once and for all.

Regaining her composure, Celeste opened her eyes. ''I couldn't see the man's face. I only heard an angry voice shouting…'if you get in our way again, I'll kill you, old man.' I—I was so afraid that whoever was attacking Jeremiah meant those words. I tried to stop him. I called out, begging the man to let Jeremiah go. But he wouldn't listen. I don't think he even heard me. He was so intent on hurting Jeremiah, I knew I had no choice—''

Celeste lifted her trembling hands and stared at them. ''My hands were shaking so badly, I don't know how I was able to hold the gun straight. But I knew I had to do something, before Jeremiah was killed. So I closed my eyes, and I pulled the trigger on the Colt.'' Tears poured down her face. ''At the same time, th-there was a clap of thunder outside. It shook the house, and scared me so. I thought it was God's way of condemning me. Then I smelled smoke, coming from the gun in my hand…it was so strong and bitter, it made me sick to my stomach. I opened my eyes and dropped the Colt on the floor, appalled by what I'd done. That was when the intruder slumped to the floor and I finally saw his face. Jeremiah was safe, but I had killed Raven Hunter.''

Summer looked away, seeming unwilling to let Celeste see the tears filling her eyes. Though Jasmine's own eyes remained dry, they burned with unshed emotion.

"Somehow, Jeremiah got to his feet. He told me to stay put while he examined Raven's body," Celeste said. She shook her head, giving a quick bitter-sounding laugh. "I was so shocked by what had just happened, I couldn't have moved even if I'd wanted to. When Jeremiah told me Raven was dead, I lost what little control I had and became hysterical. I never meant for anything like that to happen. Jeremiah tried to calm me, he told me he'd take care of everything. He said it would be our little secret, that no one would ever find out that I'd killed Raven."

Her shoulders slumped as she heaved a defeated sigh. "I never knew what he'd done with the body. I did know what I had done was wrong, but I tried to push the memory of that night from my mind. Over time, I succeeded. It wasn't until Raven's remains were found that I began to remember that night."

"That was why you could never say no to Jeremiah," Yvette said softly, shaking her head. "Why you never could stand up to him when he tried to control your life."

"He held all the cards," Celeste admitted. "He knew the worst secret in the world. If I didn't do what he wanted, I knew he could ruin me. That was why, when Ty Monroe came to town and asked me to marry him, I agreed. The thought of moving as far away as Baton Rouge was like a dream come true. At that point, I'd have done anything to get away from Jeremiah."

Celeste looked anxiously at each of her daughters. "Don't misunderstand me. In my own way I loved your father. He was a good man. Being with him saved my sanity."

At last Jasmine's tears found release. Teardrops fell unchecked down her cheeks. The last of the puzzle had fallen into place. She now understood her mother's fascination with the spiritual hereafter, her frantic pursuit of peace and solace. All these years she'd repressed a traumatic event. But the tragedy had never completely disappeared. What had occurred in the study that night had haunted Celeste's dreams and her subconscious every day of her life. It wasn't any wonder that she'd sought alternate means to find absolution.

"What happens now?" Yvette asked, looking to her son for an answer.

David made his way to Celeste's side. Crouching on a bent knee, he looked her in the eye and said, "We'll need to make a report. The police will have to be notified."

Celeste nodded. "I know. That's what I want. I've lived too many years with this secret. It's time to tell the truth."

"Then I'll go with you." David clasped her hands in his. "I'll be with you every step of the way."

"So will I," Yvette said, a determined look on her face. "You'll always have my support."

Edward nodded. Cleo and Summer murmured their own agreements. Everyone stood, voicing their opinions, making suggestions on the best way to handle the tenuous situation.

Jasmine remained motionless at the kitchen counter, unable to join her family, torn between her loyalty to her mother and her newfound feelings for Storm. She knew Storm would be shocked by the news. He would be angry and upset, and rightly so. How could she ever convince him that she hadn't intentionally kept the truth from him?

But if he didn't believe her, the fragile bond they'd built between them would be destroyed.

Jasmine felt overwhelmed by what might be lost. Before she'd met Storm, she'd dated many different men. But no one had ever caught her heart. No one she could say that's him, he's the one she'd spend her life with. She'd watched with an envious eye as others in her family had found happiness with their one true love. All the while, wondering when it would be her turn.

Then Storm had come crashing into her world and she knew something special was about to happen. He'd given her life meaning, a new purpose. She finally understood what it meant to care about someone so deeply that nothing else in the world mattered but him.

For her, it was love at first sight. From the moment they'd first met, she'd had no doubt that they were meant to be together.

But fate seemed to be working against them.

Knowing she had no other choice, Jasmine pushed herself from the kitchen counter. Slowly she made her way to her mother's side. Sensing her presence, Celeste turned to face her. Jasmine saw the painful glimmer of remorse in her mother's eyes and the heart-wrenching plea for understanding.

No one but Celeste would know the effect her confession would have on Jasmine's life. Her voice trembling, she said, "I'm so sorry, Jasmine."

"I know, I know…" Jasmine folded her mother into an embrace. "It'll be all right, Mother," she whispered. "We'll work this out together. Everything will be fine."

Jasmine wished she believed the words to be true in her own heart.

Shortly after noon, Storm felt the first inkling of unease. Jasmine had told him that she had to work in the morning, that she couldn't see him until that afternoon.

He took a steadying breath, struggling to get a hold on his impatience. It was still early, he told himself.

There was no need to start worrying yet.

When one o'clock came and went, he knew something was wrong. For the past thirty minutes he'd been pacing the floor, trying not to let his imagination run away from him. Jasmine should have called or stopped in by now. She was too honest and open. It wasn't like her not to let him know that her plans had changed.

Unless her family's objections had finally gotten to her. Unless she'd decided she couldn't see him again, after all.

The grim thought spurred him into action. He strode to the phone, picked up the receiver and started punching in the number for the B and B. The possibility of Celeste answering stopped him. The last thing he wanted was to make trouble for Jasmine. At least, no more than he'd already caused.

Frustrated, Storm slammed the receiver back onto its cradle. He pushed the hair from his face and smacked his palm flat against the wall. The sound reverberated throughout the quiet room. His hand smarted, doing little to help his foul mood. He'd been cooped up inside too long. He had to get out. He had to do something.

He needed to find Jasmine—even if it meant climbing the walls of the bed-and-breakfast to get to her.

Grabbing his keys, he headed for the door. Just as he was about to open it, three sharp raps sounded on the other side.

Jasmine....

Relief poured through him, easing the tension from his muscles. He shook his head, feeling foolish for letting his insecurities get the better of him. With a sheepish smile, he opened the door.

And was greeted by the somber face of Gretchen Neal. Behind her stood a tall, brown-haired, blue-eyed man, dressed in the uniform of a deputy sheriff.

Storm's smile fled. He stared at them, his heart lurching in his chest. His first thoughts were of Jasmine, that something had happened to her. She'd been hurt, injured, and the police had come to tell him the bad news.

As soon as it surfaced, he discarded the unlikely thought. No one knew of his fledgling relationship with Jasmine. As far as the town of Whitehorn was concerned, he'd be the last person to be notified of a Kincaid's demise.

The police were here for a very different reason.

Which meant only one thing—Raven.

"What is it?" Storm demanded in lieu of a greeting.

Gretchen Neal winced at his gruff tone. Looking as though she were struggling to control her own impatience, she inhaled a steadying breath. With a nod toward the man behind her, she said, "Mr. Hunter, this is Deputy Reed Austin. If you have a moment, we'd like to talk to you."

"About what?" Storm said, not budging from the doorway, his hand still clenching the doorknob in a death grip.

"There's been a development in your brother's case." She glanced up and down the hotel walkway, as though checking for eavesdroppers. "Would you mind if we came inside and talked about it?"

Storm stepped back, letting them enter the room. A development... The words brought a quivering of trepidation to the pit of his belly, making him even more keenly aware of Jasmine's absence. He refused to consider the possibility that she could be connected to this new development in any way. All he knew for certain was that without her at his side, he felt exposed, vulnerable to whatever news Detective Neal was about to give him.

He wasn't sure if he could handle this on his own.

Refusing to give in to his fears, he said, "What sort of development?"

Gretchen nodded toward the room's only chair. "Would you like to sit down, Mr. Hunter?"

Storm crossed his arms against his chest and planted his feet firmly on the carpeted floor. He looked at her, challenging her to delay the news any further.

At his uncooperative response, Deputy Reed Austin shifted uncomfortably, one foot to the other, his gaze narrow, his stance wary. Obviously the man's presence was a result of the confrontation between Storm and David Hannon, which had occurred when he'd first arrived in town. Storm decided the deputy must be here in a show of support to his comrade, to make sure that no harm would come to Detective Neal from a "hotheaded Indian."

Choosing each word with care, Gretchen said, "There's been a break in the case. We're holding a suspect at the county jail."

"A suspect?" Storm frowned, unable to believe what he was hearing. All these years he'd thought Jeremiah Kincaid was the one who'd killed his brother. But Jeremiah was dead. Now this woman, this detective, was telling him that someone else committed the crime. He wasn't sure what to think.

"It's a solid lead," Gretchen said, her tone defensive, as though she'd read the doubts in his mind. "This person... They've confessed to the shooting."

Storm almost wished he'd listened to her advice and had chosen to sit, after all. His legs felt weak and wobbly.

He wasn't sure if they were strong enough to hold him. His voice sounding hoarse with suppressed emotion, he said, "Who is it? Who killed my brother?"

Hesitating, Gretchen glanced at her partner. Deputy Austin nodded his encouragement. Turning back to Storm, she said stiffly, "Celeste Monroe came in early this morning. She's confessed to the crime."

Celeste Monroe.

Jasmine's mother.

The news struck like a blow, winding him. This time Storm did sit down. He collapsed into the wooden straight-backed chair, stunned by the revelation.

Gretchen continued, but the buzz of disbelief running through his head made her voice sound odd, as though she were speaking to him through a tunnel. "Mrs. Monroe is being held in the sheriff's custody, until her arraignment tomorrow morning. If you have any further questions, please feel free to call me, or Sheriff Rawlings, at the station."

Storm realized she was winding down her speech, preparing to leave. Riveting his gaze at her, he said, "There's got to be some mistake."

Gretchen looked at him, and the wooden expression she'd worn since stepping into his hotel room slipped from its place. He saw the uncertainty in her gaze and remembered that she, too, had a connection to the Kincaid family. The word around town was that she and David Hannon were engaged.

She shook her head. "It's a strong lead. Mrs. Monroe was able to give us a detailed account of the crime. Plus, she's turned over the murder weapon."

The last of Storm's doubts dissolved. Unable to stop himself, he recalled Celeste's initial reaction to his presence in Whitehorn. It must have been his resemblance to

394   STORMING WHITEHORN

Raven that had brought the shocked look to her face before she'd collapsed into a dead faint. Time and again,
Jasmine had professed her mother's normally liberated
views. Now Celeste's objections to his seeing Jasmine
made more sense. She had murdered his brother. It wasn't
any wonder that she wanted to keep them apart.

"Mr. Hunter, are you listening to me?"

Storm blinked. Startled, he glanced up at the detective.
He'd been so lost in his own thoughts he'd forgotten her
presence.

Frowning, Gretchen said, "We're leaving now, Mr.
Hunter. If there's anything more we can do..." She let
the words fade.

"There's nothing more to be done. It's over." Storm
shook his head, giving a mirthless laugh. "It's finally
over."

Gretchen hesitated, studying him, her concern obvious.

Deputy Austin cleared his throat, motioning toward the
door. Gretchen turned to leave. With her hand on the
doorknob, she paused and said, "I'm sorry the investigation didn't go as quickly as you'd hoped. A lot of time
has passed since your brother's death. There just weren't
that many leads to follow."

Storm nodded, unable to answer. His frustration at the
police department's lack of progress seemed minute compared to the crippling sense of betrayal that was growing
inside him. Now he understood Jasmine's absence.

Without another word, Detective Neal and Deputy
Austin left his hotel room, closing the door behind them.

For a long moment Storm remained in the chair, im-
mobilized by shock and disbelief. He felt crushed, as
though he'd been run over by a semitrailer. For thirty
years, Celeste had kept her guilt a secret. He didn't understand how she could have lived with herself.

Was the killing of an Indian so unimportant that it didn't bother her?

The acrid taste of bitterness rose in his throat, making him feel sick to his stomach. The chasm he'd always felt between the whites and the Native Americans deepened. His heart thudded painfully against his chest. What hurt most, even more than Celeste's callous indifference, was Jasmine's betrayal.

As Jackson Hawk had predicted, Jasmine had kept the truth from him. How long had she known of her mother's guilty secret? Was her pledge to help him nothing more than a ruse? Just a way for her to throw him off track?

A surge of self-disgust propelled him to his feet. He paced the floor, giving vent to his growing anger. Like a sheep, he'd allowed her to lead him astray. Certainly his desire for her had been a potent distraction. Jasmine had used him and his own weaknesses to keep him from discovering the truth.

How could he have been so blind?

As he struggled with a growing bout of self-recrimination, a hesitant knock sounded at the door.

Storm froze, stopping midpace. He stared at the door. His first impulse was to ignore the knock, giving the unexpected visitor no choice but to leave. He was in no mood for more bad news.

But a higher force overrode his good judgment. Ignoring the voice of reason, he moved to the door. Deep in his heart, he knew who had come calling. He told himself that delaying the confrontation would only prolong the inevitable heartbreak.

It was time he faced what fate had brought him.

Bracing himself, he opened the door. And found Jasmine waiting for him.

* * *

Jasmine's breath caught painfully in her throat. From the look in Storm's eyes, she realized she was too late. He'd already heard the news. He knew the truth about her mother.

Nervously she licked her lips. "Storm—"

"Whatever you have to say, I'm not interested," he said, cutting her off, his voice hard and unforgiving. "I've heard enough lies to last me a lifetime."

"I didn't lie to you, Storm," she said, slowly shaking her head. "You have to believe me. I didn't know about any of this until this morning."

"This morning?" He glanced at his wristwatch. "It's almost two o'clock in the afternoon. It's certainly taken you long enough to find me to tell me the news."

"Storm, please—"

The hotel's housekeeper walked by, pushing a cleaning cart, her gaze curious. The plump, dark-haired woman paused outside the room next door, busying herself with checking inventory. But more likely she was giving herself a chance to eavesdrop.

After the frustrating morning she'd spent at the sheriff's office waiting to hear the outcome of her mother's fate, the last thing Jasmine needed was to be further humiliated by being caught in a heated argument with Storm outside his hotel room. With all the pride she could muster, she lifted her chin and said, "If you don't mind, I'd prefer to discuss this in private. May I come in?"

Jasmine steeled herself for a rejection.

To her surprise, without arguing, Storm stepped back and allowed her to enter.

Jasmine's legs felt unsteady as she made her way into his hotel room, her strength gone. Memories of the first time she'd been here, of the steamy embrace they'd shared, crept into her mind. She brushed away the untimely image, knowing she needed her full wits about her to convince Storm of her innocence.

The door closed with a loud click, setting her nerves even further on edge. Slowly she turned to face him.

His steely gaze flitted over her before he pushed past her to stand at the opposite side of the room, putting distance between them. Jasmine's heart sank further when he refused to look at her.

Not allowing herself to give up, she made her plea for understanding. "Storm, my mother never confided in me. Her confession… It's been just as much a shock to me as it must be to you. I didn't know about any of this until this morning. You have to believe me."

"I don't have to believe anything," he said, his icy tone sending a shiver down her spine. "I don't know why you bothered to come here. You're wasting your time, Jasmine. I want nothing more to do with you, or your family."

The sharp words cut her to the quick, leaving a raw and open wound in her heart. Despite the blow, she refused to admit defeat. She refused to believe that the bond they'd built, the precious moments they'd shared, had been for nothing.

If he thought she would give up so easily, he was wrong.

"That's it?" she demanded, letting the anger rise in her voice. "One thing goes wrong, and you're ready to toss aside everything that we've shared?"

"It's more than just one thing," he said, biting out the words. "Your mother killed my brother."

"But I didn't know—" Her voice broke. Tears of frustration blurred her vision. She blinked hard, refusing to allow anything to stop her. "I've never lied to you, Storm. You have to know that's true."

He remained stubbornly mute. Standing with his hands on his hips, his face set in a harsh line, he wouldn't meet her gaze.

Jasmine shook her head, letting the tears of frustration fill her eyes. Her voice trembling with emotion, she said, "You can't let yourself believe me, can you? If you do, then you'd have to let go of all that hate and resentment you've built up all these years toward my family. You said you'd come back to Whitehorn to see justice done for your brother. But that isn't true. This isn't really about Raven, is it?"

A vein pulsed at his temple. His jaw clenched and unclenched. But he refused to answer.

"This was never just about Raven," she said, forcing herself to continue. "Raven's just an excuse you've used to push everyone out of your life. I know you were hurt deeply. But you've used your past as a reason never to let yourself get close to anyone else."

Still, he wouldn't answer.

Despite the helpless frustration rising inside her, Jasmine knew she had to finish what she'd started. "Raven wasn't the only one who died all those years ago. A part of you died, also. The part that's capable of caring about others. Can't you see? You've got your feelings so bottled up inside, you can't allow yourself to love someone enough to forgive even the worst of mistakes."

Storm's silence spoke volumes. He turned his head and looked away, not saying a word.

Feeling the sting of his rejection, Jasmine took a quick, steadying breath. She had tried to get through to him and had failed. There was nothing more for her to do.

Gathering her shattered pride, she wiped the tears from her face and said, "I want you to know something, Storm. No matter what's happened here today, I won't forget the time that we spent together...or what could have been between us. I will always care about you.''

With her heart feeling as though it had split in two, she turned to leave.

Eleven

"Jasmine, wait."

The words escaped his mouth before he had a chance to think them through. It wasn't like Storm to act on impulse, to let his heart rule his actions, but right now his heart wouldn't let her walk out that door.

To his relief, Jasmine stopped. Slowly she turned to face him.

For the first time he really looked at her. The red, cap-sleeved T-shirt was coming untucked from the waistband of her black slacks. Her dark hair looked mussed, as though she hadn't taken the time to comb it into place. Her makeup was nonexistent, emphasizing the paleness of her complexion, the weariness etching her face and the dark circles beneath her eyes. And he knew she hadn't told him the complete truth.

She, too, was suffering.

Her mother had kept a devastating secret from her and her family. A secret that had destroyed the balance of their lives, as it had his. Jasmine, of all people, understood the pain and disillusionment that he felt.

But she understood more than just his pain. She knew of his weaknesses, as well. What she'd said, it was as though she had looked into his very soul and had seen his worst fears.

She knew why he had never allowed himself to get close to anyone else. The only person he'd ever truly cared about had been Raven. When Raven disappeared, he'd felt his loss as a rejection. That was the real reason he'd run away from his life on Laughing Horse. Because he couldn't allow himself to acknowledge just how much his brother's "abandonment" had hurt.

She was right about his resentment toward her family, too. When Raven left, instead of letting himself accept the worst, that his brother simply didn't care about him, Storm had blamed the Kincaids for his disappearance. Being proven correct seemed little compensation for the years he'd wasted, allowing his resentment to fester into a crippling distrust of all whites.

And now Jasmine stood in front of him, the same woman he'd waited so anxiously to see only minutes before. The same beautiful woman who had the power to set his blood on fire with a single look.

The same woman with whom he'd allowed himself to fall in love.

Silence echoed in the room. Fear tightened his chest, making it hard to draw a breath. Even now, he couldn't put into words what he felt in his heart. He couldn't run the risk of another abandonment.

He would rather be safe and live his life alone.

But that didn't stop him from wanting her, from needing to feel the reassuring warmth of her body next to his. Unable to stop himself, he crossed the room and closed the distance between them. For just a moment he studied her, memorizing the sculpted lines of her exotic face, the gut-wrenching tears that she tried so hard to hide, and the stubborn yet fragile pride in the tilt of her head.

Storm bit back an oath, his anger directed at himself. She'd come asking for understanding. Instead of listening, he'd pushed her away. His behavior had been inexcusable. He didn't deserve her forgiveness. He didn't deserve a second chance. Still he longed for the sweet redemption he could find only in her arms.

His voice thick with emotion, he whispered, "Jasmine, I'm sorry."

Something seemed to melt inside her. The tension gripping her body loosened its hold. Fresh tears welled in her eyes as a sob of relief escaped from her lips. With a shake of her head, she said, "Oh, Storm."

He wasn't sure who reached out first. But it didn't really matter. Somehow they found themselves wrapped in each other's arms, clinging to each other for support.

Relief poured through him as he held her close, savoring the feel of her slender body next to his. He buried his hand in the short strands of her dark hair, cradling the back of her head. He tipped her face upward to his, forcing her to look at him. With the pad of his thumb, he wiped the trail of tears from her cheek, then showered the spot with soft, delicate kisses. His lips grazed her temple, the hollow of her cheek, the tip of her chin, before settling on her irresistible mouth.

Beneath his gentle assault, she closed her eyes and inhaled a shaky draft of air. Her quiet exhalation sounded in his ears, her breath fanning his skin.

He lowered his hands to measure the narrow width of her waist. His fingers skimmed her breasts, stroking the turgid centers. Her body quickened, tensing beneath his touch. Through the thin fabric of her shirt, he felt her nipples contract and harden.

His own body responded in kind. A warm rush of heat flooded his groin. He moaned, as Jasmine shifted her stance, brushing her tummy against his arousal. Never before had he felt such sweet misery.

He took her mouth in a greedy kiss, plunging his tongue into her moist heat, finding his own taste of heaven. She gave as much as she took, opening her mouth to his, staking her own claim.

The last of his self-control evaporated in a blaze of red heat. With his arms still firmly around her, he back-stepped toward the bed, half carrying, half leading her every step of the way. The edge of the mattress caught the backs of his knees. He fell, sprawling spread-eagle against the soft bedcovers.

Jasmine landed on top of him, one leg wedged between his thighs, her body straddling his. The boxspring sighed in protest at the unexpectedness of their combined weight. She dug her elbows into his chest and lifted herself to look at him. Her gaze was so wide-eyed and innocent that for a moment second thoughts caught up to him. His mind raced with all the reasons he should put a stop to this, before they went any further.

Then a slow, tentative smile touched her face. Slowly, deliberately, she lowered her head and kissed him. Just a fleeting touch of her lips against his. A kiss meant to tease, to test his willingness. She nibbled on his lower lip, tugging it through her teeth. Her tongue lashed against his mouth, making him close his eyes against a growing desire.

Following the chiseled line of his jaw, she dropped butterfly kisses onto the smooth skin of his face. Pushing his long hair out of her way, she nuzzled his neck and bit down onto the lobe of his ear, giving it a gentle tug.

Storm let her have her way, until he could stand no more. With a growl of impatience, he anchored his hands around her waist and rolled her onto her back. She fell against the tousled bedcovers, staring up at him, with a look that only fueled his desire. She was an irresistible combination of innocence and seduction.

Tacitly they acknowledged that both of them were

wearing too much clothing. Storm pulled the ends of her shirt out of her waistband, lifting it over her head. The black lacy brassiere gave him pause. Recovering his composure, with a quick, deft movement, he unhooked the center clasp, exposing her beautiful body for him to see.

With an impatience of her own, Jasmine struggled with the buttons of his shirt. Her fingers fumbled over the openings, wasting much too much precious time. Obligingly he tore the shirt open, the buttons popping their threads in protest. Tossing the ruined shirt aside, he focused his attention on more important matters. Gently he circled the tips of his fingers around one rounded breast, then the other, noting the contrast of his dark, coppery skin against her pale, creamy flesh. Lowering his head, he suckled one aroused tip.

Her reaction was reflexive, primal. She arched her back against the bed, gripping the sheets in her hands, inhaling deeply through clenched teeth. Dragging one leg slowly upward against his thigh, she pulled him close, cradling him in the softness of her body.

Storm unhooked the clasp of her slacks. The zipper rasped as he tugged it open. Snagging his thumbs around the waistband, he lowered her slacks over her hips. The matching strip of black lace panties soon followed. Her cowboy boots proved a challenge. Impatiently he raised himself from the bed to tug one, then the other off her feet. Finally she wore nothing—but a locket around her neck and a demure, almost uncertain look on her face.

Biting anxiously on her lower lip, she watched as he undressed in front of her. When he stepped out of his jeans, she caught her breath, her eyes widening—with second thoughts, or simple appreciation, he wasn't sure which.

His fears were put to rest, however, when they melded

into a steamy embrace as he rejoined her on the bed. Their hands impatiently explored each and every inch of their bodies, leaving no secrets. He marveled at the firm tautness of her breasts, the flatness of her stomach, the softness of her skin. Lowering his hand past the mound of dark curls, he found her warm to his touch, moist as he tested her readiness.

It took only a moment to reach for and use protection. But she tensed when he fitted himself between her thighs, forcing him to hesitate. Brushing the hair from his face, he saw the uncertainty in her eyes. "Jasmine? What's wrong?"

"Nothing's wrong. It's just…I want our first time to be special. I don't want to disappoint you."

"Disappoint me?" He frowned and started to pull away. "Jasmine, how can you think I'd be disappointed?"

"Never mind," she said, shaking her head. Before he could reconsider, she clasped her hands around his narrow waist and raised her hips off the bed, silently urging him to finish what they'd started.

Knowing he was lost, Storm released a ragged breath and eased himself inside her, penetrating the last of her resistance.

And heard her soft gasp of pain.

He froze, holding himself still. His frown returning, he looked down at her, searching her face. Swearing softly beneath his breath, he already knew the answer to his question. Now he understood her hesitancy. He hadn't realized that he was her first.

Overwhelmed by the ramifications of what was happening, he whispered, "Jasmine, I can't. We shouldn't—"

"No," she said, her voice an urgent whisper. She held

him tight, refusing to let him go. "It's what I want. I need you, Storm."

Unable to fight the power of both of their desires, Storm closed his eyes and gave in to his own wants. He plunged himself the rest of the way into her tight, virgin flesh.

Jasmine's body quivered beneath him. A flush of heat spread across her skin. She wrapped her legs around his hips and clung to him desperately.

He moved inside her cautiously. Her body gloved his, adjusting to the new demands. His heart pounded in his chest as his own need grew. Mindful of his responsibilities, he checked his urgency and brought them both slowly, carefully, to the edge. Then, when she was ready, with sharp, quick strokes he carried them to the point of no return.

She shuddered at the moment of climax, closing her eyes and crying out her pleasure. He followed her over the crest, finding release in her warm, giving body.

When it was over, he held her in his arms until her breath returned to normal and her heart slowed its rapid beat. Then, releasing her, he rolled over onto his side and sat on the edge of the bed. Dropping his elbows to his knees, covering his face with his hands, he allowed the guilt to flow over him.

He'd acted without thinking.

For a stolen moment he'd found solace in her sweet body.

But for the rest of his life he would have to live with the knowledge that he'd taken advantage of Jasmine at a time when she needed him most.

At his withdrawal, a chill settled over her. For the first time in her life Jasmine allowed her insecurities to get the better of her. Without thought of her inexperience, she'd given of herself. He'd told her that he was a man of many, many experiences. It wasn't any wonder that she'd disappointed him.

Her body warmed with the heat of embarrassment. Unable to face him, she clambered off the bed and hurried for the bathroom. Closing the door behind her, she came face-to-face with the evidence of her own folly. In the mirror, she stared at her too bright eyes, the pupils dilated with lingering excitement. Her lips were red and swollen from his caresses, as were her breasts. In the most private of places, she still throbbed with wanting him.

Choking back a sob, she turned from the mirror and wrenched the faucet on. The water drummed against the porcelain sink, masking the sound of her tears. Her hands shaking, she splashed water on her face and tried to control her runaway emotions. Grabbing a cloth from the towel rack, she washed away the evidence of their lovemaking.

It wasn't until she turned off the water that she realized she hadn't brought any clothes with her. The thought of facing him naked and exposed nearly overwhelmed her. Knowing she couldn't hide from him indefinitely, she wrapped herself in a towel and stepped toward the door.

But she couldn't do it. Jasmine froze, her hand on the doorknob. She couldn't face him. Not now, not knowing just how much of herself she had revealed.

With her back against the door, she sank to the floor, clutching the towel around her breasts. Fresh tears spilled down her cheeks as she lowered her head to her knees and gave in to the unwanted show of weakness.

She wasn't sure how long she stayed there, sitting on the floor, feeling alone and miserable. It wasn't until she heard the knock on the door that she roused herself from the depths of self-deprecation.

"Jasmine?"

The sound of Storm's concerned voice almost proved to be her undoing. She didn't trust herself to speak.

He knocked again, harder this time. "Jasmine, open the door."

Her voice muffled with emotion, she said, "Go away, Storm. I need a moment."

"You've had more than a moment," he said with a tone of impatience. Thumping the door one last time, she heard the helpless sound of his sigh. "Jasmine, why didn't you tell me? If I'd known that you were a—" He stopped abruptly. Cursing softly, he said, "Jasmine, did I hurt you?"

Heat scorched her face. Jasmine bit her lip against a flood of new tears. She'd never felt so mortified, so ashamed, in her life. "No, Storm. You didn't hurt me. It's just… I need my clothes. Would you mind—"

"Of course not," he said, sounding relieved at being given something to do. She heard his footsteps move away from the door, then return seconds later. "Jasmine, I have your clothes. But you have to open the door to get them."

Weak from crying, she struggled to her feet. She took in a breath of courage, then opened the door, her hand shaking on the knob.

Storm stood in front of her, dressed only in his faded jeans, an unreadable expression on his somber face. But his eyes told a different story. There was concern in their dark recesses. Assessingly, he took in the tears staining her cheeks, the embarrassed flush of her face, the fist that held the thin towel around her body. In his hands, he held her rumpled clothes.

Jasmine averted her eyes, unable to face him. With her gaze focused on the bathroom's linoleum floor, she held out her free hand for her discarded clothes. "May I have my clothes please?"

"Not until you talk to me."

Stunned, she looked up at him, dropping her hand to her side. "There's nothing more to discuss."

"Bull. I'm not letting you go. Not like this. You're upset, and we need to talk about it."

"Upset? Why would I be upset?" Jasmine noted that the rising pitch of her voice only gave credence to his observation. But she couldn't stop the agitated flow of words. "First my mother confesses to a crime I had no clue she'd committed. Then I go to bed with the man whose brother she killed." She gave a hollow laugh, knowing she sounded on the verge of completely losing control. "It's just been one of those days, Storm."

Silence strained between them.

Then, quietly, he said, "It isn't like you to be bitter, Jasmine."

"I'm not bitter, Storm. I'm just being honest. This wasn't one of my finer examples of good judgment. But don't worry, I'm not blaming you for what happened. We both got..." She swallowed hard, struggling to hold on to what was left of her pride. "...carried away. We simply made a mistake."

"Is that what you think it was? A mistake?"

The coolness of his tone sent a shiver down her spine. She considered sidestepping him, pushing past him to freedom. But along with her clothes, he held all the cards in this game of truth or dare. He had strength and size on his side.

"What do you want me to say, Storm? That it was my fault I didn't tell you the truth? You didn't know it was

my—'' Her voice broke. She hesitated, looking down at
her bare toes before saying, ''My first time. I don't blame
you for being disappointed. I'm sure you were expecting
so much more.''

''That's what this is all about?'' He sounded incred-
ulous. ''You think I'm disappointed?''

She lifted her trembling chin in a stubborn show of
pride, but remained silent, not trusting herself to answer.

''Aw, Jasmine,'' he said, shaking his head. Before she
could react, with a quickness that took her breath away,
he reached out, linked his hand with hers and tugged her
into the bedroom. Capturing her waist with his free hand,
he pulled her close, holding her snug against him.

Startled, she clung tightly to the ends of the towel,
looking up to see the steely determination in his eyes.

''You're wrong, Jasmine. What happened between
us…it wasn't a disappointment. It was special, more than
I could ever explain. But you are right about one thing,
though. I didn't know it was your first time. Not until it
was too late. If I had…'' He left the thought unfinished,
letting her imagination run wild. Sighing, he said, ''If I
gave you the wrong impression, then I'm sorry. But what
I felt wasn't disappointment, it was guilt. I took advantage of you at a time when you needed comfort. I didn't
deserve to be the first. I didn't deserve the gift you gave
me.''

Blinking in surprise, she searched his face for the
truth—and found nothing but sincerity mixed with remorse hidden in his eyes. Unable to stop herself, she
lifted a hand and smoothed a wayward strand of hair from
his face, tucking it gently behind his ear. Letting her hand
linger against his neck, she felt his strong pulse beneath
her fingers.

Looking him straight in the eye, she whispered,

"You're wrong, Storm. What I said before, about making a mistake, it wasn't true. You're the one I've waited for. The only one I've ever dreamed of being with. Don't you see? We were meant to be together. You have nothing to feel guilty about."

He lowered his head, pressing his forehead against hers. "I won't make any promises that I can't keep, Jasmine. Too much has happened. I don't know what the future holds for us."

She closed her eyes against the sting of disappointment. Fate might have brought them together, but it was working to keep them apart, as well. Struggling for control, she lifted her head and looked into his eyes. Her voice a whisper, she said, "I've never asked for a commitment. I only want what you can give me. Even if it's only a single night in your arms."

He stared at her, letting the silence gather between them. His dark-eyed gaze sent a trembling of awareness through her body. She held her breath and waited for him to answer.

Finally he nodded and said, "I can give you tonight."

For now, she told herself, that would have to be enough.

Twining her fingers through his hair, she tugged him close. She settled her lips upon his and felt the tension flow from her muscles. A new rush of desire billowed inside her as she let go of the pain of uncertainty in her heart, refusing to give in to her doubts. She gasped when Storm lifted her from her feet, cradling her in his arms.

As he carried her back to the bed, she told herself for now she felt safe and wanted.

Tomorrow would be soon enough for second thoughts.

Instead of the darkness and gloom she had expected, tomorrow greeted her with sunshine and brightness. As the early morning light seeped in through the cracks in the curtains, the sound of quiet, careful movements roused Jasmine from a sound sleep. Lazily she stretched a hand across the bed and discovered it empty.

Slowly opening her eyes, she blinked away the sandy grit of sleeplessness, feeling understandably tired and groggy. She hadn't slept much the night before. Too intent on making the most of each precious second of their stolen time together, both she and Storm had found little time to rest.

She sat up in bed and switched on the nightstand's lamp. Her breath caught at the unexpected sight that met her eyes.

Fully dressed in a pair of khaki pants and a long-sleeved, buttoned-down shirt, his hair still wet from a recent shower, Storm was in the midst of packing a suitcase. He stopped what he was doing and glanced over at her, his gaze wary.

"You're packing," she said needlessly.

"There's nothing more for me here." His voice sounded cold, emotionless. He picked up a shirt and slammed it into the case. "I've finished what I came to do. It's time for me to go back to New Mexico."

Pain zigzagged through her heart. She inhaled a sharp breath. "I see."

Stopping midreach for another shirt, he studied her, as though sensing her disappointment. He made his way to the bed. The mattress sank beneath his weight as he sat beside her.

Jasmine struggled to hide the tremors of apprehension that shook her body. The night she'd just spent wrapped in his arms seemed like a distant, almost forgotten dream.

The ecstasy and fulfillment they'd shared seemed like nothing more than a broken memory.

Though she longed for his touch, he rested his elbows against his knees and kept his hands clasped firmly together. "Jasmine, I told you last night I couldn't make any promises."

"I know," she said, her trembling voice doing little to ease the anxious look from his face.

His frown deepened. "Too much has happened between us. Your mother, what she did to Raven—" His voice caught and he stopped, staring down at his fisted hands.

Jasmine swallowed at the growing lump of disbelief that had lodged in her throat. She felt the sting of tears and blinked hard, refusing to give in to the lure of vulnerability. Now was not the time for weakness. She must be strong. She must face the future. Even if that future promised only loneliness and heartache.

He took a breath, releasing it on a sigh. "There's just too much to forget, too many obstacles to overcome. We would never be able to put everything that's happened behind us. It would always stand in our way."

Not we, Jasmine answered silently. You, Storm. You are the only one who cannot forget.

Jasmine knew without question that if the roles were reversed and Storm's brother had been the one to hurt her family, she would find a way to forgive him. She would not allow a mistake from the past, something that he had no control over, to ruin their chance at happiness. She would do whatever it took for them to be together.

But she wasn't Storm.

She hadn't lived a life void of love and security.

Her family had cared deeply for her. They'd built her life on a foundation of concern and confidence. Unlike

Storm, she'd never experienced the pain of being alone and unwanted.

Jasmine looked at him, her resolve melting as she saw the uncertainty that lined his face. His eyes moved restlessly, unable to meet her gaze. While the words he spoke were cold and flat, she knew there was a firestorm of emotion burning in his heart.

But it was hopeless. For thirty years Storm had survived by avoiding the very thing she longed to share with him—a close and loving relationship. She would not try to change his mind. No matter how much she wanted it to be different, she wouldn't beg him to stay.

Instead she stroked the powerful lines of his face. "It's all right, Storm. I understand."

He lifted his eyes, his gaze hesitant.

She smiled, despite the pain tearing her heart in two. "We'll always have last night. Just don't forget what we shared."

"That would be impossible," he said, giving her an uneasy smile.

She unclasped the compass from around her neck, the one her mother had given her. Taking his hand in hers, she placed the gold-plated compass on his palm and closed his fingers around it. At his questioning look, she said, "I want you to keep this, in case you ever need to find your way back to me. The compass will guide you, so you won't get lost."

With a sigh, he brushed his fingers through her hair, then cupped her chin in his hand. For a moment he stared at her, letting the regret shimmer in his eyes. Then, with a tenderness she would forever cherish, he bid her one last good-bye with a kiss.

Twelve

Two hours later, Storm approached the outskirts of town on Highway 191, heading for the airport in Bozeman. He'd left early, giving himself more than enough time to catch his four o'clock flight to Albuquerque. He saw no reason in prolonging his stay in Whitehorn.

He'd had his fill of the bad memories the town held for him.

Storm frowned. Not all the memories were bad, he admitted. Absently, he touched the breast pocket of his shirt, feeling the outline of the compass Jasmine had given him. Some were just destined to remain bittersweet.

He reached inside his pocket and fished out the compass. Holding it by its chain, he watched as the antique gold caught the sunlight, sending sparkles throughout the interior of the car.

He hadn't wanted to accept Jasmine's gift.

He'd wanted to push her and everything that reminded him of the time they'd spent together out of his mind. Coming to Whitehorn and searching for the truth behind his brother's death, had been one of the hardest tasks he'd ever had to face. Meeting Jasmine and losing his heart had only complicated matters.

Though he'd succeeded in finding his brother's murderer, once again he'd lost at love.

Closing his hand around its cool metal casing, he gripped the compass tightly. Despite her gift and her stoic show of pride, he knew Jasmine had been hurt by all that had happened.

Even worse, he knew that he'd been the cause of that pain.

Because of him and his relentless pursuit of the past, Jasmine had lost her mother, her innocence and her reason to hope. In less than two hours Celeste Monroe would be arraigned on the charges of murdering his brother. Instead of staying and facing what he'd wrought, once again he'd run away, unable to witness the final tableau.

He felt like the worst kind of coward.

His mood plummeting, he tucked the compass back into his pocket, telling himself he had no reason to feel guilty. He wasn't the one who'd pulled the trigger and taken a life. No, his crime was much more subtle. He'd come seeking revenge on the Kincaid family. And revenge he'd found....

He'd shattered their peaceful little family.

So why didn't he feel vindicated? Why did it feel as though he'd destroyed his last chance at a normal life?

Fighting the rising tide of bitterness, he told himself Jasmine was better off without him. He'd been on his own for too many years. Even if he wanted to, he wouldn't know how to care for someone the right way. He'd only end up hurting her more if he stayed and tried to make a life with her.

Thump. The loud noise came from out of nowhere, startling him. Something large and dark had hit the windshield. Storm slammed on his brakes, swerving reflexively from danger and sending the car careering into the oncoming lane of traffic. Thankfully, the highway was deserted. No other car was in sight.

His heart pounding, he corrected his mistake and

guided the car back into the right lane. The experience had left him shaken, not sure if he could drive. Besides, he needed to pull over to the side of the road to check for damage.

His tires whipped up a cloud of dust as he lurched to an unsteady stop. Shifting the gear into park, he tore open the door and stumbled out of the front seat. Relief settled over him at the feel of solid ground beneath his feet. Feeling as though he'd just sprinted five miles, he struggled for a breath and stared at the cracked windshield.

The morning air wafted over his flushed skin, cooling his agitated senses. Out of nowhere, an object had appeared and had smashed the windshield of his rented car. The safety glass had splintered, but held in place. There'd been no cars in front or behind him. Nothing that could have kicked up a loose rock from beneath its tires. Storm frowned. The impact had been too strong for just a pebble. It had to have been something large and heavy.

A flap of wings caught his attention.

Storm tore his stunned gaze from the windshield and squinted up into the sun-drenched sky. Soaring up above him was a large, dark bird. A raven.

Goose bumps prickled his skin, raising the hairs on the back of his neck. His mind was spinning with confusion. He glanced back at the damaged car and saw for the first time a single black feather lodged beneath the windshield wipers.

"Impossible," he murmured, feeling dazed as he reached for the unbroken feather.

Running his fingers over the soft, downy tufts, he considered the possibility. He'd been traveling close to sixty miles per hour. If a bird had hit the windshield at that speed, it never would have survived the impact.

But if it wasn't the bird, then what was it?

"Forget it," he said through clenched teeth, his voice lost on the wind that swept the empty expanse of road. "It doesn't matter if it was a rock, a boulder or a house that landed on the car. The car's insured. It's not a problem."

Still clutching the black feather, Storm slung himself into the front seat. He slammed the door too hard, causing the rearview mirror to vibrate, pushing his nerves even further on edge. Rocks and dirt spewed from the tires as he swung back onto the highway.

Tossing the feather to the seat beside him, he concentrated on the road ahead. The speedometer trembled as he pushed down on the accelerator. Fifty…sixty… seventy miles an hour and still climbing. No matter how much it felt like it, he refused to admit that he was running away.

The miles sped past in a blur. The wind ruffled his hair as it streamed in through the open window. Storm stole a wary glance at the feather. If he were a practicing, traditional Cheyenne, he'd say he'd been given a sign from the spirits. That his brother Raven was trying to communicate with him from the afterworld.

The morbid thought sent a shiver down his spine.

Even if he believed in the mystical powers of the spirits, which he didn't, what sort of message would they be trying to send him? That he was driving too fast? Or that he'd taken the wrong road?

Or maybe that he shouldn't be leaving, after all?

Stunned by the thought, Storm eased his foot off the pedal, slowing the car. If it was Raven trying to communicate with him, then why wouldn't he want him to leave Whitehorn? Raven, of all people, should know the heartache that the town represented. Surely he wouldn't want Storm to prolong his suffering.

Or could it be that he'd left unfinished business behind him? Storm admitted he'd left in a rush, leaving too many loose ends. First, there were Raven's remains. Once they were released from the coroner's office, he'd have to call and leave word on a proper burial. And there was Summer. He never did have a chance to tell his niece goodbye. Once again, he was abandoning the only living link to his brother.

Even more importantly, there was Jasmine.

The heavy hand of guilt pressed against his heart. As his brother had done before him, he'd allowed the Kincaid family to keep him from the woman he loved. Unlike Raven, however, it was his pride, not his courage that had finally defeated him.

Raven had stood up to Jeremiah Kincaid. He'd lost his life defending his right to be with Blanche. Storm had given up Jasmine without even a fight.

It wasn't any wonder he felt so guilty.

He couldn't leave, he realized, not like this.

Setting his jaw in a hard line of determination, Storm checked his mirrors for traffic. Assuring himself that both lanes were empty, he made a quick U-turn and headed back to Whitehorn.

"We're terribly sorry about the cancellation," Gladys Humphrey said, her round cheeks flushing with discomfort. Her hands fluttered to her throat as she gave a nervous laugh. "Our daughter insists that we come a few days early to visit her in California. Family…I'm sure you must understand."

Her husband remained noticeably silent. An impatient frown creasing his bulldog face.

"Yes, Mrs. Humphrey. I understand," Jasmine said

softly. Her hand felt as heavy as lead as she handed Mrs. Humphrey the credit card receipt for their visit.

Without another word, the pair turned from the front desk and hurried for the exit. She watched as they stepped outside into the cool morning sunlight, leaving the door open behind them. Once they were out of sight, Jasmine let her shoulders slump in defeat, feeling too tired and drained of energy to even get up and shut the door herself.

In the past hour, two other guests had checked out early, unexpectedly canceling the rest of their stay at the Big Sky Bed & Breakfast. While their excuses were inventive, as well as polite, Jasmine knew the truth.

No one wanted to stay in the house of a confessed murderer.

Out of habit, Jasmine reached for the reassuring weight of the compass around her neck, and felt nothing but smooth, unadorned skin. She inhaled a quick breath as the memory of giving Storm the compass flashed in her mind.

Though it had been only a few hours since she'd last seen him, it seemed like a lifetime ago.

After her night away from the B and B, since returning home, she'd been in a rush, hurrying to catch up on neglected chores. After a quick shower and change, she'd made breakfast for their guests. Now, with the house almost empty, it was time to prepare herself for another ordeal. Her mother's arraignment.

"Did they leave?"

Aunt Yvette's quiet voice startled her. Jasmine glanced up to meet her aunt's crestfallen face. With a sigh, she nodded. "That's the last of them. The Humphreys, the Sterlings…they've all checked out, canceling the rest of their stay."

Yvette clucked her tongue in disapproval. "I don't know how to tell your mother. She's going to be so upset. Running the B and B has always been her pride and joy."

"Then we won't tell her that people are canceling their reservations. She's fragile enough, Yvette. I don't know if she can handle any more bad news."

"I don't know if I can handle any more bad news, either." Tears glistened in Yvette's eyes. She attempted a smile, and failed.

Jasmine covered her aunt's hand with hers, squeezing it gently. Good sign, or bad, they hadn't heard from her mother or the sheriff's office this morning. According to Yvette, no one had called the night before, either. Even David, their source of information, had been unusually quiet since her mother's confession. Not knowing what was happening seemed to make everything that much worse.

When Jasmine had returned this morning, Yvette hadn't questioned her absence. Though from the troubled look in her eyes, Jasmine knew Yvette had a good idea where, and with whom, she'd spent the night. However, she was grateful for her aunt's discretion. Storm's unexpected departure had been devastating enough. The last thing she needed was to face one of her family's well-intended inquisitions.

From the doorway, the sound of a car coming fast down the gravel lane caught her attention. Jasmine frowned, glancing impatiently at her wristwatch. It was getting late. They'd have to be leaving soon for the courthouse. Now wasn't the time for a visitor.

Yvette stepped toward the large front window. Her brow furrowed into a worried frown as she stared outside. "Jasmine, I—" She hesitated, uncertainty shadowing her voice. She looked at her niece. "I think you'd better come here."

The urgency of her aunt's request sent shivers of trepidation down Jasmine's spine. She rose on unsteady feet and crossed the room to the window. Glancing outside, she blinked in surprise, unable to believe her own eyes.

Traveling at a quick clip, Storm's silver-gray luxury car was approaching the B and B.

"Were you expecting Mr. Hunter?" Yvette asked, searching Jasmine's face for her reaction.

Jasmine shook her head, feeling numb. When they'd parted hours earlier, she hadn't planned to see Storm ever again. He'd made his intentions perfectly clear. He was leaving Whitehorn and her, and he wasn't looking back.

She had no idea why he'd returned now.

The car skidded to a stop in front of the B and B. Not waiting for the dust to settle, Storm stepped out onto the white rock drive. He seemed oblivious to the fine coating of grit powdering his navy blazer. He stood with his hands on his slender hips, staring up at the house. With his hair slicked back from his face, and his chiseled jaw set in a determined line, he looked every bit as formidable and as devastatingly handsome as she'd remembered.

Her tummy fluttered. She tried not to let her hopes get too high. But his coming here…it was a good sign, wasn't it? Perhaps he'd changed his mind, after all. Given a little time, maybe he'd decided he could live with everything that had happened between their families. Would it be too much to hope that he was finally ready to let go of the past?

Not waiting for him to seek her out, she turned from the window and hurried out the door. It wasn't until she stepped closer and saw his somber face that she slowed her step. Her heart thumped painfully against her chest. Instinctively she knew that whatever he'd come to tell her, it wasn't the happy ending she'd hoped for.

Not trusting her own willpower, she left a safe distance between them. Feigning a casual tone, she said, "I thought you had left."

"I did." His deep voice echoed in her ears. His eyes never leaving hers, he said, "But there's something I forgot."

She licked her lips, her throat suddenly dry. "What was that?"

"You."

His blunt answer rocked her. The ground shifted beneath her feet. Her world felt as though it were spinning out of control. Reflexively she flinched when he stepped toward her.

He stopped, looked at her, seeming confused by her reaction.

Jasmine took a steadying breath. "I—I don't understand."

"There's nothing to understand. I'm not leaving Whitehorn, not without you."

She shook her head. "You can't be serious. I can't just...leave."

"Yes, you can, Jasmine." His voice rang with determination. "I want you to go upstairs and pack a bag. There's a four o'clock flight to Albuquerque. We can both be on that plane."

"You want me to leave Whitehorn," she said, still trying to make sense of the words. "Now? But what about my mother? The arraignment? How could I possibly leave her at a time like this?"

"There's no reason to stay, Jasmine," he said, his tone urgent. "We've both been hurt by what's happened. It's time for a fresh start. I love you, Jasmine. I want us to make that new start together.''

"Oh, Storm," Jasmine said, her voice breaking under the weight of strained emotion.

She of all people knew just how difficult his coming here must have been. In a show of trust, Storm had finally put his fears behind him. He'd taken that giant first step toward making a commitment. He'd admitted just how much he cared.

If only it wasn't too little, too late.

"I love you, too, Storm. But I can't leave," she said, looking at him with all the regret she felt in her heart. "Not now, not like this. Not when my mother needs me."

Pain flickered in his eyes before a stony mask of indifference slipped into place. "She lied to you, Jasmine."

"Not on purpose. She made a mistake, Storm. I can't abandon her. Surely you can understand that."

He didn't answer. From the hard expression on his face, Jasmine knew he hadn't a clue what she was talking about.

Anger and frustration rose up inside her. Nothing had changed, not really. Just as before, Storm wouldn't allow his emotions to interfere in his life. When his own family had disappointed him all those years ago, instead of trying to help them, to change the fate they'd been handed, he'd abandoned them. He had run away and hadn't looked back.

Now he wanted her to do the same.

"Maybe you can't understand, after all," she said, suddenly too tired to argue. "You've always seen things in black and white, haven't you? You've never been able to forgive and forget, even the smallest of mistakes. But I can."

Her voice broke. Tears blurred her vision. She swallowed hard, struggling to find the strength to finish what must be said. "I'm sorry, Storm. But I can't go with you to Albuquerque. My home is here in Whitehorn. I wish you could understand. My mother needs me. I won't abandon her. Not now, not ever."

With that, she turned her back on him. Striding to the front porch, she climbed the stairs, taking them two at a time, hurrying to put a safe distance between them. But in her heart she knew she would never be able to outrun the memory of his confused, pain-lined face.

Thirteen

The courthouse was unusually crowded.

Throngs of spectators milled in the halls, waiting for the show to begin. Despite the short notice, Jasmine wasn't surprised by the large turnout of local citizens. Whitehorn was a small town. Bad news traveled fast.

Besides, her mother had a reputation as an oddball. It wasn't any wonder that her latest example of eccentric behavior had drawn curiosity seekers. And, thanks to Jasmine's late uncle, Jeremiah Kincaid, and his ability to stir up trouble, people around these parts would travel far and wide to see what further trouble he could wreak, even from the grave.

A sudden hush fell across the courthouse as Jasmine made her way through the crowd. Bystanders scattered, making room for her, staring as she passed. Keeping her eyes focused straight ahead and her head held high, Jasmine was determined to not let the people of Whitehorn see the devastating effect her mother's murder confession had had upon her. No matter what the cost to her pride, she was here to support her mother.

Even if it meant losing everything she held dear—including the man she loved.

Jasmine strode to the front of the room, anxious to join her family. Aunt Yvette and Uncle Edward scooted over, making room for her in the first row behind the defendant's table.

Cleo leaned forward from her seat in the second row. "You're late," she whispered.

"I couldn't help it," Jasmine said, grimacing. "The parking lot was full. I had to park the Jeep a block past the movie theater and walk the rest of the way. Have I missed anything?"

Cleo shook her head. "Nothing's happened yet. There's been a delay."

"A delay?" Jasmine frowned, her stomach churning with unease. "What sort of delay?"

"They won't tell us," Yvette chimed in, keeping her voice hushed. "All I know is that Ross Garrison, the attorney we hired for Celeste, came out and told us there was a meeting going on in the judge's chambers. And that as soon as he heard anything, he'd let us know."

"Is that good news or bad?" Jasmine asked, her frown deepening.

Yvette shrugged. "It's anyone's guess."

The tall, silver-haired figure of Garrett Kincaid caught her eye. Ignoring the curious stares of the crowd, he strode toward Jasmine and her family. Resting one hand on the back of her seat, Garrett leaned forward and whispered, "Something's going on. The sheriff and his deputies were out at the ranch house last night. They spent the whole night searching my study. Made a damn mess, too." He grunted his dissatisfaction. "Even tore a hole in the wall behind my desk."

"Did they say anything?" Jasmine asked, trying not to let her anxiety show through.

"Not to me they didn't," he said, giving his head an impatient shake. "But I'd never seen such a bunch of grim faces. If you ask me, things weren't going as smooth as the sheriff had planned." Frowning, he glanced around the crowded room. "Well, I'd better be going if I want to find a seat. You tell your mama that if there's anything I can do, she should just call.''

Jasmine gave a polite smile, but didn't answer. At the moment there was nothing any of them could do. Her mother had confessed to the crime of murder. It would be in the hands of the court to decide her fate.

The minutes passed excruciatingly slowly. The din of excited voices reverberated through the courtroom, echoing off of the walls. The noise gave Jasmine a pounding headache, making the ordeal even more discomfiting. When a sudden hush fell across the room, she wasn't sure whether to be relieved or even more worried.

Something, or someone, had gotten the crowd's attention.

The buzz of voices resumed, only louder this time. Though she was dying of curiosity, Jasmine refused to turn around to look to see who, other than her mother, could be causing such a stir in the crowd. Which is why she jumped in her seat when someone tapped her shoulder.

Jasmine whirled to face the newcomer. Her breath caught in her throat, her eyes widened in surprise as she stared up into Storm's hesitant face.

''If it isn't too late,'' he said, loud enough for those around them to hear, ''I'd like to sit beside you during your mother's arraignment.''

Her mouth opened to answer, but the words of acceptance wouldn't form. For a heart-stuttering moment Jasmine couldn't answer. She was still too stunned by his unexpected appearance to speak.

Her heart racing, she tried to make sense of it all. Instead of leaving town, Storm had stayed. He was here, in the courthouse, wanting to join her at a time when she needed him most. The implication of his change of heart was obvious.

He was telling her in his own way that he was ready to forgive and forget the past.

He was ready to stand beside her, and her family, no matter what the outcome of today's arraignment.

Tears of relief prickled her eyes. Biting her lip to stop the maudlin show of emotion, Jasmine nodded and scooted over to make room for Storm beside her on the bench.

It was a tight fit. Jasmine had to tuck her arm beneath Storm's wide shoulder. The rest of their bodies—hips, thighs, and legs—were pressed together, not an inch of space to spare. But she didn't mind. She savored the warm, secure feel of his body next to hers.

With an audible sigh of relief, Storm picked up her hand in his, linking his fingers with hers. No other words were necessary. His supportive actions spoke volumes to her, and to those around them.

If it wasn't for her mother's impending arraignment, Jasmine had never felt happier or more contented. If she hadn't been certain of the future before, she was sure now. Despite the obstacles standing between them, Storm had found his way back to her. He'd proven to her that he was her soul mate, her one true love. In her heart, she had always known they were destined to be together.

Once again, a hush fell across the room.

This time her mother's appearance in the courtroom had caused the reaction. Dressed in a pale, peach-colored tunic and matching pants, Celeste looked tired and frail. Without makeup, the dark circles beneath her eyes were even more obvious. Her hair, normally so carefully styled, hung limp and unkempt around her face. She wore a confused, almost dazed look.

Jasmine's heart lurched at Celeste's disheveled appearance. She stood, reaching out to her mother. But before she could murmur a word of reassurance, the Blue River County district attorney, followed closely by the presiding judge, entered the courtroom. The bailiff called out the opening of the session, warning the crowd to stand and be silent.

Obligingly the crowd grew quiet. Only the shifting of feet as the crowd stood sounded in the room.

Taking his seat at the bench, the judge picked up his gavel and rapped it sharply. "Be seated." Over the noise of settling bodies, he narrowed an impatient glance at the district attorney. "Mr. Corwin, do you have a motion for me?"

Clearing his throat, the D.A. rose to his feet. "Yes, Your Honor. If it pleases the court, the state requests that all charges against Celeste Kincaid Monroe be dropped."

A roar of astonishment swept the courtroom.

Jasmine's heart leaped in her chest. Her shocked gaze traveled from her mother's confused face to Storm's startled look. Everyone seemed surprised by the turn of events.

The judge rapped his gavel, once, twice, three times before the uproar subsided. His expression stern, he said, "Motion granted. All charges are dropped. The case is dismissed."

After a final tap of his gavel, the judge stood and left the courtroom, disappearing through his chamber doors. With his departure, all hell broke loose throughout the courtroom. From the four corners of the room, the crowd speculated with various degrees of surprise and outrage on this unexpected turn of events.

Despite the confusion spinning in his own mind, Storm

put a protective arm around Jasmine's shoulder, shielding her from the startled outburst of the crowd. He leaned close and said, "Do you have any idea what's happening?"

She shook her head. "No, I haven't a clue. I'm just as much in the dark as you are."

Sheriff Rawlings, accompanied by Detective Gretchen Neal, approached the defense table. Spotting Storm and Jasmine's family in the crowd, he motioned for them to join him. Pointing to a side door, he said, "I think it'd be better if we waited out the crowd in one of the conference rooms." He nodded at Storm. "It'll give me a chance to explain the situation to you, Mr. Hunter. As well as to Mrs. Monroe's family."

Storm didn't bother to argue. Any protest would have been lost over the excited voices of the crowd. Instead, along with Jasmine and her family, Storm allowed himself to be shepherded into a nearby conference room.

The sudden stillness of the room felt as welcome as a cooling breath of relief. Looking exhausted, Celeste collapsed into a nearby chair. Yvette and Cleo took chairs on either side, flanking Celeste in a show of support. The rest of the family hovered nearby, leaving Storm to feel like an intruder in this private scene. Instead of joining her family, to his grateful relief, Jasmine remained beside him.

At the opposite end of the room, Sheriff Rawlings conferred with Gretchen Neal in a whispered conversation. The detective shook her head, her response too quiet to overhear. Then, with a quick nod, Sheriff Rawlings turned his attention to the small group. "I guess you must be wondering what's going on. Before I give you the details, I want to apologize for springing all of this on you on such short notice. If we'd been given more time, we would have informed you of the new developments in the case before the court appearance today.''

"What new developments, Sheriff?" David Hannon demanded. He stood at the opposite end of the conference table, keeping a discreet distance from Storm.

The sheriff sighed, looking tired and worn out. "Yesterday, after hearing Mrs. Monroe's confession, Detective Neal and I went out to the ranch house to take another look at the crime scene.''

Crime scene...Garrett's study at the ranch house. Jasmine glanced up at Storm. From the startled look in her eyes, Storm realized that for the first time she'd finally gotten the connection between the study and his odd behavior on the day they'd visited Garrett Kincaid. She now knew that he'd had one of his feelings during their visit, that he had sensed the study as being the place where Raven had died.

Storm met her gaze with a steady look of his own. Sensing her surprise, he reached a reassuring arm around her shoulders and pulled her close.

Giving Celeste an apologetic glance, Sheriff Rawlings said, "I'll be honest with you, Mrs. Monroe. Something about your confession just didn't ring true.''

"But I told you everything just as it happened," Celeste said, shaking her head and looking confused.

"Just as you *thought* it had happened," Sheriff Rawlings said, his words firm, brooking no argument. "Let me tell you what we found. First of all, the gun you gave us didn't match the type of bullet that we'd found lodged in Raven Hunter's remains.''

A murmur of surprise rose from the group.

Ignoring the reaction, the sheriff continued. "In the ranch house study, we examined the wall exactly opposite of where you told us that you stood on the night

Raven Hunter died. After a little digging inside the wall we found the bullet that you'd fired. Also, hidden behind the wallboard, we found another gun. A gun that we believe to be the murder weapon." The sheriff glanced across the room, looking directly at Storm. "There was only one set of fingerprints on that gun. And they belonged to Jeremiah Kincaid."

Storm flinched at the news. Jasmine placed a hand on his arm, glancing up at him with a look of concern. Then, just as quickly as it had taken hold, he felt the tension gripping his muscles slowly relax. Along with the truth finally came acceptance. Storm had always believed Jeremiah to be the murderer. That was why he'd been so shocked by Celeste's confession. Now, despite everything, he found comfort in the fact that he hadn't been wrong, after all.

Sheriff Rawlings heaved a sigh. "It's my and Detective Neal's opinion that, in the course of the fight between Jeremiah and Raven, Jeremiah used the distraction of his sister's entrance into the study as an opportunity to pull a gun from hiding and shoot Raven point-blank in the stomach. The trajectory of the bullet lodged in Raven's rib cage confirms this theory. Given the new evidence, we had no choice but to let Mrs. Monroe go free."

A stunned silence filled the room.

Then Cleo let out a whoop of disbelief, breaking the stillness. "That nasty old bastard. I only wish Jeremiah hadn't died so we could nail his ornery old hide to the wall."

"Cleo, really," Celeste said, a shocked look on her face. But the look quickly dissolved into a wan smile.

The ice had finally been broken. Hugs and congratulations were exchanged among Jasmine and her family.

Storm stood at the fringe of the group, feeling out of place, overwhelmed by what had just occurred. He'd been ready to support Jasmine and her family, no matter what might have happened. But the charges had been dropped, the mystery was solved, and all had been accomplished without the tragedy of tearing Jasmine's family apart.

The worst was over. Now all that was left was to wait to see if Jasmine's family would be able to accept him as a part of her life.

As though sensing his unease, Jasmine crossed the room to rejoin him. A slow smile lit her face as she wrapped her arms around his neck and pulled him close. "It's over, Storm," she whispered. "It's finally over."

Without waiting for a response, she stood on tiptoe and kissed him. A long, sultry kiss on the lips. A kiss that promised so much more to come.

Lost in Jasmine's embrace, Storm didn't notice Celeste's approach until he heard a discreet clearing of the throat. Abruptly he ended the kiss. Not quite as intimidated by the intrusion, keeping her arm anchored at his waist, Jasmine turned to face her mother.

Looking from her daughter to Storm, Celeste took a deep breath, then released it with a sigh. "First of all, I'd like to apologize to you, Storm. My behavior toward you since your return to Whitehorn has been abominable. I can only hope, under the circumstances, you understand why I felt the need to distance myself from you."

Storm opened his mouth to answer.

Celeste held up a quieting hand. "Before you say anything, hear me out. At first I tried to convince Jasmine that you and she were ill-matched. With good reason, I might add. Not only is there a difference in your ages, but the history between our families seemed to be working at odds against the two of you. But now…" Her voice broke. She swallowed hard as tears of remorse filled her eyes. "Now, seeing the two of you together, I realize that standing between you and Jasmine is wrong. Just as it was wrong for Jeremiah to keep Blanche and Raven apart."

Storm felt his heart catch with surprise. He'd never thought he would hear a Kincaid admit that she was wrong. Perhaps there was such a thing as a miracle, after all.

With a trembling smile Celeste said, "My daughter is a very determined woman. She's told me that you are the man she's meant to be with. I believe her. So much so that I'd like to be the first to welcome you into our family…if you'll have us."

For the first time in his life Storm felt the power of love. Despite the differences between them, Jasmine's mother was ready to forgive and forget, all for the sake of her daughter's happiness. He envied Jasmine and her family for the closeness they shared.

"I'd like that very much, Mrs. Monroe." He glanced at Jasmine, raising a questioning brow. "That is, if Jasmine still wants me to be a part of her life."

"Don't be silly." Jasmine laughed. "Of course, I still want you in my life. I'd never given up hope, Storm." A twinkle of mischief lit her eye. "Why do you think I gave you my compass? I knew it would lead you back home, where you belonged."

Home. The word had never sounded so good. It described perfectly the way he felt in his heart. It was as though, after a long and trying journey, he'd finally found his way home.

Home, in Jasmine's arms.

Epilogue

The crowd spilled out of the living room of the B and B and into the large front lobby. Unlike the grim courthouse scene of just two months earlier, this gathering was a celebration of new beginnings.

Today, Jasmine and Storm's wedding day, there were no unhappy endings allowed.

Jasmine had chosen a simple white dress for the occasion. It was a form-fitting style, with a flared hem that ended just above her knees and emphasized the slender curves of her body. In deference to the day, instead of her usual black cowboy boots, she wore a special pair of white ones. Hand-tooled, of course. In place of a veil, tiny sprigs of mountain wildflowers were pinned in her hair. Other than the gold-plated compass around her neck—the gift Storm had returned when he'd decided not to venture beyond Whitehorn's boundaries ever again— she wore no other jewelry. As of yet.

Jasmine frowned. Maybe she'd taken back the compass too soon, she mused as she searched the crowd for the wayward man of her dreams.

Storm was nowhere in sight.

By the living room fireplace, she spotted David and Gretchen Neal, deep in a conversation with Cleo and Ethan Redford. Frannie and her husband, Austin Parker, sidled up to join the boisterous group. As Jasmine passed by, they raised their champagne glasses in a mock toast.

With a grin and a wave, she continued past, determined not to be deterred from her goal—finding Storm.

Her mother, Aunt Yvette and Uncle Edward were stationed at the front door, greeting their guests as they arrived. Celeste raised an eyebrow in question as Jasmine neared.

"Storm?" Jasmine mouthed in a silent question.

Celeste shrugged, looking beautiful and refreshed, more like her old self in a gauzy dusty-rose caftan.

Yvette pointed to the back of the house, toward the kitchen. "I think I saw him heading that way just a few minutes ago." A mischievous smile touched her face. "Actually, I believe it was more like he was led against his will. The group he was with looked very persuasive."

Jasmine sighed her impatience. Though she wasn't usually a stickler for punctuality, this was one ceremony she didn't want to be late for.

Her boots thumped against the wooden floor as she strode down the wide hall and made a beeline for a group of guests who were lingering in the corridor outside the kitchen. Among them she recognized a smiling Summer and Gavin Nighthawk. Garrett Kincaid stood next to Jackson Hawk and his wife, Maggie. In the center of the group, she finally spotted Storm.

He smiled when he saw her, looking much too handsome in his dark suit and starched-white shirt, making it hard to stay impatient with him. The whiteness of his shirt contrasted nicely with the coppery hue of his skin and his long, dark hair. His eyes twinkled with amusement at her exasperated expression.

Instead of irritation, a hot surge of longing thrummed through her veins. Jasmine sucked in a steadying breath, getting a grip on her runaway libido. Later, she told herself, there would be plenty of time to satisfy her more lustful needs.

For now there was a wedding that was about to begin without the bride and the groom.

She plunged through the group and found her way to his side. "Storm," she said, her calm voice belying the butterflies dancing in her stomach, "do you have any idea what time it is?"

"Funny you should ask," Jackson said, interrupting her demand. "We were just trying to convince Storm to adopt the more traditional ways of the Cheyenne. Unlike the Anglos, keeping an eye on the clock just isn't as important to our people. We follow a more natural time rhythm." He made a waving motion with his hand. "You know…go with the flow?"

"I'm sorry, Jackson. But time's important when you have fifty guests and a minister waiting for you," Jasmine countered, smiling through clenched teeth.

Maggie Hawk gave her husband's arm a playful swat. "Don't listen to him, Jasmine. Jackson is the most impatient man I've ever met. He's more of a stickler for schedules than he'd ever own up to."

Jackson glowered at his wife before planting a loving kiss on the tip of her nose.

"Now, don't you be mad at Storm, Jasmine," Garrett Kincaid drawled. "If he got a little sidetracked, trust me, it wasn't his fault. We've just been discussing a little business with him."

"Business?" Today of all days? she added silently.

As though he'd read her mind, Storm reached out and pulled her into his arms. His breath tickled her ear as he whispered, "I didn't exactly have a choice."

Jackson slapped Storm on the back, a wide grin splitting his face. "Storm has just agreed to act as tribal counsel for us on the Laughing Horse Reservation."

Jasmine blinked in surprise. While they hadn't discussed future plans in detail, Storm had assured her that he had no intention of leaving Whitehorn and forcing her to choose between her family and him. She'd been grateful for his decision, but she'd wondered what he intended to do now that he had closed his law office in New Mexico.

Storm was watching her closely, measuring her for a reaction. Jasmine considered the possibility. The thought of him returning to his roots on the reservation warmed her heart. It was where he was born, where he belonged. It was another important step in his acceptance of the past.

She smiled up at him. "I think that it's a wonderful idea. Congratulations, Storm."

His smile of relief sent a shiver down her spine. He truly was a most amazing man. In the past two months he'd seemed to change in front of her very eyes. He was more open with his feelings. She'd noticed a gradual letting go of his inhibitions. When, as a wedding present, her mother had given them a parcel of land along Blue Mirror Lake to build a house, the last of his insecurities seemed to have vanished. She'd even caught him smiling, relaxing, truly enjoying himself in her family's company.

Yes, she told herself, her smile deepening, the future did indeed look bright.

"Don't you two take too long on that honeymoon," Garrett said, interrupting her thoughts. "We've got a lot of work to do to get this casino/resort back on the right track before winter sets in. Now that we've moved to the new site and gotten away from that stubborn vein of bedrock, the construction's moving along full-steam-ahead."

"The casino/resort's going to represent an unusual alliance between the whites and Native Americans," Jackson ventured.

"A lucrative one, I hope," Garrett added with a nod and a smile. "I predict that in the near future, Whitehorn's going to become quite a popular spot."

Jasmine sighed. "That's all well and good, gentlemen. But right now I've got more important things on my mind...like a wedding."

No sooner had she said the words than she heard the sound of her mother's voice directing their guests into the side parlor, where they'd set up chairs and a makeshift altar in front of the windows facing Blue Mirror Lake and the peaks of the Crazy Mountains.

The group broke apart, joining the milling crowd as they followed Celeste's instructions.

To her relief, Jasmine finally found herself alone with Storm. She looked up at him, feeling suddenly nervous. "It's been a short two months. Are you sure you're ready for this?"

"I couldn't be any more certain if I'd had two years," he said, his expression somber. "I want to marry you, Jasmine. I want to spend the rest of my life with you here in Whitehorn. Nothing will ever change my mind."

She breathed a sigh of relief. "That's all I needed to hear. I love you, too, Storm. I can't wait to be your wife."

Without another word, she leaned forward and settled her lips on his, sealing the promise with a kiss. Then, releasing him, she twined her fingers in his, holding his hand tightly as they made their way into the parlor, ready to face their future together.

*   *   *   *   *

*Silhouette presents an exciting
new continuity series:*

**When a royal family rolls out the red carpet
for love, power and deception, will their
lives change forever?**

The saga begins in April 2002 with:

The Princess Is Pregnant!

by Laurie Paige (SE #1459)

**May: THE PRINCESS AND THE DUKE by Allison Leigh
(SE #1465)**

**June: ROYAL PROTOCOL by Christine Flynn
(SE #1471)**

Be sure to catch all nine Crown and Glory stories: the first three appear in
Silhouette Special Edition, the next three continue in Silhouette Romance
and the saga concludes with three books in Silhouette Desire.

And be sure not to miss more royal stories,
from Silhouette Intimate Moments'

Romancing
the Crown,

running January through December.

™ *Silhouette*®
Where love comes alive™

*Available at
your favorite
retail outlet.*

Visit Silhouette at www.eHarlequin.com

SSECAG

Coming soon from

SPECIAL EDITION™

The continuation of a popular miniseries from
bestselling author

SUSAN MALLERY

**DESERT
ROGUES**

Escape to the City of Thieves—a secret jewel
in the desert where seduction rules and romantic
fantasies come alive....

The Prince & the Pregnant Princess
(SE #1473, on sale June 2002)

Desert Rogues:
Passions flare between a tempestuous princess and a
seductive sheik prince.... How hot will it get?

Available at your favorite retail outlet.

Where love comes alive™

Visit Silhouette at www.eHarlequin.com   SSEDR022

Start Your Summer With Sizzle
And Silhouette Books!

In June 2002, look for these HOT volumes led by *New York Times* bestselling authors and receive a free Gourmet Garden kit!

Retail value of $17.00 U.S.

THE BLUEST EYES IN TEXAS by Joan Johnston
and WIFE IN NAME ONLY by Carolyn Zane

THE LEOPARD'S WOMAN by Linda Lael Miller
and WHITE WOLF by Lindsay McKenna

THE BOUNTY by Rebecca Brandewyne
and A LITTLE TEXAS TWO-STEP by Peggy Moreland

OVERLOAD by Linda Howard
and IF A MAN ANSWERS by Merline Lovelace

This exciting promotion is available at your favorite retail outlet. See inside books for details.

Only from

Silhouette®

Where love comes alive™

Visit Silhouette at www.eHarlequin.com   PSNCP02

magazine

♥———————————————————— **quizzes**

Is he the one? What kind of lover are you? Visit the **Quizzes** area to find out!

♥———————————————— **recipes for romance**

Get scrumptious meal ideas with our **Recipes for Romance**.

♥———————————————— **romantic movies**

Peek at the **Romantic Movies** area to find Top 10 Flicks about First Love, ten Supersexy Movies, and more.

♥———————————————————— **royal romance**

Get the latest scoop on your favorite royals in **Royal Romance**.

♥———————————————————————— **games**

Check out the **Games** pages to find a ton of interactive romantic fun!

♥———————————————— **romantic travel**

In need of a romantic rendezvous? Visit the **Romantic Travel** section for articles and guides.

♥———————————————————— **lovescopes**

Are you two compatible? Click your way to the **Lovescopes** area to find out now!

where love comes alive—online...

Visit us online at
www.eHarlequin.com

SINTMAG

When California's most talked about dynasty is threatened, only family, privilege and the power of love can protect them!

THE COLTONS

Coming in May 2002

THE HOPECHEST BRIDE

by

Kasey Michaels

Cowboy Josh Atkins is furious at Emily Blair, the woman he thinks is responsible for his brother's death...so *why* is he so darned attracted to her? After dark accusations—and sizzling sparks—start to fly between Emily and Josh, they both realize that they can make peace...and love!

Available at your favorite retail outlet.

Silhouette ®

Where love comes alive ™

Visit Silhouette at www.eHarlequin.com   PSCOLT12

Silhouette Books is proud to present:

Going to the Chapel

**Three brand-new stories
about getting that special man to the altar!**

featuring

USA Today bestselling author

SHARON
SALA

It Happened One Night...that Georgia society belle
Harley June Beaumont went to Vegas—and woke up married!
How could she explain her hunk of a husband to
her family back home?

Award-winning author

DIXIE BROWNING

Marrying a Millionaire...was exactly what Grace McCall was
trying to keep her baby sister from doing. Not that Grace had
anything against the groom—it was the groom's arrogant
millionaire uncle who got Grace all hot and bothered!

National bestselling author

STELLA BAGWELL

The Bride's Big Adventure...was escaping her handpicked
fiancé in the arms of a hot-blooded cowboy! And from the
moment Gloria Rhodes said "I do" to her rugged groom, she
dreamed their wedded bliss would never end!

Available in July at your favorite retail outlets!

Silhouette®
TM
Where love comes alive™

Visit Silhouette at www.eHarlequin.com   PSGTCC

Coming in May 2002

**Three Bravo men marry for convenience—
but will they love in leisure? Find out in
Christine Rimmer's *Bravo Family Ties!***

Cash—for stealing a young woman's innocence, and to
give their baby a name, in *The Nine-Month Marriage*

Nate—for the sake of a codicil in his beloved
grandfather's will, in *Marriage by Necessity*

Zach—for the unlucky-in-love rancher's chance to
have a marriage—even of convenience—
with the woman he *really* loves!

BRAVO
FAMILY TIES

Where love comes alive™

Visit Silhouette at www.eHarlequin.com   BR3BFT

Silhouette Books presents a dazzling keepsake
collection featuring two full-length novels by
international bestselling author

DIANA PALMER

Brides To Be

(On sale May 2002)

THE AUSTRALIAN
*Will rugged outback rancher Jonathan Sterling
be roped into marriage?*

HEART OF ICE
*Close proximity sparks a breathtaking attraction between a
feisty young woman and a hardheaded bachelor!*

You'll be swept off your feet by Diana Palmer's BRIDES TO BE.

Don't miss out on this special two-in-one volume, available soon.

*Available only from Silhouette Books
at your favorite retail outlet.*

Silhouette®

Where love comes alive™

Visit Silhouette at www.eHarlequin.com   PSBTB